"You can go to hell, Carrick des Marceaux," Glynis whispered up at him.

He smiled grimly. "Then I'm taking you with me, Glynis Muldoon," he promised, drawing her hard against him.

His kiss deepened with a speed that sent her senses reeling. She felt his heat and power everywhere their bodies touched, felt the incredible urgency that drove them both. The scent of leather and wind and the night clung to him, filling her senses and leaving her wanting more. She stripped the gloves from her hands, letting them fall, and twined her fingers through the hair at his nape, reveling in the silken feel of it and the way her touch made him tremble.

"Glynis," he demanded, blazing a trail of kisses to the hollow behind her ear. "Tell me to stop."

"No." She couldn't.

"Then God help us both. . . ."

Lady
Reckless

Leslie LaFoy

BANTAM BOOKS

NEW YORK TORONTO LONDON SYDNEY AUCKLAND

LADY RECKLESS

A Bantam Fanfare Book / August 1998

FANFARE and the portrayal of a boxed "ff" are trademarks of
Bantam Books, a division of Bantam Doubleday Dell Publishing
Group, Inc.

ISBN 0-553-57747-6

Published simultaneously in the United States and Canada

Bantam Books are published by Bantam Books, a division of Bantam
Doubleday Dell Publishing Group, Inc. Its trademark, consisting of the
words "Bantam Books" and the portrayal of a rooster, is Registered in
U.S. Patent and Trademark Office and in other countries. Marca
Registrada. Bantam Books, 1540 Broadway,
New York, New York 10036.

PRINTED IN THE UNITED STATES OF AMERICA

OPM   10   9   8   7   6   5   4   3   2   1

For my parents, Donald and Joyce Voss

Who taught me that life without dreams is empty
and that without hard work and perseverance
even the smallest of dreams are for naught.

And for David and Garrett

Whose love, patience and understanding support
made pursuing the dream possible.

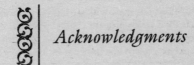 ## Acknowledgments

No author ever achieves even the smallest portion of their success without the hearts and hands of others. To my friend Marti, thank you for your incredible patience with my frequent obsessing. To my former students and teaching colleagues, thank you for the years of laughter and precious memories. To my agent and my editor at Bantam Books, my deepest appreciation for the tender care you take in shaping this rough diamond.

And last, but certainly not least, my loving thanks to the Ladies of the Lounge for their wit, wisdom, faith and friendship.

Prologue

Castle O'Connell
County Kerry, Ireland
December 1817

Carrick des Marceaux shielded the candle flame with his hand and glanced down the hall at his cousin. "Is anyone coming?" he whispered.

"No," Robert answered, moving away from the top of the stairs. "They're all still at the table. Except for your mother. She just went into the kitchen."

Carrick nodded and motioned toward his parents' bedchamber. "Then come on. We don't have much time."

"You know we're going to get in trouble if we get caught, don't you?" Robert whispered, reaching for the latch.

"*If*, Robert," Carrick countered. "*If*. But even if we do, it won't be nearly as bad as our punishment after the egg fight we had last week." He waited until the door closed behind them before he dropped his hand and allowed the flame to fully cast its light. "You look under the bed," he instructed, crossing the room to set the candleholder down on the bedside table. "I'll go through the chest by the window."

"Christmas is only two days away, Carrick. We could wait."

"As though you have any more patience than I do," Carrick retorted, hunkering down beside the oak trunk in which his mother stored the more personal of her belongings. "Having a mother from the twentieth century has its advantages, Rob. And to my way of thinking her Christmas customs are some of the better ones. I can't stand not knowing. So, if I were going to hide Christmas presents . . ."

He raised the lid of the trunk and peered inside. Carefully lifting the edge of a blue wool cloak, he peeked beneath it and saw nothing that interested him. Perhaps his Christmas present had been hidden under the next layer.

"We're supposed to get our horses back tomorrow," Robert reminded him. "We'll lose them for another week if we get caught."

Carrick looked over his shoulder at his cousin. "So?"

"You can sneak out at night to ride all you like. My father would flail me alive if he found me slipping out. Your father always lets you off easy."

There would be no point in denying the truth of Robert's claim. No point in discussing it, either. "Are you just going to stand there or are you going to look under the bed?"

"You search. I'll stand by the door and listen for someone coming."

Leave it to Robert to be the careful one, the one prepared for the worst. He always was. "Well, listen sharp, then," Carrick said, going back to searching his mother's oak trunk. "And give me enough warning so that we can get out of here in time, all right?"

"Don't forget to look in your father's sea chest. That's where mine keeps his special things."

"Good idea. And I'll look under the bed."

"The Land of the Dust Bunnies." Robert grinned.

Carrick smiled back and shoved his hand into the darkened back corner of the chest, then ran his fingers along the wooden seams. They brushed something cold and hard. Hoping that it might be a fitting for the pistol he so desperately wanted, he quickly brought the object out into the meager candlelight.

The object, softly glinting silver and red, practically filled the palm of Carrick's hand. Not pistol fittings, but certainly something fascinating, something that made his heart race. "Look, Rob!" he called, turning and rising to his feet. He held out his hand so his cousin could see. "I'll wager you a new saddle that this is the Dragon's Heart."

"Really?" Robert came away from the door with a bound, his eyes wide. "The magic Dragon's Heart? You think so?" He stopped a good two paces away from Carrick and stared at the ancient pin. "Can you see anything in it?"

Carrick turned it around in his hand. "It just looks like a plain ol' ruby to me. Maybe you have to hold it a certain way." He lifted it toward the candle and positioned it so that the light danced through the stone. Still, he saw nothing in it. No people. No places. He scowled. All the whispered stories about the magical Dragon's Heart had been simply that: stories. And he had actually believed them. It wasn't magic at all. It couldn't *really* show you the future.

"Why do you suppose Aunt Alanna put it away?" Robert asked, edging closer.

"Mother's a girl," Carrick answered. "She doesn't like scary things."

Robert snickered. "It's just a dumb ol' brooch. It doesn't look so scary to me."

"Me either." But even as he agreed, a milky cloud rose from deep within the ruby. Through the eddying, swirling mist he could see the vague outlines of various and odd shapes. He bent closer and tried to make sense of what he was seeing.

"What is it, Carrick? Do you see something?"

Carrick heard his cousin's question, vaguely felt his shoulder pressed against him, but answering was beyond him. He needed to concentrate, to make the mist go away, to make whatever was within the Dragon's Heart come into focus.

The picture came slowly, a bit at a time. First a dirty cobbled street and a scaffold made of new lumber. An executioner's scaffold. Then the milling crowd. As the vision took shape, he saw a slab of stone lying against a wagon wheel, the dates 1807 and 1832 carved in an arc across the top.

And then the white mist rolled away to reveal, beneath the dates, the name of the man for whom the scaffold had been built and whose death the people had come to see. Carrick blinked, certain he had seen it improperly. But when he looked again the name remained the same: Carrick des Marceaux.

Then the image in the Dragon's Heart changed. Carrick held his breath and watched as British soldiers escorted a younger version of his father, hands bound, up the steps of the scaffold. A younger version of his father or an older version of himself. Carrick stared into the Dragon's Heart, paralyzed by the images. The tall wooden gallows, the hangman and his noose, the sight of himself standing stoically as the hemp circle was tightened about his neck. . . .

He forced back his horror and closed his eyes, clenching the brooch tightly in his hand. But his mind refused to let go of the image, keeping it before him, branding him with the certainty that he'd seen his own death.

"No."

Robert threw open the door and ran down the hallway. But Carrick didn't move. He couldn't do anything but stand where he was, clutching the Dragon's Heart.

The Dragon's Heart wasn't real. And even if it really could show the future, that didn't mean this particular future was unavoidable. His mother was a Seer of the Ancient Find. She had magical powers and she would make things right. And if she couldn't, then his father would. His father was *the* O'Connell, the head of the clan. No one would dare hang his son.

"Carrick!"

The sound of his mother's voice filtered through his panicked thoughts. She stood just inside the room, her skirts still swirling about her ankles, her long blond braid lying over her shoulder, her chest rising and falling as she tried to catch her breath. For an instant she met his eyes and then her own dropped to his hand. She paled and seemed to falter before she looked back up at him.

"Oh, dear God. What have you seen, Carrick?"

The words came wrapped in tears. "Am I going to be hanged, Mother?"

She took a deep breath before she spoke over her shoulder. "Robert. Go down and tell your Uncle Kiervan that I need him up here. *Right now.*"

"Yes, ma'am," his cousin answered. Robert's footsteps echoed down the stone corridor.

"Mother?" Carrick pressed, trying to take a deep breath. She looked so sad. "You can make it different, can't you?"

She came to him and gathered him in her arms. Rocking him gently back and forth, she hugged him as though she would never let him go. But she said nothing.

Carrick felt the Dragon's Heart slip from his fingers, heard it hit the carpet at their feet with a soft thud. The sound struck the center of his soul. And in that instant he knew that no one could save him.

1

The Rocking M Ranch
Chase County, Kansas
April 1997

Glynis Muldoon reined in her mount and glanced between the wagon train of tourists winding across the valley floor and the darkening sky. A gust of wind tipped the brim of her Stetson in warning. Tucking a wayward strand of auburn hair behind her ear, she drew up the collar of her drover's coat.

"Well, Bert, ol' boy," she said, leaning forward to pat her Appaloosa on the neck, "they paid for a cowboy adventure and I reckon it's what they'll get." She straightened and studied the ominous green-black wall rolling in from the southwest. "Looks like fifteen minutes . . . tops."

For a long moment she sat there on the crest of the hill, appreciating the stark beauty of the world around her, marveling at the openness of the space, the violent promise of the coming storm contrasted against the brilliant green of the spring tallgrass. The wind gusted over the prairie, sending ripples across the verdant landscape.

A smile touched the corners of her mouth. It had been a wet spring and the tallgrass had again proven itself properly named. Even now the grass brushed against the soles of her boots as she rode, and rippled as the cool winds blew across it. By early summer the seed heads would trail over her thighs as she rode across the land.

The land was eternal and endless, the sky forever and beyond. Here thousands of acres stretched between remote ranch houses, and roads were nothing more than widened cow paths across rolling plains. Here life was lived on nature's terms. Those who couldn't brave scorching heat and raging storms, cutting winds and bitter cold, either fled or perished. That was the way it had always been; the way it should be.

This was her place in the world. As it had been for four generations of Muldoons born to care for this precious piece of God's creation. And like all those before her, she would die here. That, too, was the way it should be; the way of the Flint Hills.

Bert snorted suddenly and flattened his ears. Glynis glanced first at the near-distant wall of clouds and then at the wagon train below. What had him so high-strung? They'd ridden out storms before. The Appaloosa didn't like them any more than she did, but the storm bearing down on them certainly didn't look any worse than was typical for this time of year. Maybe something in the wagon train had spooked him.

She watched as Chuckie drove the supply wagon out of the rutted pathway and headed up the draw, toward the wide spot on the other side of the ridge. As the other two wagons followed him, she studied the tourists visible through the rear opening in the canvas covers. Well, they looked like they had enough good sense to be concerned about the weather and the hasty, bumpy ascent of the hill, but they didn't look exactly panic-stricken. Those who had paid to make the two-day trip on horseback were being herded up the hill by Uncle Lloyd and Aunt Ria.

Glynis stood in the stirrups and peered toward the far end of the valley. Nothing. She looked toward the near end. Only the grass moved before the gusting wind. "C'mon, Bert," she said, settling back into the saddle. Gathering the reins, Glynis shifted slightly in the saddle and nudged her horse in the flanks with her heels, clearly conveying to him her decision to move on down the hill.

He wheeled to the right instead and fought the bit as she tried to turn him. Even as she brought him back under control, she noted that the wind had suddenly ceased, that the smell of rain had thickened the air.

Again she nudged her horse forward, but he stood as though rooted to the center of the earth, withers quivering, eyes wide. Glynis shivered. With one hand she reached up to snap closed the upper portion of her coat and then drew her hat down low across her brow. On the other side of the valley, she saw her uncle pause at the crest of the ridge. He motioned for her to come along and she waved an acknowledgment.

"Okay, Bert," she chided her skittish horse. "One more time. And let's get it right, okay? We're going down this hill and up the next."

As the horse backed up, she wheeled him sharply to the left, brought him around, and then pressed her heels into his flanks. "Yah!"

He leaped forward and Glynis smiled in satisfaction. Her sense of victory came to a sudden end when, halfway down the ridge, the wind blasted through the valley and the skies opened up. Bert plunged down through the blinding sheets of cold, silver rain as though pursued by demons.

Despite his speed, by the time they reached the center of the valley, streams of rain were pouring off the brim of her Stetson and the water had found its way beneath her leather chaps. She clenched her teeth against the cold and reminded herself how fast this kind of deluge could create flash floods. The ridge ahead would offer some protection once she reached the top and dropped down on the other side.

Beneath her the Appaloosa's muscles suddenly bunched and Glynis, sensing his intent, leaned forward and rose slightly in the stirrups. God only knew what he intended to jump, but she couldn't see through the rain and knew better than to fight his instincts. They sailed up, and even as she marveled at the length of his leap, they returned to earth with a dull ring of steel horseshoe against stone. Knowing she needed to pick the quickest way to the top of the ridge or risk being caught in fast water when the draw turned into a muddy sluice, Glynis settled back into the saddle and lifted her head to sight on the hill ahead.

There was no hill.

She swiped the water from her eyes with the back of her hand and looked again. No hill; only rock-studded, rain-battered, mildly rolling grassland spread out before her.

"What the hell?" she gasped, reining in Bert sharply. He skittered to a winded halt. Glynis hesitated before wheeling him in a tight circle, searching the landscape in an attempt to get her bearings. The rain stopped as abruptly as it had begun. The tang of a distant sea sharpened the air she drew into her lungs.

"Where in . . . ?" she whispered, her heart thundering as she twisted around in the saddle. "That was one helluva jump. Where in blue blazes are we?"

She looked around again, puzzled, and quickly swung down from her mount.

"This isn't tallgrass," she exclaimed, squatting down to examine the soggy ground. "And there isn't a bit of flint in the limestone, either." She pulled up a bit of the turf and examined the soil beneath the shallow roots. "The topsoil's thin enough to be Flint Hills. But it's different, not like any I've ever seen."

Tossing away the bit of sod, she brushed her hands clean on her coat and then gathered up the reins. Back in the saddle, she looked around, desperately fighting back her fear. "And with this much open range, you'd think I'd be able to see somebody's stock. Where are the cattle?"

Bert's ears flicked forward and his attention focused on something he apparently heard in the far distance. Glynis ignored the prickling at the nape of her neck. "Okay," she said, giving him free rein. "Let's go find something we recognize. But let's make it a quick discovery. I'm feeling really creepy about this whole thing."

She judged that they'd covered just over a mile when she heard the hoofbeats. Drawing Bert to a halt, she held her breath and listened to the rhythm rising from over the next hillock. Too measured to be cattle running, she decided. Obviously horses. Big ones, if the fullness of the sound was any indication. And a bunch of them, too. Coming pretty fast.

Part of her wanted to believe that it would be her Uncle

Lloyd and Aunt Ria, and maybe some of the tourists riding out in search of her. But she knew it wasn't. She glanced about the open country around her. She'd always found the solitude, the barren isolation of the Flint Hills comforting. But while this place wasn't all that much different in physical terms, she couldn't escape a sense of being dangerously exposed.

The hoofbeats stopped amid a clatter of metal and murmuring voices. Glynis turned and her jaw dropped. A half-dozen men sat on their mounts on the hillock before her, a British Union Jack fluttering above them in the soggy breeze. Their scarlet coats and brass buttons were bright against the greenness of the landscape, and in the cloudy light a bayonet glinted dully. Judging by their expressions, they were as stunned by her appearance as she was by theirs.

"Bert," she said, her voice tight and low. "Let's get the hell outta here."

Even as she turned him and kicked him in the flanks a voice rang out across the rocky grassland. "You there! Hold for the King's men!"

Panic hit her. Half-standing in the stirrups and leaning out over her horse's neck, Glynis urged the gelding into an all-out gallop. In the next second came a chorus of angry shouts, the high whinnies and rolling rumble of horses given a vicious spur.

She made for the highest of the hillocks before her, knowing that she'd have only a split second, once she reached the top, to choose the best direction. She prayed for anything but a wide-open expanse of rocky grassland.

Bert paused at the crest and in that second, Glynis surveyed the landscape and made her decision. The land fell away steeply, the ground rocky and loose and dropping into a narrow, thickly treed valley that appeared to wind up and through a tight course of hills. Hearing the rapid approach of the British soldiers, she urged the Appaloosa forward and gave him free rein. As the gelding skittered down the moraine on his haunches, Glynis leaned back and rammed her feet into the stirrups. A grim smile touched her lips when she realized the other horses had stopped.

Thoroughbreds. Weak ankles, she thought.

She had barely reached the bottom of the hill when a bullet whistled past her shoulder. As the Appaloosa found his footing, Glynis leaned close to the foam-flecked neck of her horse, trying desperately to make herself a smaller target. Glynis heard the whine of another bullet and instinctively snapped the reins to the right. Bert instantly pivoted and the ground beside them spattered beneath the impact of the leaden ball.

Glynis swore through clenched teeth. The bastards had stopped at the crest and were trying to find their range. Her only hope lay in running her horse in a serpentine pattern across the last of the open expanse and hoping that the soldiers couldn't anticipate and adjust quickly enough.

Another boom, more splattering sod. And then another. Glynis lost count of the number of rounds, but not the increasing frequency or accuracy of the shots. So far she'd been lucky. If that luck would only hold.

In the same moment she heard the shot, the bullet hit, tearing through her left shoulder with the fire and force of a lightning bolt. A blinding wave of pain radiated out from her arm, making her queasy. She took little pleasure in having finally made the grove of trees at the end of the draw.

Through the red wall of pain, she urged her horse forward, doing her best to stay on. She needed to find the creek running through the valley and follow it. Glynis blinked, trying to stave off the encroaching dizziness. She said, hoping the sound of her own voice would ground her, "North, I think. But I'm not sure. I'm so turned around. I don't know where we are."

By sheer will Glynis struggled to make her way. For a moment she thought she heard the red-coated pursuers in the woods behind her. Still, she wasn't quite certain whether they were any more real than the small flickering fire ahead and the dark shapes darting around it.

"Bert," she whispered, "Somehow . . . I don't think we're in Kansas anymore."

As her focus finally faded, she toppled from the saddle, heard a very human, very angry voice swear. Dimly she knew that the sound of her hitting the ground was small in comparison to the muffled din reverberating through the woods.

"You've been a good horse, Bert," she whispered. "You're on your own now."

2

County Wexford, Ireland
April 1832

Carrick des Marceaux spared only a glance for the heap of leather and cloth that had landed in their encampment, even less for the strange horse that had dumped its blood-soaked burden so unceremoniously at their fire. The sound of approaching British voices mattered far more to him at that moment. There was no time to run, no place to hide.

"Douse the flames," he commanded, his voice low and hard. "Fall back into the trees. If they move against us, take them all."

As his companions quickly melted into the shadows of the forest, he grabbed the reins of the horse standing by its fallen rider and quickly drew it with him out of the coming line of fire. Pulling his flintlock pistol from the waistband of his trousers, he crouched down in the thin scrub and waited.

Meyler had had the watch. How had he let the rider get that far without a warning? And who the hell was that lying out there and how had he found them? Carrick considered the hapless pile.

A triumphant cry sent his gaze back along the path the stranger had ridden into their camp. His muscles tensed at the flash of British red among the greens and browns of the forest.

Patience, lads, he urged silently.

"He's here," called one of the soldiers, dashing into the small clearing and making straight for the fallen man in the center. "Shot clean through!"

Don't you smell smoke, you idiot? Can't you feel the muzzles trained on your heart?

Four other British regulars rushed heedlessly to the side of the first. "A helluva rider, he was," said one.

"Dead he is now," said a soldier wearing the stripes of a sergeant. He viciously kicked the mound lying motionless at his feet. "Damm good shooting, Renfro."

Another of the soldiers, looking over his shoulder into the trees circling them, asked, "Do you suppose he was one of the Dragon's men?"

As one, the redcoats looked around warily, studying their surroundings.

It's a bit late to consider that now, isn't it? Carrick admonished grimly.

"Then it's a shame he died so quickly," growled the sergeant, kicking the body again. "The bugger might have—" Whatever else the man had been about to say was bit off as the figure at their feet groaned and struggled feebly to rise.

"Christ Almighty!" one of the British exclaimed, jumping back and whipping the muzzle of his musket toward their victim.

Carrick's stomach knotted in revulsion as the sergeant kicked the hapless, bloody figure again. "So you're not dead. Maybe if you tell us what you know about the Dragon we'll get you to the regimental surgeon."

Stepping from the shadows, his pistol held at arm's length and aimed at the sergeant's head, Carrick calmly observed, "More likely it is that you'll put a bullet in his brain or leave him to bleed to death no matter what he does." He waited until he saw their fear, then continued, "Allow me to save you the trouble of torturing the poor man. I am the Dragon. I understand you're looking for me."

For a scant second the soldiers' eyes widened, and then their muskets snapped up. The blast from Carrick's flintlock was lost in the deafening roar that issued from the woods all around him. He stood unmoving through the thickening pall of gun smoke until he saw every one of the redcoats fall.

With teeth clenched, he stepped into the circle of bodies. Using his feet, he shoved the muskets beyond the reach of lifeless hands. As he did, his men scrambled from their hiding places, their expressions as grim as his own.

"Don't bother with going after the sixth man. Take these to the river and let it carry them back to their own," he ordered quietly. "Their mounts must be at the edge of the woods. Keep the horses, the best of the tack, and their weapons. Toss the rest into the river with them. Let's be quick about it, lads. When we're done, we move on." After a pause, he added, "And someone find Meyler!"

The men went quietly about their grisly task. Carrick reloaded his pistol, then tucked it into his waistband at the small of his back. God, this business sickened him. But the rare, small justices he and his men won for the people of Ireland made it worth the fight.

Robert St. John knelt beside the blood-caked stranger. As Carrick watched, his cousin rolled the smallish man over. As the figure landed on his back, Carrick suddenly thought of the images he'd seen in the ruby depths of his mother's brooch some fifteen years earlier. The tall wooden gallows, the hangman and his noose, the sight of himself standing stoically as the hemp circle was tightened about his neck.

Carrick considered the stranger through narrowed eyes. His arrival had necessitated the killing of the British patrol. Until that moment the Dragon and his men had been but minor considerations for the British, the price on their heads not worthy of the effort it would have taken someone to turn them in. Now the situation had been drastically altered. Five British soldiers had been killed. The British would hunt them relentlessly now. Carrick sensed that the stranger's sudden appearance had set the course ahead.

"He's an oddly dressed fellow, isn't he?" Robert observed.

Carrick dragged his fingers through his thick, shaggy mane, shaking his head to dispel the dark thoughts.

"Aye. Odd indeed," Carrick agreed, dropping to his knees beside his cousin. Robert pressed his fingers against the man's neck. "He's still alive," he said after a moment. Carrick shrugged his shoulders and accepted fate's decree. "Strange clothes they may be, Robert, but they apparently protect him from the weather. Skin as soft and smooth as a baby's bottom."

Carrick leaned closer, his gaze tracing eyelashes and lips and a jawline too finely chiseled to be anything but female. Overlooking such obvious things, even for an instant, could get a man killed. "He's a she," he said simply. "Get my rucksack out of my saddlebags, would you?"

Robert rose smoothly to his feet and strode across the forest floor. As he did, Carrick pulled open the front of the woman's coat and shirt and then pushed back the edges just far enough to work. He slipped his hand behind her and felt the rough, sticky edges of the exit wound.

"How's her shoulder look?" Robert called from the trees.

"The English bastard was right," Carrick answered. "The shot went clear through. For the most part the bleeding's stopped. The ball doesn't seem to have flattened much as it went. Just the same, it tore a hole big enough that she's lost a great deal of blood. She appears sound enough of limb to weather the injury and heal with time."

Robert returned, handed Carrick a cloth bag, and then dropped down beside him to sit cross-legged. Carrick withdrew an old but clean linen shirt and the silver flask containing his whiskey from the bag. He tore a half-dozen long strips from the shirt. After folding them into thick squarish pads and setting them aside, he pulled the cork stopper from the flask.

"Miss," he said, lifting up the silver vessel, "you'll owe me for the consumption of my precious store. And I hereby advise you that I'll expect repayment at the first opportunity."

"I don't think she hears you," his cousin offered.

"But the warning has been issued nonetheless."

"Cad," Robert admonished with a wry grin.

Carrick shrugged as he placed one of the folded linen squares in back of the woman's left shoulder. "Brace yourself," he whispered, leaning close. "This is going to burn like the devil." Holding his own breath, he carefully trickled the amber liquid around the edge of the wound.

She came to with a harsh gasp. *What beautiful green eyes,* he thought in the same instant that she swung her right fist into his jaw.

Had she been healthy and sound, the blow might have

hurt, but in her weakened state it was no more than glancing. Carrick caught her wrist easily and gently pinned it to the ground beside her head. With his gaze locked on the steady light blazing within hers, he cautioned quietly, "Take care, miss. I'm not a forgiving man."

He continued firmly, "A few questions while you're conscious, if you don't mind. I would know your name, why the British attempted to kill you, and how you came upon our camp."

She studied him through narrowed eyes. "Irish?" she asked finally, her voice low and soft, like dark velvet.

"Aye," Carrick answered with a rueful smile. "Now the answers to my questions, if you please. We haven't much time and I have decisions to make."

"Glynis Muldoon," she answered weakly. "I don't know, and it was dumb luck."

He saw her swallow hard, saw the muscles around her eyes tighten with the pain. Telling himself that the game of questions and answers could be played later, he released her hand. "Miss," he began gently, "I wish I had the time to be tender with your person, but your sudden arrival here necessitates our equally hasty departure. I'm going to doctor your shoulder as it need be at the moment and I'd appreciate it if you'd refrain from taking another poke at me while I do it."

She'd barely nodded when he tipped the flask and poured a steady stream of alcohol into the bullet hole. She instantly stiffened and squeezed her eyes closed as she gathered a handful of the forest floor into a whitened fist.

Carrick nodded. "Not many a man could endure that without crying out," he offered in approval while corking the flask and turning to gather up the long strips of linen from the ground beside him. "'Tis a brave and strong spirit you possess, Glynis Muldoon."

"Save the flattery for another time, Carrick," Robert said dryly. "Can't you see the poor girl's gone unconscious again?"

He considered the dark lashes lying along her pale, high cheekbones. "Probably just as well," he answered after a moment. "Binding this tight enough to do some good would have been just as painful for her as the whiskey. Give me a hand and help me get her upright."

Robert maneuvered himself until he knelt above her shoulders. On the count of three they eased her into a sitting position. Carrick eased her clothing even farther off her shoulder and then deftly bound the cloth squares with the lengths of linen.

Robert looked over Carrick's shoulder as he worked. "Meyler's peeking through the trees. And looking more than a little reluctant, I might add."

"Meyler!" Carrick called as he secured his work with a quick, tight knot and pulled the woman's clothing back into place. "You've some explaining to do, lad."

"Are you truly angry?" asked the slight, redheaded boy as he edged closer.

Carrick examined the strange fastenings on the woman's shirt and, while tentatively pressing the two metal halves together, gently admonished, "You assured me that you were responsible enough to take the watch. How is it that she got through without a warning?"

"She?"

"Aye. She. Where were you?"

"I was watchin'," the boy replied, his voice suddenly full of wonder. "He . . . er, she came down the steep side of the ridge at a full run. 'Twas amazin' to see; truly ridin' like I've never set eyes on before. By the time I realized she'd be comin' into the woods, I couldn't move without the British seein' me. I didn't know what to do, so I thought it best to do nothin'. You should have seen her ride, Carrick."

"Perhaps she'll give us a demonstration of her skills when she's stronger," Robert suggested.

"Are you goin' to ever let me have the watch again, Carrick?"

Carrick looked weary as he answered, "I've always thought that twelve wasn't old enough, Meyler. You've proven me right."

"Carrick," Robert whispered. "As Aunt Alanna has said often enough in your defense: Cut the boy some slack. His warning wouldn't have changed events in the least and he's learned a lesson from this."

"I don't like being surprised."

"It won't ever happen again," Meyler pledged earnestly. "On my heart and hope to die."

"Spare me from fools and children," Carrick muttered, rising to his feet. At the boy's crestfallen expression, he relented. "We'll see, lad," he said, and glanced about the woods. "Get our horses saddled and ready to travel, Meyler. Be quick about it. The others should be done with their tasks soon enough and we need to be on our way. Another British patrol is likely to come in search of the other."

"Yes, sir." Meyler was beaming as he ran back into the shadows of the forest.

Robert watched him go. "It takes so little to make him happy."

"And so little to get us hanged," Carrick countered.

Robert didn't look at him. "If you've lost your stomach for it, we could always go back to sea. It would greatly relieve our mothers and perhaps even earn us a bit of grudging respect from our fathers."

"I haven't lost my stomach for our task," Carrick replied, snatching up his rucksack. "And since nothing I do will please my father, I might just as well please myself."

Robert shrugged. "Uncle Kiervan's anger usually stems from seeing so much of himself in you. Your mother says it scares the bejeezus out of him."

Bejeezus, Carrick silently grumbled. *Just one of many colorful twentieth century expressions we've picked up from Mother.* "I don't care to discuss it further, Robert," he said to his cousin matter-of-factly. "If you want to leave the band, I'll understand and make no move to stop you."

"I didn't suggest anything of the sort," Robert retorted. "I was merely putting forth alternatives should we tire of the noble pursuit of outlawry."

Carrick glared at his cousin and then, deliberately looking away, changed the subject. "There had to be some reason the Brits were chasing her; why they shot her through. Since we can't very well leave her behind to their mercy, we'll take her with us. Her mount seems docile enough. But even if she rides as well as Meyler says, she can't stay in the saddle unconscious. She'll ride with me until she can ride on her own."

"How long do you intend to keep her with us, Carrick?"

"Until she's strong enough to go her own way."

"And if in the meantime she's marked as one of us?" Robert persisted. "As one of the Dragon's band? She won't be able to leave. At least not safely. You know that the patrols usually number six men. If this one did, then one's on his way back to the regiment."

"We'll leave her behind when we conduct our raids and hope for the best. Perhaps they'll think she's dead," Carrick countered smoothly, handing his rucksack to his cousin. Bending down, he slipped one arm beneath the woman's shoulders, the other under her knees, then straightened with her cradled in his arms.

Carrying her toward his horse, he said, "We don't have the luxury of time at the moment, but at the first opportunity we need to go through her belongings to see if there's anything in her bags to tell us of her family, the place where she belongs, or what brought her here."

Robert followed. "Maybe she'll tell us herself when she regains consciousness," he observed dryly.

Carrick nodded solemnly. "Aye, that she will, for certain sure. But the less we tell her about ourselves," he said, turning and handing the woman into his cousin's arms, "the better for all concerned." He swung up and settled in his saddle. Reaching to take the woman back, he added, "If she can leave us after a time, what she can't tell anyone lessens our chances of hanging."

"Agreed." Robert strode toward his own horse. "I'll pass the word for caution among the lads."

"And while you're at it, pass the word that the woman's under my protection," Carrick instructed. "I'll not have the band distracted by her."

Robert grinned. "What if there's a challenge and you have to prove your claim, Cousin?"

Carrick grinned back at him. "Tough job, I know. But somebody's got to do it."

"Ever the soul of sacrifice."

"Aye," Carrick agreed, his grin fading. "Up for sainthood, I am."

3

She'd said her name was Glynis Muldoon. A good strong Irish name. Carrick looked down at the slight woman cradled in the curve of his arm. The strands of hair that had escaped from beneath her broad-brimmed hat were a shimmering auburn. They framed a delicate oval face which he suspected would be porcelain pale if Glynis Muldoon were to protect her skin from the sun. Faint freckles dusted the bridge of her nose and the upper edges of her cheekbones; he remembered the brilliant green of her eyes. She certainly had the look of a sweet Irish flower.

He smiled ruefully as he remembered how she'd swung at him when she'd come to in the clearing. Glynis Muldoon apparently had a bit of an Irish temper, too.

But she wasn't Irish and he knew it. He recalled the precise sound of her speech. Glynis Muldoon didn't have the lilt of Erin. Not a trace of it. She spoke with a kind of slowly rolling, sandy-edged softness that made him think she came from a place where every word was appreciated and savored.

As his gaze swept down the length of her, he noted again the odd construction and materials of her clothing. He couldn't say precisely why, but he had a sneaking suspicion that this woman and his mother had a great deal in common—not the least of which would be magically traveling across a continent, an ocean, and more than a century in time.

Carrick scowled. He didn't need this complication in his

life at the moment. He had things to do, important things that didn't involve cradling a slender woman in his arms as he rode across the Irish countryside and tried to keep the British from hanging him a few months too soon. The fact that he found himself wanting to trace the delicate line of her cheekbone with his fingertips was beside the point.

Damnation. He couldn't afford such a dangerous distraction. It was high time Miss Glynis Muldoon woke from her nap and found the strength to ride her own damn horse. He deliberately moved the arm under her head.

Glynis's consciousness returned with a painful jolt. It took only a second to realize that she was being held in someone's arms. The scents of sunshine, horse, and leather mingled with musky male to wrap around her senses. *Eau de Cowboy.* For a moment she panicked, but then forced herself to remain calm and to try to make sense of her situation.

She was definitely cradled in some cowboy's arms while his horse carried them along. But which cowboy? She remembered the man with the black hair and brilliant blue eyes, the man who'd been kneeling over her when she'd come to in the clearing. What was his name? Had he even told her?

The horse's gait shifted, jarring her. God, she hurt. Everywhere. But especially her shoulder. She couldn't let the pain distract her, though. The world had apparently turned upside down and she needed to find a way to turn it right.

She tried to focus beyond the sensations of her body. There was a boy with them; she could tell his voice by its higher pitch. In addition to him, she heard the distinctly different tones and speech patterns of maybe five other men. All but one of them rode ahead of her. The odd man out rode behind, apparently leading a string of extra mounts. The muffled sound of the hoofbeats and the shadows lacing her eyelids told her that they weren't traveling over prairie, but winding their way across the matted floor of a forest.

What she hadn't heard was the one voice she would have recognized. She hadn't heard the blue-eyed stranger, and the man holding her hadn't spoken. She put two and two together. And came up with a rock-hard chest, a steel-banded arm, and a lap into which she was nestled in a manner . . . well, in a manner that if not downright obscene, was at least damn inviting. *Think of something else, Glynis.*

The man had said he was Irish. Judging from the voices she heard, they all were. Irishmen. British soldiers. Union Jacks. What in heaven's name was going on? Surely there had to be some logical explanation for the incredibly strange circumstances in which she found herself—an explanation *other* than the looming likelihood of insanity. What it might be, she couldn't even guess. But, she assured herself, if she listened and watched long enough she'd figure it out.

Still feigning sleep, she peeked through her lashes, noting that the shadows had lightened and the scrub growth had thickened. She risked another quick glance around, hoping to see a familiar landmark. Three men and the boy rode into the rolling green hills stretching before her.

"About damn time. My arm's gone to sleep."

She looked up . . . into impossibly blue eyes. *Breathtaking.* Thick, dark eyelashes. Strong nose. Sharply planed cheekbones. Wonderful, full lips. What would they look like when he smiled? She remembered a flash of straight white teeth and knew that he'd smiled at her at least once before.

Glynis impatiently quelled her wayward thoughts. What was she doing taking inventory at a time like this? She had to be nuts. She knew with absolute certainty that she needed her wits about her to deal with her current circumstances. She looked out over the verdant fields and took a steadying breath. She could handle this.

The stranger reined in his mount as he asked her, "How's your shoulder?"

"I'd be lying if I said it didn't hurt," she replied evenly. "But I'll live."

"Can you ride?"

She met his gaze and nodded. "With my eyes closed and both hands tied behind my back."

He motioned to the man behind them, who came forward instantly as commanded, giving Bert's reins to Blue Eyes and then wordlessly leading the string of riderless horses past them to join the others ahead.

"My name's Carrick," her companion said, his tone cool as he swung down off his horse.

An odd name, she thought, but it sounded hard and no-nonsense and she sensed that it fit him perfectly. "Just Carrick?" she offered.

"Aye. Just Carrick. Would you like to climb down from there?"

Looking down into his eyes did funny things to her insides, made her feel off balance. "Yeah," she answered, trying to pull her thoughts together. She ignored his outstretched hands and inched herself forward, sliding down the side of the horse.

It was a mistake and she knew it the minute her feet hit the ground. Pain, white-hot and blinding, enveloped her.

"Stubborn, aren't you?"

The amusement in his words anchored her as she struggled through the fog of pain. She was standing in the circle of his arms, her hands holding his coat sleeves in a white-knuckled grip.

"I'm all right," she said, releasing her hold on him and trying not to collapse at his feet.

He stepped back only a little and then carefully led her around to Bert's left side. He wasn't the least bit condescending, but his assistance still rankled. Glynis refused to feel like a half-wit on a weekend excursion. She squared her shoulders as best she could and took the reins from his hands. "I can handle it from here," she announced, reaching for the stirrup.

"Yes, I can see that," he said at the same time his hands came around her waist and he lifted her up. Glynis was still mustering words of protest when he gently settled her across the saddle.

"I gather this is the first time you've been shot," he said, heading for his own mount.

"Oh, no. I try for a bullet wound every six months or so," she replied flippantly. "It keeps life interesting. And you?"

When he swung up into the saddle without a reply, she asked, "If you don't mind my asking . . . was there some particular reason those men wanted to shoot me?"

"The British don't have to have a reason," he answered quietly. "This is Ireland."

"Ireland?" Glynis muttered, "Yeah, right. Wanna buy the Brooklyn Bridge?"

"Aye, Ireland," he answered, looking at the land spreading before them. A small smile played at the corners of his mouth as he added, "And the Brooklyn Bridge isn't yours to sell."

His manner said that he found her frivolous. For the second time in minutes her pride rankled. She took another steadying breath. "I haven't thanked you for helping me."

"I did nothing beyond the requirements of humanity."

"Well," she replied, determined to get their conversation rolling smoothly, "I appreciate the effort. Thanks for patching me up and helping me to escape."

"It's hardly a difficult task to escape dead men."

She kept her voice cool. "You killed those soldiers?"

"You left me with no recourse," he replied. "I wasn't about to surrender either myself or my men simply because you'd led them into our camp. I value living a bit more than that."

Glynis fought the guilt. She hadn't deliberately chosen her way into the woods.

"What breed of horse is that you ride?" Carrick asked, half-turning in his saddle to study Bert.

"He's an Appaloosa," she answered proudly. "He's surefooted and quick. Great bursts of speed on the short haul. Of course, he can't outrun your thoroughbred in a distance race, but then that's not what he's been bred for."

"And for what task has he been bred?"

"Working cattle." She smiled with satisfaction. "He can turn on a dime."

Carrick turned and considered her. "Are you a traveler?" he asked finally, his gaze locked with hers, his eyes darkening to the color of a twilight sky.

Glynis looked down at her drover's coat and then back at him. She answered with a half-smile, "Don't you think that's pretty obvious?"

"I don't mean in the common sense," he countered impatiently. "Have you come across time? Are you from a century other than this one?"

The question struck her like a well-aimed hoof. She settled herself more comfortably in the saddle before replying noncommittally, "It sorta depends on what century this one is."

"The year is 1832," he stated flatly. "Which makes it the nineteenth century. Would you happen to be from the twentieth? Perhaps even the twenty-first?"

Glynis swore under her breath and stared at the grassland ahead as she quickly reassured herself that reason and logic would ultimately prevail, that she could make some sort of sense of her situation without resorting to the impossibility of science fiction.

"Would you happen to know a woman named Saraid Concannon?" Carrick continued. "Or one named Alanna Chapman?"

Something in the tone of his voice prompted her to look back at him. His own gaze was fixed on an invisible pathway before them, his jaw hard and unyielding.

Definitely wound tighter about something all of a sudden, she decided. "No," Glynis answered. "Should I?"

He shrugged, but his expression didn't ease. "You're not Irish," he said after a few moments. "Where are you from?"

"Kansas." Glynis added, "The heartland of America."

He nodded. "And where is this Kansas in relation to Colorado?"

"One state to the east," she answered, studying the clean lines of his profile. How did he know about Colorado? she wondered. Had it even been a state in 1832? She frowned, realizing how easily she'd accepted the incredible notion that she'd been transported through time. She couldn't afford to go over the edge. She was the last of the Muldoons. Her ancestors were probably watching from heaven. They would expect her to carry on their legacy. She couldn't do that if she went nuts.

"And what is it that you do in your Kansas, Miss Muldoon? How is it that you make yourself useful?"

She replied coolly, "First off, I want it understood from the git-go that I don't believe for one minute that I've been transported across time and space. It's not scientifically possible. Second, I'm not at all used to being put through an inquisition by strangers and I don't much appreciate how you're asking questions. Where I come from we have a code. You listen if someone wants to tell you about themselves, but you don't ask."

"Miss Muldoon," he interrupted, "I happen to know for a fact that time travel is indeed possible. If you don't recall boarding a ship and actually sailing from America to Ireland, if you awoke on a recent morning in a year other than 1832, then you have traveled."

Glynis shook her head, wincing at the flash of pain the effort sent tearing through her shoulder. "I don't believe you," she answered through clenched teeth. God, this had to be the most mangled encounter she'd ever had with anyone in her life. What was it about this Carrick that put everything out of kilter?

"I don't give a flying rat's ass what you believe or don't believe, Miss Muldoon. It's irrelevant to the matter at hand. Your blundering into my encampment put me and my men in considerable danger. I could have very well left you where you lay . . . and all things considered, probably should have. I'd suggest that you might be a bit more appreciative of what we've done for you. And as for my manner, I'm not at all accustomed to being upbraided . . . and especially by a woman."

Glynis reined in Bert. "Look, Carrick Whatever," she began evenly. "I honestly appreciate that you took care of my shoulder, but I didn't ask to be brought along with you. And since, for some reason, we seem to grate on each other's nerves, I think it would be for the best if we simply parted company at this point."

He leaned toward her, his nearness adding impact to his words. "Trust me, Miss Muldoon, when I tell you that I most fervently wish we could. Unfortunately, the circumstances dictate otherwise."

"What circumstances?" Glynis asked, arching a brow, any effort of civility gone.

"How many men were in the British patrol that chased you?" he demanded.

The man's sense of superiority apparently knew no bounds. She met his gaze squarely as she shot back, "Six."

"Five came into the woods after you. Five died because you left us no other choice. Care to hazard a guess as to the whereabouts of the sixth Brit?"

"On his way back to his company," she reluctantly admitted.

Carrick shook his head. "He's already there. With a full description of you, the fate of his patrol, and the location of my camp. Care to give odds on your chances for survival once you leave the protection of my band?"

"I guess that's my problem, isn't it?" Glynis replied defiantly. "I wouldn't want to inconvenience you any more than I already have."

His voice flat, he said, "Miss Muldoon, you aren't going anywhere but where I say. Were you to fall into the hands of the British authorities you could have us all hanging from the gallows before the week is out."

Glynis fought back her panic and offered, "They'd have to catch me first."

"Do you think catching you would be particularly difficult?" he demanded, amused. "You're an American, a woman dressed in strange clothing, riding a strange horse with a distinctly different saddle. You won't be able to go anywhere without being noticed. How long do you think it would take the British to pick up your trail?"

"I could—"

"Blend in?" He cut in grimly. "You're not of this time, Muldoon. You could change your clothing, shoot your horse, and bury both it and your saddle, and still be readily identified as an outsider. You don't have the manner of a woman of this century and I doubt very much whether all the time of eternity would be enough for you to adjust your ways. Not that the British are going to give you that long anyway."

Her nerves raw, her body and mind beyond exhaustion, Glynis groused, "So I'm supposed to stay with you?"

He straightened in his saddle and considered the open country for a long moment before replying, "Neither of us has any choice in the matter for the time being."

God, she was so tired. Bone-weary. And her shoulder throbbed so painfully that she wondered if maybe cutting it off would be less trouble. " 'For the time being' suggests that there'll eventually come a point when we can go our separate ways."

" 'Tis magic that brought you here," he replied. "And if the magic can be reversed, then I shall see it done at the first opportunity."

Glynis tried to summon the energy to deal with the impossible reality he presented her. "What do you mean, *if* it can be reversed?" she asked, exasperated. She hurriedly added, "Not that I'm believing any of this, mind you."

"I say *if*," he retorted, "because only magic gone wrong in the worst way imaginable could account for my having been plagued with your presence. Mistakes of such incredible magnitude are difficult to correct at best. If you believe in God, Miss Muldoon, I would strongly encourage you to pray for a miracle. I'll do my best to see that it comes to pass as soon as is humanly possible."

"And in the meantime?" Glynis inquired, too tired to even bother trying to be pleasant. "What am I supposed to do? Play Snow White to your Six Dwarfs?"

He turned toward her, his gaze boring into hers as he answered in measured tones, "In the meantime, I expect you to do as you're told, Miss Muldoon. Try not to endanger us any more than you have already. And above all else, try not to irritate me any more than you absolutely must."

With that salvo he cantered away. Glynis glared after him. "I don't give a damn if you are one of the best riders I've ever seen," she muttered. "You're still an arrogant, chauvinistic son of a bitch." What he'd suggested about time traveling was impossible. She shook her head and finally allowed her body to relax. "And you're a certified lunatic to boot."

Carrick eased his horse's pace as he rode up beside Robert. "Drop back and keep your eye on her," he commanded. "I'll take the point."

Robert chuckled and cocked a dark brow, but he didn't say anything as he wheeled his horse about and went back to ride with Glynis Muldoon.

Carrick moved up the hill ahead of the others. He

scanned the land around him, listening for the smallest sound, looking for the smallest movement that didn't belong to the quiet afternoon.

She was a time traveler like his mother; of that he was absolutely certain. And the oddest creature he'd ever encountered, to be sure. As well as the most intriguing. Somehow, despite the fact that she dressed in the manner of a man, despite the fact that she squared up to the world with a spirit of blazing defiance and self-assurance that most men could only envy, somehow, during every second of their conversation, he'd been acutely aware of her as a woman.

And that kind of awareness made her more dangerous than any woman he'd ever known. Good judgment said he needed to be rid of her at the first opportunity.

4

Glynis chewed at the inside of her lip. Could she really be in Ireland in 1832? While the topography was similar to Flint Hills, the soil and the grass were decidedly different. And the accents of everyone in Carrick's band were undeniably Irish. All the evidence seemed to indicate that at least part of an impossibility had indeed occurred.

But 1832? She did the math. Crossing the span of a hundred and sixty-five years in an instant? Too bad her college degree had centered her in the biological and economic sciences. What she needed at the moment was a solid background in quantum physics and modern European history. She sighed and shook her head. The how wasn't as important as deciding whether she truly had been transported back in time.

She studied Carrick's back as he rode ahead. His clothes were well tailored, but without argument well out of fashion by the standards of 1997. His knee-high boots were molded to his calf and were low-heeled. Though scuffed and worn, they bore the unmistakable mark of quality workmanship. She noted that the man leaving Carrick's side and moving back toward her wore the same style of tailored clothing. The others were dressed in rather shapeless, bulky garments made of a coarse-looking woven cloth. None of them wore bright colors. Various shades of green and brown seemed to be the favored colors.

Glynis considered Carrick's saddle next, and then the

others' in his band. They all seemed to have a fondness for English riding tack. What was it Carrick had said? Something about her strange horse, her strange saddle? Bert was obviously the only quarterhorse in the bunch, the only Appaloosa, her saddle the only western one. The English soldiers had ridden thoroughbreds as well . . . and carried muskets with bayonets, if she remembered correctly from that one quick glimpse she'd had of them at fairly close range.

Surely English soldiers of the twentieth century didn't ride around the Irish countryside on horseback while wearing their ceremonial-dress red uniforms. They'd be cruising along in something like a Humvee and wearing the latest in camouflage fashion. Unless, of course, she observed with grim humor, they'd seriously strayed from the Queen's parade route.

Glynis sighed in exasperation. If only a couple of the pieces of this puzzle would go together in a plausible way. Maybe the man reining in and turning his horse to ride beside her could provide some desperately needed answers.

She returned his smile even as she mentally compared him to Carrick. She figured that if the two of them were to stand side by side, they'd be roughly the same height. This man's build was slighter, though, his shoulders not nearly as broad, his neck not quite as muscled as Carrick's. Their sunburnished skin, raven-black hair, and finely chiseled cheekbones were so strikingly similar that she wondered if they might be brothers. Something about this man's presence, however, suggested that he played Abel to Carrick's Cain.

"Allow me to introduce myself," he said. "My name is Robert. Robert St. John."

"Glynis Muldoon," she replied, carefully tucking the reins into the curve of her left hand before extending her gloved right hand.

"A bit awkward attempting this on horseback," he offered with a grin, raising her hand to his lips. "But never let it be said that a St. John was less than chivalrous."

"I must say that you're far more gracious than your brother," she observed dryly.

"Carrick?

Glynis glanced toward the leader riding well ahead of them. "Yeah, Mr. Snarly."

"Legally we're cousins," Robert supplied, "but we were raised in the same house, our respective parents feeling free to discipline and school us both as the need arose. We know each other as would brothers."

Glynis smiled at him. "You seem to have fared better in the educational process, Mr. St. John."

He chuckled quietly. "I'll make no excuses for him except to say that Carrick carries responsibility heavily on his shoulders. It tends to make him a bit gruff when he's not consciously playing another part."

"You're actors, then?" she asked hopefully.

He smiled knowingly. "On a fishing expedition, Miss Muldoon? It is Miss, isn't it?"

Glynis sighed in resignation. If she wanted to know something, she had no choice but to ask for it. There would be no subtle information-gathering. Like his cousin, Robert was no dummy. "It is Miss," she supplied. "And, yes, I was fishing. Your cousin doesn't seem to want to tell me anything beyond the fact that the year is 1832 and that this is Ireland. In fact, he even refused to tell me his last name."

"Carrick's . . ." He studied the back of his cousin. "Well," he said finally, "cautious isn't the right word. Perhaps *calculating* might be a better choice."

"As in Machiavelli?" Glynis inquired dryly.

"Oh, I didn't mean that Carrick's calculating in a politically ruthless sense," Robert protested. "No politics for Carrick. He hasn't the patience or the willingness to bend. I should have said that he's always considering, always contemplating his options and the likely outcome of his actions."

"Be that as it may, Mr. St. John," Glynis countered evenly, "it doesn't explain either your cousin's subtle hostility or his unwillingness to be forthright."

"Well," he said, "I'm not about to apologize for his rudeness. He's a grown man and, sooner or later, he'll get around to eating that crow on his own. As for his lack of openness . . ." He glanced at his cousin before turning back to her and saying with an easy smile, "Tell me what you'd like to know, Miss Muldoon, and I'll do my best to compensate for Carrick's stinginess."

She began with the simplest of the matters confounding her. "Where am I?" she asked.

Robert St. John looked a little regretful as he answered. "He may have his faults, but Carrick doesn't lie. You are in Ireland, Miss Muldoon. The year is indeed 1832. Just as he said it was."

Glynis calmly counted to ten before she said evenly, "And what if I told you that was impossible?"

He searched her face for a moment and then asked, "And what if I told you that my Aunt Alanna, Carrick's mother, came to Ireland from Colorado in the year 1997?"

Carrick had mentioned an Alanna Chapman. Glynis shook her head. "I'd have to say that you aren't pitchin' from a full loft."

He shrugged. "I suppose it would be difficult to believe, had you no experience with the possibility. However, I suspect you'll have a chance to meet Aunt Alanna before this whole thing's over and done with."

"What thing?"

"Your misadventure among us."

"Forgive me, Mr. St. John," she said with a weak smile, "but where I come from, the term *misadventure* implies something along the lines of tipping over Porta Potties at the county fair. I tend to view being shot and hauled across country by strangers as something just a tad more serious."

"I didn't mean to make light of your situation," he offered. "I assure you that Carrick and I are quite concerned about your presence here."

"So, just for the moment assuming that I have traveled across the better part of two centuries, half a continent, and the Atlantic Ocean, how exactly did I get here?"

"Well," he began, "I'm just guessing, mind you, but I think you're here through magic gone awry. That would make me think of my Cousin Saraid. She's always practiced magic with a bit of an unexpected twist. Actually . . ." he paused, grinning, "I don't think Saraid's ever pulled off a spell without it going royally wrong. Assuming that to be the case, it's going to take someone with Aunt Alanna's powers to straighten it out."

Geez. This was getting better by the second. "Are you saying that your cousin and your aunt are witches?" she asked incredulously.

"No," Robert hastened to supply. "Aunt Alanna's not a witch in the sense that most people tend to think about them. She's a Seer of the Ancient Find, a practitioner of the ancient Goddess religion. And Saraid would like to be but doesn't have the gift for it."

"Let me see if I've got this straight," Glynis grumbled. "I'm in another time and place because of a bumbling wannabe witch? But I'm not to worry because Aunt Alanna's going to wave a magic wand over me, mumble some spell, and return me to where I belong?"

Her poor attitude didn't seem to faze him in the least. "It rather depends, I think, on the particular spell that brought you here. We'll have to find Saraid before we'll know what must be done."

"This is Saraid Concannon, right?" At his quizzical expression, she explained, "Carrick asked me if I knew her. He also asked about an Alanna Chapman. I presume that's your Aunt Alanna, the time traveler."

He seemed to take her measure before saying, "Carrick seems to think we should withhold from you all the information we can. Frankly, I think he's already let most of the cat out of the bag and I can't see the point in trying to convince you it's a dog. You don't have a malicious heart and—"

"Forgive me, Mr. St. John," she interrupted quietly, "but I don't see how you can make that judgment. You don't know me very well."

He shook his head. "I see confusion and intelligence in your eyes, Miss Muldoon. But not a spark of evil or cruelty. Your heart's a good one. You'll bring no ill fortune upon us by deliberate choice."

"Tell that to Carrick. He seems to think I'm the devil incarnate."

Robert grinned widely. "I suspect my cousin doesn't quite know what to do with you, Miss Muldoon. You're well outside his considerable experience with women. And his surname, by the way, is des Marceaux. Carrick des Marceaux. Fourth child and second son of Alanna and Kiervan des Marceaux; second son by mere minutes, I might add, and a twist of fate which makes him a man very much adrift in the world. That, in part, explains his nature."

"Perhaps to you, Mr. St. John, but I'm afraid that . . ." Her words froze as a red dot rose on the distant hillock and then disappeared. She turned toward Robert. "Did you see . . . ?"

"Yes, as did Carrick," Robert St. John answered, his gaze quickly moving over the members of the troop regrouping ahead. He looked at her dubiously and then asked, "Can you manage a gallop?"

Glynis inwardly groaned but gave Robert St. John a wry smile. "Considering the circumstances, I guess I'll have to."

"Good," he shot back, wheeling his horse sharply. "Stay close to me."

At first she had to hold Bert back as they flew across the rolling grassland or risk leaving the others behind. With every thud of her horse's hooves, arrows of pain radiated out from her shoulder. Glynis focused on the forest ahead, on the protective trees and shadows they'd left such a short time ago. God, she was running from redcoats who seemed hell-bent to have her dead by sunset. How had she gotten into this mess? How was she going to get herself out of it?

"We'll go only a short way in," she heard Robert call from behind her. "Prepare to draw up and wait for Carrick's command."

"Gotcha," she replied, nodding grimly and hoping that the apparent leader of this group did indeed have commands to issue. Inspired commands, she decided, would be especially nice at this point. If the rider on the hillock just behind them brought a patrol after them—and if the one who'd escaped the death trap in the woods earlier had brought his uniformed brethren back in search of justice—surely Carrick des Marceaux knew they were being sandwiched?

She glanced about her as Bert carried her past the first of the trees. All seven riders had dashed into the woods almost abreast. Robert St. John rode on her right, Carrick des

Marceaux on her left. For the length of a football field the group rode on, ignoring the path, each rider choosing his own way, dodging trees and low-hanging branches, crashing through the underbrush heedless of the noise.

"Far enough," Carrick called, his voice low. Every horse and rider came to an immediate skittering halt.

"Eachann, you know what to do with the extra mounts," he said, wheeling his high-spirited horse about in tight circle. "Robert, take Meyler with you." His gaze stopped on Glynis for only a moment. "Muldoon, you'll ride with me." Then, nodding to each man in turn, he said decisively, "Tomorrow night at the three-quarter moon! Take care, gentlemen, and Godspeed."

The sandy-haired man called Eachann rode through the trees, heading east and leading the horses they had taken from the dead British soldiers. Robert St. John gave her a reassuring smile before he, too, turned his animal. The carrot-headed boy fell in beside him and together they angled through the woods in a southeasterly direction. The other two men rode off as well, one to the west, one to the southwest.

"That leaves the northeast or the northwest for us," she observed, bringing Bert around. Carrick remained motionless, his gaze moving between his departing men and the woods to the north and south of them.

"Miss Muldoon, are you a betting woman?" he asked thoughtfully after a moment, his gaze boring into her as though searching for some great truth.

"Not really," Glynis answered honestly. "Gambling's always struck me as a waste of good money. I prefer sure things."

"The only sure things, Miss Muldoon," he countered with a grim smile, "are death and British abuses. Everything else is a gamble. We go north."

"North?" Glynis repeated in stunned disbelief. "Won't that take us straight at a British patrol? The one looking for me?"

"It very well might," he said, turning his horse about. "But if either patrol reaches this point, they'll see the directions everyone went. If they get this far, they'll pursue my friends and kinsmen. But if one patrol finds a fox to chase, the odds are the other will join the hunt and neither of them will ever reach this particular place. I owe my men a diversion if I can create one. And since you created the problem in the first place, it's only right that you take the risk with me."

Controlling the urge to remind him that she hadn't deliberately created the situation, Glynis urged Bert after Carrick. "I'll give you points for loyalty and courage," she retorted as she drew abreast Carrick, "but you're also insane."

He didn't spare her a glance. "You're hardly the first to point that out, Miss Muldoon."

"We go north and I could very well be the last."

She saw the hard line that came to his jaw. Still, she was unprepared for the chilling bitterness of his words.

"Should you ever have an occasion to meet my father, Miss Muldoon," he said, "do make a point of sharing your opinions with him. It will gratify him to no end to know that you agree with his judgment of me."

Glynis said nothing more, but dropped back a half-length. Tomorrow night the band would meet. All she had to do in the meantime was endure the growing pain in her shoulder, stay astride Bert, elude British patrols apparently intent on killing her, and keep from angering any further the unpredictable, ill-tempered bastard with whom she was forced to ride. From the looks of things already, she thought tiredly, the last of the bunch was going to be the toughest.

Glynis considered her options. Part of her was tempted to leave her surly companion on his own. If she cut a wide arc to the southeast she'd catch up with Robert St. John and the boy sooner or later. It would certainly be a far more pleasant experience to ride with them than it would to follow Carrick des Marceaux. At least Robert had good manners.

She watched Carrick riding before her through the woods. He was, among other things, a true enigma: handsome in a roguish cowboy sort of way, but with a chip on his shoulder the size of Mount Rushmore. She had no doubt, however, that he possessed a gentility that would rival Robert's if and when he chose to haul it out of mothballs.

But, from what she'd been able to piece together, the

man was obviously an outlaw. Why had he given up his lofty social position to become a hunted man? Perhaps the choice hadn't been his. As she well knew from her own life, circumstances sometimes jumped up and left you without options. Carrick hated the British. *That* he'd made abundantly clear. And he and his father were on the outs. The why for both issues remained to be discovered.

"Are you always so silent?"

Glynis glanced up to see that he hadn't bothered to look back at her before he spoke. "Depends on the situation," she answered. "Right now I don't feel much like talking."

"You strike me as the kind of woman who doesn't say much under any circumstance," he countered.

"Yeah, I'm a different breed of critter," she shot back.

Carrick didn't bother to look back. "That's a given, Miss Muldoon."

"Not that it matters to me, but I gather that you don't approve."

"I don't give a damn about you one way or the other, Miss Muldoon. You're simply a problem that has to be dealt with . . . as expediently as possible."

Despite her abused pride, Glynis responded evenly, "I hope you don't mind if I consider you in the same manner, Mr. des Marceaux."

He reined in sharply and she brought Bert to a halt beside him. His eyes were the color of blued steel as they glared at each other. There was a long moment before he spoke. "Robert, I presume?"

"What about him?"

"I assume he told you my surname?" He considered her through narrowed eyes, then asked, "What other information did he give you?"

Glynis knew damage control when she heard it. "Nothing of any earth-shattering importance, I assure you. He told me that you're cousins. Your mother's the Alanna Chapman you asked me if I knew, and she comes from Colorado in 1997. That sort of stuff. I don't think any of it will threaten national security."

His face hardened. "It's enough to get all of us an appointment with the hangman," he countered, his voice low and even. "Miss Muldoon, permit me to be blunt. If I even so much as *think* there's a possibility you might fall into British hands, I'll put a bullet in you myself. And you may rest assured, Muldoon, that I'm a far better shot than the last man who tried to kill you."

"I'll keep that in mind," she replied, resisting the impulse to check the scabbard laced to Bert's saddle. She met his steely eyes without flinching, determined to hold her own despite his attempt to intimidate her. She'd faced rustlers and unscrupulous cattle dealers. The only way Carrick des Marceaux was going to get the best of her was if he physically wrestled her to the ground.

He looked away suddenly, staring into the far distance. Glynis instantly heard what had caught his attention. "Large group," she said, half to herself. "Moving fast. And straight toward us."

He nodded in agreement and measured the distance between them and the on-coming riders.

"This way, Muldoon," Carrick said, wheeling his mount toward a thinning in the trees and the open ground visible beyond.

Glynis sent Bert flying after him, wondering even as she did whether she was running from the lesser danger.

5

Carrick glanced back over his shoulder, noting that they were outdistancing the British patrol and that Glynis was managing to keep up. He could tell by her face that the pounding ride across the Irish countryside had taken its toll. Lines of pain were etched between her beautifully shaped brows. Her lips were compressed and bloodless. And still, despite the bullet hole in her shoulder and the pain that obviously gripped her entire body, she rode like the proverbial wind.

Glynis Muldoon hadn't begged him to slow their pace or ease their course, hadn't so much as whimpered once. While there was much he needed to learn about his green-eyed companion, he already knew she had more grit than the vast majority of sailors he'd captained, more than all the men he now led against the British on land. He'd tested her mettle, and by all measure, she'd passed. The time had come to end their flight from the patrol, for a much-needed respite.

"Muldoon," he called over his shoulder, motioning for her to come up beside him. She was there before he'd completed the gesture. "Had enough?" he asked, smiling grimly.

He saw her take a deep breath before she answered, "I can stay in the saddle."

Carrick wondered if, at that point, riding might be easier for her than standing on her own two feet. "We've led them far enough astray. It's time to lose them."

"I don't like running Bert this hard, this long," she offered.

To his way of thinking it was most probably the closest she would ever come to admitting she needed to stop. She obviously had a prideful streak, one that might rival his own. "You've got pluck, Muldoon."

"If it's all the same to you, I'd rather have a spell that'd take me home."

"All things in their time," he countered with a tight smile. "Getting rid of our persistent British patrol gets first priority."

She nodded, her lips set in a thin line. Again his conscience nagged him. "There's a narrow draw tucked into the folds of the land about a mile from here," he explained, angling his tired mount toward the hillock. "When the shadows get long, the entrance becomes hidden. We'll slip in there and the Brits'll think the earth has swallowed us up. Can you make it that far?"

"Piece of cake," she replied, her voice tight.

"There's plenty of water and I've got food in my packs. Are you hungry?"

"No."

He looked her over critically and decided that she probably couldn't feel anything except the pain in her shoulder. He knew from experience that it would lessen a bit when she got something solid in her stomach. It would be more bearable if she got some sleep as well. The dark patches beneath her eyes and the weary lines that etched her mouth made him wonder if she'd be able to stay awake long enough to eat. If he wanted thoughtful answers to the questions he needed to ask her, he would undoubtedly have to wait for tomorrow.

As he guided her into a narrow valley and toward the darkest of the shadows at the end of it, Carrick felt the tension in his neck and back begin to ease. "We need to slow up," he said even as he drew in his mount. "The terrain gets very rough, very soon. We don't need to lose a horse at this point in the game."

"If they've got a decent tracker," she observed tautly, dropping in behind him, "they'll still be able to follow our trail."

"Don't worry, Muldoon," he assured her with a wry chuckle. "The British don't consider Irish outlaws worthy of a tracker's efforts. We'll be safe and snug in less than five minutes."

"No need to hurry on my account."

Lord, but she was indeed a breed of woman different from any other he'd ever encountered. Either she was made of steel or she'd come from a place and time where the age-old lines dividing men and women had ceased to exist.

Unbidden, memories of his parents came to him; the tenderness and love in his mother's eyes when she looked at his father, the curve of her smile when her husband wrapped his arm about her waist and drew her to him. How many years separated his mother's other life from the one Glynis Muldoon knew? Carrick shook his head. Certainly buried somewhere inside his stoic companion were the softer instincts of a woman. Finding them could be a wonderfully intriguing pastime until he could get Saraid to reverse her bungled magic, he decided.

Or the stupidest thing he'd ever contemplated. He had a mission to complete and people who counted on him to keep a clear head and a steady purpose. Judging by the resolve he'd seen her display so far, he sensed that getting Miss Glynis Muldoon into his bed would very likely take both greater time and greater effort than most women demanded; the concentration it would require made the task inherently dangerous, decidedly foolhardy. A single second of distraction could mean the hangman's noose for himself and his kinsmen, as well as the end of Irish hopes to break the yoke they'd so long worn.

There was no choice. His life at the moment didn't allow for the luxury of a romantic seduction. If she asked for his favors, he'd be happy to oblige. But that was all the effort he could afford to expend on the matter.

"We have to lead the horses in. It's a low, narrow passageway," he said, reining before an apparently solid rock wall and swinging down from the saddle. "Are you up to it, Muldoon?"

"I can hold my own," came the terse reply from behind him. "There's nothing wrong with my legs."

"Throw the stirrups up over the saddle," Carrick instructed. "I'll lead. You follow."

"The appropriate three paces?"

Carrick let her caustic remark pass, telling himself that anyone hurting as much as she probably did deserved more tolerance than he might otherwise show. Flipping the reins over his horse's head, he stepped forward into the passage. He'd gone no more than a half-dozen feet when a most unfeminine oath came up the stone corridor behind him.

"Muldoon?" he called, trying without success to see around his animal. "Is there a problem?"

"Nothing I can't handle," she yelled back. "Go on. I'll be there in a minute."

"Unless the rump end of that horse is in here before the Brits crest the rim of this valley—" he began.

"I know that, dammit! You don't have to tell me," she shot back impatiently.

With the sound of clinking metal, creaking leather, and her labored breathing came understanding. The entrance to their haven wasn't wide enough to allow for her horse and the extra bulk of her strange tack at the same time. "Let me get Molan in here and then I'll come back to help you," Carrick said, quickly moving down the passage.

Whatever she said in response was lost in the reverberations of his horse's shoes against stone. Carrick took his mount just far enough into the rocky enclosure to clear the opening and left him there. Halfway back down the corridor he stopped in his tracks.

She came toward him with her jaw set, the edges of her coat fluttering about her long legs as she walked, her right hand hooked through the pommel of her saddle and supporting its weight across her good shoulder and down her back. With her left hand she led her horse. Yes, he decided, Glynis Muldoon was well-honed and hard-tempered steel. All the way to the center of her soul.

"Here," he said, stepping forward to take the saddle from her.

She kept moving, ignoring his outstretched hand. "I don't need any help," she said matter-of-factly. "I can get it on my own. If you'd just kindly get out of my way."

He did as she requested, knowing that if he didn't, she'd

simply trample him. The light in her eyes had gone out. He recognized the look, had experienced himself the kind of numbed determination that overcame a person who had been pushed beyond his physical and mental limits.

He pictured her healed and riding with his band against the British but quickly quashed the notion. The battlefield was no place for women. Their presence made men lose their focus, lose their willingness to sacrifice all for a noble end. No, he told himself, Glynis Muldoon needed be left in some safe place until she could be sent back to where she belonged.

He found her too distracting; his thoughts went to her too often for his own safety. He had to put her beyond his reach for his kinsmen's safety, for the sake of his own temporary survival. A convent would be appropriate, he decided quickly.

A wry smile lifted the corners of his mouth. What Glynis Muldoon could undoubtedly do to the sensibilities of pious nuns might very well border on unholy. He'd fry in hell for unleashing that kind of terror in their midst. But what a sight it would be.

Glynis tried to mask her relief as she led Bert from the stone tunnel into a small, rocky enclosure. Daylight was almost gone and the back of the enclosure was already bathed in deep shadows. The air was colder than it had been in the valley and she knew that Bert, lathered and tired, would soon be fighting muscle cramps. She had to rub him down before she could rest.

"This way," Carrick said, picking up the reins of his own horse and leading the animal to the last patch of light in their lair.

Glynis nodded but carried her saddle to the wall and left it before she followed him.

"Here. . . ."

It took her a moment to push past the curtain of pain clouding her awareness. He was holding out a set of saddlebags. She stared at them, knowing that he must want her to take them and angry that he considered her his minion.

"Deal with them yourself," she mumbled, turning away and heading toward her own packs for Bert's brush.

He was behind her within seconds. She marveled at his speed, at the forcefulness of his hand on her good shoulder, at the gentleness of the power he used to turn her around to face him. She glared up into dark eyes blazing with an anger as fierce as her own.

"Muldoon," he grated, "put away your pride." He shoved the saddlebags into her chest and she instinctively wrapped her good arm around them. "Open them up and find yourself something to eat. You look half-dead. I'll take care of the horses."

God, she was too battered to take even the smallest measure of kindness. If she eased back for even a fraction of a second, she'd collapse and never get up again. "Thanks," she offered, stepping back, "but Bert's my horse and my responsibility. I'll eat after I've seen to him."

"God, but you're a stubborn woman. Can't you exercise good sense?"

She ignored him and put the leather pouches down beside her upended saddle. When she bent to open her own packs the world reeled around her. Her unsteadiness worsened when she straightened. She held on to Bert's brush with all her strength, using it to anchor her.

And then Carrick was there. He swept her up in his arms in a quick, fluid motion. Disoriented, she clung to him in sheer desperation. The warmth from his body spread like liquid silver into her numbed limbs, and the strength of his arms calmed her. It felt good to have him hold her.

Warning bells went off in her head. In that instant she knew that Carrick des Marceaux was the most dangerous man she'd ever met, that he had the power to reach the places she had kept safe from other men. Even her ex-husband, Jake Reimer, hadn't been able to worm his way into her soul. Thank God. She couldn't let Carrick do this to her. She had to stand on her own, to be strong. She'd learned that lesson the hard way. In that respect, Jake had been a good teacher. "Put me down," she demanded with all the strength she could muster, pulling her arms from around his thickly muscled neck. "I'm all right."

He tightened his hold on her and said dryly, "Oh, yes, I can see that."

"Put me down. I'm serious," she insisted breathlessly, hating herself for her weakness.

"So am I, Muldoon," he replied, settling her into the dirt with her back propped into the curve of the saddle. "You're going to stay where I put you, woman. And you're going to do as you're told."

"You can't make me." Glynis threatened defiantly.

"The hell I can't," he countered, opening his saddlebags. She watched as he pulled out a rucksack. From it he took a chunk of dried meat and a hard biscuit, and thrust both into her right hand. "Now eat before I have to take the time to bury your carcass. I'll bring you some water in a minute."

"Take care of the horses first," she answered, suddenly too weak to protest. "I'll be fine."

"I'm going to have a look at that wound of yours before we call it a day," he said as he walked away.

Glynis sighed. Where had her sense of self gone? She was sitting in the dirt of a rocky, roofless hole in a canyon wall, letting some man tell her what to do. Tearing off a chunk of the spiced meat, she chewed and considered the longest hours of her life.

Her shoulder pounded hotly, distracting her. She pulled off another bite of the meat and deliberately shifted her focus beyond her physical self. She watched Carrick rubbing Bert down. The man obviously knew what he was doing; his strokes were sure and well-practiced. Glynis smiled weakly when she heard him murmuring to the Appaloosa as he worked.

Okay, maybe Carrick des Marceaux wasn't such a demon after all. He rode extremely well, respected good horseflesh, and seemed to possess an understanding of horses. Still, he was a chauvinist, she added, unwilling to cave in completely. And an outlaw with an attitude.

She studied him openly as she nibbled on the incredibly hard biscuit he'd given her. Now that he was off his own mount, his shoulders seemed broader and his legs seemed longer. The dust of travel coated the shoulders of his dark jacket and the smooth leather of his boots. His dark hair curled slightly over his collar at the nape and she wondered how long it had been since he'd had a haircut.

"Eat!"

Glynis rolled her eyes. He hadn't even glanced at her. How could he have known she'd paused? She shook her head, tore another bite of the meat, and then laid the meager provisions in her lap while she removed her Stetson. Placing it crown down in the dirt beside her, she moved the meat and biscuit into it and sat up straighter.

She didn't know much about him, but she didn't have the slightest doubt that Carrick would keep his word, that he fully intended to check her shoulder when he finished working with the horses. The thought of his hands peeling back her coat and shirt, of him touching her bare skin, sent an unsettling wave through her. Knowing that a greater degree of safety lay in doing the task herself and being done by the time he was ready, she worked the drover's coat off.

The combined effects of partially rising and working her injured shoulder made the world swim around her again. Glynis clenched her teeth and straightened her back to still the swaying world. Sweat beaded her body and she shivered.

"Christ Almighty, Muldoon," Carrick whispered, the solid comfort of his arms coming around her shoulders. "What some women will do to have a man take them in their arms. All you have to do is ask, you know."

"I don't want to be held," she retorted, knowing that the words weren't wholly true at the moment. "I want you to take care of Bert."

"Strange name for a horse, Bert."

"No odder than Molan," she countered as he finished removing her coat sleeve.

"It means 'Servant of Storm,' " he explained while settling her back in a sitting position. "I think it quite fitting, don't you?"

"I suppose it is. He's black and Lord knows you can be a thunderhead when you want to be. For a man who promised to shoot me a few hours ago, you're being awfully nice right now. Why?"

He shrugged and began opening the snaps of her shirt. "What does Bert mean?"

" 'Bright,' " she answered, keenly aware of his fingers brushing against her skin. "And Bert is bright, in case you're wondering," she rushed on, feeling desperate to escape his competent hands. "He needs to be brushed. And your horse needs to be cared for as well."

Carrick looked grim. "I don't need instruction in how to properly care for my animals. Or when to do it."

Glynis failed miserably in her attempt to control her breathing while he worked at the knot of the cloth holding the bandage in place. She could see his pulse thumping in the hollow of his throat, could feel the warmth radiating from his body. And the gentleness of his long fingers. . . . God, she needed to put some distance between them. She reached behind her with her right hand and found the leather sheath on her belt.

"Here," she said, drawing her Buck knife out and handing it to him. "Use this so we can get this show on the road."

Carrick's eyes widened as he took in the wicked-looking knife she was holding out to him. "Damnation, woman," he said quietly. "How did you come by that?"

For the first time since the storm Glynis felt as though she had a handle on things. "I got it from the sheath on my belt," she replied, a smile lifting the corners of her mouth. "It's pretty much standard issue for ranchers. Cut the blasted bandage and let's get this over with."

Carrick returned her smile. "If it's all the same to you, Muldoon," he said, studying her, "I'd rather work at the knot. I don't have another shirt to sacrifice on your behalf. Unless you want the one off my back?"

The shadow of his beard teased her, inviting her to brush her fingertips over the dark stubble on his jaw. She gave herself a mental shake. Geez, she had to be really out of it to be thinking like this.

"Such gallantry won't be necessary, des Marceaux." She motioned to her saddle. "In the bottom of my right-hand saddlebag is a first-aid kit. Big white plastic box with a red cross on the top. You can't miss it."

He leaned across her to open the buckle and lift the flap.

Glynis held her breath and tried not to marvel at the muscles beneath the strained fabric of his jacket, at the wonderfully tapered line of his hips. Finally, she closed her eyes and simply hoped he hadn't noticed her regard, hoped she'd get her act together soon.

"What manner of binding is that you wear?" he asked, straightening to kneel before her again.

Glynis opened her eyes and stared at him, unable to recollect her scattered thoughts. "Binding?"

His gaze dropped to her chest and his smile broadened. "That pink lace across your breasts."

She flushed crimson before she answered, "It's called a bra." She added hastily, "And I don't normally wear either pink or lace. Things have been kinda busy around the ranch lately and the laundry's been piling up. It was the only clean thing left in my drawer. Normally I wouldn't even buy something like this. I had a weak moment."

A mischievous light danced in his eyes when he looked up at her. "Have I embarrassed you, Muldoon?"

"No, des Marceaux," she retorted, arching a brow. "Despite your deliberate and rather transparent attempt to do so."

Again he studied her. "You're blushing."

"Well, maybe I'm getting a fever," she retorted blithely. "If I'm really lucky it'll be lead poisoning and I'll die quick."

He grinned, cut the bandage from her shoulder with one deft stroke of the knife, and drew away the wrapping as he asked, "Any last requests?"

"Yeah. Take care of my horse."

"Like I would my own, Muldoon." He picked up the first-aid kit, considered it for a half-second, and then popped it open.

"God, that's reassuring," Glynis scoffed, watching him set the box aside. She looked over at the horses as she added, "Molan's still standing there waiting to be—"

The pain came so suddenly and intensely that it took her breath away.

"Sorry," she heard Carrick say. "Better to tear it off quickly than to prolong the agony."

"You're a sadist," she muttered, wiping the tears from her eyes with the back of her right hand. "You're a damn Nurse Ratched."

"A who?"

"She's a really mean nurse in a book I once read. Heart of stone. Just like yours."

"Hardly," he countered, drawing himself up as though she'd insulted him. If it hadn't been for the amusement in his eyes, she might have believed him. "And you've wounded me grievously by saying so, Muldoon."

"Well, you'll just have to get over it."

"Actually, speaking of wounds, yours doesn't look too bad," he said, inspecting her shoulder. "I've seen a lot worse."

"Thanks," Glynis replied flippantly, glancing down at the raw-edged hole. Her stomach rolled and she quickly looked away. "You're a real comfort, des Marceaux. Where'd you get your medical training?"

"At my mother's knee." He winked. "Mostly as her patient, though. She always said it was a miracle I lived through childhood." He leaned across her again to retrieve something from his own saddlebags.

Glynis watched as he unstoppered a flask and poured part of the contents over his hands. The sharp scent of good whiskey tickled her nose. "Wait," she said, stopping him as he lifted the silver bottle toward her shoulder. "Give me that for a minute."

He relinquished the flask to her, looking puzzled. Glynis smiled and held up the flask in mock salute. "If you're going to pour more of it into the hole in my shoulder, I want some of it coursing through my veins first." Then she took several long, fiery swallows. She gasped, and shuddered as the heat of the whiskey ignited her insides.

"You've rendered me speechless, woman."

She drew in a ragged breath. "Apparently not for long enough."

"Do all the other women you know slug back whiskey with such fierce abandon?"

"Naw." She smiled and took another drink, a much smaller one this time. "They dilute it first, stick a paper umbrella in it, and then sip it daintily, their pinkies raised."

"And what do they think of you, Muldoon?"

She took yet another sip for medicinal purposes. "They don't know what to make of me, des Marceaux, and that's the way I want it."

"And the men?"

Glynis studied the intricately carved pattern in the silver as she answered. "Half of them don't think I can do the job and are waiting for me to cash it in." She balanced the flask on her thigh as she finished, "The other half want to marry me for my assets."

"Well, at least they're not blind." he said blandly.

She looked up at him and smiled as she shook her head. "Not those kinds of assets, you letch. My land and cattle."

He cocked a brow. "Must be considerable if they're willing to look past your rather glaring peculiarities."

"Yeah," she said, deciding that one more sip of Carrick's whiskey couldn't hurt. "I suppose most men would be willing to put up with a lot in order to get their hands on seven thousand acres and all that goes with it." Beyond the end of the flask she saw his eyes widen and his jaw go momentarily slack.

"*Seven thousand?* That's over seventeen thousand hectares!"

"Ah, des Marceaux," she said impishly, handing back the whiskey, "I see I've caught your attention."

"Do you have any idea how much land that is; what can be done with it?"

Feeling the effects of the whiskey, she laughed. "Hell, yes. Do I strike you as an idiot?"

"You have cattle? What kind? How many head?"

"You know, des Marceaux," she observed, suddenly more sober, "I thought you'd be a bit more original. Do you have any idea how often men have asked me those questions? Have you any idea just how irritating it is to be viewed as a capital conquest?"

"I take it that you've been fairly successful in beating them off."

"Yep. I keep a big stick right inside the kitchen door. Been known to use it from time to time, too. And when that's not enough, I unleash my attorney."

"Muldoon, you're an odd woman."

She winked at him. "You just hold that thought, des Marceaux, and we'll do just fine."

Bemused, he shook his head and set about rebandaging her wound. "Has there ever been a man in your life?" he asked while he worked.

Was the ground swaying or was she? Glynis wondered. She squinted at Carrick, trying to focus more clearly on his face. Now was not the time to tell him about the god-awful experience of being Mrs. Jake Reimer. "This is getting kinda personal, don't you think?" she muttered.

"Then don't answer. I'm not going to twist your arm."

Whether it was the irony of his statement or the fact that everything sounded like it was coming through a cotton-packed pipeline, Glynis smiled and sighed. "My father died in a plane crash when I was seventeen. The insurance money paid off the ranch itself. My Uncle Lloyd's been there ever since I can remember, helping me make the taxes, the overhead. Thank God. He'll keep the place going until I can figure out what's going on and get back where I belong."

"That's not what I meant. Have you had no suitors?"

She grinned. "Tons of 'em."

"Lovers?"

She laughed quietly to herself. "Tons of 'em."

"You're shoveling it, Muldoon."

"Maybe," she admitted, trying again to focus. "Then again, maybe not."

She thought he might be smiling at her when he asked, "Are you feeling any pain?"

"Oh, yeah," she said with a wobbly nod and a lopsided smile, "but I'm to the point of not really caring about it. You may proceed, Nurse Ratched."

6

His limbs were chilled to the bone by the time he returned with a blanket-load of carefully foraged grass for the horses. The expedition had taken him only a short distance beyond the rocky valley, but far enough to see that the British patrol had camped within a mile of their hideaway. Carrick scowled. With their campfires, the bastards were considerably warmer than he and Glynis Muldoon would be that night.

He looked over at Glynis. She remained exactly as he'd left her, curled into her bedroll, the blanket tucked tightly beneath her chin. Carrick shook his head as he carried the fodder to the waiting horses, the memory of her laughter warming him from the inside out.

The whiskey had hit her hard and fast, no doubt the result of exhaustion, blood loss, and a virtually empty stomach. Everything he'd done seemed to have amused her. She'd sobered when he'd smeared some of the liniment she called Neosporin around the edges of her wound, but her pain had been apparently forgotten as she watched him try to tear the sticky strips of cloth from the not-so-damn-handy dispenser.

Her amusement had unsettled him, had stirred his hunger for gentleness and fed his attraction. "And it's likely to get worse before sunrise," he groused, knowing the night would be too cold for either of them to sleep alone. The British were far too close to risk building even the smallest fire. He needed Glynis Muldoon's body warmth as much as she needed his.

"Give me strength," he muttered to the stars. Then, with the blanket in hand, he headed toward the still-warm wall of the rocky enclosure and his hopefully still well-inebriated companion.

God, he was warm; too warm. His next sleep-befogged thought was that they'd slept away most of the morning. The sun had to be straight overhead for him to be baking as he was. Carrick tossed aside the blanket even as he opened his eyes. He blinked, startled to find himself staring up into inky darkness. He glanced at the position of the stars and judged that it couldn't be more than an hour or two past midnight.

Glynis moved against him, flinging her good arm outward and muttering restlessly. Carrick pressed his fingertips to her forehead and frowned at the heat radiating from her skin.

His mother had always set him in a tub of tepid water whenever he'd been laid low by a fever, he remembered. He glanced between the woman lying at his side and the small pool of water at the base of the spring that trickled from the rock wall. Aside from the amount of it being insufficient to immerse a child, he knew that a truly cold-water bath would do more harm than good to the patient.

He considered her again. Perhaps if he simply removed a few layers of her clothing the night air would bring down her fever. Knowing it to be the only practical course he had, Carrick eased his arm from under her head, offering a mumbled apology when her brows furrowed during the process.

"It's okay," she whispered groggily. "Where you going?"

"Right here. You're burning up, Muldoon," he explained as he worked one of her boots from her foot. "We need to get you out of some of those clothes."

"Yeah. I am kinda warm." She touched her forehead and then squinted in the darkness to stare at her fingertips. "Why don't you just turn down the thermostat?"

"The what?"

"The heat," she replied, clearly exasperated. "Turn down the heat. Uncle Lloyd always does when we go to bed. He must have forgotten tonight."

"Muldoon?" he called, reaching for her other foot.

"What?"

The boot came off with a quiet pop. "Are you still drunk or are you delirious?" She stared at him, but her sleepy green eyes didn't provide him with an answer. "You are, without doubt or argument, the most troublesome woman I've ever laid eyes on."

"Sorry," she offered, blinking and smiling broadly. "Does that help?"

"No."

She shrugged her right shoulder and then laid her forearm over her eyes. "You should go on without me. Leave me to die."

He ignored her comment. Her socks were red, and woven into them were several identical black and white cats; cats standing on their hind feet, each clutching a little yellow round-headed bird in its fist. The expressions on the cats' faces were of surprise and utter dismay.

"Better put my boots back on me," she warned from beneath the sleeve of her coat. "Cowgirls always die with their boots on. Tradition must be upheld."

Carrick cocked a brow. "Can you sit up?"

"No. I'm dying, remember? Why bother?"

"Christ, Muldoon," he said, grabbing the lapels of her coat. "Sit up so I can get this thing off you."

"Aunt Ria warned me about men like you," she said, swaying slightly before him. "You'll use any excuse to take advantage of a helpless woman."

He pushed the heavy canvas garment down her right shoulder as he countered, "You're hardly helpless, Muldoon."

"Did your mother warn you about women like me?"

"No, but my father certainly did." He grabbed her by her shirt and eased her backward. She went without resistance. "Do you feel any cooler yet?" Carrick asked, taking in the spectacular narrowness of her waist and the luscious curve of her hips.

He glanced over at the coat lying discarded beside her. The thing might protect her from the elements, but it also hid her from the speculative appreciation of men. He wondered if she wore it more for the first benefit it afforded or the latter.

Carrick reluctantly repeated his question. "Muldoon? I asked if you were cooler. Would it help to take off something else?" *Please God,* he offered up silently, not at all sure which answer he prayed to hear.

"I doubt it," she said quietly, bringing her good arm up to cover her eyes again. "I think it's more than the fever."

He let his gaze sweep the length of her again. "What are you saying, Muldoon?"

"It's you."

He rocked back on his heels. "Me?"

"Yeah. You."

"Would you care to explain?"

"Not particularly. Are you coming back to bed now?"

"Muldoon," he said quietly, "if you know what's good for you, you won't say another word. I may be a gentleman, but I have my limits. Right now you're pushing them."

"Sorry." She yawned, daintily covering her mouth with the back of her hand. "How 'bout I go to sleep again?"

"That's the best idea you've had since I met you," he grumbled, angry with himself for his lack of control.

"Say good night, Gracie."

Who the hell is Gracie? "Good night, Muldoon," he said sternly. He watched her roll onto her side and pillow her head on her forearm. As she drifted off, a secret smile played at the corners of her mouth.

Carrick also smiled. He hadn't stopped in the course of the day just past to consider Muldoon more than in passing. Now that she lay curled up without her coat, he could see that her auburn hair had been bound into a single braid and that it reached midway down her back. If the thickness of the plait were any reliable indication, it would make a glorious, shimmering cascade when loosened.

The vision came without warning, as they often did. In it he clearly saw he and Glynis Muldoon, together, firelight dancing across their bare skin. His breath caught at the image and he banished it quickly with a shake of his head.

"Damnation," he muttered, pulling away the top blanket

and wrapping it around his shoulders. He hadn't asked to have the gift of a seer. Saraid would have given anything for the power he possessed. He closed his eyes and shook his head. It was a curse, pure and simple. He didn't need the Gift any more than he needed Glynis Muldoon in his life.

Carrick felt her brow, noting that the fever had lessened. With a long sigh of resignation, he rose to his feet.

What was it that his father had told him? Something about the fascinating power of female time travelers. Something about not knowing what had hit you until it was too late to save yourself.

"Not with me. I'm smarter than that," Carrick muttered as he paced the rocky enclosure. He was a dead man. He wouldn't live to see another summer pass. There was no point in becoming involved with her. Saying goodbye to his family and friends was going to be difficult enough. Taking a lover just before heading to the gallows was sheer masochism.

"Besides, I have important things to do. I have no time for this kind of foolishness. Before we leave here in the morning, Miss Glynis Muldoon and I are going to come to a very clear understanding."

He went back to her and checked the fever. Finding it considerably less than when he had awakened, he drew her coat back over her and then walked away. Carrick next checked the horses and then resumed his aimless pacing, practicing what he'd say to her in the light of dawn and resolutely pushing away thoughts of lying down with her each time the temptation came to him.

Glynis couldn't remember the last time she'd been so sore or so hungry . . . or had such a pounding headache.

"Sleep well, Miss Muldoon?"

From the tone of his voice she knew he'd spent a miserable night. Mr. Snarly was back in full force. She sat up and began to gently work the kinks from her back, saying as she did, "I don't think I slept any better than you did."

He muttered something under his breath that she didn't quite catch before he said clearly, "It is a new day, Miss Muldoon, and we need to have a clear understanding."

"Were you up all night thinking about this, des Marceaux?" she asked, reaching for one of her boots.

"That is the first of the matters we have to discuss . . . the use of my surname. You will call me Carrick henceforth. Des Marceaux is a well-known name, and I'd prefer to keep it from being associated with my present activities."

She watched him while she pulled on the boot and wondered whether he'd swallowed a lawyer sometime during the night. "How 'bout Snarly instead?" she proposed. "It'll add to your outlaw persona."

He glowered at her. "Carrick will suffice. And as to your own activities—"

"Geez, do you always wake up so grouchy?"

"You will follow orders as do the rest of my men. You will do as you are told until such time as I can find my sister and get her to reverse the magic that brought you here. Do you understand, Miss Muldoon?"

"Yeah, and I'm hungry," she retorted. "Got any more of that jerky you gave me last night?"

"It's in the rucksack. Help yourself. And while I would like to allow you time to gather some of your strength, we don't have that luxury. Be ready to ride in ten minutes."

With that he walked away, moving with purposeful strides toward the entrance of their hideaway. Glynis watched him go as she pulled on her second boot. Whatever seemed to have infected his mood had soured hers. She rose to her feet and resolutely worked the stiffening fingers of her left hand, then her wrist, then her elbow. Lifting her entire left arm brought tears to her eyes, but she gritted her teeth, cursing Carrick des Marceaux and his mercurial moods all the while. If the bits and pieces of what she recalled from last night were any indication, he could be pleasant, even downright amusing if he had a mind to be.

A few minutes later, and with several pieces of jerky stashed in her coat pocket, she picked up her saddle, eased it over her good shoulder, and went to get Bert. She found Carrick sitting on a boulder just outside the opening into the valley. His expression was resolute as he stared into the distance.

She didn't say a word as she methodically began to

saddle her horse. The pain and limited use of her left hand made the task not only awkward but damn difficult. She swore softly in frustration and looked up to see Carrick watching her. She deliberately turned her back toward him.

"I'll do that for you," he said gruffly.

"Don't bother yourself," she shot back. "I can manage perfectly well without assistance from you or anyone else."

He stormed past her, slipping like a black cloud into the narrow passage and disappearing. By the time he'd returned with Molan, she was in the saddle and chewing a piece of jerky. He, too, mounted and then without a word started down the valley. For a moment Glynis considered letting him go on without her.

In the end she nudged Bert forward. Carrick des Marceaux was her only connection to the woman who apparently had the power to return her to where she belonged. That made him a cross she had to bear for the time being. Nothing said she had to enjoy it. Nothing said she had an obligation to be any more pleasant about the forced association than he was. And nothing, *nothing,* could make her endure one more minute of Carrick des Marceaux's company than absolutely necessary.

They'd ridden in silence for the better part of the morning when Carrick motioned for her to ride beside him. She hesitated long enough to make him wonder, to make him glance back at her.

"The tracks are getting fresher," he said when she finally drew alongside him.

"I'm not blind," she replied evenly as she studied the broad path of hoof-turned earth they rode over.

"There's a crofter's cottage up ahead. It looks as though that's where the Brits are going."

"And so . . . ?" she prompted.

"Stay close to me, wait for my instructions, and don't do anything foolish."

I'm with you. It doesn't get any more foolish than that, she grumbled silently as she nodded and fell back.

Geez, he had an attitude about him that drove her to distraction, confidence that bordered on arrogance, and an ability to command that rankled her pride. It didn't help matters much that he was so damn good-looking, either. Every time she'd work up a good head of steam, she'd notice something else about him and all her anger would fade away. At one point it had been his square jaw. Another time it had been his mesmerizing eyes. And once she'd even found herself wondering how his lips would feel against hers.

Glynis worked her left shoulder, an activity that had already proven useful in diverting her wayward thoughts. Pain was good in that respect, she told herself. It certainly drove away any possible thoughts about impossible pleasures.

As they neared a curve in the gentle slopes of the country-side, Carrick raised his hand and drew Molan to a stop. Glynis quit torturing herself and reined in Bert.

"We'd best take a look on foot," Carrick said, pointing toward a clump of trees clinging to the high side of the hillock rising to their right.

Glynis nodded and together they climbed the easy slope, slipping silently into the thin shadows afforded by the young oaks. Using one of the thicker trunks to shield her from view, Glynis studied the tiny farmstead below.

The British were filing out of the yard on their mounts. A nonuniformed man rode at their head and the last man in the column dragged at rope's end a balking, bawling cow. The Irish family, a stooped-over man, a long-skirted woman crying into the hem of her apron, and six dazed-looking, rag-dressed children, watched the procession leave with what was undoubtedly their cow.

"It's the tithe processor," Carrick explained, his voice soft against her ear.

"Why are they taking one of that family's cows?"

"Not *one*, Muldoon. Their *only* cow."

"But that means the children won't have milk to drink. And how will their mother cook anything without milk? You can't make so much as a decent biscuit without milk."

"The British don't care about leaving them with food, Muldoon," he explained, his dark eyes angrily following the British. "The law allows them to collect ten percent of every

Irishman's annual worth and to determine and take what they deem to be the proper payment."

"Why?"

"To support the Church of England," he supplied, bitterness adding an edge to his explanation.

"But doesn't the church, in turn, take care of the people?" Glynis pressed. "Can't these people go to their pastor and get some help?"

"These people," he said matter-of-factly, "like ninety-five percent of Ireland, are Catholic. Even if they swallowed enough of their pride to go ask for it, the Anglican clergy wouldn't help them." His expression dark, he added, "Unless, of course, they renounced the evils of papacy."

Glynis frowned and looked back toward the farm. The man had slipped his arm around the woman's shoulders. The children clung to her skirts. "That doesn't seem right," Glynis whispered. "If the people are Catholic, why should they be forced to support a church that isn't theirs? And to make them give up what they obviously need to survive?"

"Fair has nothing to do with it. It's British law." He, too, studied the family in the yard below. "The people have to obey. If they don't, they can be transported or hanged. Starvation is the lesser of the possible consequences they face."

"I'm not a student of Anglo-Irish history, but I assume that someone has explained to the British how unfair these policies are."

Carrick crossed his arms over his chest and scoffed, "My father has spent the last thirty years doing that. You can see how effective he's been at getting London to be more humane."

"And so his son's chosen a different path to the same destination; a path his father opposes."

"Aye. I'm simply one among many, Muldoon, but all of us make it unsafe for the tithe processor to travel without a military escort." He pointed toward the distant line of British redcoats. "We make his life uncertain and his debt collection even more so."

Glynis leaned back against the trunk of the tree. "And how have the British responded to this campaign of yours?"

Carrick didn't look at her. "They've sent more troops to

support the processors and steal from the people. They've put bounties on the heads of the leaders."

"Hence your understandable obsession with my presence." She sighed and shook her head. "Don't worry," she assured him softly, "I'm not going to rat you out."

"Rat me out?"

"I'm not going to betray you or your noble cause."

He continued his contemplation of the scene playing out below them. "The British have been known to be rather ruthless in their pursuit of information. Rather creative, too, if the stories are to be believed."

"They've gotta catch me first," she countered.

He turned to face her squarely, his stance and manner no less resolute than a moment earlier. "Which brings me to something we neglected to discuss this morning."

"We didn't discuss a damn thing," she pointed out. "You pronounced and I let your head swell with self-importance. In hindsight, that was a mistake."

His voice came low. "I don't suffer impertinence well, Muldoon."

She met his steely regard without blinking. "And I don't suffer pomposity well, des Marceaux."

"Between now and the time when I can safely leave you with Saraid," he said flatly, "you'll not participate in my activities, Muldoon. I'll not be responsible for a price on your head."

"I sorta think that's my decision to make," Glynis countered evenly. And then she smiled impishly. "Now, how can I go back to my time knowing that I rode with Robin Hood and didn't lift my hand against the tyranny of Prince John?"

He rolled his eyes heavenward even as he retorted, "Your sense of history is horribly confused."

"Maybe," she conceded. She straightened from the tree and slowly worked her left shoulder. "But I have a finely honed sense of justice and I'm not about to walk away from a fight that needs me. I may be here for only a short while, but I want my time to count for something."

A cynical smile touched his mouth. "And just what is it that you think you might be able to contribute to a fight, Muldoon?"

She refused to let him bait her. "You might be surprised by what I can do," she said cryptically, walking away from him and back down the hill to their horses.

"Alas, I'll never get to know," he rebutted, coming after her. "We're meeting the others tonight and then making straight for Saraid's."

"I think we ought to meet the others and then get that cow back for those people."

"It's already been branded with the Crown's T," he said. "It would be readily identified as an animal marked for the tithe and the farmer would pay the consequences when the British come this way in search of it."

"Then we run the brand," Glynis countered, swinging up into the saddle. "Not that I have personal experience doing it, of course," she added quickly. "But every rancher knows how it's done."

Carrick shook his head. "We go to Saraid's. Then *I'll* deal with the needs of Irish justice. The discussion is at an end."

"Fine," Glynis retorted angrily. "Have it your way. Far be it for me to interfere in your private little campaign for Truth, Justice and the Irish Way."

He nodded, satisfied.

The ease of his acceptance prodded her already bruised pride. "Besides," she added, "it's not like I'm going to be around here long enough to do anything anyway. I'm going home as soon as it can be arranged."

Hearing her words made her suddenly thoughtful. What was wrong with her? When had she accepted having traveled through time? When had she bought this whole thing, hook, line, and sinker? This wasn't like her at all.

She thought back through her experiences of the last twenty-four hours. Glynis shook her head. Geesh. It was all so incredibly bizarre. How had this Saraid person managed to transport her through time, and why? How in hell's name were they going to get her back to the Flint Hills where she belonged?

There were far too many questions and not nearly enough answers. Going with the flow was an essential occupational skill for anyone who made a living in agriculture, and especially for those who ranched. But, somewhere along the way, one simply had to dig in her heels and refuse to be a doormat. If you didn't, you got trampled by life. She hadn't let god-awful circumstances defeat her in the past. And she had absolutely no intention of blithely surrendering now; not to the craziness of time traveling, not to the cruelty of British Ireland, and certainly not to the self-assured command of Carrick des Marceaux. Common sense said that in at least one respect he was absolutely right, though: The fight for Irish justice wasn't hers.

At the precise moment, she didn't have any options beyond making the best of being with Carrick, but sooner or later she'd find some running room. And when she did, she had every intention of doing the smart thing and getting the hell out of Dodge.

7

The moon had risen by the time they neared the rendezvous. At Carrick's signal they reined in their horses. He watched his companion silently scan the dark valley, noting her narrowed eyes as she considered the dilapidated, long-abandoned crofter's cottage.

"Aye," he said softly. " 'Tis the three-quarter moon site."

"I was expecting it to be a bar, a tavern."

"That's what I wanted you to think." He felt her gaze slide over his face and he smiled. "There existed the possibility that you might bolt on me, Muldoon. Had you gone to the British, I wanted them looking where we weren't."

"So now you trust me?"

"I didn't say that." He stood in his stirrups, cupped his hands around his mouth, and mimicked the call of a night bird. A second passed before a similar sound came back to him from the shadowed shell of the building.

"It's clear," he said, nudging Molan forward. "Let's hope they've managed to forage something warm for supper."

"Really," she agreed. "I don't know about you, but my belly button's been rubbing against my backbone for the last couple of hours."

"Muldoon"—Carrick chuckled—"that has to be one of the most unique expressions I've ever heard. Slightly bawdy. Highly descriptive. And from what I can tell, so typically you."

"Well, as much as I'd like to take credit for coining it,

I'm afraid it's a fairly common expression where I come from."

"You know, Muldoon," he mused, turning in the saddle to study her. "At some point before the end of this outrageous adventure of yours, you've got to tell me about your Kansas. I get the impression that it's quite a bit different from my mother's Colorado."

"Well, it sort of depends on which part of Colorado she was from."

Carrick swung down from the saddle as he told her, "She was living in a town called Durango. Have you ever been there?"

"Yeah." She dismounted as well. "But the answer to your question really depends on what she did for a living in Durango."

"She was an accountant," Carrick explained, realizing even as he did that he was sharing too much of his family with her. "Which I gather from her description is a rather glorified bookkeeper."

"Then we're talking about a difference of night and day."

Carrick drew Molan's reins over the animal's head and led him toward the rear of the nearly collapsed building. "We stable the horses back here." He passed beneath a tilted lintel and into a pitch-black room, pungent with the smell of horses and fresh-cut grass. Two sets of whinnies welcomed them.

"We don't unsaddle them, Muldoon. If we have to ride, there won't be time for dealing with tack," he explained, loosening the girth slightly and tossing his stirrups over the saddle as his companion likewise settled her animal.

"We were beginning to worry about you," Robert said, lifting the blanket that separated the makeshift stable from the dimly lit room which served as their inn.

Carrick walked into the light and his cousin's back-pounding embrace. Stepping away, he explained, "Muldoon and I took the long way around. Saw the sights."

"Miss Muldoon," Robert said brightly. "You're looking a bit better than when we parted company. I trust Carrick's taken good care of you in the interim."

"It's been an interesting thirty hours or so," she replied, entering the dirt-floored room.

Carrick saw her take in the interior, saw her note the tiny peat-fed fire and the battered, blackened pot bubbling in the embers. She smiled at the boy crouched beside the fire, a wooden spoon in his hand. For some reason he'd expected to see her wrinkle her nose or frown at the humbleness of her surroundings. Instead she looked relieved as she nodded to the boy and moved closer to the fire.

Robert followed her to the fire. "And what fair Irish sights did your guide take you to see?"

"Well, there was this rocky little hole in the back end of an equally rocky little valley," she said, easing down to sit cross-legged by the fire. Carrick studied her in the soft light, seeing the lines of pain etched at the corners of her mouth.

"Ah, that little hideaway would be the Wolf's Den," his cousin replied, settling in beside her. "I've spent several nights hidden in there myself. Where else did Carrick take you?"

Carrick watched the byplay from a corner of the small room. Robert was being his typically charming self. Carrick had long ago learned the fundamental truths about his cousin. Robert found women fascinating. And as a result, women would give Robert everything and forgive him anything. Robert never had to exert himself to have a woman in his bed, never had to work to extract himself from a liaison. Then again, neither had he. Carrick was always careful to avoid entanglements with substantive women—women like Glynis Muldoon.

"This morning we tracked the British patrol that had followed us the afternoon before," Glynis explained. "We arrived at another valley just in time to watch them haul off some poor family's milk cow."

Robert smiled. "I gather that you didn't approve of their actions, Miss Muldoon."

"I pretty much reckon, Mr. St. John, that right's right and wrong's wrong no matter the year or the country." She removed her hat and laid it beside her, the crown nestled in the dirt, and began to work her coat from her right shoulder as she added, "The idea of children going hungry doesn't sit very well with me."

Carrick frowned as Robert leaned over to assist her. He had just begun to wonder whether Robert was smitten with Glynis Muldoon when she turned her head and the firelight fell full across her face. No, Robert wasn't smitten. His cousin had simply seen what Carrick hadn't. Muldoon was past exhaustion. Her smiles and slow movements weren't entirely evidence of natural grace and civility. They were also the result of the fact that she was fall-over tired.

"Did he make you take the oath right there on the spot?" Robert asked, neatly pooling the bulky garment around her.

She looked wary. "What oath?"

Robert pressed his hand over his heart and looked up through the hole in the thatch roof. "The one where we pledge our lives to the end of the insidious tithe laws."

Carrick shook his head and intervened. "There's no oath, Muldoon. Robert's being overly dramatic."

"He has a flare for it," piped up the boy.

"That's Meyler." Carrick nodded toward the redheaded youngster. "A kinsman by proximity and a runaway for the cause. His mother will have our hides if she ever finds us. He's the one responsible for letting you stumble without warning into our camp yesterday."

"I said I was sorry," the boy protested before turning his attention to their feminine guest. "I got to watching you ride down that slope and forgot what I was supposed to be doing. You ride good, ma'am."

"She rides well," Carrick and Robert corrected in unison.

Meyler went on as though they hadn't bothered. "Can you teach me to ride like that, Miss Muldoon?"

"She's not going to be with us that long, Meyler," Carrick answered, settling himself more comfortably against the wall. "We're heading to Saraid's at sunup. If there's truly a benevolent God in heaven, Muldoon will be back where she belongs by sundown tomorrow."

"Talk about your whirlwind tours," she joked. "Just out of curiosity, Mr. St. John . . . exactly which part of Ireland am I in? I'd hate to go home and not be able to tell anyone where I'd been."

Her laughter warmed Carrick. He realized that his bones were chilled until that moment.

"You're in County Wexford," Robert supplied.

"And would that be north, south, east, or west?"

Carrick answered, "East and a bit south." He came away from the wall, determined to take control of the conversation. "Do you honestly think anyone would believe such a tall tale, Muldoon?" he asked, moving across from her and the others.

"My Aunt Ria will." When he looked dubious, she added, "Ria's a shaman's daughter. She won't even so much as bat an eye."

"What's a shaman?" Meyler asked earnestly.

She paused and Carrick knew that she was choosing words the youngster might understand. In the meager firelight her cheekbones were hollowed, her lips dark and full. His thoughts went back to the firelit vision he'd seen the night before.

"A shaman is an Indian holy man," she explained after a moment, shattering Carrick's thoughts. "He's someone who can speak to the spirits inhabiting this world and those who wait just beyond it. He knows special spells and rituals that heal the sick. He also knows how to look into the future so that he can guide his people with wisdom. Ria has the powers of her grandfather."

Meyler nodded solemnly. "Like Aunt Alanna. And Carrick."

"Yes, like Aunt Alanna," Carrick murmured, considering their companion anew, wondering if the mysterious Aunt Ria had had some hand in her niece's passage across the years. What if Saraid were actually blameless in the matter? How would he get things set right if the magic had come from the other side of time?

Glynis Muldoon turned and met his gaze. Instinctively he knew that she searched his own for some hint of his thoughts. He slowly smiled at her, confident in the impervious wall he'd spent a lifetime building around his heart. No one had ever breached it. No one ever would. Only fools allowed others the chance to betray them. *Search to your heart's content, Glynis Muldoon,* he silently challenged. *I won't let you find anything of value.*

"I find this interesting," Robert said.

She blinked at the sound of his cousin's voice and Carrick saw her confusion and hurt in the instant before she turned to Robert.

"Forgive my lack of good manners, Miss Muldoon," his cousin continued, "but I'm curious. Are you saying that your aunt is one of the American savages we've read accounts of? And if she's your aunt, then surely the same blood must flow in your veins?"

"That savage thing ended a long time ago," she said after a time, her voice distant. "You'd know Ria was Indian just by looking at her, but in any other way she's just like the rest of us." She seemed to pull herself together when she added, "And we're not blood relations. My mom divorced my dad when I was a baby and Ria helped raise me."

"So she's not really your aunt," Meyler chimed in. "Like I'm not really Carrick's and Robert's cousin."

"I guess," she agreed.

Robert looked pensive. "Are you saying that your mother abandoned you, Miss Muldoon?"

She gave him a reassuring smile. "It wasn't like she left me on the doorstep of an orphanage with a note pinned to my blanket. She just went back East to visit her relatives and decided not to come back. She couldn't face the loneliness of the Plains, I guess. You kinda have to be born and bred to it. My dad never talked about her very much. And then he was killed in a plane crash."

Robert still looked concerned. "Haven't you asked her yourself?"

"She was killed when I was five," Glynis said with a shrug. "I never met her, never spoke to her."

Meyler's eyes were wide as he asked softly, "How'd she die?"

Robert gave him a sharp look of disapproval.

"Oh, it's okay," Glynis assured them both. "It doesn't bother me to discuss it." She leaned forward until her gaze was level with Meyler's. Gently, she explained, "She was mugged. Someone beat her up on the street so they could take her money."

Meyler looked upset as he asked sadly, "Didn't you miss having a mother?"

She shook her head and replied, "I had my Aunt Ria."

He whispered, "If something like that happened to my mother, I'd cry forever."

Robert laid a hand on the boy's shoulder. "Forever's a long time, Meyler," he said softly.

"About as long as it's taking you to offer us some of this stew," Carrick grumbled, determined to move them toward less troubling topics and to ease the hollowness of his insides.

"It's rabbit," Meyler supplied, his mood brighter as he lifted a spoonful of the mixture for Carrick's inspection. "Snared and skinned it all by myself."

"And the potatoes and carrots I see in there?" Carrick asked, leaning forward to give the meal the consideration it fully deserved. "Did you grow those as well?"

"Robert met this lady . . ."

Carrick grinned mischievously. "Oh, Cousin. Do I sense a story begging to be told?"

"She was an old woman," Robert countered with a grin.

Carrick chuckled and picked up the game. "Ah, by your concept of the term, she'd be just past sixteen. And how was it that you chanced to make this lovely creature's acquaintance?"

"That's *your* definition of old, and she was ninety-five if she was a day," Robert contended, holding the wooden bowls while Meyler ladled generous helpings into them. Handing them to Carrick and Muldoon, he went on, "She was traveling from her cottage with a basket of produce for market. We stopped and offered to lighten her load and shorten her journey."

"What else did you offer the poor, unsuspecting wench?"

"Miss Muldoon," Robert said with a roguish grin, a hand over his heart. "I assure you that I routinely conduct myself as a proper gentleman ought to. You should believe nothing of what this . . . *brigand* . . . is intimating."

Carrick rolled his eyes and laughed outright. "He's the proverbial wolf in sheep's clothing, Muldoon. Don't fall into his *proper gentleman* trap. He uses it with all the ladies."

"All the time," Meyler added, nodding vigorously.

"Now see here! I protest!" Robert offered in mock offense.

"A bit too much, don't you think?" Carrick observed.

Glynis batted her lashes coyly. "It seems to me that Robert's conducting a perfectly reasonable effort at self-defense."

"I'm stunned, Muldoon," Carrick countered. "I wouldn't have thought you the kind of woman who could be so easily duped by fancy words and pitiful fawning."

She gave him a superior look, a look he instantly recognized as being wholly feigned. With a jolt he realized that Glynis not only understood, but could well practice the fine art of male banter. He was intrigued by the possibilities.

"I know who the wolf is around here," she said. "I didn't just fall off the turnip wagon, you know."

Carrick met her gaze square on. "Oh? And who might the wolf be?"

"Meyler."

The boy squealed in pure delight. Muldoon considered the redheaded Meyler with narrowed eyes and drawled, "Yes, sir-ee. That boy's a heartbreaker. It's written all over his innocent little face."

"Robert taught him everything he knows," Carrick assured her.

"Which wouldn't fill a thimble," Robert countered. "If Meyler's cutting a wide swath through feminine hearts, he's taken his lessons at Carrick's knee."

Meyler fairly bounced with excitement as he turned to Carrick. "Aren't you going to deny it?"

Carrick tried to look as though he were considering his options. "Nope," he said with solemn finality. "I've put a great deal of time and effort into cultivating my dastardly reputation. For the moment I'm going to bask in wholly undeserved glory."

Glynis muttered loudly enough for everyone to hear, "Talk about pitiful fawning . . ."

Robert slipped his arm around her shoulder and whispered conspiratorially, "And to think, Miss Muldoon, that I actually harbored some small concerns that you'd fall prey to Carrick's predatory tendencies while alone with him. I apologize for having so underestimated you. I can see now that you are a woman of great intelligence and precise discernment."

"Which has undoubtedly led her to conclude that you're a bag of wind," Carrick observed, grinning. He picked up a dirt clod and threw it at his cousin, forcing him to pull his arm from Glynis's shoulders in order to deflect the missile.

"On the contrary, des Marceaux," Glynis countered with a soft chuckle. "I think your cousin is wonderfully witty and delightfully entertaining."

Robert winked at her and reached for the stew ladle. "Might I offer you a second portion of our evening's fare, Miss Muldoon?"

"Why, thank you, Mr. St. John," she said, extending her near-empty bowl. "How very kind of you to offer."

Carrick held his bowl forward, too. "I'll take some more while you're at the task."

Robert didn't even bother to look at him. Instead he smiled at Glynis and replied, "Get it yourself, Cousin. I'm otherwise engaged."

Unfazed by his cousin's dismissal, Carrick leaned forward to get more of the stew. "Where are Eachann, Sean, and Patrick?"

Meyler grinned in a roguish, twelve-year-old way. "They're off a-wenching."

"Sean has a cousin in the next village," Robert supplied. "He went to call on her. The other two went along to see what might develop."

"Is that wise?" Glynis asked, looking from one cousin to the other.

Robert offered her a shrug that spoke of a pointless struggle abandoned. "Given that they don't have the sense of a goose between them, probably not. However, they couldn't be stopped. I did my best."

"Robert's exaggerating," Carrick countered. "All three are actually quite capable of exercising good judgment."

Robert looked grim. "Oh, yes. I recall quite clearly Sean's good judgment of two weeks past."

Carrick swallowed a bite of stew before he smiled and

retorted, "She claimed to be widow and he but took her at her word. You can't fault him for being a trusting soul."

"If he's so trusting, why, if you'd be so kind as to explain, did he have Eachann and Patrick serving as look-outs the night in question?"

"Prudence," Carrick explained with a flourish of his spoon. "Yet another sign of their common sense. Imagine what the outcome would have been had he not had the fore-sight to watch for a husband suddenly returned from the dead."

Robert struggled to contain his smile as he turned to Glynis. "Miss Muldoon, I beg your forgiveness. We've embarked on a subject no lady should be forced to consider. If I may be allowed to offer a defense, please permit me to say that I have long served as the voice of conscience for this wayward band of men but that over time their considerable sins have proven stronger than my virtues. I do what I can to keep them civilized, but they frequently draw me into unforgivable lapses of good manners . . . such as the regret-table conversation to which you have just been subjected."

Carrick snorted. "Don't believe a word of that elegantly served drivel, Muldoon."

"Don't worry, Mr. St. John," Glynis offered, patting the man on the forearm. "It was one of the tamer discussions on the matter I've heard. I don't think nineteenth century men are all that much different from those of the twentieth when it comes to"—she grinned—"wenching."

Robert laughed outright. "I must say that you've ad-justed quite well and very quickly to having been trans-ported across time, Miss Muldoon."

A shadow passed briefly over her features before she smiled. Carrick thought the effort looked forced. "I don't know that I've fully accepted it, but I'm a rancher, Mr. St. John. The first job requirement is the ability to adapt to unexpected changes. The second is to be selective in what you worry about. There's nothing I can do at the moment about getting back to where I belong, so there's no point in wasting the energy of getting myself worked into a knot over it. For the time being, I'm, as they say, riding the storm out. When worrying will accomplish something, I will."

Yes, Carrick thought, hearing the undercurrent in her words, *she's putting on a brave face.*

"That's a very sensible position to adopt," Robert assured her. "I'm impressed by your equanimity."

"Her what?" Meyler whispered across the fire at Carrick.

"Her poise," he supplied, not at all quietly. "Her calm manner." Carrick added, "But then he hasn't seen her after a few shots of whiskey."

"For medicinal purposes only, I assure you, Mr. St. John," Glynis explained smoothly. "Your cousin insisted on re-dressing my wound when we stopped last night, and in order to endure it with some dignity, I was forced to avail myself of the only painkiller at hand. I'm afraid that, given my exhaustion and the shock of my circumstances, I slightly misjudged the potency of your cousin's whiskey."

Carrick pretended solemnity. "I behaved myself."

"I'm sure," Robert observed dryly.

Carrick felt anger flood his veins, but his fiery defense was trampled by the sudden approach of thundering hooves.

"Trouble," he snapped, vaulting to his feet and drawing his pistol from the small of his back. "Douse the fire, Meyler. Muldoon, stay with him. Rob . . . with me."

8

Glynis stood for a moment in the dark, trying to hear beyond her own thundering heart and Meyler's rapid breathing. The earthshaking rhythm of galloping horses reverberated through the night, driving the pain and fatigue from her body. Where had Carrick and Robert gone? she wondered, fighting back rising panic.

"Look, Meyler," she said quietly, scooping her hat up from the dirt floor and settling it on her head, "I don't know the routine of this merry little band, but I think we ought to be ready to take the horses out of here. What do you think?"

"Sounds good to me," he answered, his own voice soft. "Let me gather up the cooking stuff."

"Leave it, Meyler," she said, pulling on her coat. "Unless it's monogrammed, no one will be able to trace it to anyone of you. If there's no emergency, we'll come back for it. Otherwise, it can be replaced."

"If you think so," the boy conceded, sounding doubtful.

She started toward the blanket-covered door that led into the ramshackle stable. "If Carrick has a problem with it, tell him it was my idea. I can take the heat."

"He likes you, you know," Meyler observed, following on her heels.

Glynis smiled doubtfully as she tightened Bert's cinch strap with a quick tug and pulled free the reins tied loosely about his upper neck. "I think you have him confused with Robert," she commented, moving over to prepare Molan for riding.

Meyler tightened the girth on one of the other horses. "Well, Robert does like you, but not the same way Carrick does."

Glynis gathered up the reins. "Oh, yeah? What's the difference?"

"Robert would probably kiss your hand and sigh before he laid down his life for you. Carrick would kill for you and then haul you away on his horse."

"Meyler," she said, swinging up into the saddle, "you're a little young to be such a romantic."

"That's what everyone says," he admitted.

"Ever considered that they might be right?" she asked.

"Yeah. But I like seeing things my way," Meyler replied, climbing onto his horse. "My pictures are always happier than everyone else's. Wouldn't you like to have Carrick haul you away?"

God, her shoulder hurt. Holding Molan's reins seemed to be about the limit of what she could do with her injured arm. She edged Bert closer to the door. "Frankly, Meyler," she replied absently, "I don't want anyone slinging me across his saddle and riding off into the sunset with me. I ride on my own." Outside, horses thundered to a halt and male voices came low and hard. From the distance came the sound of more hoofbeats.

"All the girls like Carrick."

"I'll just bet they do," Glynis replied wryly, listening to the muffled exchange going on somewhere in the darkness outside the stable. Carrick's rumbling voice told her that he wasn't the least bit happy.

"Wherever we go, the ladies smile at him," Meyler went on, apparently oblivious to everything but their whispered conversation. "They bring him little presents and invite him to their parties."

Glynis arched her brows. "And he eats it up."

"I beg your pardon?"

"He enjoys their attention, Meyler," she clarified, straining to hear Carrick's and the others' words clearly. No matter how she turned her ear, the sounds reaching it were nonsensical, almost as if they were a foreign language.

"Is Carrick speaking Gaelic?" she asked.

The boy nodded and then went on, his own train of thought uninterrupted. "He doesn't look too terribly pained while the girls are around, but after they leave he's always in a horrible mood, stomping about and saying that he's cursed, that all the women who are interested in him are shallow and insipid."

She arched a brow. "Do you have any idea what insipid means?"

"No, but Carrick says it a lot."

"Well, add this word to your vocabulary, Meyler . . . *chauvinist.*"

"What does that mean?"

"It's a word used to describe a man who says that the women around him are shallow and insipid."

She saw the whiteness of his teeth as he grinned. Meyler leaned closer and his voice came through the inky blackness, "I think that's mainly why Carrick likes you."

"If you don't mean to be insulting me, Meyler, you're going to have to be a bit more precise in your explanation."

"You fight back. You don't accept things the way they are. He's like that, too, you know."

Glynis shook her head. In the distance she heard the approach of more horses. "To be real honest with you, Meyler, all I've noticed about Carrick is that he tends to have a bad attitude in the morning and that the rest of the time he's quite the imperial lord. He doesn't have much tolerance for independence beyond his own." She smiled ruefully. "Given that, I really don't think I'm his kind of girl."

"Maybe you should give him a chance. I've heard he kisses good."

Glynis felt a rush of heat fan across her cheeks. "You've heard that he kisses *well*, Meyler," she corrected, not knowing what else she could possibly say at the moment.

Outside the makeshift stable the low voices suddenly ceased. The only sound was the oncoming horses in the distance. Then suddenly Carrick swore and bellowed an order in the strange-sounding Gaelic. The horses in the yard outside whinnied.

"That's our cue," Glynis said, nudging Bert quickly through the doorway and leading Molan behind her. Once clear of the tilted jamb, she urged her mount forward in order to clear the exit for Meyler and Robert's horse. Even as she did, Carrick ran toward her, reaching for the reins. Robert was a dark shadow darting past them in search of his own mount. Leaving a trail of flying sod, the three other riders disappeared into the nearby trees.

"The Brits are sweeping the countryside tonight," Carrick told them, vaulting into his saddle. "If they find us—"

"We're toast," Glynis finished, whirling Bert around so that the approaching horses came at their back. "Where do we go?" she asked even as Robert and Meyler spurred their horses and dashed into the trees behind the cottage.

"Stay with one of us," Carrick explained hastily, holding Molan back as the sound of approaching horses grew closer. "There's no time to explain."

"Got it," Glynis agreed, letting Bert have his head to race along in the wake of Robert's and Meyler's mounts. She felt Carrick hesitate and then follow.

She bent low over Bert's neck, dodging low-hanging limbs, her heartbeat thundering in her ears. Beneath the sound of her breathing were the muffled thuds of the horses before her, the horses behind her.

Glynis rode instinctively, her thoughts as erratic as her breathing. What kind of hell was this? What had she done to deserve transportation into this nightmare? Where was Carrick? If she could clearly see those racing ahead of her, wouldn't the British be able to see them, too?

She followed in their wake nevertheless, cursing her ignorance of the terrain. If she were home in the Flint Hills . . . *none of this would have been happening.* She'd be riding fence, looking for new calves, and stopping every now and then to sip coffee from a thermos.

But I'm not at home, she chastised herself. *I'm here and if I don't get through this, I'll never get home. Pay attention, Glynis!*

Ahead, Robert and Meyler and the three other riders left the protection of the trees and dashed into a moonlit, gently rolling meadow. The hair on the back of her neck prickled. The riders were coming out of the trees blind and pushing their mounts in an all-out effort to escape the British behind them. Glynis tightened her grip on the reins. If she were the hunter instead of the hunted, she'd pick that spot to set up an ambush.

Trusting her instincts, she came from the shelter of the shadows and pulled Bert hard to the right. Riding along the dappled edge of the forest and keeping the others in sight, she tried desperately to tamp down the rising sense of dread that gripped her heart. They were too exposed, too vulnerable.

You're being chicken, Muldoon, she told herself over and over. *Follow. They know what they're doing, where they're going.* But despite the hard reassurances, she couldn't let go of her fear. Her heart raced and her anxiety deepened with every inch of ground she covered.

Glynis glanced back over her shoulder. *Where's Carrick? He should have cleared the trees by now.* An image filled her mind of Carrick lying sprawled in the fallen leaves of the forest, his body broken. She reined Bert in sharply and in the next instant she had turned him about to face the way they'd come.

A sudden explosion of gunfire boomed across the meadow, followed by the raucous sounds of whinnying horses and men shouting. Glynis stared into the open field, suddenly realizing that the others had moved beyond her sight. Her heart pounded furiously, her breathing ragged. Glynis glanced first at the woods where Carrick remained and then to the meadow where the others had gone. Bert shifted beneath her, as uncertain as she as to the direction they should go.

The answer came as the members of Carrick's band came pell-mell across the silver-tinted grass; four riders, each moving away from the others, fanning out in different directions, all heading for the hillocks rising ahead of them. Meyler was the closest to her. On the far side of the group, she saw Robert. She glanced once more at the woods behind her, then pulled Bert around and set off after the boy.

"It was an ambush!" Meyler shouted when she caught up with him.

"Was Carrick with you?" she yelled above the thundering of hoofbeats.

"I thought he was with you!"

Glynis prayed that she hadn't abandoned him in the woods. Together she and Meyler raced across the turf, pelting the land behind them with torn bits of sod, putting distance between themselves and the meadow.

A gunshot rang out, and Meyler's mount shrieked and pitched forward, his life broken. Glynis watched in horror as the animal went down, as Meyler spilled from his back and tumbled across the rocks like a rag doll.

"Meyler!" she screamed, whipping Bert about. Out of the corner of her eye she saw the flash of red against the greenness of the land and understood what she had to do. Even as the boy rolled away from the bullet splitting the ground beside him, Glynis swore through clenched teeth, dropped the reins, and stood in her stirrups.

The warning caught in Carrick's throat as the two British redcoats burst from around the hillock before him and Meyler's horse went down. He leaned forward over Molan's neck, urging his mount to carry him faster, to get him within the range of the flintlock pistol clutched in his hand. Even as he pushed the valiant animal, he knew he was too far away, that he couldn't get close enough in time to help either Meyler or Muldoon.

Carrick heard the second shot, saw the belch of fire and smoke that came from the British rifle, and his heart sank. Meyler rolled safely away as the deadly lead spattered sod around the boy's head. Red rage surged through Carrick's veins. He bellowed . . . at Molan, at the British, at Meyler, at Glynis Muldoon . . . as he raced against certain death.

And then Muldoon sat Bert down on his haunches, stood up in her stirrups, and reached across herself. Carrick's eyes widened as she pulled a rifle from beneath the flapping edges of her coat and in one single fluid motion levered the weapon, brought it to her shoulder, and pulled the trigger. He saw the nearest of the oncoming soldiers fly from his saddle, saw the other raise his pistol to fire. Muldoon lowered the weapon ever so slightly, levered it again, and then snapped the butt of it back against her shoulder. The second man went down in the same heartbeat, his own weapon spewing shot in the night sky.

And then, without hesitation, Muldoon whipped about and trained the rifle on the center of his chest. Carrick's heart stopped in the second it took her to recognize him and flick the muzzle up and away. She quickly scanned the land around them while she said something that was lost amid the thundering of Molan's hooves. Meyler scrambled to his feet and raced toward her. When she pulled her foot from the stirrup and reached down for him, Carrick understood her intent.

"Well done, Muldoon," he murmured, angling his own horse toward the British animals nervously dancing about in the meadow. He caught the reins of the younger, stronger of the two and set out after Muldoon.

"Pull up!" he called as he drew near.

She eased her lathered mount to a stop and waited, Meyler sitting behind her, his arms wrapped tightly around her waist. Carrick positioned the British soldier's horse between Bert and Molan and together he and Muldoon transferred the boy onto it.

For a second his gaze met Muldoon's and he felt the overwhelming depth of her anger, her fear, and her horror. But not so much as a twinge of regret, he noted. It would come later, he knew, when the other, rawer emotions had passed and she had only her conscience to keep her company. She would need him then. And he would be there for her, just as she had been for Meyler.

None of them spoke a word as they started forward again, riding three abreast; Carrick with his unfired pistol still clutched in his right hand, Muldoon with the blued rifle lying across her lap, and Meyler riding safely between them.

Glynis handed Carrick the Neosporin-coated bandage. "Are you sure you'll be all right, Robert?" she whispered, wincing as Carrick pressed the pad of gauze against his cousin's torn side.

"It's merely a flesh wound, Miss Muldoon," Robert assured her through clenched teeth. "And all things considered, I'm damn lucky to have gotten away with just that to show for the evening."

Glynis nodded and glanced over at Meyler. The boy slept

under her drover's coat, curled up into a tight little ball, his hands clenched into fists, his wrists crossed beneath his chin. Bits of straw clung to his tousled red hair. She reached out to pluck them away and then smoothed the ruffled strands.

"Meyler will be fine, Muldoon," Carrick said softly. "The young are remarkably resilient."

"I suppose so," she replied, climbing to her feet. "If you're not going to need me for a while . . ."

Carrick paused in wrapping an Ace bandage about Robert's torso and studied her, his eyes soft and searching. He said nothing and only shook his head.

"Then I'll be back in a little bit," she finished.

Bert snorted a greeting when she reached the bottom of the loft's ladder. Patting him on the neck, she offered him a weak smile. "Wanna give me odds on what they're talking about up there, ol' boy?"

He snorted again and went back to munching his oats. Glynis adjusted the blanket that Carrick had thrown over her horse's back in a quick effort to keep him from being easily noticeable. "You know, Bert," she mused aloud, "I wouldn't blame you one bit if you bucked me off the next time I try to ride you. I've put you through hell the last couple of days."

He continued to eat and she rested her forehead against his withers.

"I'm sorry. I really am," she whispered, straightening and squaring her shoulders. She walked away, her hands stuffed in the front pockets of her jeans, the soft leather of her chaps fluttering about her legs as she wandered toward the stable's lone window. Outside, the eastern sky was beginning to lighten. She stared at the rolling hills beyond the dusty yard of the livery and wondered what had happened to the other three members of Carrick's band. Neither he nor Robert had said anything, but she knew that they were worried that Sean and Patrick and Eachann might have been captured. *Or killed, like those two—*

Glynis moved away from the window and shook her head, determined to keep her thoughts from wandering down that path. "Just keep moving," she muttered. "Keep thinking about other things." She looked around the small straw-littered stable and quickly decided that the horses needed to be brushed. With four of them, she assured herself, it could occupy her for hours.

She left the tack room a few minutes later, resolutely clutching a brush in her hand and heading across the stable toward Bert. Without warning the sharp-edged emptiness that had been safely kept at bay flooded over her.

Glynis stumbled into Bert's stall, her entire body seized by bone-numbing cold. Even as she dropped the brush and wrapped her arms across her midriff, her knees weakened and tears came from deep inside. Powerless against the onslaught, she closed her eyes and, slipping down into the straw, surrendered to uncontrollable sobs.

"I'll give her a few minutes and then check on her," Carrick offered before his cousin could ask.

Robert reached for his shirt. "What happened to her?"

Carrick repacked the supplies into Muldoon's white box of medicinals. "Two of the British caught her and Meyler out in the open; shot Meyler's horse from under him," he explained matter-of-factly.

"Where were you?"

Carrick grumbled, "Far enough behind them to be of no use. All I could do was ride like hell and watch Muldoon deal with them."

Robert eased his shirt over his head, wincing in the effort. "What did she do?"

"Killed them."

His cousin's head popped out of the neck opening, his eyes wide. "How'd she do it?"

The memory came quickly to mind. "She drew a rifle from out of that lumpy saddle of hers and dropped them," he replied, studying the mental image. "It took her less than two seconds to dispatch them both."

"Two seconds, Carrick?" Robert questioned, gingerly pushing an arm into a shirtsleeve. "Impossible. She couldn't have reloaded in that amount of time."

Carrick rose to his feet. "Let me show you something," he said, moving to the back corner of the loft. A moment later he returned to his cousin's side with Glynis Muldoon's rifle. "Take a look at this," he said, handing it over to his kinsman.

Robert hefted it in one hand, examining it from end to end with a critical eye. "Damn, it's light," he whispered after a long moment. "And look at the profile; so slim."

"Lever action," Carrick supplied, sitting cross-legged in the straw. "God knows how many shots it contains. I didn't ask and she didn't volunteer to discuss it."

"She's proficient?" his cousin asked, lifting the muzzle toward the ceiling and sighting along the length of it.

Carrick smiled wryly. "When she pointed it at me . . . my heart stopped. She's unbelievably fast. And smooth . . ." He shook his head in wonder. "Not a single wasted motion."

Robert looked at the rifle again and then handed it back, asking as he did, "Why didn't we notice this on her saddle?"

Carrick, too, lifted the weapon to his shoulder and studied the ceiling through the sights. "She carries it in a scabbard tucked beneath the skirt on the left side. That coat she wears covers it when she rides."

He brought down the weapon and shrugged. "With the butt of it dark like it is, it doesn't much show when she's out of the saddle. I've noticed the end of the stock, but it never registered; probably because it never occurred to me that she'd know how to use a firearm, much less possess such a weapon."

They shared a look and Robert observed thoughtfully, "That kind of oversight can considerably shorten a man's life."

Carrick laid aside the rifle. "Is that a thinly veiled reminder?"

"You might be willing to blindly accept the Dragon's Heart's prophecy," Robert retorted angrily, "but I'll be damned if I have to."

Carrick offered a wry smile. "Twenty-five is the magic year. You can't fight fate, Robert."

"The hell I can't."

Carrick shook his head, knowing that the time had long passed for him to be honest. He set his jaw. "Look, Cousin," he began. "I've been giving this some thought. When we killed those five Brits day before yesterday, we upped the stakes. It seems to me that it's time for Meyler to go home. I'd like for you to make sure he gets there in one piece."

Robert's eyes narrowed and bitterness drove his words. "The end draws near and you want the two of us well out of the way?"

Carrick cocked his brows. "Would you prefer to stay and watch?"

"I'd prefer to prevent it entirely," his cousin said bluntly.

"You're on a fool's mission, Rob," Carrick shot back, his own anger rising. "Go home; take Meyler with you and let me face what I have to. Once they have me, they'll forget that anyone ever rode with me."

Robert shook his head determinedly. "We'll leave Meyler at Saraid's. In the confusion of her household, it'll be weeks before she even notices he's there."

"Let me be clear," Carrick stated. "I don't want you with me, Robert."

"You haven't objected before now. Why your sudden change of thinking, Cousin?"

Brushing the straw from his pant legs, Carrick tried for patience. "Two days ago we were but an irritating splinter under the British skin. From time to time they'd remember we were here, but for the most part they left us to do our work."

He straightened and met his cousin's gaze. "Now we've festered and they're taking serious measures to rid themselves of us. It's become far more dangerous than it was before and I refuse to put you and Meyler in harm's way."

Understanding brightened Robert's dark eyes. "It's Glynis Muldoon, isn't it?" he demanded, his tone accusatory.

Carrick tamped down his anger and offered him a dismissive shrug. "Not in the way you're thinking, Rob. Her coming across time set in motion what was foreseen long ago. Because of her, because of the circumstances surrounding her arrival, the British will now hunt us until they have us dead."

"It's not her fault."

"I know that," Carrick agreed, running his fingers

through his hair in exasperation. "I don't hold her to blame. My only concern is to protect those I can, as best I can. For the moment, that means running day and night to stay ahead of the British patrols."

"And if we weren't with you, you wouldn't have to run," Robert observed, his tone acerbic. "You could turn and fight. You could let them kill you and be done with it."

Carrick glowered at him. "And everyone could finally expel the breath they've been holding since the night I came into this world."

It was a long second before Robert said quietly, "You'll not be doing any of us a favor by dying."

Why was it so damned hard for those around him to accept the truth he'd faced when he was ten years old? "How many times have we had this conversation, Robert?" he asked wearily.

"Too many to count."

"And has it ever made a difference?"

"No."

He looked into his cousin's eyes. "And it won't ever, Robert. Let's put it away and go on. You need to sleep and I need to find Muldoon. She's had long enough to deal with her demons alone."

"To my mind, that's much like trading one demon for another," Robert offered, the sharpness back in his voice.

God, Carrick inwardly moaned, *I'm too tired for this.* "She's a sensible woman, our Glynis Muldoon," he replied in what he hoped was a benign manner. "I've no doubts that she can protect herself from the likes of me."

"She deserves to be more than just another one of your little conquests-in-passing, Carrick."

The condemnation was gently spoken, but spoken nonetheless. His pride pricked at the attack. "Are you making a bid for her, Cousin?"

Robert's response was earnest and determined. "I'm not the man for her and we both know it. All I'm saying is that, for once in your life, take your heart into bed with you. For God's sakes, if you're determined to die before the year is out, you should at least go knowing that you actually felt something for a woman while you were making love to her."

Carrick hid his bruised pride behind indifference. "A most tender sentiment, Robert," he replied with a forced smile. "Unfortunately, if I were to do that, I might not be so willing to die."

"Wouldn't that be a shame."

Not trusting his anger, Carrick let his cousin have the last word and walked toward the edge of the loft, his pulse pounding in his temples.

9

Carrick found her sitting in the straw, legs drawn up against her chest and her face buried in her hands. The anger raging through him evaporated at the sight of her. He sat down beside her and after a moment said quietly, "I've heard of women who like horses, Muldoon, but I do think sleeping with them is carrying it a bit far."

She rubbed the palms of her hands over her tear-streaked cheeks. "If you wouldn't mind," she said, her voice soft with exhaustion, "I'd kinda like to be alone."

"I understand the motivation, Muldoon," Carrick replied gently. "But I'm obliged to tell you that it's not a particularly good idea. It's when you're alone with the memories that the second-guessing starts; when you wonder if you had other choices that you didn't see at the time. You can't allow yourself to do that, Muldoon. You start doubting and you'll hesitate the next time you need to make a judgment. And that's what will get you killed."

She leaned her head back against the stall and closed her eyes. "Maybe I'd rather be killed than kill."

"I'd miss you. So would Meyler and Robert."

"You'd all get over it soon enough."

Carrick studied her in silence, seeing the tightness at the corner of her mouth, the set of her chin. Wisps of auburn hair had escaped her braid and feathered around the slender oval of her face. He resisted the urge to smooth them back, knowing that the distance between them would be more effective in pushing her toward the edge she needed to confront. Time passed slowly, each second measured by his growing desire to take her in his arms.

"I can see their faces," she said softly. Her chin trembled. "I can see their surprise. Two mothers have lost their sons. Two wives have lost their husbands. God knows how many children will grow up without their father! And it's because of me. . . ." Her voice broke, but she managed to finish, "Because of what I did."

Ignoring his better judgment, Carrick reached out and took her face gently between his hands. "Look at me, Muldoon," he quietly commanded, bringing her gaze to his. "Would you have preferred that Meyler's parents, Niall and Hisolda, lose their son?"

Her eyes filled with tears, but he pressed on. "Those men had lived their lives; they had loves and maybe even families. Would you deny those pleasures to Meyler? To yourself?"

"But . . ." Tears spilled over her lower lashes. She pressed her eyes closed with trembling hands.

Her pain pierced his heart, but he kept his voice even. "The only choice you had was between saving yourself and Meyler or letting the both of you die. You chose to defend yourself and a helpless boy."

She pulled away and wiped her shirtsleeve across her cheek. "So I did the right thing," she said, sounding to Carrick's ears as though she were still trying to convince herself.

"Yes, Muldoon. You did the right thing. And exceedingly well."

"But I don't want to be good at killing people."

Carrick reached for her, his exasperation sufficient that he considered shaking her until good sense prevailed. The instant she looked up at him with grief-stricken eyes, another solution came to him.

"So how 'bout dem Yankees?"

She blinked. "What?"

"Do you think they have a chance to take the pennant this year?"

"The Marlins did last year. What do you know about baseball?"

"Virtually nothing," he admitted, smiling. "But when my mother senses that nothing she says is getting through, she throws out that line about the Yankees. Sometimes it's the Green Bay Packers. Sometimes the Knicks. And sometimes the Detroit Red Wings."

"What? No Mighty Ducks?" She grinned up at him. "Quack. Quack."

Reason faded away as he looked into her eyes. All that remained was a need that begged for a taste of Glynis Muldoon. He slowly leaned forward and brushed his lips over hers, reveling in their softness, in their sweetness. He felt her relax, felt the sigh that passed through her. Carrick eased away, conscious of how unevenly his pulse raced. He smiled down at her.

"Maybe . . ." she whispered up at him.

"Yeah, maybe."

He kissed her again, deepening his possession of her this time, sliding his arms about her shoulders and drawing her closer. She came into his embrace without resistance, her lips answering his caresses with a gentle hunger that stole his breath and warmed his blood.

Carrick shifted, turning until she lay cradled against him, her head resting against the curve of his shoulder. Her lips parted at the instant of his tender request. God, but she was beyond the wildest of his dreams. He wanted more of her, all of her. His conscience offered words of wisdom. With great effort he heeded them and slowly, reluctantly, released his claim to her lips.

She made no effort to move from his arms, but lay gazing up at him with soul-searching earnestness. He surrendered to the temptation and smoothed an auburn lock off her cheek. Her skin felt warm and soft beneath his fingertips.

"Perhaps I should go now, Muldoon," he offered, aware that she tempted him to do far more than touch her wayward strands of hair and stroke the wondrous softness of her cheek.

For a long moment she gazed up at him, the battle of her emotions evident in the sea-green depths of her eyes. "No," she finally said. "Please stay. Could you just hold me awhile?"

He traced the outline of her lips with a finger. "If I do, I'm likely to kiss you again."

"I've survived worse things," she countered, her voice soft.

Carrick studied her, noting that her lashes lay like thick dark spikes on her cheekbones. He cleared his throat. "Muldoon?"

She snuggled closer and blinked up at him sleepily. "What, des Marceaux?"

"Thank you for not shooting me."

She closed her eyes and a tiny smile hovered at the corners of her mouth as she answered, "I thought about it, you know. But then I decided that I couldn't shoot you until I knew if Meyler was right."

"Right about what?"

"About you being good at kissing."

God, would the woman never cease to surprise him? He grinned at the sleepy woman in his arms. "So . . . what do you think, Muldoon?"

She yawned and said blandly, "It's too early to make a decision. I'll have to let you live awhile longer."

"So," he pressed, "I suppose that with every kiss I'm hastening the day of my own execution."

"Pretty much so." She sounded as though she were on the verge of sleep. "Then again, I could decide that you're worth keeping."

"And then what, Muldoon?" he whispered.

"Then we see what else you might be good at."

At her words Carrick sobered instantly. Glynis Muldoon was a flesh-and-blood woman, he told himself, just like all the others he'd known in his twenty-five years. But he knew he was a liar, knew that the woman sleeping in his arms, unlike the others, had wit and humor and a will of well-honed steel. If a man weren't smart enough to turn and run, she'd have him grinning from ear to ear as she slashed his heart to irreparable ribbons. Robert was a madman if he thought it wise to risk feeling anything beyond respect and friendship for Glynis Muldoon.

"Ah, Muldoon," he whispered, placing a gentle kiss on her cheek. "With you I might come to regret that I've been a dead man since the day I was born." He smiled ruefully. "But, just the same, if the end is to come in the days ahead, I'd rather like to leave with the taste of you on my lips."

• • •

She awoke instantly at the sound of Carrick slowly cocking his flintlock pistol. Glynis lay perfectly still, her eyes closed, and tried desperately to keep her breathing even while she strained to hear the sound that had put Carrick on guard. The hinges on the stable door creaked softly.

Carrick's lips brushed her ear. "Not a sound," he breathed.

She nodded against his shoulder. She could feel his heartbeat against her cheek, its cadence strong and even. She focused on it, allowing its rhythm to fill and calm her.

"Carrick?" someone called softly from near the doorway. His voice sounded slightly familiar.

She felt a small portion of the tension ease from Carrick's body as he settled against the planking at his back. "Over here, Eachann," he answered just as quietly.

The sound of footsteps, the creaking of saddle leather, and the shuffling of hooves filled the small stable. Beneath her, she felt Carrick shift the angle of the pistol.

"I'll be damned, Carrick," the man whispered a moment later from a few feet away. "You're the only man I know who could spend the night dodgin' British patrols an' still have a willin' woman in his arms by sunup."

"Glad you made it, Eachann. And this is not as it might appear," Carrick explained. She heard the smile in his voice clearly, could well imagine the sparkle in his eyes.

"I'm sure it's not at all what we think, Captain," offered a skeptical voice from someplace farther away.

"Ah, Patrick," Carrick began. "You made it as well. Good. Where's Sean?"

While he spoke, Glynis felt Carrick slowly lower the hammer on the pistol. She realized that he'd drawn and prepared the weapon when he'd heard two riders approaching; that he hadn't lowered the muzzle until he'd been certain as to both their identities. Carrick des Marceaux was obviously a man who didn't trust easily. She shouldn't have found as much comfort in the characteristic as she did.

"Don't know 'bout Sean," answered the man called Eachann. "We waited most of the night at Swan's Cove for him, but he never got there. Could be a prisoner."

"Or could be dead," added Patrick.

She felt Carrick's tension, but not a trace of it showed in his voice when he replied, "Now, there's a couple of cheery thoughts to begin the day."

Glynis stirred against Carrick's chest and his arms tightened momentarily around her in warning. She went still again.

"Robert and Meyler are in the loft above," Carrick said. "I'll take care of your mounts. You go on up and catch a few hours of sleep. We'll move on to Saraid's later this morning."

"Of course," Eachann said. Glynis gritted her teeth. It didn't take any great imagination to see him looking between her and Carrick with an arched brow and a lecherous smile.

"Sorry to have intruded, Captain," Patrick added, his own meaning plain.

She waited until the sound of their booted footsteps crossed the loft above. Then she abruptly pushed herself from Carrick's arms.

He laughed quietly while she scrambled to her feet. "Good morning, Muldoon."

To return the simple greeting seemed tantamount to accepting the entire situation and all the implications of it. "I'm not some bimbo, you know," she retorted in a heated whisper, slapping the straw from the backs of her legs with her good arm and wishing that the others weren't in the loft. She really would have preferred to scream.

"Bimbo," he repeated, grinning. "That, Muldoon, happens to be one of my mother's favorite expressions. Come to think of it . . . it's the one she usually uses to describe the . . ." his grin widened, "ladies . . . who pass through my life."

She leaned closer to keep her anger between them. "Well, I'm not one of them!"

He gazed innocently up at her. "I never said you were."

"You allowed Eachann and Patrick to think it," she accused.

"So? Do you care what they think?"

"Yes."

"Well, don't take it personally," he replied, climbing to

his feet. Calmly brushing the straw from his legs, he continued, "They think that about all women, Muldoon. I
can't change their way of believing and I'm not going to
waste the effort trying. If you want to act prissy, go right
ahead. But fair warning, Muldoon, they'll still think you're
a bimbo."

Glynis glared up at him, her hands on her hips, furious at
his cavalier attitude. "So, in other words, I can't win for
losing."

He shook his head. "Not with them."

"I hate this," she fumed.

"Do you always wake up so sweet-tempered?" he asked,
amused.

"Oh, leave me alone," she groused, moving past him and
out of the stall.

"That's what you asked me to do last night," he called
softly. "Fortunately, you didn't mean it then. Do you mean
it now, Muldoon?"

Glynis winced as she remembered how easily she'd suc-
cumbed to Carrick's kisses. She turned back to him,
protesting, "I was past exhausted, des Marceaux. I do a lot
of stupid stuff when I get to that point."

To her surprise he tucked a strand of hair that had come
loose from her braid behind her ear. Her pulse quickened
and a delicious wave of warmth radiated through her body.

"I think I prefer you exhausted," he said softly, his
words sliding over her like the softest silk. "You're not
nearly as prickly."

Glynis resolutely pushed his hand away and then took a
step beyond his reach. "I'm going to find someplace to wash
up," she announced, failing miserably in her attempt to
sound calm.

He smiled knowingly at her. Her cheeks flooded with
embarrassment, she turned on her heel and moved to the door.

"Muldoon," Carrick called after her. "Wait a minute."

She turned back to him, keeping her gaze focused on the
center of his hard-muscled chest, determined to escape the
small room without having to look into his knowing eyes
again. She saw him draw the pistol from the small of his back.

"Take this with you and keep your wits about you," he

said, handing her the weapon. "Don't go too far. Stay within shouting distance."

She took it from him without a word and then opened the door just wide enough for her to slip through. Pulling it closed behind her, she pressed her forehead against the cool wood panel. God help her. If she wasn't careful, Carrick des Marceaux would manage to accomplish what virtually every cowboy in east-central Kansas had tried his damnedest to do . . . and destroy what little of herself she'd been able to put back together after Jake.

"No way, des Marceaux," she whispered, straightening and lifting her chin. "I'm going home come hell or high water. And in the meantime, I'm not about to become another notch in your bedpost."

Carrick stepped over to the window and watched her stalk across the hard-packed yard toward the trees. He reminded himself to ask her about the leather coverings she wore on her legs. As she walked away, the thin straps that held them in place nicely accentuated her slim hips and the shapely, tapered length of her legs. He also noted that on the woven belt that encircled her narrow waist, she wore a leather sheath fitted into the small of her back. He rubbed the sore spot on his thigh where it had pressed through the late hours of the night. It held her knife, he remembered. He hadn't suspected her of owning such a weapon and his shock at the well-practiced, one-handed ease with which she'd opened it had been matched when she'd drawn the rifle with such speed from the scabbard laced to her saddle.

Glynis Muldoon was one surprise after another. Not the least of which had been the way she'd reacted to being in his arms, to his touch. He hadn't been the first to kiss her; of that he was absolutely certain. But her experience beyond that? Carrick let out a long, slow breath.

Panic had seized her when he'd touched her hair a moment ago. She'd recognized what he'd been about and he'd plainly seen desire in her beautiful green eyes. But in the same heartbeat she'd run from them both, from what had promised to bloom between them.

Glynis had been hurt in the past. And, if he was any sort

of judge in these matters, hurt badly. Logic told him that her painful past was to both their advantages. Her determination to keep emotional distance between them would make it a lot easier for him to do the same.

He shook his head. What the hell was wrong with him? He never had trouble making decisions. He always knew whether or not he wanted a woman. He always knew whether or not he wanted to put the effort into a seduction. And God knew that emotionally involving himself had never been a consideration in the matter of taking a woman to his bed. What was it about Glynis Muldoon that had turned his black and whites into grays?

With a snort of self-disgust, he turned on his heel. The sooner he put Glynis Muldoon out of reach, the better.

Glynis dropped down onto a rock beside the trickling creek and quit fighting the tears. Could things get any worse than they already were? Disbelief aside, it sure as hell looked as if she had indeed been transported across time. And whether or not she wanted to, she was going to have to face the fact that she might not be able to get back to where she belonged. Uncle Lloyd, Aunt Ria, and the Rocking M needed her. She had obligations. She couldn't let them down. And, damn it all, she couldn't let herself down, either. She'd put a hell of a lot of plain old hard work into the Rocking M. Far too much to just walk away from it without a good hard fight.

And as if all that wasn't overwhelming enough, she had to admit that Meyler had been absolutely right: Carrick des Marceaux was a good kisser. A damn fine kisser, in fact.

But Jake had been good at that, too, she reminded herself, wiping the tears from her cheeks. But after two years of marriage, his kissing was about the only thing in his plus column. And that hadn't even come close to being enough to balance out the impressive list of minuses he'd managed to rack up.

Glynis looked up into the clear blue morning sky. She had to be the worst at picking men. She'd proven that by marrying Jake Reimer. She'd proven it again by giving him a second chance before she'd finally come to her senses and divorced him. And had she learned anything out of that whole god-awful mess? Apparently not. If she had, her heart wouldn't be turning over every time Carrick des Marceaux touched her.

"Well," she muttered, sliding off the rock, "I've just got to get a handle on this, that's all. I'm tough. I'm smart."

She was tired and sore, and that always made things seem bleaker than they really were. Things would turn out fine. Eventually. Carrick's wannabe witch sister would reverse the magic that had brought her to this unstable time and she'd get back to the Rocking M and the life she was supposed to be living. What she needed until then was a purpose, something to keep her mind off of Carrick des Marceaux.

Working cattle side by side with the ranchers and their sons had been quite effective at dousing romantic notions in the past. Since she couldn't count on having that particular opportunity with Carrick, she'd have to find something else.

Washing her face in the river, she found the solution. She'd just demand to openly assist Carrick in exacting justice for the Irish people. He couldn't very well refuse her at this point. Last night she'd crossed the line and even Carrick couldn't pretend she was a noncombatant in the war against the tithe laws. When she became a member of his outlaw band, both of them would be compelled to view the other as a comrade rather than a conquest. They'd be forced by circumstances to respect each other as equals. And if that didn't work . . . She smiled wryly. If that didn't work she could just shoot him.

10

Glynis glanced at the late afternoon sun. The day was warmer than the previous two. She brushed her sleeve across her brow to dry it and wondered whether removing her coat would be worth the effort. Her shoulder had stiffened again and moving it the slightest bit sent waves of hot pain through her. Maybe the next time they stopped to water the horses . . .

They rounded the bend and a two-story quarried-stone house suddenly loomed before them.

"Saraid's," Robert said from her left side.

Glynis's first thought was that Carrick's sister had married well. Her second was that anyone who lived in a house that fine had to have a bathtub and that basic hospitality would require that person to share it. Glynis looked down at herself and wrinkled her nose. No, she decided, Carrick's sister would offer her a bath in simple self-defense. She counted the chimneys. Four in the main part of the house. Two in the single-story north wing. One in the matching southern wing. Seven altogether. Glynis nodded in satisfaction. There'd be plenty of hot water.

"What do you think of Saraid's little cottage?"

Glynis looked over at Carrick and admitted, "I'd hate to have to be the one who got to wash all those windows."

"It's a half-sized reproduction of our parents' house." He grinned. "It's the best ol' Horace could do, but it sufficiently impressed Saraid."

Half-sized? Glynis turned and considered him. "What is it that your parents do, Carrick?"

"International shipping," he answered with a shrug. "Industrial investments. Some farming."

As long as he was being forthright for a change . . . "And before becoming an outlaw, Carrick . . . what did *you* do for a living?"

"When I wasn't much older than Meyler is now, I signed aboard one of my father's ships and set about learning the art of seamanship."

"He captains *the* ship of the Erin Line; the *Wind Dancer*," Patrick said archly from behind them. "He's in charge of the American portion of the company's trading."

"Patrick takes great pride in being the first mate," Carrick added.

"As I do in being the first officer," Robert added. "As my father did when he served Carrick's. God willing, we'll feel a deck beneath our feet again before the month is out."

Had Carrick stiffened at his cousin's comment or had she simply imagined it? She decided wisdom lay in ignoring the possibility of problems between them. Besides, she reasoned, she didn't really have the energy for figuring out puzzles today anyway. "How about you, Meyler?" Glynis asked, peering around Carrick's shoulders at the boy. "Surely they didn't leave you out of this family venture."

He grinned. "I'm Carrick's cabin boy."

"And you, Eachann?" she asked, slowly turning in her saddle to look at the big blond man who rode with Patrick behind them. "Are you a misplaced sailor as well?"

"No, Miss Muldoon." he answered seriously, "The sea has never called me. I'm a horseman. Been with the des Marceauxs all my life, I have. Born in Castle O'Connell just like the rest of 'em."

"Castle?" she asked, looking to Carrick for an explanation.

He shrugged dismissively. "My mother's English brother burned the original castle and my parents built a new manor in the first years of their marriage; all of it inside the protective walls that survived the fire. I suppose in that sense it remains a castle."

So she had been right in her initial assessment, she decided. Carrick and Robert had indeed been to the manor born.

"Ah," Carrick drawled. "We've been spotted. Prepare yourselves for the onslaught."

Glynis looked back at the house in time to see a lanky, towheaded boy dash up the front steps and fling open the front door. He stuck his head inside for a moment and then darted back out, racing back down the steps.

"Saraid's oldest," Robert explained. "Matthew."

In the next second a flurry of elbows and knees filled the doorway and tumbled down the steps. "Mark, Luke, and John," Robert supplied, pointing to each of the boys in turn.

"How biblical," Glynis observed with a smile.

"It's the only way Saraid can keep track," Carrick muttered out of the side of his mouth. "I'll ride ahead and draw their fire, men," he announced, grinning and nudging Molan in the flanks. The boys waiting in the yard jumped and waved their arms as he left the group and moved ahead.

Glynis chuckled and dragged her coat sleeve across her brow again. "I gather Carrick's something of a sensation with his nephews."

Robert nodded and smiled. "And with the nieces, too."

Glynis looked uncertain. "How many kids does Saraid have?"

"Eight at last count," Robert answered, grinning. He raised his arm and pointed toward the house, adding, "Ah, here comes the petticoat brigade. That's Eve, Mary, Sarah, and Rachel. Luke is Mary's twin, John is Rachel's."

Glynis shook her head and expelled a long breath. "How am I supposed to be able to keep all this sorted out?"

"Don't even try, Miss Muldoon," Robert said with a chuckle. "Even the family often refers to written notes to keep it straight. If I were you, I'd simply avoid calling anyone by name. If you have to single one of them out, simply run through the list like Saraid does. Eventually the one you want will turn around and you can go from there."

"It was much simpler being an only child." Glynis observed uneasily, watching the barely contained pandemonium waiting ahead.

"You have no brothers or sisters?" Robert sounded as

though she'd announced that she had six toes on one foot. "Surely you have cousins."

"Nope. Just me."

"It sounds like a very lonely circle in which to live, Miss Muldoon."

"But there's also something to be said for order and calm," she countered, watching Carrick swing down off Molan and catch all four of his nephews in his embrace. Within almost the same moment the girls tossed themselves into the squirming huddle surrounding their uncle.

"He'd make a good father, wouldn't he?" she mused, startled to hear that she'd given voice to the thought.

"Yes."

Something in Robert's tone caught her ear. She turned in the saddle to face him. "You sound as though you disapprove, Robert."

The man's expression darkened as he watched his cousin. "I disapprove of Carrick's stupidity; his fatalism."

"Now, that one begs an explanation. Fatalistic about what?" she pressed.

"He's always been convinced he won't live past the age of twenty-five. It's been the subject of many a heated exchange. Nevertheless, he's refused to commit to anything beyond the moment. As a consequence, Carrick's chosen to have no family except for the one he was born into."

It all went a long way toward explaining his rather easygoing attitude about women and his willingness to take risks. "So how old is he now?" she asked, wondering what sort of timetable Carrick held in his head.

"Twenty-five. He'll be twenty-six in early November."

Six months. That fact spoke volumes about his passion for ending the tithe laws. If she had that little time, she'd want to do something significant with it, too. "Damn," she whispered, studying Carrick as he lifted a child over his head.

"Yes, Miss Muldoon," Robert echoed, his anger and frustration evident. "Damn."

They rode up the drive in silence.

"There's Saraid, joining the parade well behind the others . . . as usual," Robert said, shattering her thoughts.

Glynis rubbed her sleeve across her damp brow again. Why

was she having such a difficult time focusing all of a sudden? Robert was speaking again and she listened carefully, her effort rewarded by the gradual return of her attention.

"That rather rotund older man coming down the steps behind her is Horace, her doting husband. A nice man, all things considered." Robert paused and stretched forward in the saddle. "Good Lord, has she got another one on the way?" he asked incredulously.

Glynis looked at the woman coming down the steps, noting the high waist on her gown and the rounded bulge beneath her breasts. "It would appear so, Robert," she agreed as they reined in their mounts.

Robert immediately swung down, saying as he did, "Remind me to have a quiet talk with Horace before we leave here."

Glynis smiled and leaned forward to rest her forearm on the saddle horn. She watched Carrick extricate himself from the arms of the little ones and step forward to embrace his sister. Robert vaulted up the two lower steps, smiling, his hand extended toward Horace. Meyler hopped down and melted into the crowd of children momentarily forgotten by the adults. Eachann and Patrick slipped past her, taking the reins of all the other mounts and drawing them away.

She watched it all, part of her knowing good manners suggested she climb down and stand on the same plane as everyone else. A wariness held her back. She didn't belong here. She wasn't family. She felt more secure staying in the saddle.

Carrick released Saraid to Robert's claim and reached out to shake his brother-in-law's hand. A moment later he laid his hand on his sister's shoulder and drew her forward. Glynis held her breath in anticipation.

"Saraid, dear sister," Carrick began, "I'd like for you to meet someone." He lifted his hand and gestured toward Glynis. "Saraid, please meet Glynis Muldoon. Muldoon, this is my sister, Saraid Concannon."

Saraid's blue eyes widened as she looked up. Glynis watched the color drain from the woman's face and her jaw go slack.

"It's a pleasure, ma'am," Glynis said, still leaning forward on the saddle horn but casually lifting her left hand to touch the brim of her Stetson in the classic western greeting.

Saraid's eyes rolled upward and, with a whispered "Ohmigod," she crumpled into Carrick's arms.

Horace and Robert dashed to Saraid's side. Relinquishing his sister to the other men, Carrick straightened and looked up at Glynis.

"I have that effect on people sometimes," she offered. She watched as the men carried Saraid into the house. "Will she be all right?"

He nodded. "Saraid long ago perfected fainting to an art form. It's her way of avoiding unpleasantness. Climb down from there and come with me."

As she swung from the saddle, he motioned for Eachann. The man reached for Bert's reins while Carrick said, "See what you can do to hide those spots on him, Eachann. And put that saddle somewhere where the casual looker isn't going to find it. Miss Muldoon isn't going to be needing it for awhile."

"Hold a minute," Glynis called, stepping to Bert's side. She untied the saddlebags, slung them over her right shoulder, then withdrew the Winchester from its scabbard. "Thanks, Eachann," she said, giving the young man a nod and patting Bert's withers before she joined Carrick on the steps.

Gulliver couldn't have felt any more out of place among the Lilliputians than she did at the moment, Glynis mused, watching everyone move around the parlor. She took up a position near the door. Conscious of the dirt clinging to every square inch of her and the bloodstains and ragged holes marking her coat, she took care not to touch the walls or anything else. Even the hole in her shoulder throbbed more than it ever had . . . just for the occasion. And being out of the sun didn't appear to have diminished her discomfort the least little bit. She shifted beneath the weight of the saddlebags on her good shoulder.

"Dear," Horace was saying, concern deepening the lines in his broad forehead as Saraid reclined on a pink brocade love seat, the back of her wrist pressed against her forehead. Robert quickly stepped from the beverage cart with a crystal tumbler of water in his hand. "Here, Saraid," he said, slipping his hand beneath her head. "Take a sip of this and you'll feel better in a minute or so."

"And then you can stand accountable," Carrick added, leaning back against the cart, a glass of whiskey in his hand.

"I'm so terribly weak," Saraid murmured.

"I think you should retire to your rooms, Saraid, my dear," Horace said. "The excitement of Carrick's unexpected arrival has been too much for you."

"Yes," Robert asserted, nodding. "Considering your delicate condition, perhaps—"

"Delicate my ass," Carrick snorted, setting aside his glass and crossing the room with a deliberate stride. Stopping beside his sister's recumbent form, he leaned down and said, "No woman who can pop out babies like you do can claim delicacy, Saraid. Now stop this farce and let's get the matter dealt with."

"Carrick," she snapped, flinging her arm into her lap and glaring at him. "You're a beast. You really are. You always have been."

Glynis hid her grin behind her hand, choking back her laughter. God, the household the two of them had grown up in had to have been something of a war zone. She pitied their poor mother.

Carrick pinned his sister with a hard stare. "And so you try to get even with me by bringing Glynis Muldoon down upon me?"

Saraid sat up abruptly and swung her legs over the edge of the love seat, looking up at her brother. "I honestly didn't bring her here, Carrick."

"Then how is it that she passed through the portals of time, Saraid? I've checked. She has no wings."

"You promised me that you'd make no more attempts at magic, Saraid," Horace said, placing a gentle hand on Saraid's shoulder.

Saraid looked at the ceiling for a moment before throwing her hands up in a gesture of resignation. She turned to her husband. "I was bathing and in the water I saw Carrick and his men sleeping in the forest. And then I saw the British patrol coming across the countryside in their direction. I was frightened at what might happen to him and Robert, so I searched in the water for a possible diversion."

She looked over at Glynis. "And that's when I saw you riding your horse, Miss Muldoon. I wished that you would draw the British attention away from my brother and cousin. I meant only to protect them. I didn't realize that you were from another time and place or that you were a woman."

Glynis shrugged and winced as pain sliced through her left shoulder. In the wake of it came a wave of heat far more intense than any she'd endured before.

"Are you hurt?" Saraid asked, jumping up off the love seat with remarkable speed for a woman so recently incapacitated. Horace slipped his arm protectively about her waist.

"At what would appear to be your request, big sister," Carrick practically growled at her, "Muldoon took a hefty piece of British shot in her shoulder."

Saraid's eyes widened. "Oh, dear. How I can ever apologize?"

"It'll heal," Glynis offered somewhat breathlessly, trying to still the suddenly swaying room. She shifted her hold on her rifle for better balance. "My main concern is getting back where I belong."

Saraid looked worried. "I don't know where that is."

"Well, I do, ma'am," Glynis heard herself reply as though from far away. "And I figure if you brought me here not knowing where I came from, you can surely send me back with the same sort of vagueness."

"But I didn't deliberately bring you here. I have no idea how I did it. I have no idea how to go about returning you. I don't have control over the magic. It just happens."

God, the room wouldn't quit moving. She broadened her stance.

"Ma'am," Glynis drawled, trying desperately to focus on Saraid's face, "I have to get back home."

"Our mother came through the time portal. She made a life for herself here. I honestly don't think she's ever regretted it. Perhaps in time—"

"Time is something I don't have," Glynis cut in, fighting

panic. She realized that Carrick had turned toward her, studying her with furrowed brows.

"It's spring," Glynis rushed to explain. "It's calving season and the pastures have got to be ridden, the cattle worked and medicated. The fences have to be checked, mended, and rechecked. Any day now the trucks will be delivering the herds from Texas for summering."

"Surely there's someone else who could see to the work."

Glynis felt her panic threatening to overwhelm her. She took several deep breaths before she blurted, "There isn't anyone else. It's my ranch and it's my responsibility. I can't stay here, Mrs. Concannon. I don't have the option of making a new life for myself. I have obligations in the old one that I can't walk away from."

"Life frequently takes unexpected turns, Miss Muldoon," Horace offered, his tone gentle. "Being able to accommodate oneself to them is a mark of one's maturity."

God, she was losing it. In a matter of minutes she'd be nothing more than a sobbing zombie. She looked at Horace as she fired her last, desperate salvo. "Another mark is being able to step up to the line and do whatever it is you have to, Mr. Concannon, no matter the inconvenience or the risk.

"Staying here would be the easiest thing. In the last two days I haven't done a lick of work. It's been like a holiday . . . a holiday in hell, granted, but a holiday nonetheless.

"My other life is gambling against the heat and the snow and the storms and the cattle market. Sometimes I win. Sometimes I lose. Either way means long hours and a lot of hard work. But it was the work of my father and his father before him. The legacy's been passed to me and I'll be damned if I go to heaven and have to explain how I took a trip through time and let all their hard work go for naught."

"Muldoon . . ."

Glynis turned at the sound of Carrick's voice and tried to bring him into focus. Was he moving toward her or did it simply look that way because of the fever? *Like a mirage.* Where had all the others gone? She and Carrick were suddenly alone in the room.

"Our mother has an uncanny knack for knowing when

we need her," Carrick said gently. "She also has powers far beyond any that Saraid might have used to bring you here. It's not hopeless, Muldoon. Mother may well be able to return you to your place in time."

He *was* closer, she decided. She'd have to change the angle of her head if she wanted to look him in the eyes; a change she quickly decided she couldn't risk. The odds were she'd fall over if she tilted her head back. "Where is your mother?" she asked. "And please tell me she's upstairs taking a nap."

"She's on the other side of Ireland," Carrick answered quietly.

"How's she at doing long-distance spells?"

"She's probably on her way here already. We'll find a solution, Muldoon."

Yes. Carrick was right. She needed to find a solution. "I'll go find her. The Castle O'Connell, right? How difficult can it be to find?" She headed toward the door.

Carrick grabbed her arm. "Not now, Muldoon."

And then he was standing before her, blocking her passage to the Castle O'Connell. "Christ," he swore, pressing the palm of his hand to her cheek, "you're burning up. How long have you been like this?"

She swayed on her feet. "I'll be okay."

He stripped the rifle out of her hand and the saddlebags from her shoulder.

"Rob, take these," she heard him say. In what seemed like the same instant she felt herself leaving the floor, felt the wonderful coolness of Carrick's shirt against her cheek, the strength of his arms cradling her.

"Saraid, point me to a room and have a tepid bath brought up. *Now*," he said, the calm command instantly easing the horrible panic that had gripped her.

Glynis closed her eyes. "I want a *hot* bath," she whispered. "With soap."

11

Glynis couldn't remember when she'd ever felt so weak, and so embarrassingly helpless. If she'd had the strength, she'd have insisted that she be allowed to walk on her own. But her pride was the only reserve she had left and its wasn't enough to force her body to move. She had no choice but to let Carrick carry her out of the drawing room, up the stairs, and down a long narrow hallway.

Saraid swept a door open and stepped into the room ahead of them. "Put her on the bed," she instructed as Carrick carried her across the threshold.

Carrick stopped in the center of the room and shook his head. His voice rumbled against her cheek. "Not unless you want to change the covers before you tuck her in for the duration."

With her hands on her hips, his sister countered, "Well, do you have a better idea?"

"Muldoon?" he said softly. She blinked groggily up at him. He smiled and asked, "Can you manage if I sit you in a chair for a bit?"

"I can do anything," she replied, trying to focus on him.

He smiled at her thin attempt at bravado. "Yes, of course you can," he agreed, carrying her to the chaise in the corner nearest the unlit fireplace. He carefully settled her on the edge and, with one hand resting on her shoulder to hold her steady, began to work the tattered, stained coat down her injured arm. Glynis closed her eyes to keep the room from spinning.

"Carrick!" Saraid protested from behind him. "What are you doing?"

He switched hands and drew the coat down the length of her other arm, letting it pool on the chaise behind her. "I'm getting her out of these clothes," he answered impatiently. "What does it look like I'm doing?"

"Engaging in most inappropriate behavior," Saraid declared as he reached for the open edges of her collar.

"You think you're up to wrestling her, Saraid?" Carrick asked, popping open the front of her Levi's shirt with a quick flick of his wrists. Glynis looked down at his work with pursed lips, knowing that she should protest Carrick's familiarity. The more practical side of her suggested that she should be grateful for his help, that she was in no condition to undress herself. She closed her eyes in an effort to hide her humiliation. She'd never needed a man to help her with anything other than occasionally handling cattle. And now . . .

Her expression struck a chord in Carrick. Glynis, hurt and vulnerable. . . . He'd never felt so helpless. He forced his mind back to the task at hand. Whether Saraid's gasp came at the clicking sound of the fastenings opening or at the pink lace so suddenly exposed, Carrick couldn't decide and didn't really care. As he had her coat, he set about stripping the shirt from Muldoon. Her shoulder looked ghastly—red, swollen, and bruised.

Saraid tried once more to intervene. "I do believe I can do this without your assistance, Carrick. I hardly think the poor woman is capable of putting up much resistance."

Glynis met his gaze and he saw the desperate request in her brilliant green eyes. "Trust me, sister," Carrick said, giving Glynis a conspiratorial wink and a smile. "She's a lot meaner than she looks."

Glynis smiled back, broadly if a bit lopsidedly. Her eyes were even brighter as she looked to Saraid and said, "I'll have you know that I'm the soul of feminine decorum, Mrs. Concannon."

Carrick chuckled and eased her to her feet. She clung to his shirtfront with both hands. "Muldoon, you're delirious," he taunted, wrapping one arm about her waist and clearing her coat and shirt from the chaise with a quick sweep of his other. Settling her back into the seat, he added dryly, "You're not going to remember a single minute of this come the next day or two."

Unfortunately he'd remember it in vivid detail for months to come: the firm, inviting swells of her breasts cradled by pink lace, the gentle ripples of her ribs, the deep, sweeping curve that led his eyes to her narrow belted waist. His blood heated in his veins.

A distraction. He needed a distraction. Carrick grasped the heel of a boot and the whole thing came off with an audible pop.

As he pulled the other boot from her foot, his sister picked the coat up from the floor where it had fallen. Holding it at arm's length with a thumb and index finger, she asked grimly, "What should I do with this?"

Carrick spared it only a glance. "Burn it."

"No way, nohow," Glynis protested, struggling to sit upright. "That's my trusty drover's coat. It can be washed and patched."

Saraid bent to retrieve the shirt. "And your . . . blouse, Miss Muldoon?" she asked. "Shall I have it patched as well?"

"You bet," Glynis replied, settling back into the curve of the chaise with a determined nod. God, Carrick was working the leg buckles on her chaps. She really should push him away, should do the task for herself. His hands were too warm, too close, too distracting.

Geez Louise. She was sitting there without a shirt, without her boots, and letting this man strip away her chaps. What was wrong with her? It couldn't all be the fever.

Carrick smiled to himself. Getting this woman out of her odd clothing was a true test of his considerable skills. At least he wasn't trying to manage the task in the dark.

When he positioned her leg so that he had access to the buckle on her upper thigh, Glynis said breathlessly, "It's my favorite Levi's shirt. It's soft as butter. I bought it at the outlet mall in Lawrence, you know," she rambled. "On sale. Right after Christmas. That's when you get the best bargains, of course. Everything's marked down for year-end clearance. Aunt Ria and I always drive up and make a day of it."

"Muldoon . . ." Carrick interrupted softly, drawing her forward so that he could reach the last of the buckles, the one that held the entire leather garment about her hips.

She slipped her arm around his neck and looked up at him. She asked ernestly, "Who's going to go shopping with Aunt Ria if I can't get home, Carrick? I'm all she's got. She never had any children of her own. She always called me her little green-eyed Indian."

Before he could think of a reply, she wrinkled her nose, and eased away from him. "You know, Carrick . . ." she began, hesitantly, "I don't mean to insult you or anything, but you could stand to have a bath, too."

He grinned and pulled away the leather garment. "Are you offering to share yours, Muldoon?"

Saraid choked behind them. "Carrick!"

"Oh, be still, Saraid," he admonished, winking at Glynis. "I'm about to get the best offer I've had in recent memory."

"Not in my household, you're not!"

"Lock the door behind you and tell Robert to entertain the children so they don't miss me for a while. I won't say a word to anyone," Carrick drawled.

"That does it!" Saraid pronounced. She pointed toward the door as she added sternly, "Get out!"

Carrick considered the strange track of metal that appeared to hold Glynis's trousers closed.

"And might I suggest you go throw yourself in the lough," his sister continued indignantly. "The water's cold enough it might help you remember some sense of decorum. Mother would be appalled."

"Oh, stow it, Saraid," he countered, tugging at the top of the breeches in the hope that they would open as simply as her shirt had. He wasn't that fortunate. "I'm not about to compromise Miss Muldoon in her present state."

"It's just bantering, Mrs. Concannon," Glynis contributed brightly. "It's all harmless fun . . . unless, of course, you don't know when to quit."

"Knowing when to quit is hardly one of my brother's strengths, Miss Muldoon."

Muldoon smiled at Carrick and with a wink added, "I like a man who can go to excess every now and then. It adds nice edges."

The sound of the metal bathtub bumping around the last corner in the back stairway called their attention to the impending arrival of Glynis's bath. Carrick quickly took the coat from Saraid and draped it over Glynis, just as a stout, gray-haired woman paused in the doorway.

"Mrs. Kelly," his sister said with obvious relief. "You're just in time. Please have the tub placed before the hearth. And when you're done here, please have another bath brought up to Carrick's room."

The housekeeper looked disapprovingly at the young woman lying on the chaise and then stepped aside to let the boy carrying the tub and the two older girls with the water buckets pass by. As they prepared the bath where instructed, she nodded to Saraid and said, "It will take a bit to warm the water for Master Carrick, madam."

"Don't fuss with it overmuch," Saraid countered. "He'll not mind if it's a bit cool." She fixed him with a pointed stare as she added, "Will you, brother dear?"

He smiled at the matronly housekeeper. "Not at all, Mrs. Kelly."

The woman barely nodded. "In ten minutes, then, sir. Your customary room."

With a broad smile, Carrick replied, "I'll be ready and waiting for you, Mrs. Kelly."

The woman made a *hrump*ing sound as she swept out of the room. The boy blushed scarlet to his ears and the girls giggled into their hands as they scurried along in her wake.

Saraid turned to him, her hands on her hips. "Must you be such a tease?"

"It's what adds sunshine to my existence," he countered with a grin. He turned from his sister and, carefully lifting away the coat, said, "C'mon, Muldoon, time to be into the tub and rid of this fever." Taking the edge of her trousers in hand again, he growled, "Help me with this damned device, will you?"

Glynis pushed his hands aside, lifted the metal tab at the top of her trousers, and slid it down. Carrick felt his lungs seize as the metal track parted to reveal a wide band of pink lace encircling the narrow curve of her hips. He took a step back and closed his eyes, willing himself to remember her fever.

"I think I can manage it from here, Carrick," Saraid offered from the hearth.

Forcing himself to take deep breaths, he turned away and watched his sister test the bathwater.

"Go lie in wait for Mrs. Kelly," she continued. "When you're cleaned up, you may stop by on your way downstairs to see if we need any further assistance."

Unsettled, he retorted, "She's quite capable of protecting herself, Saraid. You needn't play the dowager aunt."

Glynis laughed and the throaty sound played across his body. "I'll be back shortly, Muldoon," he said, turning toward the door. Offering up silent thanks that she still wore her trousers, he forced a smile and admonished, "Don't let Saraid drown you with kindness," as he fled the room.

Glynis paused at the tub, the sheet clutched around her body, and told herself that no matter how bad it seemed, it wasn't as bad as gym class. There weren't thirty-five girls running around the room; only Saraid. If only she could do this without help, without the chance that she'd pass out and drown in the first bath she'd had in days. To be found face down, naked, in half a tub of water . . . Glynis lifted her chin. She'd just have to get through it, was all. And, if she were *really* lucky, the unpredictable fever would flare up again and she wouldn't be able to make heads or tails out of what was happening around her.

Saraid stood beside her, clearly prepared to catch her if necessary. "Are you certain that you can climb in on your own?"

"I'm okay," Glynis assured her, awkwardly dropping the sheet covering her body and stepping quickly into the tub. Settling into the water, she closed her eyes, leaned into the curved back of the copper tub, and wondered if it would be possible to pretend Saraid wasn't there. It was cowardly, but pride was a precious thing and just about all she had left.

"But I'll tell you what you could do for me," Glynis said, sitting forward, determined to make the best of the horribly awkward situation. "Would you wash my hair. Please? I can't lift my left arm up high enough to do it myself."

Saraid looked relieved and began undoing Glynis's braid. "You have lovely hair. I didn't even notice it until Carrick removed that horrid coat."

"Thank you," she managed to reply.

With a sigh, Saraid scooped water from the tub and carefully poured it over Glynis's head. As she repeated the task, she quietly ventured, "You should exercise caution with my brother, Miss Muldoon. He's not the sort of man who takes flirtation lightly. And you would also be well advised to bear in mind that he avoids commitment just as diligently as he seeks his pleasures."

Glynis nodded. It seemed like it took an eternity to get her thoughts to her tongue, took entirely too much concentration to form even the simplest sentence. "Well, if I were going to die before the year's out, I think I might adopt a similar attitude."

Saraid froze. "How is it that you know? Did he tell you?"

"No. Robert did."

Soaping Glynis's hair, Carrick's sister observed, "I suppose it's knowing that his life will be short that has always softened people's perceptions and, in turn, the consequences of Carrick's actions. Everyone seems most willing to forgive him, regardless of how outrageous his transgression."

"How is it that everyone's so certain he's going to die young?" Glynis asked, closing her eyes and trying to divide what energy she had left between the conversation and the simple pleasure of having someone shampoo her hair for her. "Was he cursed by a gypsy at birth or something?"

"What has he told you of our mother?"

What had Carrick told her? "That she's a time traveler, too," Glynis answered simply. "That she came from Colorado and that she was an accountant before her life got twisted around and she ended up here."

Saraid rinsed away the soap. "Our mother came through time unwittingly but at the specific behest of her Aunt

Maude. It is Mother's destiny to live her life in this century, not the one in which she'd been born."

Adding more soap to Glynis's hair, she repeated her washing, saying as she did, "Mother's certain of this because when Aunt Maude set her plan in motion, she made sure that Mother had the Dragon's Heart, a ruby brooch in which Mother can see distant events—distant both in the sense of miles and time."

Glynis concentrated, knowing that she needed to hear every word of Saraid's explanation. Mercifully, the fever seemed to have eased.

"The Dragon's Heart always tells the truth, and while the course it predicts hasn't always been smooth, Mother has been able to accept what is destined to be." Saraid's hands went still. "Except when Mother was carrying Phelan and Carrick and she saw Carrick's death in the Dragon's Heart."

"How did she know it was him?" Glynis countered, refusing to patently accept Carrick's death. "Maybe it's his brother instead. I gather from what Robert said that Carrick's a twin."

Saraid sighed and explained sadly, "Phelan is slender and fair . . . as is our mother. Carrick favors our father. As they came into the world she knew it was Carrick she saw killed."

Glynis felt a surge of anger. "I don't think I'd want to know anything like that," she muttered. "It would be too hard."

"Yes," Saraid acknowledged, toweling Glynis's hair with a large linen sheet. "Mother put away the Dragon's Heart the night Phelan and Carrick were born, and to my knowledge hasn't sought its magic since. She and my father try to live each day as though they don't possess the knowledge of his fate and try to keep the managing of Phelan and Carrick even-handed."

"Damn difficult task," Glynis offered. She didn't know whether it was the distracting conversation or the tepid bath working its magic, but she felt cooler and the world wasn't nearly as fuzzy as it had had been.

"Impossible, actually," Saraid agreed. "By the time they

were ten both boys were certain that something dark lay beneath the surface of things. But Carrick is the more demanding of the two and it was he who pressed for the truth."

Glynis whispered, "And they told him?"

"They didn't have a choice in the matter," Saraid admitted. "Carrick found the Dragon's Heart and saw the future for himself. All our parents could do then was comfort him as best they could."

This new information about Carrick was intriguing and somehow hopeful. "So Carrick has the same gifts as your mother for seeing things in the brooch?"

Saraid looked annoyed. "He's the only one of us that inherited the gift and he's always refused to develop it. He says there's no point. It doesn't seem quite fair, does it? I've spent a lifetime trying to cultivate the skills required to be a seer and the best I can do—"

"Is drag some poor, unsuspecting woman off the Kansas prairie, spin her through time, and then drop her into an Irish version of hell on Earth," Glynis finished, smiling ruefully.

"I am so very sorry," the other woman offered, soaping a sponge and handing it to her. "I truly didn't mean to involve you in Carrick's life."

More like his death, Glynis corrected silently. She smiled at her hostess. "I'm willing to forgive you as long as you get me back to where I belong."

With a frown, Saraid clasped her hands beneath her coming child. "If only it were that easily done." Both women looked sober.

"We would welcome you, make you one of the family," the Saraid offered, brightening.

Glynis squeezed water from the sponge and trickled it down the length of her arm. She met Saraid's gaze and tried to keep her voice calm. "I want to go home, Mrs. Concannon. My family may not be as large or as extended as yours, but it's mine."

"Please call me Saraid," the other woman offered. "And I promise that I will do my very best to see that you're returned to your proper place in time, Miss Muldoon."

"Turnabout's fair play. Call me Glynis. Miss Muldoon sounds too formal to be me." Even as she spoke, Glynis reached up and yanked the bandage from her shoulder. Through the thin veil of her tears she could see that Saraid was concerned.

"That shoulder is ugly."

"Why, thank you very much," Glynis replied, summoning a halfhearted smile.

"No," Saraid replied, holding out her hand. "I mean that the wound has become infected. Give me that horrible bandage."

"I figured as much," Glynis admitted. The fever suddenly took hold again and her vision swam. She managed to say, "I have some ointment in my saddlebags."

"I'm afraid the treatment is going to be a bit more complicated and painful than would be involved in simply slathering a balm around the edges of it," Saraid countered gently. "Had Carrick taken proper care of it earlier, I doubt you would be in this situation."

"He did the best he could," Glynis assured her. "The circumstances of the last few days have been less than ideal for any real doctoring."

"Granted," Saraid conceded with a brisk nod. "You finish your bathing while I go and gather my medicinals. I doubt very much that your fever is going to break until we put a poultice on that wound. And don't try to remove the bandage from the back of your shoulder while I'm gone. I'll soak it off when I return."

"Are you pretty good at this doctoring stuff?" Glynis called after her, trying to focus on the other woman.

Saraid turned back at the doorway and smiled. "I'm far better at it than I am at magic."

"Thank God," Glynis replied with a grin.

"Do you have a high tolerance for laudanum?"

"I have no idea," she admitted.

"Then I suppose we'll simply have to discover that as we go along. I'll return in a few minutes."

"Thank you," Glynis answered, reaching for the soap. When the door closed behind Saraid, she allowed herself to slump back into the curve of the tub. She told herself that the chills wracking her body were nothing more than a sign that the water was growing cold, nothing more than one of the symptoms of her fever. She assured herself that they had absolutely nothing to do with the fear that she might not see her Flint Hills again, or that she'd come into this world just in time to watch Carrick des Marceaux die.

Carrick studied the sleeping woman for a moment before he pressed the back of his hand to her forehead. Her skinned burned hot against his. "How much of that stuff did you give her, Saraid?"

"Quite a bit, actually," his sister replied, stirring the embers in the hearth. "I wanted her to feel no pain while I cleansed the wound. Now that she's finally sleeping, though, I suspect that it's as much from exhaustion as it is from the laudanum."

"How did her shoulder look?"

"Horrible," she said bluntly. "Oh, don't furrow your brows, Carrick des Marceaux. Glynis is young and strong and otherwise healthy. I've cleaned and packed the wound to draw out the poisons. What the herbs can't be rid of, the fever will. She'll be well on her way to mended in a matter of a few days."

Despite the fact that he held serious doubts, he acknowledged her assurances. "I'll stay with her tonight," he said, half to himself. "In case she needs anything or awakens and is confused by her surroundings. She'll appreciate a familiar face."

Saraid turned to study him. "You care for her, don't you, Carrick?" she asked.

"Not in the sense you're implying," he countered with a dismissive snort.

"Then enlighten me," Saraid invited.

"I can't explain it." He shrugged and grudgingly gave her the closest he'd come to discovering the truth for himself. "Okay. Let's simply say that I respect her strength."

"All women have a certain kind of strength, Carrick," she observed. "Perhaps you've never paused long enough to look past their other, more obvious attributes to see it."

He studied the figure lying beneath the covers and shook his head. "Other women aren't remotely like Glynis Muldoon."

"I have to agree with you on that observation," Saraid said, smoothing the blankets around her patient. "It's quite easy to forget that she's a woman."

Carrick took in the long, shimmering hair that fanned out across the pillow, the high, delicate cheekbones, and thick, dark lashes. "Perhaps easy for you to forget," he commented dryly.

She came around the end of the bed, chuckling. "Carrick, just once in your life you should try to see a woman as something other than a temporary, albeit pleasant, physical diversion."

Carrick looked shrewdly at the woman standing beside him. "Do you and Robert work together to come up with these little homilies?"

"Perhaps you should listen to us." She patted his arm and then walked away. "If you need me during the night, simply knock on our chamber door."

Carrick nodded absently and the door softly closed behind his sister, leaving him alone with Glynis and his thoughts. The room was silent except for the low crackle and occasional pop of the fire. In the flickering light he watched Glynis Muldoon sleep and thought back over the days since she had tumbled into his world. So much had happened.

Carrick leaned down and gently brushed an errant auburn strand from her cheek. "What is it about you, Muldoon?" he quietly asked. "Why do I look at you and feel as though . . ."

Carrick looked grim. "Why is it that I feel as though I should be seeing something that I'm not?"

12

Glynis lifted her head from the pillow and gazed toward the bedroom window. From the other side of the dark green curtains came the sound of raucous laughter. Saraid's children. She let her head fall back into the pillow. How many days had it been? she wondered. Carrick had been there once when she'd awakened. He'd given her something to drink, brushed the hair off her cheek, and said she'd been sleeping for three days. Had that been yesterday? Or the day before?

She laid a hand across her brow. No fever. A small smile lifted the corners of her mouth. Now if only she didn't feel like the entire British army had ridden across her bed while she'd slept. "Small price," she murmured, "for coming back to life."

Even the act of reaching for the edge of the bedcoverings taxed her strength, but in the end she managed to get them pushed aside enough to work her feet toward the edge of the feather mattress. Actually climbing from the bed took her another good five minutes and left her weak. She rubbed the back of her stiff neck and then pulled aside the heavy brocade curtains for her first glimpse of midmorning light in God knew how long.

All of them, the boys and the girls, Saraid's eight and Meyler, were dashing about the front yard. And in the midst of them ran Carrick, a lumpy sack tucked beneath his arm. Glynis leaned her forehead against the cool pane of glass and smiled as the boys caught up with him first and wrapped their arms about his legs in a determined effort to bring their uncle down. Even from her distant vantage point, Glynis could tell that Carrick's struggles to free himself were exaggerated. The girls joined the tangle of arms and legs, and, encircled by the giggling mass, Carrick bellowed in mock rage and then toppled over into the grass.

She smiled and settled into the window seat to watch. The melee took a few minutes to sort itself out. When at last they had all righted themselves, they formed into two grossly unequal opposing lines. On one side stood Carrick and Saraid's eldest son, the towheaded Matthew. On the other were all the rest.

As Glynis watched, Matthew walked up to the line of his brothers and sisters with the leather sack. To her amazement, every single child hunkered down as though on cue, setting themselves in a manner that would have been the envy of any pro lineman. For a moment Glynis considered them, then she grinned in understanding. Apparently Carrick's mother had decided not to leave football on the other side of time.

Still grinning, she watched Carrick take the snap, watched him fade back and search for a downfield receiver. She laughed outright when his own center turned and came after him. He scrambled away from them, darting this way and that, rendering a credible Heisman performance as he picked his way across the yard. His dash for glory ended slightly better than his last. With much embellished effort, dragging his nieces and nephews every inch of the way, he managed to stumble onto the dirt drive before he allowed himself to succumb to the superior strength and numbers of the opposition.

Glynis laughed again as Carrick extricated himself from the dusty pileup and threw his arms skyward in victory as the children scrambled to their feet, clamoring in protest, pointing back to the grassy lawn. Carrick shook his head and pointed to the ground.

"God, he should have a whole houseful of his own." She chuckled.

Her amusement faded as the import of her words sank in. Carrick was supposed to die before the year was out.

He'd never have a chance to play football with his own children in his own yard.

"It's not right," she whispered, watching them scamper back to the center of the front yard and set themselves up in their lines again. "It's just not fair. Carrick should have more."

The solution came to her in the same heartbeat. As long as she was in limbo . . . as long as she was just hanging around waiting for the miracle that would get her back to where she belonged . . . justice for the Irish people was an abstract sort of thing. Justice for Carrick was another matter entirely.

Glynis nodded. "There's no way in hell, Carrick," she said determinedly to the figure through the window, "that the Dragon's Heart had me factored into the prophecy."

Glynis stared incredulously. "All of that? You expect me to wear all of that just to go check on my horse?"

Saraid nodded firmly. "Your own clothes are inappropriate. They reveal entirely too much of your form."

"My clothes are comfortable. Practical. They don't weigh a ton."

"And neither will these garments," Saraid smoothly countered while sorting through the pile. "You cannot run around here dressed in a manner that will call attention to you."

"Ohmigod," Glynis gasped. "Is that a corset?"

"It is the most fundamental piece of a woman's wardrobe," Carrick's sister explained, placing the stiff article to the side. "Without it, the dress cannot possibly be closed."

Glynis shook her head and slowly leaned back into the pillows. "What? Is there a fabric shortage or something? Make the dress bigger."

Saraid replied, "A proper lady has a tiny waist."

"And deformed internal organs." Glynis crossed her arms and said stubbornly, "I'm not going to let you cinch me into that. It qualifies as a torture device. I could report you to Amnesty International."

"I am also compelled to mention," Saraid continued evenly, "that a lady does not consume a large breakfast, as you did only moments ago. It makes the corset even more difficult to lace. A proper lady eats only the very smallest of quantities."

"And then dies of starvation," Glynis muttered.

Saraid straightened with her hands on her hips. She studied Glynis for a moment before she said, "I do believe Carrick was right . . . as much as it pains me to admit it."

"Oh?"

"He told me that once the fever had broken I would see that you are not insane, but merely aggravating beyond belief."

Glynis sat forward. "I'm aggravating because I insist on exercising good sense?"

With a sigh Saraid came to sit on the edge of the mattress. "Glynis," she began softly, "you have come from another time with very different beliefs and attitudes from this one. I fully understand that. However, you must make some effort to adapt to your hopefully temporary circumstances. Carrick is involved in dangerous activities against the Crown and we protect him best if we do nothing that will attract attention to ourselves and thus to him."

Glynis knew that she'd been defeated in the matter. "You don't play fair, Saraid," she conceded.

The other woman smiled and patted the back of Glynis's hand. "I know," she agreed. "I have a husband and eight children. I play to win."

Glynis studied her shadow as she walked along the row of outbuildings. She wasn't ready to go back inside yet. Something told her that Saraid had just begun the feminine deportment lessons and she couldn't bear them at the moment. She'd been cooped up too long with her shoulder, with the fever. What she needed was fresh air and open space and the luxury of being herself.

Deciding that an afternoon spent exploring would be a far more pleasurable alternative than what undoubtedly awaited her in the house, Glynis wandered between two low-roofed outbuildings. Halfway down the lane she passed an open doorway and stopped, curious about what the building was used for. She stepped inside and paused just on the other side of the doorway, allowing her eyes time to adjust to the dim interior.

Carrick worked at a center table, his shirtsleeves rolled up to his elbows, the wood shavings curling up over his hands as he pushed a hand plane over a piece of wood with long smooth strokes. She watched in silence as he paused and traced the course he'd just worked, watched as a slight smile of satisfaction lifted the corners of his mouth and he nodded to himself.

Carrick . . . a carpenter. Somehow the task seemed to fit him. In fact, it suited him far better than the image she had of him as a farmer or a ship's captain, Glynis decided, moving toward him. A carpenter, a damn good horseman, and an outlaw. Now, why did that combination make her feel so ridiculously lighthearted? It had to be the corset. She wasn't getting enough oxygen to her brain.

Carrick saw the swing of sky-blue satin skirts from the corner of his eye. He straightened instantly and set aside the plane. If Glynis Muldoon's intent had been to create a visual feast for him, she'd outdone herself. His gaze took in everything about her. She'd distracted his senses while wearing her twentieth century clothing; she consumed them now in her borrowed finery. His instincts urged him to sweep her into his arms and see how far his desire could take them. Better judgment told him to take his time and let her lead.

"Muldoon. How are you feeling?" he offered in greeting as she stopped before him.

She arched one slim brow and drawled, "Fine, and one snide remark, des Marceaux, and I'll make you very sorry."

Carrick shook his head and reached up to push a loose hairpin into place. "God help me," he replied. "You're absolutely beautiful."

Her dainty brow arched higher. "God helps those who help themselves."

Carrick grinned as he slowly, deliberately, brought his arm back to his side. "Woman, why do you persist in inviting me to take advantage of you? I'm a mere mortal. I have my limits."

"I wasn't issuing an invitation," she retorted, gathering

her skirts and stepping around him. "I was simply offering a classic rebuttal."

He watched her, noting the long slender column of her neck and wanting very much to taste its sweet promise, to trace his fingertips along the edge of the low-cut bodice, to—

"What are you making?"

He blinked and brought his errant thoughts back to the woodwright's shop. She stood before the unfinished shell of the Queen Anne highboy. "A chest of drawers for Saraid," he explained, drawing a deep breath and picking up the plane again. He needed something to distract him. "I started it last spring when I came to visit," he added, running his fingers down the edge of the drawer front under construction. "It occurs to me that I should be about the finishing of it."

She turned to study him and then said softly, "Sorta like the tying up of all the loose ends, huh?"

His blood ran cold through his veins. "Aye."

"Carrick . . . ?"

He drew a steadying breath and prepared himself for the questions he sensed she intended to pursue. "What is it, Muldoon?"

"How do you know you're going to die?"

He'd been right. Damnation. "Everyone dies, Muldoon," he reminded her, running the plane down the edge of the wood. An almost transparent wood curl wrapped over the back of his hand.

"Yeah, I understand that." She stepped closer, looking up into his face as he worked, and his heart slammed against his chest. "What I don't understand is how you can know that you're going to die this year."

Carrick met her gaze square on. "Was it Robert or Saraid?"

"Both," she supplied quietly. "Neither one of them wants to see you die."

He offered her a half-smile. "Truth be known, Muldoon, I'd prefer not to see it myself."

She countered, "But you've accepted it."

He pushed the plane across the edge, creating yet another

thin, long curl as he said, "I think there's a greater dignity in accepting it than kicking and screaming in a point-less attempt to change one's fate. Wouldn't you agree, Muldoon?"

She laid her hand on his arm and stepped closer; close enough so that the heady, velvet scent of roses swirled around him. "I don't want you to die, either," she mur-mured, her eyes filled with sadness as they searched his.

"Muldoon . . ." he warned.

"How do you know it's this year?" she persisted, not moving away. "How can you be so certain?"

"I saw my headstone propped against the dead wagon, waiting for me," he said bluntly, half-hoping that his state-ment would send her running.

"Geez . . ." she breathed, closing her eyes for a moment. Then she gazed up at him, a determined look in her eyes. "There has to be a way to prevent it, Carrick."

He couldn't help but smile at her fierceness. God, but she had will and fire. It never ceased to amaze him, to fill him with an odd sense of pride. "Stop fretting about it, Mul-doon," he advised, reaching up to gently tap the end of her nose. "Events will unfold as they're destined to be."

"But I've been thinking about this," she persisted, her fingers tightening urgently about his forearm as she leaned closer. "Surely my being here wasn't part of the formula when you saw the vision of your death. Maybe my com-ing through time has had an effect that no one could have anticipated."

He replied slowly, "Or perhaps it was that event that triggered all those that will lead to my end."

Her eyes widened. "I didn't think . . ."

"I don't resent you for it, Muldoon," Carrick offered softly, covering her hand with his own. "It's not your fault."

Her chin trembled and she continued to look stricken. Carrick shook his head and, ignoring his good judgment, lightly traced the column of her throat with the tip of his finger. "Don't cry, Muldoon," he murmured. "I'm not worth the tears."

"Stop being so damn passive about this!" she cried, suddenly defiant and angry. Her spirit proved to be his undoing.

"All right, Muldoon," he pronounced, slipping his arm about her waist and pulling her against the length of his body. She gasped at the sudden embrace and he smiled as he captured her parted lips with his own. For a moment she struggled against his possession and then, with a low moan, she relaxed into him, her lips claiming his in equal measure. She slipped an arm about his waist, holding him with a fierceness that ignited the blood pounding through his veins.

His senses were filled with the delight of Glynis. He reveled in the sweet taste of her lips, willingly surrendered to the heat her touch sent through him.

Glynis's good sense was swept away as sensations crashed over her. Carrick's lips, his hands, sent desire swirling through her. Nothing mattered but the fire he stirred to life within her.

Glynis sighed and leaned into him, whispering his name as he pressed a trail of searing kisses from her lips to the hollow behind her ear. She closed her eyes and clung to him.

"Uncle Carrick!"

The childish voice shattered the moment.

"God as my witness, woman," Carrick rasped, his breathing every bit as labored as her own as he released her from his embrace. His dark gaze held hers before he offered her a wry smile. "We do that too many more times and I'm likely to sob with regret when they hang me."

Carrick's words ravaged her heart even as her anger reignited. Nothing Jake had ever said had hurt as deeply as Carrick's words. How had she let him get close enough to do that to her? Hadn't she made a solemn vow to protect herself from that kind of heartache?

"Uncle Carrick! There you are!" A dark-haired boy popped around the door of the shop. "Mama said to tell you that Mrs. Conroy has come to call and has asked after you. You're to wash up and present yourself. Mama said I was to tell you . . . posthaste."

"Oh, God, the cheek pincher," Carrick muttered under his breath. "Thank you, Mark. Tell your mama that I'll be in attendance shortly."

Glynis marshaled her wits and smoothed her skirts. When she and Carrick were alone again, she managed a reasonably affable smile and said, "Ah, I see that Meyler was right. You show up and so do the ladies. Is she going to invite you to one of her parties?"

He replied absently, "Julia Conroy is one of Saraid's elderly neighbors. And yes, she'll invite me to her party. Hell, she'll probably have one just so she can invite the county notables over to watch her pinch my cheeks in her drawing room."

Glynis smiled. "Damn," she offered with a whistle of appreciation. "Meyler *is* right. You are good. Even little old ladies."

"Muldoon," he began, looking confused, "what are you talking about?"

"I think I'll hide this one out in my room," she said, still smiling. She didn't wait for his response. Instead, she quickly turned and walked away from him. "Have fun."

He watched her leave, mesmerized by the inviting swing of her skirts. What had changed with their kiss? He'd intended only to silence her protests, to let her see for herself the folly of trying to save a man too shallow to be worth the effort. But it hadn't turned out as he'd intended. He frowned and stared blankly at the wood shavings littering the tabletop. What was happening to him? How had she found those feelings he'd so carefully locked away? How had she so effortlessly touched him?

The voice of reason called him the worst of fools and opened a flood tide of memory. He'd ridden with her for three grueling days, had seen her courage and resolve. He'd watched her face danger without flinching. He'd held her in the aftermath of the violence and dried her tears. They'd argued countless times over any number of things. And she'd made him laugh just as often. He'd sat at her bedside for four days, feeling powerless as the fever ran its course through her body.

Glynis Muldoon had been a part of every moment of every day since she'd tumbled into his life. Her steely will and passion for life had turned him upside down in a thousand tiny ways. And she'd done it without his awareness, until this moment.

Carrick faced the truth square on. If he cared about Glynis Muldoon any more than he already did, he wouldn't be able to step blithely into the hangman's noose when the time came. He would regret his dying, would pass into the next world mourning for a life that had unexpectedly become worth living. He sure as hell didn't want that kind of an end. And he wasn't going to let it come to that.

Brushing the wood shavings from his sleeves, he set off to make his appearance before the Widow Conroy. He'd find Glynis afterward and they'd come to a clear understanding of their relationship.

Eating had always been her way of stifling worry. Glynis emerged from the pantry with a jar of what, after inspection, appeared to be some sort of pickles. Good. Her mood was certainly sour enough. Her stomach should come close to matching it. She was trying to pull the wide cork from the top of the jar when Carrick came through the door at the rear of the kitchen.

He hesitated at the sight of her, as though he were trying to make up his mind about something. "Glynis," he began, crossing to where she stood at the worktable. "Give me just a moment, will you please?"

Pretending the cork was his neck seemed to do the trick. It popped loose as she replied, "You don't have to explain anything, Carrick."

"Yes, I do. You need to understand. I'm not being fatalistic. I'm being realistic. And all I'm asking is that you try to be sensible, too."

"Well, there you are, Carrick," called a feminine voice from the dining room door.

Glynis turned, the jar in one hand and the cork in the other, in time to see the slightly bent woman who came across the flagstones, her hands reaching for Carrick's face. She didn't have the slightest doubt as to the woman's intent. Good thing Carrick was stoically willing, she thought. Otherwise it could have gotten messy. Julia Conroy might be sixty if she was a day, but she didn't look like the kind of woman who had ever taken resistance well.

"Saraid went to check on one of her children," Julia Conroy explained, pinching Carrick's cheeks. "Something about splashing around in a mud puddle. I thought I'd see that a bath was prepared.

"And in the midst of my Good Samaritan effort, look what a wonderful treat I find for myself." She pinched his cheeks again tightly, apparently unaware of Carrick's wince. "You are such a handsome and charming boy."

"Mrs. Conroy," Carrick said, returning the woman's smile and taking her hands firmly in his own. "How nice to see you again."

"You must remember your manners, Carrick des Marceaux." She looked at Glynis and smiled kindly. "Aren't you going to introduce me to your pretty young friend?"

Glynis saw Carrick quickly consider his options. Of course, Glynis thought. Explaining her presence would be a tad dicey. Before Carrick could make the decision for her, she put the jar of pickles and the cork on the table, smiled sweetly, and sallied forth on her own.

"I'm Glynis Muldoon—one of Carrick's American cousins," she said. "It's a pleasure to make your acquaintance, Mrs. Conroy."

The older woman pulled her hands from Carrick's and turned to face her squarely. A smile crinkled the corners of the woman's eyes. "You are from the American South, I gather," the other woman offered.

The South? Well, okay. I can work with that. "Of course," Glynis replied, noting that Carrick had subtly moved beyond Julia Conroy's reach. "My family owns land to the north and west of New Orleans. Have you ever had an occasion to visit my country, Mrs. Conroy?"

"Unfortunately, I have not, Miss Muldoon," she replied regretfully. "And I doubt that I ever shall." Her expression brightened. "I hear that it is full of savage Indians and wild beasts who drag you from your bed while you sleep."

Glynis smiled and observed, "Far better to be dragged by

a beast *from* your bed, Mrs. Conroy, than *into* it. Wouldn't you agree?"

A sparkle came to the older woman's eyes. She looked to Carrick and then back to Glynis. "Well, my dear child," she said, smiling wickedly, "I suppose it would very much depend upon the nature of the beast doing the dragging, wouldn't it?"

Carrick stared at the ceiling, rocked back on his heels, and said nothing.

Glynis bit the inside of her lip and hoped her cheeks weren't as red as they felt. "Well, I should leave you two to yourselves," she offered. "You must have so much to talk about."

Julia stepped to Carrick's side, slipping her arm beneath his and laying her blue-veined hand on his forearm. "I would so love to hear some news of your mother and father," she said, smiling up at him. "And how is your sister Maude doing these days? Didn't she marry a Scotsman? I seem to recall Saraid telling me that she's living near Aberdeen."

Carrick's gaze flicked from Glynis to Julia and back again. Glynis heard his unspoken plea loud and clear. She decided not to show him any mercy; he didn't deserve it.

"It's been a pleasure, Mrs. Conroy," Glynis offered politely. "I hope to see you again before I return home."

Julia returned her smile even as she steered Carrick toward the kitchen door. "I'm having a small party in a fortnight. You must make Carrick bring you over."

"I wouldn't miss it for the world," Glynis drawled.

The door had barely closed behind them when she fished a pickle from the jar. Yep, she mused, taking a bite of it. That unexpected encounter had gone beautifully and had suited her purposes surprisingly well. Glynis took another bite of the pickle. Julia Conroy, Sweet Old Lady Extraordinaire, would dotingly monopolize Carrick's time for the next few days. And given that certainty, Glynis now had the running room she needed to figure out how she could keep the son of a bitch from dancing at the necktie party the British Crown intended to have in his honor.

13

She should have accepted Saraid's offer and had dinner in her room. Fat lot of good hindsight did her. She was trapped at a table with thirteen other people, one of whom seemed determined to pretend she wasn't there—no doubt in retaliation for having tethered him to Julia Conroy earlier that day. Glynis toyed with the food on her plate and told herself that her appetite had simply been squeezed to death by her damn corset. Carrick's dismissal had nothing at all to do with it. And neither did the memory of their moments together in the woodwright's shop.

It had been those damn memories that had practically been her undoing as she'd entered the dining room. Even now, separated by the table and surrounded by his family, Glynis found herself too keenly aware of Carrick's every movement, his every expression. And, as it had been among the shadows and wood shavings earlier that day, she ached with a longing she couldn't name.

What she needed was to get out and burn off some energy. She'd been cooped up too long inside the house, had been too long from her normal levels of activity. Tonight, when everyone had gone to bed, she would take Bert for a ride. The disquiet she felt would be under control if she could manage to be herself for just a short while. Yes. Tomorrow she wouldn't feel nearly as close to exploding as she did now. All she had to do in the meantime was get through dinner and the rest of the evening without going publicly berserk.

Glynis took a breath as deep as the whalebone contraption encircling her would permit and focused her attention on the conversation going on around her.

"William McKenna is the latest among the British lackeys," Horace said around a bite of roast beef. "He has no compunction whatsoever about doing their bidding."

Robert paused with a bite of potato halfway to his mouth. "Is that the William McKenna over by Stonecroft?"

"The same. I always said he had no conscience when it came to putting the coin of the realm into his pockets. And he's proven me right yet again. For the paltry recompense of a new corral he's now willing to help starve his neighbors' children."

Venturing into the men's conversation, Glynis observed, "I gather that Mr. McKenna is the tithe collector."

Horace started visibly at her comment and then quickly glanced about to see who else might have been listening to him and Robert.

"The other evening Carrick and I watched a tithe collector and a British patrol take away a family's milk cow," Glynis continued. "Am I to understand that one of Ireland's own sons is a willing participant in these crimes?"

Horace carefully stabbed a piece of meat with his fork and nodded, his expression a mixture of anger and embarrassment.

Carrick lifted his wine glass and studied the world through its ruby hue as he answered, "William McKenna isn't alone in his predation, Muldoon. There are many more, all across Ireland. I've come to think that a man willing to steal from his countrymen for a few British farthings is a lesser form of life." He took a slow sip of the contents before adding darkly, "And I have also come to view them as being a growth which must be ruthlessly cut away if Ireland is to survive."

"And, of course," Robert added, lifting his own glass, "it's the banding together of men with similar beliefs that has led to the present state of unrest and to increasing British frustrations."

Horace nodded and reached for his goblet. "It seems only right to me that the British should have to work to steal from the people of Ireland." He extended his wine glass and cleared his throat. "May the Dragon long bedevil the English blackguards who prey on the helpless and poor among us."

The Dragon? Like in the Dragon's Heart? Glynis's gaze darted between the men. She watched as Carrick and Robert lifted their glasses in silence.

Even as they did, Matthew whispered, "I hear that the Dragon has killed fifty of the British soldiers."

Carrick laughed and ruffled his nephew's blond hair. "It sounds to me as though you've been listening to the old men who have nothing better to do than spend their days drinking ale at the pub and making up stories for wide-eyed children."

Mark shook his head. "No, Uncle Carrick. When Matthew and me took the grain into town yesterday we saw the notices the soldiers were posting. They're offering a thousand pounds to the man who can tell them who and where the Dragon is. It's so much because he's killed so many of them."

"They caught one of his men, too," Matthew added. "But he died. We heard all about it when we were in town."

Carrick froze and Glynis saw the fury in his eyes before his expression eased. Then he shrugged and tossed back the last of the wine in his glass. "Well, with a price of a thousand pounds on the man's head, his days are undoubtedly numbered," he said blandly. "Poor blighter. He'll pay a high price for his success."

Glynis chewed the inside of her lip. It didn't take a brain surgeon to figure this one out. She would bet this year's tax money that Carrick was the infamous Irish Dragon; the dead man, Sean.

It all made perfect sense. She'd add the insurance money to the bet that his nephews were ignorant of his outlaw identity. It would be safer for both them and Carrick that way. Boys caught up in hero worship didn't always use good sense in who they tried to impress.

Her thoughts were in turmoil as Carrick rose to his feet. "Saraid," he said, smiling and offering his sister an abbreviated bow, "my compliments to Mrs. Kelly, the cook, and to yourself. The meal was the best I've had in recent memory."

Saraid placed her linen napkin beside her plate. "Thank you, little brother. Am I to assume you're now leaving us to our own company?"

"Julia asked me to ride over and take a look at one of her horses that has come up lame. I should be about it before it gets too much later." He came around the table, tousling little heads as he went, to plant a quick kiss on his sister's cheek.

Glynis watched him leave the dining room, feeling worried.

Carrick adjusted the cloth hiding the lower portion of his face and silently slipped through the French doors. He wandered about the parlor for a minute to let his eyes adjust to the dim interior and to absorb the feel of the house itself and the man who occupied it. Judging by the new breakfront and the velvet-upholstered chairs, William McKenna was profiting nicely from his British servitude. With his flintlock pistol in hand, Carrick cautiously made his way up the central staircase, keeping to the innermost edge of it and praying that the boards didn't squeak beneath his weight.

At the top, he paused and considered the line of doors before him. Now, which one would the master of the house choose for himself? The carved brass lion's head or one of the four plain ones? Such a difficult choice. . . .

He let himself into the room without a sound. Then, noting the poorly banked fire flickering in the hearth and the single figure in the massive four-poster bed, he crossed the carpet to the room's only window. Reaching beneath the drawn curtains, Carrick worked the locking mechanism, then eased the lower portion of it up enough to allow for a quick escape should the unlikely need arise.

He crept back across the room to stand beside the bed and the man sleeping in it. How could anyone stand to wear a nightcap? he wondered. The strings, tied as they were beneath the chin to hold the damn thing on, tended to choke a man and too frequently awaken him during the night. And the mere appearance of it was far less likely to send fear through the heart of a midnight intruder than it was to dissolve him into gales of laughter.

But apparently William McKenna was as much a slave to

the folly of fashion as he was to British gold. Carrick shrugged and gently settled himself on the edge of the bed before pressing the muzzle of the pistol to the sleeping man's head. Slowly drawing back the hammer brought McKenna's eyes open with a start.

"I'd not move or make a sound, friend," Carrick said quietly, putting a full measure of Irish brogue into his voice. " 'Tis a hair-fine trigger this pistol's got on her. 'Twould be a most unfortunate mess yur wife would be a cleanin' up in the mornin'."

"What do you want?" William McKenna asked, his words raspy with sleep and fear. "We have no gold or jewelry of any value."

"Yur crime is not bein' a rich man, McKenna. 'Tis the manner in which ya go 'bout the makin' of yur coins."

The tithe collector's face paled to match his linen nightcap. "You're the Dragon."

"I might be," Carrick answered. "Then again, I might not. Suffice it that I come bearin' the same message as he carries 'cross Ireland. Ya collect the tithe an' starve our children at yur own peril, McKenna."

"I have no choice. The British make—"

" 'Tis a lie," Carrick snarled, pressing the muzzle tighter against the man's temple. "Every man has a choice in his master. Ya buy yur fine furniture an' yur fancy nightclothes at the cost o' yur neighbors' sufferin'. 'Tis a wonder that ya can sleep at night. How do ya go 'bout lookin' people in the eye while awake, McKenna?"

The man said nothing as he stared, wide-eyed with fear.

" 'Tis a warnin' I'll be a leavin' ya with this evening, tithe collector. Heed it well. Find another master. One that doesn't steal the milk an' bread from the hands o' helpless children. One that doesn't grind the poor 'neath the heel o' its heartless boot."

"I can't. I'm bound by contract," McKenna sputtered.

"Then 'tis a certainty that yur headstone will say ya died in service to the Crown."

"I have a wife," the man pleaded. "I have three daughters. Please have mercy."

"Ah, yes, mercy," Carrick said softly. He leaned closer to

add, " 'Tis a fair enough request ya make o' me, McKenna. 'Tis a matter o' honor that I show ya as much mercy as ya've shown for the wives an' children o' others."

The man squeezed his eyes closed as a sob broke past his pale lips.

Carrick nodded and rose to his feet, his teeth clenched and his fingers white around the butt of the pistol. "Find a new master, McKenna," he said, low and hard. "Or see that yur wife an' daughters purchase their mournin' clothes with the next forty coins the British toss at yur feet."

Carrick left the room as he'd entered it, leaving behind a man trembling beneath his covers, his knuckles white as he grasped the edges of the bedclothes.

The night was still and the sky speckled with glittering stars as Carrick swung up into the saddle. Molan shifted impatiently beneath him while he studied the house he'd just left. As he knew it would, a light suddenly flickered behind the drapes of an upper window. He smiled grimly. William McKenna wouldn't sleep another moment this night, perhaps for several nights to come. The man would undoubtedly spend his days looking over his shoulder and warily avoiding the shadows. And if the man had a brain in his head, he'd find a way to separate his life from British efforts to rape the people of Ireland.

The Dragon's work for the night had gone well. Now all he needed to do was establish an alibi for himself should the British decide to ask questions. He thought of going to Glynis and spending the rest of the night in her arms. Carrick shook his head. Wanting and wisdom were two very different things.

Halfway to the safety of the Widow Conroy's stables, he crested a hill to find a British patrol stopped halfway up the other side. He stopped and for a long moment they simply stared at one another in silence. When the command came for him to advance and explain his business, he knew he had no choice but to try to outride them. With a grim smile, he whirled Molan around and the race began.

Glynis reined Bert in sharply. He skittered to a halt and danced beneath her, pulling at the bit, wanting to resume their run across the hills. She held him in check, watching the scene below through narrowed eyes. The lead rider could be no one but Carrick. No one rode like he did. Those following him were clearly British soldiers.

She swore beneath her breath and marked Carrick's course. If she guessed correctly, he intended to bring them up the relatively narrow valley below her and then lose them in the labyrinth of wooded draws that radiated out along its length. "What do you say we give him an edge, Bert?" she asked, studying the moonlit course below her.

By the time her horse had carried her to the bottom of the hill, she had loosened the tie holding her rope to the saddle. The thunder of approaching hooves set her heart racing and she quickly maneuvered her horse into position, dropping the reins across his neck. Glynis shook out the rope and a moment later the circle of hemp dropped neatly around a sturdy rock outcrop on the other side of the meager road.

Playing out the rope so that it lay like a pale snake across the path, she backed her horse into the deeper shadows of the trees, wrapped the other end of the rope around the saddle horn, and settled in to wait.

It didn't take long. Carrick came past her, Molan a streak of lather-flecked black, his rider a dark vision of muscles and leather focused only on the way twisting before him. Glynis spared him a quick glance before giving her attention to the riders coming hard in his wake. Six of them, and each jockeying for the position of leader. If they were still riding abreast as they came past her . . . Glynis counted the seconds, her heart pounding in her ears.

When less than ten feet separated the British from her position, she gave Bert the signal. Like the best of cow ponies, he vaulted backward and sat on his haunches, drawing the rope taut with a snap.

One moment there were six red-coated riders racing their horses in pursuit. The next, the horses pranced about in confusion and the six redcoats lay in the dirt.

Glynis patted her horse on the neck as she unwrapped the rope from the horn and quickly re-coiled the hemp as she worked her way toward the stone outcropping.

A low moan came from the haphazard pile of red lying to her right. Glynis settled herself back into the saddle and turned toward the milling British mounts. "Let's move them, boy," she commanded, nudging him forward. He needed no further encouragement.

Glynis smiled broadly as Bert ably took up the task for which he'd been bred and trained. God, but it felt good to be doing what she did best. The riderless horses resisted herding for only a few yards and then fell into a tight bunch. Glynis considered the draws ahead and then chose the farthest one, the one with the easiest ascent. When she got the thoroughbreds to the top, she'd scatter them. The redcoats wouldn't be pursuing Carrick any farther tonight. They'd be damn lucky to find even one of their horses before daybreak, and in all likelihood they'd be limping and moaning as they walked all the way back to their headquarters. To her way of thinking it was a much better fate than being shot from the saddle.

The British mounts turned back on themselves and stopped when they reached the open grassland of the hills above the valley. Glynis reined in Bert, dropped the coiled rope over the saddle horn, and quickly swung down. Knowing the horses would go farther and be even more difficult to catch if she stripped them of their saddles, she set about the task with what speed her injured shoulder allowed and without the least concern for the fate of the tack that fell to the ground. One by one she slapped the horses on the rump and sent them galloping across the grassland.

As the last of them departed, she settled her Stetson lower across her brow, tugged her gloves back on, and turned back toward Bert. She froze in midstride. Carrick, his eyes blazing, his jaw hard, sat less than ten feet away.

"Hi!" she offered, trying a smile. "Nice night for a ride, isn't it?"

"What in the name of hell and all the Irish saints are you doing here?"

Saving your butt? She stopped beside Bert and lifted the rope from the horn. As she tied it back into place, she answered, "Given your luck of late, des Marceaux, it's probably not a good idea to mention hell and the Irish saints in the same breath."

The quick creak of saddle leather was the only warning she got. She'd barely turned toward him when his hands came about her upper arms. She gazed up into the icy fire of his midnight eyes and felt the familiar ache.

"I don't need your interference!" he growled, his grip tightening about her arms.

"Well, God forbid the words 'thank you' should come past your lips, Carrick des Marceaux," she retorted hotly.

"What are you doing out here?" he demanded, giving her a rough shake. "Why aren't you back at Saraid's tucked into your safe, solitary bed?"

Glynis lifted her chin stubbornly. "I have just as much right to go for a ride as you do. I don't have to ask your permission for anything. I come and go as I please." She pressed her hands against his chest, trying to force some distance between them. His heart hammered against her palms; the heat of his body burned away her restraint, leaving her weak.

Panic swept over her and she pushed harder against him, determined to be free of his possession. "Let go of me," she demanded, hating the fear she heard in her voice.

"The hell I will," he snarled as he reached for the brim of her Stetson. "And take off that goddamned hat," he continued, roughly accomplishing the task for himself. He tossed it aside without looking as he added, "I want to see your eyes."

Glynis took a deep breath. It failed to steady her shaking knees. "You son of a bitch." She glared up at him. "You can go to hell, Carrick des Marceaux."

He smiled grimly. "Then I'm taking you with me, Glynis Muldoon," he promised, drawing her hard against him.

His kiss deepened with a speed that sent her senses reeling. She felt his heat and power everywhere their bodies touched, felt the incredible urgency that drove them both. The scent of leather and wind and the night clung to him, filling her senses and leaving her wanting more. She stripped the gloves from her hands, letting them fall, and twined her fingers through the hair at his nape, reveling in the silken feel of it and the way her touch made him tremble.

"Glynis," he demanded, blazing a trail of kisses to the hollow behind her ear. "Tell me to stop."

"No." She couldn't.

"Then God help us both," he murmured, his teeth grazing her earlobe.

His kisses made her heart beat too quickly, made her ache with longing. She realized that Carrick had opened her shirt. His hands, strong and callused, flowed gently over her skin and pure pleasure washed over her in their wake.

Carrick eased her down into the grass and drew her against him, cradling her in his arms as he savored the hollow at the base of her slim throat. She murmured his name and arched back, offering him whatever he cared to take. In that moment he knew that if there was a heaven, it could exist nowhere but in this woman's arms.

His conscience cautioned him to stop. But, even as he struggled against his desire, her hands slipped beneath his shirt to caress the planes of his back and he was lost. His lips tasted her delicate skin, leaving behind the invisible marks that forever branded her as his own. Gently pushing aside the edges of her coat and shirt, he pressed a fevered, lingering kiss to the swell of her breast just above the tantalizing pink lace.

Her fingers twined through his hair, tightening gently in a wordless plea as old as desire itself. He bent lower and blew slowly over the dark crest tempting him from under the nearly transparent lace. It pebbled beneath his gentle attention and Glynis moaned softly, a sound that quickened his need as she arched into him. He blew gently across the hardened peak once again while he slipped his hand beneath her and plucked loose the fastening.

Easing the lace aside, he lowered his head to tease the tight bud with the tip of his tongue, then slowly circled the hardened peak. She cried his name feverishly and arched up, her hands gently pressing him to fully take the sweet treasure. He obliged, tasting her with light licks until he couldn't prolong the pleasure any longer and took the pebbled whole of her into his mouth.

Glynis gasped for breath and at the overwhelming pleasure. Nothing had ever felt so wonderful. Awash in sensation, she knew only that Carrick excited her senses as no other man had. Where his touch took them, she didn't care. She wanted to go on feeling this way forever, knew instinctively that only Carrick could ease the ache and make her whole.

"Damnation!"

Glynis started as Carrick covered her body with his and whirled about, swinging his fist. Her heart racing with fear, she frantically searched beyond Carrick's shoulder for British soldiers and bayonet points.

All she saw was Bert backing away, an expression of indignation on his face, his ears flattened.

"Damn horse of yours," Carrick muttered, turning to her incredulously. "It nuzzled my neck."

Glynis laughed softly and slowly traced the line of his jaw with a fingertip. "It's his job to worry about me when I'm flat on the ground."

Carrick caught her hand in his and, turning his head, pressed a lingering kiss to the inside of her wrist. "He can't tell the difference between an injured woman and one being pleasured? I distinctly remember you telling me that he was an intelligent animal."

"He is smart. He just lacks any experience with seeing the latter. He'll know better next time."

Carrick grinned wickedly. "Might I suggest we see just how quickly Bert learns?" he asked quietly, tucking a strand of hair behind her ear.

She sighed, regaining control of her common sense. "I think it might be a good time for us to move to our respective corners and think about this."

"I don't need to think, Glynis," he countered. "I know what I want. And I'm fairly certain that you wouldn't be opposed if I were to press the issue."

"Yeah . . . well . . ." she replied softly. "The morning after could be a real downer."

Carrick saw her resolve and knew the moment had been lost. If he pressed the matter she would no doubt eventually surrender, but he realized that he didn't want her to come to him in that way. Her willingness mattered far more than easing his hunger for her.

Carrick rose smoothly to his feet and extended his hand to her.

Glynis allowed him to pull her to her feet and then stepped back. She quickly straightened her clothing, being careful not to look at Carrick.

Carrick said nothing. She had gotten closer to him than he'd realized, and he was unsettled by the range of emotions he felt. God knew his relationship with Glynis Muldoon was complicated enough already.

Glynis finally asked, "Would you be so kind as to hook my bra for me? I can't reach that far back with my shoulder yet."

Carrick controlled a smile and stepped forward to slide his hands beneath her coat and shirt. Her skin felt warm and satin-soft against his knuckles. Trying to ignore his rekindled desire, he focused instead on the question of how she'd gotten into the thing in the first place. He carefully slipped the metal hooks into their eyes and observed, "I find this sudden obliqueness of yours fascinating, Muldoon."

"What obliqueness?" she challenged, quickly stepping away from him.

He smiled at her, knowing that she'd been just as jolted by his touch as he had been by the touching. "Your uncharacteristic unwillingness to be blunt, Muldoon. To say, 'People will talk and my reputation might be tarnished' and 'I might find myself carrying your child.' "

"I don't give a damn whether people talk," she said, brusquely snapping the front of her shirt closed. She shoved her shirttail into the top of her pants and continued, "It's the looking you in the eye afterward that might be difficult."

"It wouldn't be difficult on my part. I like looking into your eyes." He cocked his head to the side as he added, "We've covered one possible set of objections. What about the other? Would it upset you to become pregnant?"

She didn't look at him. "Well," she said brightly, "I suppose it's one way of ensuring an heir for the Rocking M."

"Ah, there's my Muldoon," Carrick observed with a chuckle, tucking his own shirttail into his trousers. "I was concerned that she'd disappeared, never to be seen again."

She bent down to scoop up her hat and gloves. "In case you haven't noticed," she countered with a wry smile, blocking the brim with her fingers before she settled it on her head, "I don't have that kind of luck."

"Glynis . . ." he said softly, reaching out to lightly trace the curve of her kiss-swollen lips. "When you've thought about it, when you're ready to set aside your reservations . . ."

In the shadow of her hat brim, he saw a dark brow raise slightly. "You're ready, willing, and able, huh?" she said.

"Aye," he answered, nodding. "Something like that."

As she walked past him he thought of staying her, of telling her that she could trust him, that he'd be there for her no matter the consequences of their lovemaking. But he knew the words for the lies they were. He was a dead man. She was a time traveler who would soon return to her own life. What consequences there would be, they were destined to handle alone.

But, he decided, watching her swing up onto her horse, if anyone had the pride and determination to do it, it would be his Glynis Muldoon. His felt a disquieting sense of pride. Calling himself the worst kind of fool, he crossed to Molan and said, "I'll see you safely back to the house."

She shook her head. "I appreciate the offer, but there's no need, Carrick. I'll be fine. I'm sure you have things you need to be about."

"I can't think of any," he admitted, settling onto his mount.

She studied him from beneath the brim of her dark hat. "You've already seen to Mrs. Conroy's horse?" she asked dryly.

Carrick looked chagrined. "You didn't believe that, did you?"

"Not for a minute."

He shrugged. "Well, it's too late to go over there now."

"I'm sorry if I ruined your plans for the evening. It was accidental, you know," she assured him.

Moving closer and tilting her face into the moonlight, he quietly insisted, "No apologizes are necessary, Muldoon. I'd much prefer to roll around in the grass with you than have Julia pinch my cheeks. It was to have been a convenient alibi. The Widow Conroy would have sworn I'd spent the evening in her stable, tending her favorite mare." He grinned and touched his thumb to her lower lip. "Now, if questions are asked, my sweet Glynis Muldoon, you'll have to be the one to tell them what I did with my late-night hours."

She laughed softly. "Just which parts of the truth am I supposed to tell them?"

He drew her toward him and, against the softness of her willing lips, whispered, "Tell them whatever you want, Muldoon. I trust your judgment."

14

He trusted her? She remembered when he'd threatened to put a bullet in her himself. They'd come a long way. The realization triggered an internal warning. Part of her denied it; Carrick wasn't anything at all like Jake. The cynical side of her scoffed. Jake had only publicly embarrassed and tried to bankrupt her. Carrick would break her heart. If she let him. The trick was to be his friend and nothing more. She could manage that, she assured herself. She'd be firm about holding the limits. She'd carefully avoid those situations where anger swept away their good judgment. Like moments ago when they'd been rolling together in the grass.

Her blood warmed at the memory. She looked for a distraction as they started back toward Saraid's.

"So," Glynis began, "did you do anything interesting while I was off touring the land of the fever-ridden and unconscious?"

Carrick, riding at her side, grinned. "I'm happy to report that we found a cow for the family who had theirs taken. A few other families also discovered a new milk cow in their barns one morning. Rather like Christmas in April."

"You don't hand it over to them personally?" she asked, thinking that the conversation was going along in a wonderfully neutral way. "I'd think you'd like to have the satisfaction of seeing their faces. Half the fun of giving a gift is watching someone open it."

"Normally, that's true, Muldoon," he answered quietly.

"But in these situations their desperation and gratitude are not easy to witness. I always feel as though I should be doing far more for them than I am, that I should have done it a long time ago."

"And that's why you became the Dragon," she observed softly. "To do for them."

"I'm sorry to disillusion you, Muldoon, but my motives are more selfish than that." He shrugged. "I've traveled the world and I've seen too many men live aimless lives and die pointless deaths. I want mine to count for something. I don't care whether they carve a litany of noble deeds on my headstone. I'll know I tried to accomplish something worthwhile in the time I had."

She considered his words and their import. He'd given her a glimpse of what went on in his heart and mind. A friend wouldn't back away from the opportunity to make a difference. "Have you ever considered that being the Dragon is what gets you killed? Maybe if you chose another course it wouldn't happen."

"A man can't alter his destiny, Muldoon. But he sure as hell can choose how he gets there." He gazed out over the hills before he asked, "Have you ever seen a rat trying to find a way off a burning ship?" He didn't wait for her reply. "I refuse to hide from my fate or pretend it isn't going to happen. I'm not going to make pathetic, empty bargains with God. I'll die on my feet and I'll die for a just cause."

"So you'll die like a man," she countered sarcastically. "With nobility, dignity, and grace."

He replied evenly, "Only the truly fortunate get to die that way, Glynis. You can bet Sean didn't."

That hurt. "I'm sorry about Sean."

"If I'd known the British had him, I'd have done whatever it took to free him. Robert began making discreet inquiries the same day we arrived at Saraid's. The Brits kept their secret well."

"If you had known, what would you have done? Turned yourself in, in exchange for his release?"

"If it had come to it . . . yes." Glynis snorted disgustedly. He turned to smile at her. "I might have accepted the fact that I'm going to die, Muldoon, but that doesn't mean I don't enjoy living in the meantime. I do think I might have tried to break him from the cell before I resorted to handing over my weapons and making a confession."

"Robert wouldn't have let you do that, you know. Turn yourself in, I mean."

"He's predictable," he admitted, his smile fading. "Too much so. It's time he went home and took Meyler with him."

"I kinda think he's of a mind to stick it out, Carrick. Robert knew the risks when he signed on to the campaign. Just like Sean did; just like I did."

His heart missed a beat. He pulled Molan to a halt. "Stop right there, Muldoon. You're not involved in this. Understand? It's my fight."

"Oh, yeah. Right," she countered, reining in Bert. The moonlight did nothing to soften the fire in her eyes. "Let's see . . . I've killed two British soldiers. I've dehorsed six others who were pursuing you after what I suspect was a visit you paid to Mr. William McKenna, tithe collector, this evening. Face it, Carrick, I'm an accessory after the fact. It seems to me that I'm pretty much committed to your tithe war whether you like it or not."

"I won't have your blood on my hands, Glynis."

"Oh, get over it. I'm a big girl and I make my own decisions." With that she sent her horse cantering ahead.

Carrick went after her. "Do you have to fight me on everything?" he demanded as he drew abreast.

"Not everything," she answered over the thudding of the horses' hooves. "Just this. Well, and there's the destiny-of-death thing, but that's not what we're talking about at the moment. For the life of me I can't figure out why you're being so pigheaded about me helping you. I should think you'd be glad to have me along on your crusade for justice. I hardly qualify as an albatross around your neck."

Carrick swore under his breath and looked out over the moon-tinged hills. God help him, he *did* want her riding at his side, *did* want her help. Defeating the world was a ridiculous notion, he told himself. He had to exercise reason. And he owed it to Glynis to see that she did, too.

"So why don't you want me along?" she pushed.

"There are a number of experiences I'd gladly share with

you, Glynis Muldoon. Dying isn't one of them. And in the event that you haven't noticed, people around me tend to do that. I'd prefer to go to the Great Beyond knowing you were safe on this side of it."

"That's terribly chivalrous of you. But let me tell you from experience that being left on this side of the Great Beyond isn't all it's cracked up to be. The death of people you care about tends to leave a big hole in your life."

"That's something else we should discuss, Muldoon," he said, determined to make her keep her distance. "All of this will be much simpler for both of us if you don't care about me."

"I'm working on it," she retorted, irritated. "And the longer this conversation goes on, the easier it's getting."

She reined in Bert and he brought Molan around so that they faced each other.

"I've got an idea," she said, pushing her hat back off her forehead. "Why don't you take a good swing at me? That ought to pretty much take care of any tender feelings I might be harboring for you." She tapped her chin with her finger. "Right here. Take your best shot."

He threw back his head and laughed. God, he'd never met a woman like this one. She never ceased to surprise him, never failed to turn the tables on him. He shouldn't enjoy the experience, but there was no denying that he did.

"What man was fool enough to let you go?"

Glynis started. She hadn't expected his laughter. Nor the way the sound of it had warmed her. But his question came like a bucket of ice water. "What?" she asked, trying to gather her senses. "Where on earth did that come from?"

His gaze continued to hold hers, watching her intently. "What was his name?"

Oh, God. Too close. Way too close. "Billy Martinez," she answered flippantly, urging her horse forward. "We were five," she continued as Carrick rode beside her. "One day he just stopped putting his rug next to mine for nap time and it was over. No explanations. Frankly, while he never had the guts to tell me straight out, I think he wanted to have a fling with Debbie Mercer, Little Miss Blonde Banana Curls and Tap Dance Class. Let me tell you, it made the sandbox one tough place to be. All those memories, all those hopes . . ." She sighed for effect. "Dashed on the rocks of infidelity."

"And after Billy Martinez?"

She tightened her grip on the reins. "There wasn't anybody serious after Billy," she lied, keeping her tone light. "I mean, geez, once you've shared your milk and cookies and then been burned by the guy, it's hard to risk your heart again."

He smiled tightly. "So there's the solution. Don't put your heart in it."

Just go through the motions. Like I do, she finished for him. "I can't do that, Carrick," she replied, figuring there was nothing to be lost in being at least that honest. "I'd rather be alone than with someone and lonely."

"But if you're always looking for a forever, then you sacrifice all the todays you might have. Seems like a very empty life to me."

"And you are the expert on no forevers and empty lives."

For a moment there was only the sound of hooves against sod, and then he said quietly, "If you meant for that to hurt, it did."

She *had* meant for it to hurt, but there wasn't the least bit of satisfaction in knowing she'd succeeded. Relating to Carrick des Marceaux was a complicated proposition. It had never been this complex with Jake. But then Jake had been a relatively simple man compared to this one. Carrick was like one of those wooden 3-D puzzles; lots of carefully crafted pieces that fit together in ways you didn't expect. Straight on seemed to be the only way to deal with him.

"It just frustrates me to hear you so blithely accept some death vision as gospel. Don't you want to live, Carrick?"

"Seeing is a curse. Seeing your own death, doubly so. I've lived a long time with knowing the end, Glynis. Part of me is damn tired of waiting for it to get here. And yes, living to be an old man would be nice. Only it isn't going to happen that way, so I simply make the best of the days I do have."

Straight on had its drawbacks, she decided. "Just out of curiosity . . . generally speaking, do women respond well to the I'm-a-dying-man-and-don't-you-want-to-make-me-happy-before-I-go ploy? Or is it more of a make-me-forget-what-awaits-me-on-the-morrow gambit?"

He gave her a grin that could melt steel. "Well, there is the matter of their Christian duty."

Damn, he was a great rogue. She couldn't contain her own grin. "And it warms their hearts to send you off smiling."

"I would assume so. I've never asked." His eyes twinkled. "Wouldn't you like to make me smile?"

"Never let it be said you give up a fight too easily, des Marceaux," she countered. "Have you given any thought to what you're going to do if your death vision doesn't come to pass? If it's all a big mistake?"

"No. There isn't any reason to; there's no mistake. And you didn't answer my question, Muldoon."

"Have you ever thought of returning the favor? Of making someone else happy?"

"I'll have you know, madam, that I make every effort to leave the ladies smiling and content. It's a point of pride and reputation."

She knew a dodge when she heard one. She'd done it too often in her own life not to. He might have let her get away with an evasion a few minutes earlier, but she wasn't going to return the favor. "Stop being a rogue for a minute, willya? I'm serious. You're not a callous man, Carrick. I've ridden with you long enough to know that. You haven't gone through your whole life not caring about those around you. Hasn't there been a special woman for you?"

His smile disappeared as he considered her. "Truthfully, Muldoon?" he finally answered. "No, there hasn't. And it's not a matter of having deliberately shut away feelings. No woman has ever stirred them. And while I hope I have left the women in my life content, I know for certain that I have dealt with them honestly. I've never pretended to feel something I didn't, never promised a tomorrow I couldn't give."

Carrick frowned. What he'd just said wasn't wholly true. He knew that if someone were to ask him that question a month or six months from now, he'd remember Glynis and that if he were answering honestly, he'd admit that being with her had made him a different man than he would have been otherwise. How would she remember him?

Uncomfortable with the direction of his thoughts, he smiled and said, "Actually, I've always tried to affect the people around me as little as possible. I'd prefer to avoid a lot of weeping and wailing at my grave. I'd rather not see a lot of leaping and dancing, either. Truth be told, I'd be quite happy if no one noticed I was gone."

"What about your family, Carrick?" she asked gently. "You can't really expect them to not care what happens to you."

Lord, but Glynis Muldoon had persistence. And something told him that she could be trusted with an honest answer. "Part of the reason I went to sea when I was fifteen was to put some distance between my life and theirs. I thought it would be easier on all of them if they didn't really know the man that died." He smiled ruefully. "It doesn't seem to have worked out that way, though. Robert matches my every step and nothing I do to him seems enough to drive him away. And I've certainly tried."

A memory came to him and he laughed. "I sold him one time. About three years ago. To a Charleston socialite old enough to be our mother. He had a helluva time escaping, but damned if he didn't eventually catch up to me."

"And when he did, did he beat you to a pulp?"

He chuckled. "It took me weeks to recover. He cracked my jaw and broke two ribs." He fell silent and then said quietly, "Six minutes separate my brother and me. There's a year between Robert and me and yet it's as though he were my twin, not Phelan."

"Robert once told me you were a second son and that it explained a lot about you. What did he mean?"

She'd finally asked him an easy question. "By law the eldest son inherits all his father's worldly goods. The second son is the spare male, educated and groomed for leadership in the event that some horrible fate befalls the first. I'm an absolutely unnecessary second son because nothing horrible is going to ever befall Phelan."

Fairness compelled him to add, "I probably should take that latter statement back. He could cut himself with paper. Or drop a book on his toe. He's a good and decent man, mind you, but in my opinion just a bit too complacent for regular company. Robert, on the other hand, and despite his gentlemanly protests otherwise, knows how to properly enjoy himself."

"Surely your parents don't think of you as unimportant. I realize that I don't know them, but I just can't believe that any parents would think that of their child."

Damn. He had tried to steer her away, but she'd arrowed right back to her course. There seemed to be nothing he could do but give her enough to satisfy her curiosity. "Actually, when I reached an age where I had some perspective on it, I realized that my parents always treated me as though I were going to die young." At her wide-eyed look, he smiled and added, "Oh, they saw to it that I was well educated and had a broad range of training, but they frequently indulged me when they probably shouldn't have."

"It seems to me that you didn't turn out all that badly."

The unexpected compliment warmed him. "God, Glynis. Please share that observation with my parents when you meet them."

"So you really think they're on their way here?" she asked as they ambled into the Concannon yard.

He nodded, relieved that they'd finally reached a relatively benign topic of discourse. "Enough so that the day we arrived here I sent Patrick to await their ship. And Mother will find the means of sending you back to where you belong. She's a remarkably resourceful woman."

Looking at him sitting so comfortably in the saddle, it suddenly came to her. Carrick on the Rocking M. She and Carrick riding side by side just as they were now. The two of them heading into the yard at the end of a day, getting ready to stable their horses. If Carrick's mother could send her back where she belonged, why couldn't she send Carrick, too? If he went with her, then he wouldn't be here to die. It was the perfect solution to the problem. And it was so incredibly simple.

She stopped before the open door of the stable and waited until Carrick had reined in Molan. In the lantern light his eyes were ebony dark. Her heart tightened. "When your mother sends me home, Carrick . . . come with me."

"I can't," he replied instantly, swinging down off Molan. In the next second he'd pulled the reins over the horse's head and started into the stable.

The finality of his response left her stunned. What had happened to the man she'd been with just a minute ago? Why was he so suddenly distant? "Carrick!" she called after him. When he didn't look back, she swore and hurried after him.

"You didn't even consider the possibility," she accused as she lead Bert into the stable.

"And you shouldn't, either," he answered without looking up.

"Why?"

"If you hope," he replied as he loosened the girth strap, "you hurt when it's lost. I refuse to be that cruel to you or anyone else. And if you were sensible, you wouldn't do it to yourself."

"But—"

"Go inside, Muldoon." He tossed Molan's saddle over the edge of the stall and then gave her a look that brooked no argument. "I'll take care of the horses."

Glynis couldn't remember the last time she'd felt such frustration. She desperately wanted to throw something at him and demand that they go back out into the yard and find a better ending for their evening. She wanted to stomp her feet. But she wouldn't give him the satisfaction. She refused to let him know just how hurt her feelings were. "You're absolutely impossible sometimes," she declared, turning on her heel. Striding toward the door, she fired her final shot. "Good night and sweet dreams."

"Good evening, Miss Muldoon."

"Hi, Robert. Bye, Robert."

Carrick looked up just in time to see his cousin step out of Glynis's path as she stomped away. Carrick began to strip the saddle from Bert as he waited for Robert to join him.

"How'd matters go with McKenna?"

"Fine. What were you able to learn in Greystones?"

"The interrogating officer's name is Cunningham. Captain James Cunningham. It seems that he's more than a tad pissed that Sean cocked up his toes during his inquiry. No one is hiding their opinions of the sadistic son of a bitch. He's as loathesome to the Brits as he is to the locals."

Carrick nodded crisply and set about brushing Molan. "I'll take care of the bastard."

"Or I can," Robert countered, picking up a brush and beginning work on Glynis's mount. "It doesn't matter which of us does it. Either way, retribution needs to wait. The British are expecting it. To have them a bit less vigilant would lessen the risks." Changing the subject, he asked archly, "How is it that you came in with the fiery Miss Muldoon?"

Carrick gritted his teeth. Robert was every bit Glynis's equal when it came to persistence. Since there could be no dignified escape, his only hope lay in carefully choosing his words and saying little. "I picked up a British patrol between McKenna's and Julia Conroy's. Muldoon happened along and took care of them for me."

"And your words of gratitude inspired her to a fit of pique."

"Christ, Rob," Carrick groused. "Don't start on me. It's been a long evening."

"And her leaving you to take care of the horses has you frustrated and angry. Would you like to know what I think about you and Glynis?"

"No."

"For the first time in your life, you've found a woman who won't let you hide."

"What the hell are you talking about?" Carrick demanded, turning to face his cousin.

Robert continued to work. "I was with you the night you saw the vision in the Dragon's Heart, Carrick. I was there the next morning, too. And I saw what knowing did to you; how it changed you. I've watched you almost every day since, Cousin. I know you better than you know yourself. Taking women to your bed isn't just a matter of physical pleasure for you. Lovemaking's a distraction, a way to escape the uncertainty and doubts. Having a woman in your arms lets you pretend that your heart's not numb from loneliness."

"Thank you for your insight," Carrick drawled as he resumed brushing Molan. Why had the people in his world suddenly taken it upon themselves to reproach him?

"I'm not through yet, Carrick."

"I'm done listening."

"Suit yourself. I'm saying it anyway. You've spent the last fourteen years living behind a masterful facade, and I've let you get away with it. I shouldn't have. Throwing yourself into the rigging during a storm isn't an act of reckless bravery. Others can think that if they like. I know better. You do things like that because, for just a few precious moments, it frightens you more than the vision in the Dragon's Heart."

Carrick controlled his anger, keeping his face a bland mask.

"And for the first time someone you respect has squared up to you and looked right through your facade of certainty and command," Robert continued without pause. "Glynis Muldoon expects more of you than anyone ever has. She expects you to face yourself, your fear. For the first time in your life you've met someone who doesn't believe in unchangeable destiny. Glynis Muldoon believes in *you*."

"With your brilliance and her determination, the two of you would make a lovely couple." Carrick said tersely.

"I'm not the one she loves."

"I don't need or want her love," Carrick snarled, pitching away the brush and taking Molan's reins in hand.

For several seconds the only sound in the stable was of the horses being returned to their stalls, of creaking wood and the latches dropping into place. Carrick crossed his arms along the top of Molan's gate and watched his horse settle in. He felt Robert studying him but refused to look at him. To acknowledge his cousin would invite yet another round of pointed commentary. He'd had enough tonight to last the rest of his life.

"Jesus, Carrick," Robert said softly, stepping away from Bert's stall. "Glynis can save your life. Let her."

Carrick watched his cousin leave the barn and then expelled the breath he had been holding. Christ, he'd never guessed that Robert knew so much about his demons. Carrick sagged against Molan's stall and stared blindly at the straw-covered floor. Was his cousin right about all the rest of it, too?

15

The noonday sun beat down on his bare shoulders and back, heating his skin. Carrick leaned against the shovel. Drawing his forearm across his brow, he paused to study his efforts. He'd set a good twenty-five feet of stone walkway around the lough; a considerable accomplishment, one that should have taken the entire day. That it represented only this morning's labor spoke of the frustration driving him.

He turned at the sound of hoofbeats, his heart leaping with the hope of seeing Glynis riding toward him, memories of their moonlight kisses flooding his senses. Then he recognized the dark phaeton being driven toward him. He winced and rubbed his cheeks before going back to work.

"Carrick, my boy," the Widow Conroy called as she reined the carriage to a stop beside him. "I had hopes of seeing you yesterday evening."

Carrick groaned and reluctantly stopped his shovel work. "My apologies, Julia," he answered. "Family considerations kept me here last night. By the time I was free, it was well past a reasonable calling hour."

Mischief sparkled in her blue eyes. "Might I hope that you were kept here entertaining your delightful American cousin?"

"And what brings you over again today, Julia?"

"Why, Carrick des Marceaux," she chided, laughing. "That wasn't the least bit subtle. But we'll come back to Cousin Glynis in a moment." Her expression sober, she indicated the two-wheeled carriage with her gloved hand. "I've trotted myself over today because my home has been invaded by the British army."

"So they've finally caught you smuggling whiskey, have they?" he asked, hoping he sounded much more casual than his interest had suddenly become.

Her face brightened. "How you do tease, Carrick. Unfortunately, the more adventurous years of my life seem to be well past." She whispered conspiratorially, "But what I wouldn't give to have something to hide right beneath their patrician noses. It would be ever so thrilling, don't you think?"

Carrick crossed his arms over the end of the shovel handle and settled in for what he prayed would be a profitable discussion. "So, Julia, if it's not your nefarious activities, why have the British quartered themselves in your home?"

She settled back into the seat and arched a pale brow. "It seems that the Dragon is active in the region. Not that I eavesdrop, mind you, but I could scarcely help overhearing several conversations among the officers. It would appear that the Dragon broke into the home of the tithe collector last night and threatened his life and the lives of his wife and daughters."

"How shocking. And the British think you may have something to do with this Dragon fellow?"

"Oh, Carrick," she admonished with a quick laugh. "To think that such a dashing rogue would have anything to do with a woman of my years." She leaned slightly forward again. "Actually, they explained that they were about a thorough investigation of persons in the area that might be opposed to the Crown's tithe laws and that they needed commodious quarters for the officers in charge of the whole affair. I suppose that since my third husband, God rest his soul, was an Englishman, they believed I'd be a bit more hospitable than other landowners."

"A logical assumption, I suppose."

"Logical, perhaps, but incorrect," the Widow Conroy replied indignantly. "I've always had a low tolerance for men puffed up with a sense of their own importance. Combined with their belief in inherent British superiority, these particular men really are quite insufferable. But there's little to be gained from baiting them directly, so I've chosen a more discreet form of subversion. I've decided that I shall simply visit my neighbors and casually mention the British presence in the area. Surely in my doing so the information will reach the Dragon and he'll know to be careful. A brilliant plan, wouldn't you say?" she finished mildly.

Did Julia suspect him? Good God, did she actually know? He forced a smile and said dryly, "You should seriously consider taking up smuggling, Julia. You'd be very good at it."

"And speaking of pursuit . . . how is your Cousin Glynis this morning?"

Lord, this topic wasn't any less disturbing than the last one. "Julia, are you playing at matchmaker?"

"Playing?" she repeated with feigned horror. "Good heavens, no. Matchmaking is a very serious business. Why, in London the social reputation of women my age rests almost entirely on their ability to bring together suitable young men and women."

"Well, Glynis and I aren't suited for one another," Carrick observed, hoping to put an end to Julia's well-meaning interference. "You'd be wasting your time and risking your reputation to pair us."

"What utter nonsense," she countered tartly. "I haven't married four times without learning to recognize passion. You and Glynis are destined to be together. Why, dear boy, the two of you are obviously on the brink of falling in love."

"Julia, that's simply not possible," he said, a harder edge to his voice. "You're seeing what you'd like to see."

She waved her hand airily. "Oh, men always protest. Tell me, she is a cousin far enough removed to avoid scandal, isn't she?"

Recognizing his defeat, Carrick resigned himself to enduring Julia's questioning. "Cousin Glynis is only very distantly related."

"This is very good. The two of you will have the most wonderful children."

"Oh, yes," he agreed with a short laugh. "They'd also be the terrors of the county."

"Oh, but placid children are so utterly boring, don't you think? I'll take a high-spirited, mischievous little rascal over a studious, well-mannered one anytime. That's why I so adore Saraid's mob. They make me feel young again."

"Young? They make me feel old."

"Really? And how does Cousin Glynis make you feel?"

His face flamed. Good God, she had him blushing like a schoolboy. "Julia, you are a most persistent woman."

She smiled in agreement. "Then save yourself the time and aggravation and tell me what I want to know."

"I don't know how Glynis Muldoon makes me feel," he admitted reluctantly. "May we now leave this topic of conversation?"

"Of course not. Since your mother is presently absent it falls on my shoulders to serve as her proxy to help you arrive at a clear perspective on this important matter. Does Cousin Glynis make you laugh?"

"Yes," he grudgingly admitted.

"Would you sometimes like very much to strangle her?"

He laughed outright. "How did you know?"

She leaned forward another degree. "And do you find yourself envisioning the moment when you sweep her into your arms and carry her off to your rooms?"

"Julia . . ." he warned.

"Well, do you or don't you?"

The image of making love to Glynis Muldoon flashed briefly before him. "Not the sweeping and carrying part."

"Oh, that's even better." She paused, her eyes twinkling with amusement. "And so much more inspirational, don't you think?" She considered him a long moment before adding, "Well, if you're not already in love with the woman, you're certainly well into infatuation. I say you should pursue the path and see where it leads. I think you'll discover quickly enough that Miss Glynis Muldoon of America is the perfect young lady for you."

Carrick shook his head and took up the shovel again,

intending to resume his work. "You don't know Glynis very well at all. You've only met her the one time."

"True. But I'm certain she has very serious feelings for you. I could see that quite clearly in the way she looked at you."

"Please, Julia. Glynis probably wants to strangle me only slightly less than I would like to strangle her."

She dismissed his protests. "Oh, pish. What do men know about these matters? If it weren't for the wisdom and persistence of females, you'd all stumble blindly through your lives, poorly dressed and lamenting your lack of direction."

"Thankfully, you take pity on us hapless creatures."

"*Undeserving* hapless creatures," she corrected with a smile as she took the reins in her gloved hands. "And now that I've done all that I can here, I do believe I shall go to the house and visit your sister and your sweet little American cousin."

Carrick watched Julia drive on toward the house and wondered just what it was about Glynis Muldoon that she saw as being so right for him. Lord knew Glynis had more pluck and intelligence than most women. Actually, he quickly corrected, she had more than most men he knew. She had a temper as well. And stubborn? Once Glynis dug in her heels, there was no moving her. He mentally tabulated the column. They were relatively positive traits in a human being, male or female.

But Glynis was more than the sum of her traits. There was something about her that touched him as no other person ever had. What was it? Maybe it was her innate sense of optimism. She honestly believed that she could shape her destiny, that she could triumph over any circumstance.

How he envied her faith. And how much he wanted to believe as she did. But his future had been foretold in the Dragon's Heart and there was nothing any mortal could do to alter it. All he could hope for was to die for a noble cause and with some dignity.

He looked back at the manor house, wondering where Glynis might be at that moment, what she might be doing. If he were to go to her, would she wrap her arms about him and lend him some of her faith? Would she help him to pretend, just for a while, that all things were indeed possible?

No, his good judgment said. There was no point in pretending; it would only worsen his regrets when the time came to die. Carrick turned deliberately away from the house. Damn the muddy mess Glynis Muldoon had made of his resolution. Before she had tumbled into his life, he hadn't had to think twice about anything. Now nothing seemed as simple as it had once been.

The waters of the lough rippled gently in the faint breeze of the early afternoon, inviting him to seek solace within them. Tossing aside his shovel, Carrick pulled off his boots and took two long strides before launching himself into the cooling waters.

When several laps of the lough had finally brought him some measure of peace, Carrick rolled onto his back to float and watch the clouds move across the sky. If he judged correctly, a storm would develop in the early hours of the night ahead. If he didn't want to shovel the same dirt tomorrow as he had today, he'd best get the stones set. Reluctantly heading for shore, he glanced toward the edge of the lough.

His heart swelled at the sight of Glynis standing there, holding Rachel on her cocked hip. A light breeze caught loose tendrils of her auburn hair and wreathed her face. She brushed them back with one hand and smiled as his gaze met hers.

"Hi!" she called. "And here I was feeling sorry for you out here working yourself to death."

He chuckled and, offering no apologies or explanations, asked, "And what brings you down from the house, Glynis Muldoon?"

"Mrs. Kelly has lunch ready and the general consensus appears to be that your presence is required."

Carrick swam lazily toward her, fascinated with the way the breeze lifted the hem of her skirt, by her naturalness with Rachel. It came to him that Glynis Muldoon needed children of her own. And he wished he could be the man who gave them to her. Shocked, he instantly quashed the urge and cursed Julia Conroy for planting the insidious seed.

"And how did you get the honor of summoning me?" he asked, trying to divert his dangerous thoughts.

"Saraid isn't feeling well," she answered with a quick, meaningful glance toward the child balanced on her hip. "She's gone to bed. Robert took charge of the boys and I seem to have inherited your nieces. Everyone's a bit unsettled by it all and I decided a temporary escape might be a good idea."

The taut undercurrent in her voice prickled his concern. "Where's Horace?" he asked, reaching the grassy edge of the lough.

Glynis again glanced at Rachel before answering. Quietly, she said, "Against Saraid's objections, he went to get the doctor."

"How long ago?" Carrick demanded, snatching up his shirt.

"Maybe a half hour or so," she replied, looking worried. "Mrs. Conroy is looking after Saraid."

Shoving his arms into the sleeves of his linen shirt, he looked up at her. A smile teased the corners of her mouth as her gaze came up the length of his body.

"Why, Glynis Muldoon," he chided, grinning.

She blushed prettily and, fighting to control a broad smile, she retorted, "I was momentarily distracted. I've got a grip now."

Carrick pulled the shirt over his head, stifling the invitation tempting his tongue. Lord, if only she didn't have Rachel with her.

"I'll carry her, if you'd like," he offered, reaching for his sister's youngest daughter.

Glynis transferred the child to him with the ease of a woman who had done the task for years. Again he was struck by the thought that the child should properly be one of their own making. Again he set it aside as a fool's dream and an old woman's meddling. There would be enough regrets in dying without adding fatherless children to the list.

Gathering her skirts in one hand, Glynis picked up Carrick's boots with the other and headed toward the manor.

Why on earth did she suddenly want Rachel to be her child? she wondered. She'd never given the slightest thought to having a family beyond the practical necessity of having an heir. The Rocking M had always been enough to consume her thoughts, her dreams. But as she'd handed Rachel over to Carrick she'd been filled with longing. And now as she walked beside him, she found herself struggling against tears. She was tired of fighting her heart. It would be easier to surrender and let the future turn out as it might.

The future. She and Carrick had no future, she reminded herself sternly. She had to find her way back through time. And unless she succeeded in altering the fabric of his destiny, Carrick was going to die. God, but her heart ached. Why couldn't she have met Carrick at a Stockmen's Association meeting? Or at the sale barn? Or any of a thousand different places on her side of time?

Carrick moved closer and gently slipped his arm around her shoulder. Instinctively she slid her own about his waist. Their closeness brought the threat of tears nearer and although she wanted to with all her heart, she didn't dare risk meeting his eyes.

"Everything will be fine, Glynis," he said softly as they continued walking together. "There's no need to worry about it."

For a wild moment she wondered if he could read her thoughts. Then she realized Carrick had simply interpreted her silence as concern over Saraid's sudden illness . . . as it should have been.

With no small measure of guilt, she took a steadying breath. "I'm sure it will," she answered. "Robert said the same thing to Horace as the poor man was dashing about trying to decide what he should do."

She felt Carrick tense, and his step faltered for a moment. Then, without another word, he drew her even closer to his side. In her heart, Glynis knew that these moments were as they should be between her and Carrick, and that her memory of them would have to sustain her through the heartbreak certain to come.

"Glynis? About last night . . ." he said softly. "I'd like to apologize for being so abrupt. I should have explained that there are some . . . things . . . I need to do. I can't walk way from them any more than you can walk away from your obligations to the Rocking M."

"Apology accepted," she managed to say around the lump in her throat. God, it was so much easier to fight with him. She knew how to deal with the angry man. The gentle one scared the hell out of her. The gentle one was so easy to love.

16

Glynis sat on the sofa and watched as Horace mopped his brow with a handkerchief and declined the glass of brandy Carrick offered him. Through the windows of the parlor he watched the black carriage roll down the drive and after a moment of silence turned back to the room and said absently, "The doctor said Saraid should be up and about and as good as new within the next few days. In the interim, she should be kept abed and given clear fluids. He also said we were to try to keep the children occupied elsewhere as best we can so that she can rest."

Robert, observing his cousin's husband, said, "You don't look too well yourself, man. If you don't mind my saying so, you appear to be rather washed out."

Horace shrugged and drew the linen square across his upper lip. "It's just a chill. I'm sure it will pass."

"Horace," Glynis offered softly, "I hate to mention the possibility, but maybe you're coming down with the flu. How does your stomach feel? Are your joints achy?"

He groaned and sat heavily on an upholstered chair opposite her, his expression pained, his misery obvious. "The doctor said that the entire village is down with it. There isn't a tenant left on his feet."

Glynis nodded, wondering how long it would take the malady to sweep through the Concannon household. With eight children it could very well be a grizzly day or two. "I think you had better head off to bed yourself, Horace," she suggested, crossing to press the back of her hand to his brow. His skin felt hot and moist to her touch. "I don't mean to sound insensitive, but if you're in bed you're not as likely to get the rest of us sick."

Carrick, leaning back against the cherry sideboard with one booted ankle casually crossed over the other, studied the brandy he swirled about in his glass. Without looking up from it, he said quietly, "A storm's going to break in the next few hours and from the look of the sky it's likely to give us heavy rains. Where are your cattle, Horace?"

With great effort and a long sigh, Horace hauled himself up from his seat and answered, "Those that the Crown has left me are in the westernmost pastures." He looked dubiously out the parlor windows at the leaden clouds building overhead. "Perhaps they should be moved to higher ground," he admitted, sounding for all the world like a man about to undertake his last act on earth.

"It might not be a bad idea," Carrick agreed, setting his glass on the sideboard. He smiled at his brother-in-law. "You go to bed where you belong, Horace. Since none of your retainers is up to the task, Robert and I will see to getting them moved."

Robert nodded enthusiastically and placed his glass beside his cousin's. "Who needs tenants? I'll get changed. It'll take only a moment. Why don't you have Eachann saddle our horses, Carrick?"

Glynis cleared her throat. "If I might put in my two cents' worth?" Getting their attention, she continued, "With Horace and Saraid both down with the flu, someone's got to be here for the children. If there's going to be a hellacious storm, the children, especially the younger ones, are probably going to be frightened. They'd do better with someone they know well to comfort them. I'm a stranger to them. Don't you think they'd prefer to have Robert here?"

Robert looked at her, perplexed. "Carrick can't possibly move the cattle alone."

A smile slowly spread across Carrick's face as his gaze met hers. "She doesn't intend for me to do it alone, Robert. She's about to suggest that she go in your stead. Am I right, Muldoon?"

Glynis nodded. "Yes. As a matter of fact, that is precisely

my suggestion. Bert and I are both experienced at herding under less than ideal conditions. We can help you make quick work of the task."

Horace mopped his sweaty brow again and rasped, "I can see the wisdom in—"

"You're not leaving me here to play nanny," Robert interrupted. "The work is dangerous and shouldn't be undertaken by a woman. Not when a man is willing and perfectly capable of doing it."

"Robert . . ." Glynis chided, shaking her head sadly. "I love you dearly, but at the moment you're being a sexist pig. Please stop. It's most unbecoming."

Carrick laughed and ignored his cousin's glower. "You're going to get drenched before the night's done, Muldoon."

She shrugged. "I won't melt."

"Damn," Carrick replied, his eyes bright with mischief. "I rather hoped you would. Perhaps if you were to get cold enough and a bit frightened . . ."

She considered him for a moment, then retorted archly, "That's why a girl has a reliable horse under her."

Carrick laughed outright. "Go get changed, Muldoon," he said, motioning with his head toward the foyer and the stairs leading to the upper floor. "The sooner we get the cattle moved, the sooner we can be back."

Robert stepped forward, looking worried. "I'm going to object one more time," he offered hopefully.

"Go right ahead," Carrick shot back. "It's not going to do you any good."

"My Aunt Ria always has hot coffee and warm cookies waiting for me when I come in from a night like this," Glynis suggested, smiling brightly at Robert. "Peanut butter cookies are one of my favorites."

His dark brows furrowed. "Peanut butter?"

"Okay. How about chocolate chip? Or maybe some oat-meal raisin?"

Robert snorted. "There's no point in adding insult to injury." He looked between her and his cousin as he added pointedly, "Might I suggest that you try to exercise both good judgment and restraint while you're out and about?"

Carrick grinned and patted his cousin on the back.

"You're welcome to suggest whatever you like, Robert. Now get Horace upstairs before the poor man collapses, will you, please?"

He saw the look in Robert's eyes, and he braced himself as his cousin came toward the beverage cart with his empty brandy snifter.

"If you find the opportunity for it," Robert said quietly, "you might try to engage in some honest conversation. You might listen to her and think about what she says."

Even as Robert and Horace left the parlor, Glynis felt Carrick's attention on her. She looked at him and noted that his expression had darkened. "I'll see to the horses, Muldoon," he said thoughtfully. "Join me in the barn whenever you're ready."

Deciding that there were more important considerations at hand than his unfathomable thoughts, she offered him a jaunty salute before lifting her skirts above her ankles and following in Horace's and Robert's wake.

"This is a frog strangler!"

Carrick finished latching the gate and looked over at her, noting the water that ran in a steady stream off the brim of her black hat. "Frog strangler?" he yelled back above the sound of the rain.

She grinned. "Think about it!"

He should have been utterly miserable. He was soaked to the skin and cold. But he was happy. Honest-to-God happy. And he knew it was simply because Glynis rode beside him. He grinned back at her, letting her inherent good humor carry him along.

"Does it ever rain like this in Kansas?" he asked.

"Yep. Especially in the spring. We get hail, too. And sometimes even tornadoes."

"What's a tornado?"

Her eyes sparkled from beneath the brim of her hat. "Lots of fun. Well, I suppose the cattle don't much enjoy them, but they're awesome to watch."

"You still haven't answered my question."

"It's a spinning column of wind we get when a warm air mass comes in from the south and collides with a cold front dropping down from the north. They suck up and spit out everything in their path . . . which can be up to a mile wide."

"And you think watching this is an enjoyable pastime?"

"Well, yeah. There's nothing quite as amazing as Mother Nature running amuck. You have to be smart enough to get the hell out of her way, of course. Watching one coming straight at you isn't an occasion for giggles."

"Doesn't anything scare you, Muldoon?"

He saw the shutters come down, noted the slight straightening of her shoulders, and knew without a doubt that he'd trespassed. And then she recovered and smiled at him.

"Well, bull riding comes to mind. I think you'd have to be nuts to do that."

"I'm serious, Glynis," he persisted, recognizing her attempt at evading the issue. "What scares you?"

She reined in and faced him squarely. "The thought of not being able to get home." Her gaze held his for no more than a second, but it was long enough for him to clearly see that she had put a wall between them. She looked away and said carefully, "The cattle will have dropped down into the draws to get out of the wind. I'll head over to that one and see what I can gather up. How about you take that one over there? I'll meet you back here in a few minutes."

She wheeled about and was gone before he could answer. He watched her ride away for a moment and then glanced up at the sky. What meager daylight they had was quickly fading and the clouds overhead showed no signs of lightening or parting. If it continued to rain as it was for very much longer, it would soon be impossible to cross the stream between them and the manor. He and Glynis would be stranded on the high ground with the cattle until the water levels dropped.

Carrick nudged Molan in the flanks. If he remembered correctly, there was an old, single-room stone house tucked among some gnarled old trees in the uppermost pasture. Luxurious it probably wasn't, but if the roof was still good and the chimney intact, it could provide them with shelter for however long they were marooned. He smiled. Putting up with the cold rain and moving cattle were small prices to pay for the possibilities ahead.

He'd had time to think on Robert's words and Glynis's graceful acceptance of his apology that morning. He'd decided that there was no need to make things more complicated than they already were. There was no denying that he and Glynis were physically drawn to each other. And as long as they both made a conscious effort to avoid any discussion of the future, that attraction would be enough to pleasurably pass their hours together in the shepherd's cottage.

Glynis pushed the wooden gate until it hung up on a clump of sodden grass and then backed Bert away from it. The cattle trotted through the opening with determination, pushing and jostling each other for the right to be the first into the pasture that swept gently upward. She watched the lead cows for a moment and then looked to the rear of the herd she and Carrick had assembled in the last hour. Carrick rode across the back edge, pushing the animals forward. Glynis tilted her head so that the brim of her Stetson blocked the worst of the rain driving against her face and watched Carrick work. He had a good sense of cattle, could anticipate what they were likely to do. If the man ever had a good quarterhorse under him and a western saddle, he'd be a decent cowboy in no time at all.

Would Carrick be content with a role as hired hand? Probably not. Would he want a more intimate, more permanent relationship? Over her dead body. She'd done the waltz down the aisle once already and the consequences had been disastrous. So what was the solution? She certainly wasn't willing to give up on him, to leave him behind to die.

She needed to think on it before she broached the subject with Carrick again. The *things* he'd spoken about needing to do obviously concerned fighting the tithe laws. But the son of a bitch was so resigned to an early death that he wouldn't listen with an open mind unless she had all her ducks in a row before going in to the discussion. Half of the herd had passed through the gate when she rode back to join Carrick.

"They seem to know where they're going," she said, reining in beside him. "Why don't you take them on for a bit by yourself? I'm going to ride back and check to see if we missed any. Some of the brush is pretty thick and one or two could be caught."

He shook his head, droplets flying from the ends of his dark hair. "No. The water's rising too fast to do anything about it even if they are. Let's get what we have settled in."

"You go ahead," she persisted, turning her horse and nudging him forward. "I'll catch up with you in a minute."

"Glynis!"

She wheeled her horse back just long enough to shout, "I don't leave stock behind. It won't take me long. I'll be just fine."

Okay, so maybe she wouldn't be just fine. Glynis leaned out in the saddle and peered over the edge of the cut bank again. The calf was too tangled in the brush to let her throw a loop over his head. If she was going to bring him up, she'd have to go down to get him. She studied the surface of the swirling muddy brown water sluicing through the narrow draw and then measured the distance between it and the trapped calf. There might be enough time. "Then again there might not," she muttered. "It's rising fast."

She pulled her rope from its thong and wrapped one end around the saddle horn. "But let's focus on the positive," she added, swinging down and drawing the rope tight. With the increased pull, Bert braced himself like any good roping pony. Glynis smiled at him as she backed toward the muddy edge of the embankment. "Let's make this an easy down and a really quick up, ol' boy."

Between the slickness of the mud beneath her feet and the calf's thrashing and bawling, Glynis had serious questions about her sanity by the time she reached the midpoint. One quick glance at the water level told her she didn't have time to second-guess herself. Deliberately letting her feet slip out from under her, she slid the rest of the way down on her knees, abruptly stopping her momentum by using her free hand to catch a sturdy branch of the scrub imprisoning the calf. Whether it was the cold and wet, or the strain of working it, her shoulder pounded unmercifully.

The calf leaped up, kicked, and tried to twist away from Glynis's outstretched hand. "Oh, stop flailing around!" she muttered through gritted teeth, wedging herself into the brush and keeping the tension on the rope. "Can't you see I'm trying to rescue you? You're too damn little to make a decent hamburger."

She caught a handful of dewlap and the frightened animal momentarily froze. She instantly flicked the loop over its head.

"Now for the elevator treatment," she said, letting go of the rope and rolling out of the way. The rope lay slack for no more than a half second and then it snapped up and quivered. The calf tried to pull against the force drawing it forward and up, but the rope held firm. With grim resolution, Glynis clambered her way through the thicket of branches to reach the calf's hindquarters.

"You could help, you know," she admonished, putting her good shoulder into the little animal's rump and shoving him forward. For one second the rope fell slack. In the next, Bert pulled it tight and popped the roped calf a good foot forward.

"Now you're getting the idea," she cheered when the calf finally figured out to help rather than hinder his own rescue. She scrambled after him, her arms tired and her breathing hard, but determined to keep her hold on him so that Bert could pull them both up the steep embankment at the same time.

They had gone no more than three feet up the slick slope when the calf slipped and fell over, kicking his legs wildly in a futile attempt to regain his footing. Glynis instinctively let go and twisted away from the sharp hooves. In the same instant her own feet went out from under her. She shot slickly down the embankment on her belly at the same time that Bert whisked the calf upward on its side.

Glynis gasped when she hit the ice-cold water. She was sinking, the weight of her clothing combining with the pull of the water to take her down. She felt her Stetson ripped away, felt a sharp twinge as the stampede cord scraped along the length of her jaw. With every bit of her strength she ripped open her drover's coat and clawed her way out of it, kicking frantically up to the surface.

Her lungs burned. Her legs and arms were leaden. Her

boots were filled with water and fighting her. Then blind panic swept away every thought. She was going to drown. She was going to die a long way from home.

She refused to go easily. She fought against the water, giving every ounce of her strength and then some to reach the surface. She finally broke through with a harsh gasp. Breathing painfully, she pushed herself farther, forcing her arms and legs to move, to propel her toward the embankment, toward a tiny clump of brush clinging precariously to the steep wall of mud and rock.

She caught it with her right hand. A quick glance around told her there was no other handhold within reach. There would be no working her way up from this point unless she could literally carve steps up the face of the cut bank. God, and she'd told Carrick she'd be all right. She glanced down the water-filled draw, searching for another place that might offer a better chance at climbing out.

Something hit her on the shoulder, the impact cutting through her numbness from the cold and fatigue. Looking up, it took several seconds for her brain to realize what was happening.

Swearing at the dullness of her thinking, she took a deep breath and transferred her hold to her weaker left hand, then quickly wrapped the rope about her right hand and wrist. She didn't have to call out. She didn't have to offer any sort of sign to say that she was ready. The rope went taut and drew her up the bank with a speed that gave her no time to get her feet under her. She managed to keep her head up as her body plowed a deep furrow all the way to the top and over the edge.

Grass . . . she was looking at beautiful, well-rooted grass. She was safe. Glynis took a shuddering breath and slowly sat up. Suddenly she was standing upright, a pair of strong hands holding her steady. A pair of fiery blue eyes glared angrily into hers. Had God ever made a more handsome man than Carrick des Marceaux?

"You stubborn fool! You damn near got yourself killed over a silly calf!"

She managed a weak smile. "But it turned out okay in the end and that's what counts."

His grip on her tightened. "I swear, Muldoon. Sometimes I could just . . ."

"Just what?"

Something inside him let go. Glynis saw his surrender in the same instant that he pulled her hard against his chest, before his mouth came down hard over hers. There was no gentleness in his possession, no tender attempt at seduction. He devoured her senses, sweeping her along with raw desire. Glynis wrapped her arms around him, wanting more of the heady sensation . . . wanting more of him and offering whatever he wanted to take in exchange.

He'd never hungered for a woman like this; so deeply, so completely. There was no point in fighting it, in trying to be rational. The devil could name the consequences. He'd pay them. In the instant that he'd seen her clinging to the bank and fighting the current, he'd known that all he wanted in the world was Glynis Muldoon. She was all that mattered to him.

He tightened his arms around her, deepened his kiss. And when her lips parted he almost cried out at the wonder of it all. Every sense sharpened. The cold rain pelted his back, but where Glynis pressed against him, there was a searing heat that took his breath away. He caressed her cheek, wordlessly apologizing for his desperation.

She winced at his touch. He drew back, still holding her tight as he searched her face for some sign of what was wrong. And then he saw the wound on the curve of her jaw.

"Oh, Christ, Glynis," he whispered, tilting her chin up so he could see better. "You're hurt."

"My hat got ripped off in the current," she explained, her breathing as uneven as his own. "The stampede cord got me as it went. Is it bad?"

"Not too. It's more a scrape than a cut." He started to examine her. "Are you hurt anywhere else?"

"I don't think so." She took a deep breath before taking a half-step back. "I'm one helluva muddy mess, though," she said, looking down the front of herself and then over at him. A weak smile lifted the corners of her mouth and she took another step away. "I seem to have shared it, too. Generously. Sorry."

"I seem to recall that it was my idea," he replied, letting

her go, hating the distance between them and feeling the chill that suddenly cut to his bones. He wanted to take her back into his arms. He wanted to kiss her again. But the confusion in her eyes kept his arms at his sides.

She crossed her arms and looked off into the rain. "I didn't exactly resist."

"No, you didn't."

"Oh," she said, suddenly remembering, "I haven't said thanks for hauling me up out of that. You're pretty impressive with a lariat. Did the calf get up the embankment all right?"

"Don't you care whether you live or die, woman?" He knew the question was a mistake the very instant he said it. He'd just given her an opening and invited her to step into it.

"That's a bit like the pot calling the kettle black, don't you think?"

"We have cattle to move," he said, turning on his heel, angry with himself for having so foolishly destroyed the magic between them.

"Sooner or later we're going to have to talk, Carrick. I'm not going to cut and run."

His earlier optimism crushed, he watched her coil the rope and then slap it against the side of her leg as she headed toward her horse. She didn't look at him but headed back toward the gate where they'd parted company earlier. Carrick went after her, deciding that Glynis Muldoon had to be a glimpse of hell. Or was she maybe a heaven he'd never reach?

They'd closed the gate behind them and crested the hill when Glynis reined in her mount and pointed to the animals crowded together on the other side of the stone wall. "Whose cattle are those?"

"The land belongs to Julia Conroy," Carrick supplied, bringing Molan up beside her. "The cattle are the Crown's. See the T? It's the brand of the tithe collector."

She leaned forward to get a better look. "Looks like he hasn't had a chance to put his mark on some of them."

She grinned, but her gaze didn't leave the milling cattle. "I was just thinking that cattle tend to stampede in a storm like this one and how difficult it would be to get them properly sorted out if they weren't branded." She straightened and looked over at him with a mischievous smile. "Some might get lost forever. Wouldn't that be tragic?"

He laughed outright, his frustration forgotten. "Muldoon, you have an outlaw's heart."

"And moments of inspiration."

Carrick gestured toward the small dwelling behind him. "Why don't you head over to the cottage? I'll be along shortly."

"And let you have all the fun? No way. It was my idea," she retorted.

He shook his head. "It's a capital offense, Glynis. If you were to be caught at it, they'd hang you."

"Well, I'm not about to ride off and leave you to risk it on your own. I'll take the same chances you do. We either do it together or not at all." She set her jaw stubbornly and waited.

Together or not at all. The words resonated through him. The sensation was much like the feeling a man got when staring down the muzzle of a pistol. His heart beat wildly and his blood ran cold. "Aren't you chilled?" he asked, as much to distract himself as to redirect Glynis's thoughts. "Aren't you tired? Hungry? Don't you want to get out of those muddy clothes?"

"I'll survive," she countered with a shrug. "It's not like anyone's ever died of discomfort."

She was unlike any woman he'd ever known; tempered steel wrapped in tempting curves. "There are times when I don't quite know what to do with you, Muldoon."

She grinned. "Well, mull it over while we decide where we're going to make a breach in the wall. Maybe by the time we're ready to head home you'll have an idea." And then she was gone, heading down the wall, inspecting it as she went.

17

The tiny cottage had far better appointments than she had expected. The roof was sound and the fireplace tight. The furnishings were simple: a table, four mismatched chairs, and a featherbed that had seen better days along with some blankets and the miscellaneous clothing they'd found in the chest at the footboard. Finding clean clothes had been a gift from a benevolent God, second only to the plainly constructed sideboard. Its assorted contents had not only allowed them both to have a quick but efficient bath but to also brew a steaming pot of tea to go along with the meat, bread, and cheese Carrick had packed before they'd left the manor house.

Carrick sat cross-legged before the fireplace, his teacup cradled in his massive hands, staring blindly at the flames. Her gaze traveled slowly across the width of his shoulders and then down the planes of his muscled back. The storm raging outside didn't come close to the one roiling inside her. Part of her wanted very much to cross the small room and settle in close beside Carrick, to ask him to hold her while they watched the flames die down in the hearth. Another part of her knew where that would lead and warned of the danger. Making love with Carrick would be tantamount to committing emotional suicide.

But it would be a glorious way to go. Glynis closed her eyes and begged her heartbeat to slow. She had to be sensible about this. She didn't love him. She appreciated his abilities as a horseman. She respected his desire to improve the lot of the Irish people and to fight against British injustice. She enjoyed his sense of humor and his company. She admired his sense of command, the sureness of his presence. She felt safe and secure and protected when with him. And Lord knew that it had been a very, very long time since she'd shared a bed with a man. It was entirely understandable that simply looking at Carrick des Marceaux made her want him. He was a handsome man, on this side of time or any other.

But he was heartbreak on the hoof and she knew it. If she let her needs and desires have free rein, she'd spend the rest of her life seeing his face in her dreams, would always hear his voice on the wind. Glynis frowned. Truth be known, he'd probably haunt her anyway. She'd never forget him, one way or the other. But remembering was a matter of degrees. As things now stood between them, her memories would be of what might have been. If she allowed herself to tumble headlong into his arms, into his bed, she would know exactly what she'd had and lost.

Of course, everything could be different if Carrick would just agree to come across time with her. It was the only logical thing for him to do. No man could reasonably refuse to save his own life. And if she were to offer herself as an inducement, well, it wouldn't be a truly noble sacrifice. Her own interests would be served in the bargain.

Glynis winced. God, she was becoming a real mercenary. Delilah had nothing on her. But then Delilah hadn't been trying to save Sampson's life. Glynis looked back at Carrick. Her pulse quickened the instant her gaze touched the ebony hair curled against his sharply honed cheekbones. Had Delilah wanted Sampson as much as she wanted Carrick des Marceaux? To hell with Sampson and Delilah, she groused. What good did it do to wonder about some long-dead biblical characters? Her problem was here and now. If she didn't find some sort of solution, she was going to explode.

"Take the bull by the horns, Glynis," she whispered.

Carrick turned at the sound of her voice. His gaze slowly caressed her face and his smile turned her blood to liquid lightning. "Did you say something?" he asked quietly.

Her heart lodged in her throat, Glynis smiled back and

answered, "I asked if you'd like some more tea. I think this has steeped long enough."

"Yes, please."

She took the chipped crockery pot from the table and carried it to the hearth. Hoping he didn't notice the trembling of her hand, she took the cup from him and filled it.

"I could get quite used to this, you know," he said, his fingers brushing hers as he took his cup back.

"To what? To having me wait on you?" Lord, had that sounded as breathless to him as it did to her?

"To sharing storms and late-night tea with you."

"Yeah, well." Oh, God. She was melting inside. Melting.

"Come sit with me, Glynis."

He didn't give her a chance to refuse. He took her hand and gently drew her down beside him on the warmed flagstones. Afraid that the words would stick in her throat if she tried to speak, Glynis silently leaned forward to place the teapot as close to the fire as she could. The diversion didn't take as long as she needed. Her heart was still racing madly when she settled beside him. Her breathing was still too quick for her to claim nonchalance.

And then he reached out and took a lock of her hair between his thumb and forefinger, his expression thoughtful.

"What was his name, Glynis? What was he to you?"

"Who?" she asked, startled.

"The one you've carefully avoided mentioning. The man you prefer not to think about but who haunts your memories anyway. Was he cruel to you?"

"Cruelty is one of those relative things, you know?" She managed a weak smile. "It sorta depends on who's telling the story."

"So who was he and what did he do to you?"

"You're not going to leave it alone this time, are you?" she answered softly, telling herself that she could handle this, that if she was going to ask Carrick to risk, she had to be willing to do the same. She took a deep breath and plunged ahead. "All right. His name was Jake Reimer and I was young and starry-eyed and I married him. It lasted two years officially, but the truth is it was pretty much over by the first-year mark."

"Did you love him?"

Usually thinking about that chapter in her life made her sad. But this time it felt like the story had been someone else's. Not hers at all. Was Carrick responsible for easing her connection to the past? Probably. She smiled at him with true appreciation. "In all honesty? No, not really. In hindsight I can see that I was more in love with the whole fairy tale of happily-ever-after. Jake was handsome, a damn fine cowboy with a big silver rodeo buckle. I'd known him all my life. He seemed like a good, practical choice."

"It doesn't sound as though there was any great passion between the two of you."

"You're sharp, Carrick. No, there was no grand passion."

"Why did you toss him out?"

"Now, what makes you think I did the tossing?" she asked, wondering how he'd known. "Jake could very well have tossed me out, for all you know."

His entire focus seemed to be on wrapping his finger with the strand of her hair and yet there was great insight when he said, "You wouldn't have married a stupid man in the first place and so that means he had to be smart enough to realize what he was losing. No. I say *you* sent him on *his* way. Why?"

"Jake . . ." Glynis tried to explain. "Where I come from it's pretty much expected that you'll marry in the rancher's circle. It keeps the land in the old families and outsiders out. Jake seemed to be the best pick of the ranchers' sons around my age."

"But Jake wasn't quite the prize you and everyone else thought. Correct?"

"Right again." There was little pain in admitting that. Not anymore. "No, Jake was no prize husband. He was wonderful in the courtship phase. I never had a clue that he was a snake in the grass until it was way past too late. No one knew."

"It's been my experience that men have three main choices when it comes to vices . . . drink, gambling, or women. Which was Jake's?"

"All three, actually," she answered easily. It felt good to let it all go. "But always in sequential order. He'd start with the drinking, then he'd begin to think he was the world's greatest gambler. When he won, the women liked the gifts he showered on them. When he lost, they liked to console him. Most of the time he lost. And he lost big. The debts were horrendous."

"And he expected you to pay them."

"It finally got to the point where I had to choose between risking the Rocking M or cutting Jake loose and taking the loss."

"So you tossed him out."

"He was already out. He had pretty much seen the writing on the wall when I refused to put his name on the deeds to the Rocking M. A couple of months before our second anniversary, Jake headed west to Las Vegas with a more . . . understanding woman. I divorced him in absentia."

"Do you regret it?" he asked, his voice soft.

"Divorcing him? No. Marrying him in the first place? Yeah." She laughed ruefully. "I don't think it says very much about my judgment when it comes to men."

He let the tendril slide slowly from his finger. "Has there been anyone since Jake?"

"Nope. But then it's kinda hard to meet anyone if you never leave the ranch." She had shared enough. "So which of the three vices is your favorite, Carrick des Marceaux?"

"Women," he answered absently, gently threading his fingers through her hair. His fingertips brushed her shoulder as he looked up and into her eyes. "I must say, though," he added quietly, "that I've recently developed a fondness for one particular stubborn, green-eyed, auburn-haired colleen."

Oh, God, here it was . . . the moment of truth. Her heart thundered. "Look, Carrick," she began honestly. "I don't know any way to approach things but straight on, so I'm just going to say what I think needs to be said, all right?"

One corner of his mouth quirked up. "Is my granting or withholding of consent going to make any difference?"

"No."

He went back to winding a tendril of hair about his finger. "Then say what needs to be said, Glynis Muldoon. What troubles you?"

"You do." At his arched brow she hurried to add, "More accurately, it's us. I . . . I . . . ." She swallowed. "Geesh, this is so hard. . . ."

He grinned and met her eyes, his shining with mischief. "By *us*, I assume that you refer to the attraction that we're each attempting to resist?"

"One of us is attempting with a bit more determination than the other," she shot back good-naturedly.

"And why is that, Glynis? I know it's not the fear of having your reputation tarnished. You don't care about that. And I sense that it's deeper than the regrets you have about Jake. He's in the past and you don't dwell there. Is it the possibility of bringing a bastard child into the world?"

"It's not that that's a minor concern."

"I agree. Would you feel better if I were to ask you to marry me?"

"Nah. Been there. Done that. Don't care to do it again anytime real soon. Besides, what good would that do, Carrick? You wouldn't be there for me or our child."

"Ah," he said slowly. He let her hair fall from his hand and sat back. His gaze went to the dying flames in the blackened hearth. "And at last we arrive at the central issue. It's the hangman's noose."

She wanted him back, wanted him touching her hair. The distance he'd put between them hurt and she felt suddenly alone. "Why must you be so fatalistic about this?" she asked, trying hard not to let her frustration show. "If your mother can transport me back through time, why couldn't she transport you as well?" She laid her hand on his forearm and leaned closer. "Come with me, Carrick," she pleaded. "Cheat the prophecy."

He quickly considered his choices. Telling her that he couldn't go because he was honor-bound to kill Cunningham and avenge Sean's death certainly wouldn't help matters. While it was the truth, he knew it wouldn't be a sufficient reason for Glynis. And it was only part of the larger truth anyway. It would have been cruel to let her think there was a way out of the labyrinth other than the one the Dragon's Heart had foretold. He didn't look away from the fire as he said matter-of-factly, "Other, more practical considerations aside, one can't alter destiny, Glynis. What is destined, will be."

"I can't accept that," she countered, tightening her hold on his arm as though by sheer physical force she could compel him to change his mind. "I refuse to roll over and surrender my free will. Why won't you even consider making an attempt?"

He looked back at the fire and asked, "And what would I do with my life in your time?"

"There would always be a place for you at the Rocking M," she promised. "You ride like you were born in the saddle. You can work cattle with the best of them. We're a good team."

Carrick heard the earnestness in her voice and knew that he'd see hope in her eyes if he dared to look at her. He didn't want to hurt her, didn't want to be the one who destroyed her dreams. As gently as he could, he said, "Glynis, I appreciate your offer, but I'd rather choose death on this side of time than live off charity on yours."

"Then fine. Don't work with me," she replied quickly. "You can build your furniture and sell it at exclusive shops and make a fortune. If you don't want to do that you can go to work at Wanda's Bait and Party Shop. I don't care. You'd be alive and that's all I want."

"You wouldn't want me in your life?" he asked without thinking. Even as he regretted having spoken, he felt her tense beside him.

"If you wanted to be, I'd like that," she said after a moment. "If you didn't, I'd accept it. It's a big world and there are lots of opportunities for a man like you. I wouldn't want to tie you down if you really wanted to be somewhere else. Or with someone else."

He chuckled quietly. "Glynis, no one else could possibly interest me in the utterly maddening, frustrating way you do."

His blood ran cold. Christ. Why had he said that? It was the truth, but it was too damn close to being a declaration of love. He rushed to repair the breach in his defenses.

"But that's neither here nor there. If I went with you, I'd be in a world I didn't know and didn't understand. I'd be the village idiot, standing about and gawking at the strange wonders all around me. No, thank you. I don't want to go through life with kind little old ladies patting me on the hand and assuring me that everything will be fine."

"God, you're a negative son of a bitch," she retorted, pulling her hand away. "Haven't you ever considered the fact that you might adjust quite well? Haven't I done fairly well adjusting to your time?"

"My world is far simpler than yours, Glynis," he replied patiently.

Color flooded her cheeks. "Give it up, Carrick," she said angrily. "Your world is remarkably like mine. Take away electricity, running water, and the combustion engine and what you have left isn't a nickle's worth of difference between the two."

"My mother's told me of some of the things that were common in the world she left behind. More importantly, I've seen how she thinks, Glynis. I see how she looks at her place in this world. She's different from all the other women in this time because her beliefs, her attitudes, were born and cultivated in another. It's more than material things that separate our times. I don't think like a man of yours, Glynis. I'd be a freak."

"Think about what you just said. You know about my world because your mother's told you. Do you honestly think that you could be your mother's son and not have some of her attitudes and beliefs? I'm telling you, Carrick, you'd do fine. Your mother being a time traveler gives you an edge. She's lived in two different centuries and, by virtue of being her son, you have the ability to do the same."

Suddenly he was tired of arguing with her. At that moment all he wanted to do was lie down with Glynis in his arms. He wanted to lose himself in the pleasure of making love with her. He turned slowly and reached out to cradle her face in his hands. Her green eyes widened and in the depths of them he saw both her uncertainty and her desire.

"Accept that our destinies lie on opposite sides of the portal, Glynis," he said softly. "Can we not make the best of the moments we have together?"

Her words came raggedly and tore at his heart. "You're asking me to make love with you and then to bury you."

He forced a smile. "And would that so be awful? It would be an expedient way to be rid of a tiresome lover."

"I'm not finding this the least bit amusing, Carrick," she cried, her eyes flashing as she pulled away from him. "Why the hell do you refuse to try?"

His own anger flared. "You think I should take the coward's way out?"

"Holster your pride, Carrick," she retorted, her hands balled into fists at her side. "It's getting in the way of your good judgment."

"And your refusal to accept that there are matters beyond your control is getting in the way of the happiness we could have together," he shot back.

She vaulted to her feet, her borrowed shirt slipping off one shoulder as she did. "You're impossible to reason with."

"As are you," he agreed, gaining his feet to face her squarely. "You're right in one respect, Glynis. We make a good pair, you and I."

"This is as frustrating as it is hopeless," she cried, flinging her arms out as she whirled about. "I'm going to bed."

He caught her by the shoulder and held her in place. "Glynis . . . please," he said, his anger slipping away and leaving him desperate to make her understand. "Can we not forget about all the tomorrows? Can we not take one moment at a time and be grateful for what it brings us?"

She turned to face him, the slow friction of her bare skin beneath his hand sending shivers of desire coursing through him.

"Only if I thought there would be a chance of slipping away together before tomorrow caught up with us."

The wanting was too much. "And if I were to agree to go with you?"

He saw the depth of her yearning, felt the tremor that passed through her. He didn't know whether he drew her to him or she stepped into his arms. She was there, her fingers tangled in his hair, her body flush against his, and that was all that mattered. He kissed her, slowly, deeply, as he slipped his hands beneath the hem of her coarse linen shirt. She was all satin smoothness and beckoning curves, and when she moaned softly at his touch his knees went weak. When her hands sought the planes of his back Carrick answered with a low cry of his own. Holding her close, his lips devouring hers, he lowered them to the flagstones, all of the world gone but for the woman in his arms.

He'd carry her to the bed in a little while, he promised himself. He wouldn't make love to her here on the hearth. But he would strip from her all her doubts while he could, where he could. She whispered his name and all conscious thought was lost in his raging desire.

He drew away, just far enough to look into her emerald eyes as he unbuttoned her shirt and pushed aside the fabric. Her eyes widened as he brushed his fingertips over the dark crest of her breast. It instantly hardened and it was everything he could do not to groan at the sight. "God, but you're beautiful," he whispered, struggling to keep his possession gentle. He cupped her in the palm of his hand and, with his thumb teasing the pebbled crest of her, bent down to lay a trail of feathery kisses from the corners of her mouth to the tip of her stubborn little chin and then down the long, slender column of her throat. Her fingers wound through the hair at his nape. She arched upward, pressing herself against his lips, against his hand. The cord of restraint frayed.

"I want you, Glynis."

"This . . . is . . . insane," she cried, her words coming on ragged breaths.

"Have I told you," he whispered, kissing his way across the creamy swell of her breast, "that I've seen the future? And that in it we're lovers?"

She put her hands on his shoulders and firmly pushed him back. "You have the Dragon's Heart with you?" she asked, suddenly wary.

Cursing himself for having brought up the matter, he lazily traced the curve of her jaw with a fingertip and answered, "The Dragon's Heart makes it simpler to see when you're first developing the gift. Once you have it, though, you simply see. Oftentimes the future shows itself in a smooth surface . . . still water, window glass, a mirror. Other times it is a flash before your eyes in a quiet moment. That's how it was with the vision of you and me."

"Was I crying?"

He smiled wickedly, remembering, "Actually, you seemed rather intent on enjoying yourself. And me."

"And these visions of yours . . . they're always accurate?"

"Yes. At least the portions of the future that I've been allowed to see. You don't always have the full event appear to you. You get snippets, enough to allow you to recognize that portion of events when it occurs," he provided patiently.

"Okay, let me see if I'm understanding this." She rolled out from under him and sat up, brushing her hair back off her shoulders with an impatient gesture.

Carrick rolled onto his back and groaned at the ceiling. She appeared not to care that she was tormenting him beyond the limits of endurance.

"You see the future but not a full-blown story," she pressed. "It's like opening a book in the middle and reading a scene. You have to figure out what led up to that point in the story and you make a best guess as to where the story's going after that. Right?"

Christ, maybe if he let her work it out she'd come back to him. Maybe she'd give him an opening and he could draw her back into his arms. With a resigned sigh, he answered, "Yes, Glynis, I suppose so."

"So you can't tell me on which day we'll become lovers, the circumstances that get us to that point, or the consequences. Am I getting this right?"

"Yes." With no small measure of frustration, he added, "But it sure as hell looks like it isn't going to be tonight."

"You can't tell me if the vision you've seen is even the first time we're lovers or the tenth, can you?"

Enough was enough. He couldn't take any more. "Glynis . . ."

"Do the same sorts of limitations apply to the vision you had of your own death?"

"Christ Almighty, Glynis," he said, wrapping his hand in

her shirttail and gently pulling her toward him. "You have the persistence of a bull terrier. Wouldn't you much rather—"

She braced her hands on either side of his shoulders and looked down into his eyes. A curtain of auburn silk fell about them both. "Answer the question, Carrick. Do the same sorts of limitations apply to the vision you had of your own death?"

"No," he said. Determined to be done with it once and for all, he grasped her by the shoulders and pushed her back. "I'll tell you all of it. I saw the crowds waiting under the noon sun, the scaffolding made of new wood. I saw the dead wagon and the horses stamping in their braces. I saw the granite headstone with the date and my name carved in it. I watched as they brought me down through the crowd, my hands bound behind my back. I watched as I climbed the stairs and took my place on the trapdoor. I saw the priest open his prayerbook and offer up words for my soul. I saw them put the noose about my neck and tighten it, saw them settle the coil into the hollow behind my left ear. I watched my mother cry, saw my father curse. I saw the trapdoor swing open beneath my feet. And then there was nothing."

Glynis pressed the heels of her hands to her eyes, trying to block out the image.

"I'm sorry, Glynis," he whispered, slipping his arms around her shoulders.

"Come with me," she begged, her hands twisted in the front of his shirt. "I'll teach you what you have to know about living in my time. I won't let you feel out of place. I'll take care of you. I promise."

She meant it. He knew that. He also knew she was falling in love with him. He couldn't let her do that. He couldn't hurt her that way. She sat before him, her shirt open, her hair cascading over her shoulders and lying softly against the curves of her breasts, her nipples still hard and budded from his touch. It was so tempting to take her, to deny the consequences and satisfy their desires. It would be so easy. He wanted to. And he knew he couldn't. Not unless she had walled her heart safely away from him.

"The sinner in me suggests that I should let you believe we can cheat my fate. The better man knows it's wrong to be anything but honest." The pain shimmering in her eyes cut him to the quick. "God, but I sometimes hate the high road."

"Carrick . . ."

"Sweet Glynis. Do you always fight so hard for your dreams?"

"And nine times out of ten I get what I want."

"This, darling, is the one out of ten. Accept it and take what you can from the time we have." He gave her his most seductive smile. "Would you deny a dying man his last pleasures on earth?"

"Low, Carrick. Low."

"But generally very effective," he replied, relieved to see the pain leave her eyes. "I'm amazed that you're still resisting me. I did mention the vision of us as lovers, didn't I?"

"You're a card-carrying letch. Have you no scruples at all?"

"Of course I do. If I had no scruples, I'd kiss you into forgetting everything but making love with me."

"But you're not going to?"

"Glynis, my sweet, there's nothing I want more than to carry you to that bed and spend the next week or so there."

"So why are you being so noble and self-sacrificing?"

"Because."

"That's not an acceptable answer."

All right, Glynis, he thought. *If it's honesty you want, so be it.* "Seeing the vision as often as I have over the years has prepared me a bit for my parents' sorrow. But I don't think I could face the hangman with any dignity if I had to see you crying as well." He let his hands slip from her shoulders and pulled the front of her shirt closed as he said, "When you can accept that we don't have forever, when you can be content with the todays we do have, then I'll make love with you, Glynis Muldoon. Not before."

"And you think I'll eventually accept it all."

"Aye. I know you will."

"When?"

He smiled wryly. "Soon, I hope. I don't think I can take much more of this."

"What if I told you right now that I understand and I won't fight it anymore? Would you make love to me?"

"You have the most beautiful eyes, Glynis. So expressive. Do you know what I see in them at this moment?"

She looked away. He reached up and cradled her face in his hands and gently brought her gaze back to his.

"I see you hoping that if you pretend to surrender, I'll come to love you enough to choose cowardice."

She jerked away from him as though he'd struck her. Her eyes blazed. "Have you ever considered that maybe it's cowardly to so blithely accept death? Dying's easy, Carrick. Anyone can do it. But finding a way to live and risking your pride by starting over again in a new life . . . that takes courage."

God. Would he ever be able to make her understand? "I'll not argue with you about this, Glynis," he said finally. "It's late and we've had a long day. You take the bed. I'll sleep here before the fire."

She scrambled to her feet. Stomping across the bare floor of the cottage, she grated, "Goddamn you, Carrick des Marceaux."

He gazed into the pulsing embers of the fire and quietly replied. "He did. Twice. The day I was born. And the day you came tumbling into my life."

18

Glynis willed the dream to stop. She didn't want to feel anymore, didn't want to deal with the maelstrom of her emotions. But the vision continued to unfold.

Carrick stood in the sunshine, the grass heads dancing in the breeze, brushing against his thighs. He laughed and opened his arms, his eyes full of mischief and promise. And then she was wrapped in his embrace, laughing and pulling his shirt from his breeches, showering him with kisses.

And then there was no more laughing. She saw Carrick's eyes, dark with passion and longing, felt his heart pounding against her. Their clothing lay scattered about them and he pressed her back into the cool damp earth, the heat of his flesh branding her.

She couldn't breathe, but it was all right. She wasn't afraid. She had Carrick and he had her. All was as it should be. She wanted this. He filled her, his possession fierce and forever. And she felt her desire taking her higher and higher.

And then he was gone and the wind, colder now, cut across her bare flesh. She scrambled to her feet, her heart racing. Panicked, she called for him. A sharp sound came from her right and she spun about.

The new wood of the scaffold stood stark against the gray sky. And from the rope hung Carrick's lifeless body, his hands tied behind his back.

Glynis woke up gasping and shaky. She lay in the middle of the bed, clutching the blanket with white knuckles, her heart racing. She had to get control of herself. She couldn't cry out. Even as she struggled, the image of Carrick hanging from the scaffold came to her again.

She bolted from the bed, nearly collapsing as she stood on trembling legs. She was shaking and only the back of a chair kept her crumpling to the dirt floor. Glynis stumbled around it and dropped onto the seat. Holding on to the edge of the table, she told herself that it had only been a dream. A god-awful nightmare. Carrick was all right. He wasn't dead.

But he wasn't there, either, she realized. She looked around the cottage. The blanket he'd slept in had been folded and placed on the chest at the foot of the bed. His half-rinsed clothes had been taken from the makeshift clothesline they'd rigged in the corner. The teapot from the night before sat near her on the table and she wrapped her hands around it. Cold. Her gaze went to the hearth. Only gray-white ash filled the opening.

Glynis went to the door. The sun shone in a brilliant blue, cloudless sky. The damp grass sparkled a deep green. Cattle stood scattered about the gentle slopes, quietly feeding. But Carrick was nowhere to be seen. Fighting back her panic, she scrambled around the corner of the cottage, making her way to the lean-to where they'd stabled the horses.

Bert had been brought outside and tethered so that he could stand in the sunlight and nibble at the grass. Molan wasn't with him. Glynis clung to the rough wooden frame of the doorway and peered inside. Molan was gone.

She wanted to cry. She wanted to scream. Somehow she found her way back to the cottage. Her hands shook as she poured herself a cup of cold tea. God, she'd never been this close to the edge before. She had to get a grip on her emotions.

She downed the contents of her cup without pause, wishing that it was whiskey she were drinking and not tea. She'd have given anything to be numb. Instead she was left afraid for Carrick and unable to ignore the ache he had left her with. She knew it for what it was. And she knew what it meant. Carrick was right. She would make love to him. She had to.

And, God help her, she also knew that no matter how insane it was, she loved him. The admission tore at her and shredded the last of her self-control. She buried her face in her hands. The tears came then.

She started and lifted her head, momentarily confused. Then she recognized the interior of the cottage and she realized where she was. She must have fallen asleep, emotionally exhausted. She straightened and winced as her muscles protested. God, how long had she been sleeping in the chair with her face cradled on her arms? It felt like it had been an eternity. A glance out the open door of the cottage told her that while she probably wasn't a candidate for this year's Rip Van Winkle Award, it had indeed been quite a while. The sun had moved well past its zenith.

Where was Carrick? Had he been back while she'd slept? The thought of him twisted the knot around her heart. No. She couldn't go down this road again. Not yet. It was time to do something, anything. If her butt stayed in the chair any longer she'd be rooted there forever.

She drank the last of the cold tea in her cup. Squaring her aching shoulders, she grasped the edge of the table and forced herself to her feet.

"Time to do what every good cowgirl does when the going gets rough . . . saddle up and ride until I'm too exhausted to think."

Carrick turned Glynis's muddy coat over so that the sun could dry the other side of it. He critically examined what remained of her battered felt hat. She'd probably have to throw it on the rubbish heap. It certainly didn't look like it could be reshaped into anything wearable. Knowing her, she'd probably keep it for no other reason than to use it to water her horse.

He had been thinking about his feelings for Glynis since he left her that morning. A single thought kept at him despite his resistance. He'd never wanted the gift of seeing. He'd never deliberately tried to call up visions of the future. The few glimpses he'd had of what lay ahead hadn't been at all to his liking. Searching for more had always seemed like an especially perverse endeavor.

But suddenly he wanted to take up the dangerous quest.

Maybe if he searched, he would find some reason to hope. He bent and carefully picked up Glynis's hat. For a moment he simply stood with it in his hands, feeling the sun's warmth on his back. Did he really want to do this? What if he found not hope, but even more devastating visions than those he'd already seen?

Making a decision, he strode along the well-worn cattle path that led down to the creek. The water level had dropped through the course of the day and, while still high, it was no longer the fierce torrent it had been the night before. He stooped and filled the crown of her hat with water.

He carefully averted his gaze until he'd settled himself into the grassy spot where he'd spent much of the day. Then, with the hat sitting before him, he closed his eyes and deliberately cleared his mind. Slowly, he opened his eyes and looked at the still water before him, not willing any specific vision to come but willing to accept whatever did.

It was there almost instantly, clear and sharp. His pulse quickened, but he kept his focus on the images in the water, concentrating on the details, trying to absorb everything he saw. Glynis was striding over rough cobblestones, the edges of her coat fluttering about her legs, the battered felt hat pulled low over her eyes. She walked with determination. He looked closer and his heart stopped. She concealed it well, but she held her rifle in her right hand.

And then the vision was gone, not a trace of it remaining.

Carrick blinked and shook his head. Looking back at the water again, he watched as another vision came. Glynis sat in a plain wooden rocking chair before a hearth he didn't recognize. As he watched she adjusted the blanket wrapped about her shoulders. Glynis smiled and gently stroked the cheek of the infant suckling at her breast. His child. He knew with absolute certainty that the child was his. He focused on Glynis's face and relief swept over him in an overwhelming wave. She was happy. She loved their son.

And then that vision went as had the first. Carrick closed his eyes and silently offered up his thanks. He now had a measure of the peace that had eluded him before. He reached for the hat, intending to spill the contents out across the ground, but something stilled his hand and compelled him to look one more time.

The cry stuck in his throat. He wanted to look away, wanted to fling the hat as far as he could. But he didn't. He forced himself to watch. Robert and Meyler were transporting his lifeless body in a wagon across the rolling green hills. Why were they stealing his body?

And then the third vision went as quickly as the others.

His happiness shattered, Carrick slowly tipped the hat, pouring the water out onto the grass. He had searched the future and found it. He and Glynis would be lovers; they would have their time together. And then he would die. And Glynis would raise their son without him.

He frowned, recalling the first of the visions. How did it fit into the sequence of events he'd seen? Bringing the images to the fore, he went through them one by one. He was fairly certain that he'd never seen the cobblestones she walked. He concentrated on the images of Glynis herself. Was she pregnant with his child? He couldn't tell. But the set of her jaw told him she was more determined than he'd ever seen her.

God help him if she was coming after him with that rifle of hers. The hangman would be cheated out of his wage. A rueful smiled lifted the corners of his mouth. Then again, the vision could be years into the future. He had no way of determining when Glynis would stride down that street with her rifle in hand. But, knowing Glynis, she wouldn't think twice about defending her child by force of arms. It was somehow reassuring to know that she wouldn't need him there to see their son safely through life.

Deciding that thought would be the most optimistic he'd manage, he gathered up Glynis's hat and coat. It was time to head back to the cottage. He didn't know exactly what he was going to say to Glynis when he got there. Nor did he know what he should do. He swung up onto Molan thinking that perhaps the smoothest course lay in letting her lead and trusting everything to work out in its own time.

The sun was near setting when he finally found her in the far end of the north pasture. She'd ridden as far as she could, as far as the fences of Horace's land would permit. As he brought his horse beside hers, he noted the lather flecking the animal's neck and knew that she'd also ridden as hard as she could.

She studied him in silence. Her eyes seemed swollen, her cheeks too pink to be from the sun and the wind.

"Are you all right, Glynis?"

She nodded and looked away. "All things considered, yeah," she answered quietly.

"Have you been crying?"

She shrugged. "Every now and then I throw myself a giant pity party. It passes and life goes on."

"Is there anything I can say or do? Or have I said and done enough already?"

She looked up at him again, a smile curving her lips. "You can be a sweetheart when you want to be, you know that?"

Her words staggered him. "I'd never deliberately hurt you, Glynis," he replied without thinking. Then, quickly changing the subject to something safer, he said, "Look what I found." Lifting her coat and hat from the pommel of his saddle, he handed them to her. "I don't know if the hat's salvageable, but I think the coat will be once it's washed."

Relief and happiness shone in her face as she took them from him. "Thank you! I thought they were lost forever. I owe you," she said softly.

Her happiness touched him. "The water's dropped quickly," he offered. "I think we can get across the stream without getting soaked." He turned back and smiled. "What do you say to a hot meal and a decent bed tonight?"

"Yours or mine?"

If he'd been standing, he'd have fallen over. "Glynis . . ."

"I've accepted, Carrick," she said, calmly. "It isn't the future I want, but I have to play the cards I've been dealt. I've looked at my choices and I've decided that I'll take what I can get and I'll take it for as long as I can have it."

He wanted her to be sure. "You had a miserable night and you couldn't have gotten much sleep. You might make a different decision once you're a bit more rested."

She shook her head. "It wouldn't make any difference. Now, if you've changed your mind, just say so."

He laughed, nudged Molan forward, and very deliberately gathered the front of her shirt into his fist, drawing her to him. She came without resistance, her hand slipping to the nape of his neck as his mouth closed over hers. He kissed her deeply. Only when she melted against him did he relent.

"Do you still think I've changed my mind?" he asked, setting her back in her saddle.

Her eyes were bright, her lips swollen. She smiled and answered shakily, "It would appear not."

"Then let's go home."

She nodded and tugged Bert's reins to move him away.

"Oh, and Glynis . . ." he said, catching her arm. He grinned. "My room. The bed's bigger. And the door has a sturdy bolt."

Glynis looked up at the night sky as they left the stables. "It's a beautiful night, isn't it?" she asked.

Carrick caught her hand and drew her to a halt on the stone walkway. "If you'd like, we could saddle fresh mounts and head back up to the cottage. No one but Eachann knows we've returned."

She laughed and placed her hand along the hard line of his jaw. "As tempting as I find the idea, Carrick, I'm even more tempted by the thought of a hot bath and clean clothes."

"Don't I figure into the temptations somewhere?"

"Oh, somewhere, I suppose," she teased, her heart light.

"If I kissed you, would it help you to remember?" he asked, drawing her closer. "I'd be happy to oblige."

"Decency compels me to tell you that you're not alone."

Carrick swore under his breath and released her. Stepping away, he turned toward his cousin, who stood framed in the light spilling through the kitchen doorway. "You look like hell, Robert."

Glynis stifled a chuckle and started up the stairs. "Hello, Robert. How are you?"

"God will get you both for leaving me here to deal with this. I'm sick of playing musical beds."

"Ah, now, there's an interesting story to be told," Carrick observed, coming up the steps behind her. "It's a damn good thing Muldoon was out with me or you might have some hasty reassurances to offer."

Robert backed into the kitchen and shook his head wearily. "The storm awakened the children, as Miss Muldoon predicted it would. Horace and Saraid's bed got so crowded at one point that I finally carried Saraid into my room so she wouldn't be accidentally jostled. We won't even discuss how many of the children came down sick while you were gone."

He ran his fingers through his disheveled hair. "Truth be told, I'm not sure I can remember. It was a long night and today hasn't been one bit better. The entire household staff's down with the malady. If you want baths and something to eat, you're on your own. As for beds, I can't tell you who's sleeping where except for Saraid, who's still in my room."

"Poor Robert," Glynis said, laying her hand on his arm. "And so you now find yourself without a place to lay your own head for the night."

"I'll find something somewhere. Maybe the barn. I'm too damn tired to be picky. Did you get the cattle moved to higher ground?"

"Aye," Carrick answered. "And well we did, too. The streams were rising quickly even as we reached the western pastures. Some of the calves could have been swept away. Muldoon decided to play hero for a stranded calf and nearly got herself killed."

Robert examined her critically. "Were you injured?"

"I'm fine, Robert," she assured him, turning about for his inspection. "Just a scratch and probably a few bruises. Your cousin rescued me quite handily."

"Oh?" Robert turned to Carrick. "Handily, huh?"

"It was a helluva storm, Robert," Carrick rebutted.

"Well, it seems to have blown itself out," Robert observed, gracefully accepting the abrupt change in topics. "Tonight should be fairly quiet in that respect. I can't promise that we won't have more sick children, though. God, it's been grizzly." He stifled a yawn with the back of his hand. "Would you think me terribly ill-mannered if I begged for some sleep now?"

Glynis shook her head. "Don't think twice about it, Robert. Go on and have sweet dreams. If anything needs to be done, we'll take care of it."

He went out the back door, saying, "Call me if you need me. Third stall on the right."

He'd no more than stepped around the corner and out of view than Carrick's arms came around her from behind. Glynis laughed and settled back against him.

Nuzzling the curve of her shoulder, he said, "I suppose only a complete cad would carry you upstairs right now."

"You suppose quite correctly, sir."

He burrowed his face beneath the fall of her hair and nibbled at her neck. "Which do you want first, food or your bath, milady?"

Desire said to hell with everything but the ripples of warmth Carrick sent through her. Glynis closed her eyes and with her last shred of willpower offered to fix a meal if he'd see to their bathwater. It was minutes later when Carrick finally wandered off to heat their water.

He came down the main stairway and dumped the load of linen atop the three other sets he'd already left in the corner of the foyer. God was one mean son of a bitch, he decided, heading into the parlor to see how Glynis was faring.

He froze just across the threshold, his heart twisting. Glynis sat on the settee, Rachel's head on her lap. As he watched, Glynis brushed the hair from the child's forehead and then smoothed the linen of the small nightshirt to cover the sleeping child's feet. There was a serenity in her expression that caught his breath and made him ache with longing.

What he wouldn't give to have forever with Glynis Muldoon. He put the thought aside and reminded himself that his destiny had been set long ago. He could not escape his fate. And he couldn't . . . no, he wouldn't let Glynis see his fear and regrets make a coward out of him. He wanted her to be able to tell their son that his father had died with dignity and courage. He wanted his son to be proud of him.

The clock on the far side of the room chimed the third hour of the morning, startling Glynis from her contemplations. Her gaze met his and held it. "How did the simple syrup work upstairs?" she asked quietly.

"It had the same effects as it seems to have had down here. Has she been asleep long?"

"Just a few minutes. You look tired."

"So do you. Shall we carry her upstairs and tuck her in?"

Glynis shook her head and stroked Rachel's dark brown tresses. "I think it's probably better to let her sleep where she is. Poor thing's been so sick. And I suspect we've got another bout left to go before it's over and done with. You go on upstairs and get some sleep. We'll be fine."

"No," he replied, settling himself into the corner of the sofa. Wrapping his arms around Glynis's shoulders, he drew her back against his chest. "I promised myself I was going to sleep with you in my arms tonight, Glynis Muldoon. And I'm going to, one way or the other."

Glynis felt the beat of his heart against her as the warmth of his body enveloped her. Nothing on earth had ever felt so good, so right. She snuggled closer and sighed when his arms tightened about her. He laid a gentle kiss on top of her head and everything inside her melted.

"I love—" She stopped herself, instinctively knowing that Carrick couldn't bear the truth. "I love it when you're like this," she said, covering as best she could.

He brushed his cheek against her hair. "Go to sleep, sweetheart," he murmured.

She relaxed, relieved to have successfully avoided what could well have been a confrontation. They'd had far too many of those. It was time to move on to better times, to make better memories.

Her breathing was slow and even when Carrick brushed his fingertip across her lips. "Don't love me, Glynis," he whispered. "For God's sake, don't give me your heart. I'll only break it."

19

Carrick awoke to a hand firmly shaking his shoulder and looked up into his cousin's smiling face.

"Comfortable, ol' boy?"

He groaned and gingerly shifted his stiff limbs. Glynis stirred against him and murmured in her sleep. Desire shot through him.

"Shall I take Rachel upstairs?" Robert asked.

"What time is it?"

"Half past six," he supplied quietly, sliding his arms beneath Rachel and gently lifting her from Glynis's lap. "Everyone seems to be coming back to life around here. It's likely to get a bit noisy fairly soon. They've got to make up for two days of lost chaos."

Carrick rolled his head and worked his shoulders while he made some sound that he hoped passed for an acceptable comment on the news.

"What would you think of putting Rachel on the lounge in Miss Muldoon's room?" Robert asked, considering the flight of stairs leading to the family level of the house. "The staff hasn't quite gotten on their feet and I doubt there's any other place to put her yet."

Carrick carefully slipped out from under Glynis without waking her, and stretched his back and legs. His gaze went to her face, relaxed and peaceful in sleep. Carrick closed his eyes, willing his blood to cool and searching for inner strength.

"Did you hear me?"

"I heard you," Carrick answered. "Put Rachel in Glynis's bed. She won't be using it."

"Carrick."

He heard the censure. "I'm not in the mood for a lecture on morality, Robert. Save your breath."

"Christ Almighty, Carrick," Robert whispered harshly. "Have you finally taken full leave of your senses?"

"No. Quite the contrary. I've finally come to them."

"You can't do this to her."

"Not only can I, but I will," Carrick replied, bending down to gently scoop Glynis into his arms. Her hand came up to rest over his heart as she curled into him, her sleep unbroken. He started toward the stairs and turned back. "And Robert . . . if you come to my door after I've closed it, I'll shoot you through it," he warned.

"Aye," his cousin groaned. "At least promise me that you'll give her a chance to say no; that you won't seduce her against her will."

Carrick stifled a rueful chuckle and met his cousin's troubled eyes. Softly he replied, "No one can make Glynis Muldoon do anything against her will, Rob. No one has the right to even try. Especially me."

Robert stared at him for a long moment and then, a slow smile brightening his face, he nodded. "You love her, don't you?"

Carrick's jaw clenched, but he said calmly, "Rob, unless you're yelling fire, don't disturb us. We'll be out when we're damn good and ready. And you can pass that on to Saraid as well. I don't give a damn about her delicate sensibilities."

Leaving Robert to follow with Rachel, he carried Glynis up the wide curved stairway and down the hall to his room. Gently kicking the door closed behind him, he carried her to his four-poster bed and gingerly deposited her atop the goose-down comforter. Without pause, he spun about and moved back to the door. The bolt shot home with a resounding click.

He stood for a moment with his forehead pressed against the oaken jamb, feeing his heart race and listening to the labored rasp of his breathing. Carrying Glynis hadn't taxed him and he knew it. Still, his limbs quivered as though he'd run a hundred miles. What in the name of all the Irish saints was wrong with him?

Frustrated, he went back to the bed and the delectable woman he'd just placed in it. She lay with her head on his pillow, her auburn hair fanning out around her head like a rich satin sheet. A small smile touched the corners of her lush lips and he found himself wondering what secrets she knew, what amusements she saw in her dreams. If he took her in his arms right now, would she awaken and share them with him?

Would she draw him into her arms and make love to him with fierce abandon? Did she need and want him with the same kind of aching desperation that he did her? What if she didn't?

Carrick ran his fingers through his hair. God, he was a wreck. He hadn't felt this mixture of fear and anticipation since his first foray into the realm of seduction. In his present state of mind, he'd rush things and make a bumbling fool of himself.

He swore under his breath. He wasn't ready for this. Perhaps his doubts would ease if he were to sleep for a while. Perhaps he'd awaken with a calmer, more certain frame of mind. Three hours had been all he'd managed on the settee in the parlor. And the night before had been too full of dreams to give him any real rest.

He pulled off his boots and eased himself down on the bed beside Glynis, taking care not to touch her. The scent of her filled his senses. The warmth of her wrapped around him and threatened his tightly reined control. With his teeth clenched, he moved to the edge of the feather mattress and rolled over, burying his face in the pillow. He willed himself to think of other matters, his too-tense body to relax. As he finally drifted off, his last thought was that it was a goddamned shame that he couldn't smother himself.

In the dream she lay in a patch of afternoon sunlight, the ground softly cradling her back, the sun warm on her skin. Carrick lay beside her, the scent of him teasing her with every breath she took. And then he rolled to his side and gazed down at her for a moment before lifting a tendril of her hair and drawing the ends gently over the swell of her breast. Glynis smiled and—

"I didn't mean to wake you."

The dream slowly faded as she opened her eyes. "Don't apologize," she whispered, cradling the hard line of Carrick's stubbled jaw. God, he was a handsome man. His eyes sparkling with deviltry, he drew the strand of her hair across her breast again, just above the lacy edge of her bodice.

"And I'll give you a half-hour to stop that," she murmured, hoping he wouldn't actually take that long.

"God, you're beautiful, Glynis Muldoon. May I kiss you?"

She smiled, tracing an invisible line down his throat and into the opening of his shirt with a fingertip. "Since when do you ask for permission?" She neatly undid the first button.

"I'm trying to be on my best behavior," he answered, his voice suddenly thick. "I want you to think well of me."

"If it's all the same to you," she replied, undoing two more buttons, "I'd rather not do any thinking."

He smiled and cocked a dark brow. "What would you like to do instead?"

"Feel."

"I might be able to do something about that."

"I kinda thought you might." She slipped her hand under his shirt and ran her fingers through the dark curls matting his chest. His gaze caught and held hers as his fingertips traced a teasing path across her breast.

"May I kiss you now?"

"Impatient, are we?"

"Good God, Glynis," he whispered, shaking his head. "You have no idea."

"Oh, I think I do," she murmured back, sliding her hand under the waistband of his trousers. From palm to fingertip, she slowly traced the hard length of him. Once. Twice.

He closed his eyes, taking a deep breath. "Jesus, woman," he swore raggedly. "Do that again and I won't care what you think of me."

"Promises, promises."

And then he finally kissed her, his possession of her mouth both desperate and gentle. And more thoroughly intoxicating than any kiss she had ever received. She moved into his embrace, her legs twining with his as she marveled at the incredible heat he sent through her. She felt the steady beat of his heart against her, felt the heavy ache low within her. Somewhere in the back of her mind a weak voice protested, saying that she wanted too much, too fast, and that unless she maintained some sense of control, she'd end up making a first-class fool of herself.

And then Carrick began to deliberately work his way down the line of hooks holding her dress closed and she stopped thinking. His fingers were quick and adept at the task, his ragged breathing matching the tempo of her own as he pressed kisses at the corners of her mouth, on her eyelids, along the curve of her jaw, and into the hollows behind her ears. Her senses reeled before the relentless onslaught. And then Carrick drew back, looking at her seriously.

" 'Tis the point of no return we've reached, Glynis," he whispered, sliding his hands from behind her and resting them on her shoulders. "Speak now and I'll stop."

She couldn't have answered had she known what to say. Reaching out, she silently pulled his shirttail from his trousers. His eyes darkened as he drew in a long, slow breath.

He didn't move, didn't make a sound until she began to unbutton his trousers. Then, with a low moan, he slid the dress from her shoulders, lowered his head, and laid a searing trail of kisses along the length of her throat and down into the valley between her breasts.

Never had she surrendered to feeling with such fierceness, such abandon. Somehow, her dress was discarded. Somehow, Carrick's shirt and trousers disappeared with it. A heady sense of freedom washed over her as she caressed the hard planes of his shoulders and back, as her hands stroked the corded muscles of his hips and thighs.

" 'Tis unfair," Carrick murmured, nuzzling into the curve of her neck, his fingers slipping just beneath the edge of the thin chemise gathered across her breasts. "Women have more layers to lose than men."

"Definitely," she managed to reply, regretting that her chemise, petticoat, and stockings hadn't evaporated along with her dress. She eased away from him, placing a kiss at the corner of his mouth and whispering, "Give me a second to even things up."

He laughed softly and caught her about the waist, gently pinning her beside him on the bed. Leaning over her, mischief glimmering in his eyes, he softly said, "No assistance is required, my love. Unless, of course, you want to deprive me of my own simple pleasures."

"I wouldn't dream of it."

"What do you dream of, Glynis Muldoon?"

She heard the erotic promise in his voice. She moistened her dry lips. "I'm afraid that my dreams are rather mundane."

"Do you know what I've been dreaming of the past few weeks?"

"No. What?"

"Doing this to you." He lowered his head and hotly suckled her breast through the thin fabric of her chemise. A bolt of pure desire shot through her. She gasped and arched her body, pressing herself to his lips with a quiet moan as she threaded her fingers through his ebony hair.

"And this," he added, releasing her breast and drawing back as he slipped his hand beneath her petticoat and up the length of her leg. She smiled when he plucked loose the ribbon of her garter. She quivered with anticipation as his hand glided still farther up and his fingers traced small circular patterns over the bare flesh of her thigh.

"And this, too," he whispered, watching her as his fingers brushed lightly over her curls.

She closed her eyes and shivered with delicious pleasure. His fingers trailed down her other thigh, sending yet another wave of glorious heat through her as he undid the second garter as deftly as he had the first.

"And, of course, this," he said huskily, lowering his head to suckle her breast again as his fingers once more slipped into the damp curls at the apex of her thighs.

Carrick heard her whispered pleas for release, felt the edge of her desire peaking beneath his deliberate seduction. He held his own burgeoning desires in check, determined to undo her composure as slowly and inextricably as he undid what remained of her clothing. She would never be able to claim that she had held back even the smallest measure of herself. She would be his to the center of her soul. She would be his forever and whatever man came after him would always make love to her in his shadow.

He removed her stockings and her petticoat, his hands sliding over the satin softness of her flesh, exploring and teasing, making her gasp and arch with breathless cries. He reassured her wordlessly, his lips pressing wet, taunting kisses in the wake of his fingertips and always returning to the tightly budded crests straining against the fabric of her chemise.

He lifted his head and gazed down at her, at his Glynis Muldoon. Her hair was a tangled auburn mass streaming out across his pillow, wreathing her face and shoulders in a shimmering halo. She lay with her eyes closed, her lashes thick and dark against her cheekbones. Her dark lips were parted and swollen from his kisses. God, but she was more than he'd ever dreamed. More than he'd ever known love-making could be. He wanted her with a hunger that no man could possibly survive. He had no intentions of denying either one of them for very much longer.

He slowly pulled the ribbon that held the chemise gathered across her breast and then smoothed the finely woven fabric down and out of his way. His gaze caught on the angry red scar on her shoulder. Regret flooded over him and he wondered if he had the right to take a chance on a scaring her heart as deeply.

He touched her shoulder gently, saying, "I'm sorry for this, Glynis."

"Don't be."

"I'm going to make love to you, Glynis Muldoon," he promised softly.

She nodded, her green eyes brilliant, and it came to him. He was in love with her.

Glynis saw the fear flicker in his eyes in the same instant that she felt the staggering trip of his heartbeat where their bodies touched. Her own heart lurched in response and her desperation made her bold. She reached for him, her gaze holding his as her hands glided down his chest and over the corded muscles of his abdomen.

He drew a harsh breath as she took him into her hands, the sound strangling in his throat.

"Make love to me, Carrick," she challenged him. "Make me remember this night forever."

"Forever," he agreed, moving over her and lowering his lips to hers.

He filled her with maddening slowness. Glynis moaned, overwhelmed by the sensation. She closed her eyes, shutting away all but this one heady reality. Never, never had it felt like this. So good. She gasped and tightened about him as he slowly withdrew; raggedly whispered in grateful assent when he drove to fill her again. With her legs wrapped around his narrow hips, she arched to meet each stroke, her desire intensifying with each thrust.

She abandoned herself to the breathless desire, feeling it building up from deep inside of her. It drew her upward, a delicious rapture that spiraled through her body and catapulted her into a wondrous universe.

Her passion ignited his own with fiery intensity. There was nothing beyond their union in that moment, nothing beyond the promise of now and the lure of sweet oblivion. He buried himself deeper and harder, and with a shuddering cry filled her with every measure of his heart and soul.

The crest broke and she was dying the sweetest, deepest of deaths, fading away with the stars, gently drifting downward. Sated. She wanted it to last forever, their bodies still joined, their passion easing.

The sound came with the subtlety of a dynamite explosion. Someone was standing in the hallway and pounding on the bedroom door. Carrick had frozen above her. His cursing instantly brought her awareness back to the bed and the intimate tangle of their limbs. But the magic in which they'd been cocooned had been shattered beyond repair. She fought back her disappointment, reassuring herself that there would be another time for them.

"Carrick!" Robert shouted from the hall.

Carrick closed his eyes in frustration. He lowered his head and against her lips whispered, "Ignore him, sweetheart. He'll go away."

"It's not a fire but damn close to it," Robert continued from the other side of the door. "Your parents are here!"

Carrick swore again and threw himself onto his back

beside her. He glared up at the ceiling, his chest rising and failing like a long-distance runner. Glynis wanted to reach out, to touch him and reassure him that nothing had been lost. Even as she lifted her hand, Robert called again from the hallway.

"Do you hear me, Carrick?"

He rose onto his elbows and directed a murderous look at the door as he barked, "I hear you, goddammit! Now go away!"

They heard the soft thuds of Robert's footsteps as he left, and then only the sound of their uneven breathing broke the silence stretching between them.

"I better go find some clothes," Glynis said quietly, easing off the bed and retrieving her dress from the carpet.

"Glynis . . ." Carrick said, scrambling across the mattress. He wrapped her in his arms and drew her against him. God, he was so warm, so strong. It would be easy to let him carry her away, back to the world where only the two of them had existed.

"Grandmama! Grandpapa!"

"Rachel seems to be feeling better," Glynis observed quietly.

"Don't go," Carrick murmured in her ear. "We don't have to present ourselves downstairs right away. The children will occupy them for a while and no one will think anything if we tarry for a few minutes."

"No, Carrick," she said, gently but earnestly pushing against his chest and putting a few precious inches between them. "Later. Please. I'm going to have a hard enough time facing your parents as it is. Please don't make this any more difficult for me."

His studied her for a long moment before he leaned down, placed a light kiss on her lips, and then gently set her at arm's length. "Don't you ever doubt how much I care about you, Glynis Muldoon. I wouldn't let any woman but you walk away from me at this point."

She managed a weak smile for him. "I'll come back."

He smiled in return, the expression caressing. "You damned well better, Glynis." Tracing her lower lip with the pad of his thumb, he added, "Or I'll come find you."

"That might be kinda interesting."

"At the very least," he countered, his grin holding a wicked promise.

He leaned against the doorjamb and watched Glynis pad down the hall, her dress wrapped around her shoulders like a shawl and concealing most of her body from all but his memory. She paused when she opened the door to her room and looked back at him. Her gaze traveled down the length of him and as his body responded, an appreciative smile lifted the corners of her mouth.

"It's not too late to come back, Glynis," he called softly.

"Go put some clothes on," she laughingly retorted, stepping into her own room. A second later she poked her head out. "Don't wait for me. I'll meet you downstairs. Okay?"

"How will I recognize you?" he teased.

Even with the distance between them he could see the spark of mischief in her eyes as she glanced down the hall. Still, he wasn't the least bit prepared when she stepped from her doorway absolutely, beautifully naked. He might have remained casually propped against the door frame, his arms folded over his chest and one ankle crossed over the other, but there was nothing casual about how the parts in between responded to the sight of her.

Smiling innocently, she half-turned to give him a tempting view of a perfectly rounded hip and said, "Imagine this in a rose brocade."

"If you don't stop that, the only thing you're going to be in are white linen sheets. *My* white linen sheets."

She grinned impishly, then winked and waved. "See ya."

He didn't return to his room until he heard the bolt on her door slide home. He calmly kicked his door closed behind him and went to the washstand.

The chill water quickly cooled his hands as he lifted the pitcher to above his head. It wasn't nearly cold enough when he turned the vessel upside down and drenched himself.

20

Glynis paused at the base of the stairs, her palms moist. Part of her wanted to rush headlong into the parlor, throw herself around the ankles of the oldest woman there, and plead to be sent home on the next available magic spell. It wasn't the lack of dignity that stopped her from acting on impulse. Rather, it was her love for Carrick and her hope for their future together.

She could see him through the wide arch of the parlor. He leaned against the liquor cart, his casual pose the same as when she'd last seen him. He wore clothes now, of course, she amended, smiling. And he'd apparently splashed about in the washbasin after her departure; his raven-dark hair was still damp, the ends curling softly against his collar.

God only knew when she and Carrick would find time to be alone again. With a household this big, this busy, it might be close to Christmas. Damn Robert and his miserable sense of timing. Damn Carrick's parents for arriving when they had.

Even as Glynis considered how to best make her entrance into the parlor, a tall, stately woman crossed to the beverage cart. She glanced toward the foyer and for an instant her blue-eyed gaze met Glynis's. A small smile touched the corners of the woman's mouth as she looked away. Glynis groaned. The woman was obviously Carrick's mother and she'd caught her son's lover standing at the base of the stairs like some lost soul.

Alanna des Marceaux obviously said something to Carrick

because he suddenly set aside his glass. Glynis met his eyes as he came to her, silently begging him to find her some means of escape. She'd never so desperately wanted to be rescued as she did at that moment.

"You look gorgeous," he said, taking her hands in his and raising them to his lips. "There's no reason to be frightened, Glynis," he whispered with a reassuring smile. "They haven't bitten anyone in a long time."

"What am I going to say to them? What if they think I'm a blithering idiot?"

"They won't. Just be yourself, Glynis. Say what you're thinking."

"Oh, yeah. Right," she countered, arching a brow. "Hello, Mr. and Mrs. des Marceaux. As much as it's a real pleasure to finally meet you, I think I'd much rather take you son upstairs now and spend the next twenty-four hours or so making love to him. Catch you at dinner tomorrow night?"

Carrick grinned. "Well, perhaps that much honesty wouldn't be a particularly good idea right at the start. Not that I'd fight being hauled away if you decide to do it."

"Geez, Carrick. I'm usually much more together than this. I'm not sure I can pull this off with any finesse."

He lifted her hands to his lips again. "I won't leave your side until you're ready to be rid of me. I promise." He pressed a long, lingering kiss to the back of each.

"That's a double-edged sword, Carrick," she replied dryly. "You're rather distracting, you know."

He smiled in his splendidly wicked way. "Good." Then he turned and escorted her through the arched doorway.

"Mother, Father," he began, drawing her before the woman with the dark blond hair and a man who was an older version of himself. "May I present Miss Glynis Muldoon. Glynis, this is my mother, Lady Alanna des Marceaux. And my father, Lord Kiervan Marceaux."

She managed to nod at the appropriate parent at the appropriate time and say, "It's a pleasure to make your acquaintance," without stammering or choking on the words.

"The pleasure is entirely ours, Glynis," returned Carrick's mother with a smile.

"Indeed," said Carrick's father, his eyes sparkling the same way Carrick's did when amused. "My wife has been telling me that you're quite lovely. I see now that she spoke with her usual sense of understatement."

She's been telling? Glynis felt a prickle along the nape of her neck, but she managed to calmly ask, "But how did you know what I look like?"

Alanna des Marceaux offered her a small shrug and another of her smiles as she answered, "The Dragon's Heart has given me several glimpses into your time among us."

The possibilities gave her pause; most of them were not fit for parental viewing. Glynis swallowed hard. "Glimpses of what exactly?"

"I assure you that I looked away when it was best to do so. There are some things a mother just shouldn't know."

"Oh, God." *Someone can shoot me now.* "Where's a British patrol when you need one?" she wondered aloud.

Carrick laughed softly and squeezed her hand. His father fought a smile as he cleared his throat and said, "Ladies, I do believe that this is the point at which we should leave you to your own conversations. We'll be out and about with the children. If you need any manly input into your discussions, you have but to call." He slipped an arm around his wife's waist and pressed a kiss to her cheek. Then he offered her a mocking bow. "We'll be at your service."

"We'll call you for dinner," Carrick's mother replied wryly. "Try not to get into any trouble."

Carrick's grip on Glynis's hand tightened and she felt his indecision. Knowing that she couldn't gracefully avoid a one-on-one with his mother forever, she turned and gave him a brave smile. "It's all right. Go with your father and do manly man stuff. I'll see you at dinner."

"All right," he agreed. "But do me a favor, will you?" He crossed to the beverage cart with two long strides and just as quickly returned with his whiskey glass. "Finish this for me," he said, pressing it into her hand. "It'd be a crime to let it go to waste."

He knew just how nervous she was. She could have thrown her arms around his neck and kissed him.

He winked, and then kissed her cheek, as his father had his mother's.

"I owe you, Carrick," she whispered in his ear.

"Yes, you do," he quietly replied before stepping away, his blue eyes twinkling.

They were still sparkling when he threw her one last look before following his father out of the parlor. Glynis watched him go and then took a large sip of her whiskey. Long seconds passed before Carrick's mother broke the silence.

"Are you finding this as awkward as I am?" she asked, crossing to beverage cart and retrieving her own drink.

"God, yes," Glynis admitted, somewhat relieved. She turned to face the other woman. "I'm sorry, but I have no idea what to say to you, Lady des Marceaux."

"Well, let's dispense with that Lady des Marceaux stuff right off the bat, shall we? Call me Alanna. I can't tell how wonderful it is to have another woman of my own time to talk with for a change."

"Carrick tells me that you came from Durango in 1997."

"Yes. I was a CPA engaged to the wrong man. A decent man, mind you, but the wrong one for me. I've been much happier here than I ever would have been back in Durango as Mrs. Bill Boyer."

She considered Glynis. After a moment she said, "I'm afraid that the Dragon's Heart hasn't shown me much of your circumstances prior to your having been brought through time. Tell me about yourself, Glynis."

"There really isn't all that much to tell," she replied with a shrug. "I'm from the Kansas Flint Hills; the fourth generation of Muldoons to ranch the Rocking M. I never knew my mother and my father was killed in a plane crash when I was seventeen. I have an ag business degree from K-State. I was married once . . . to the wrong man for me."

"You have no children from the marriage?"

"None. Trust me. That was the one smart thing I did in the whole two years."

"What year did you come from, Glynis?"

"It was early April 1997 when Saraid accidentally brought me here."

"Amazing," Alanna said softly. "Only a few days separated our coming through time. And yet almost thirty years passed between our arrivals." Carrick's mother looked apologetic. "I'm sorry that my daughter brought you here against your will. Saraid always has the best of intentions with magic, but she's just the pits when it comes to actually doing it. I hope she's apologized to you."

"Oh, she has. And, in all honesty, it really hasn't been all that bad." Glynis took another sip of her whiskey. "I'll admit that I didn't have the best attitude when I first came through, but things have changed a bit since then and I've done some adjusting."

"Glynis," the other woman said quietly, her gaze direct, "I can't tell you how very happy I am that you've come into my son's life. He's needed you for a long time."

Alanna watched the play of emotions across Glynis Muldoon's features. Relief. Hope. And then, in rapid succession, caution and determination. Alanna smiled. Carrick had found himself a woman of considerable substance. His Glynis was not only intelligent, she was strong and resilient and, from the look of her at that moment, one hell of a fighter. Yes, Carrick had chosen well. Glynis was the perfect woman for him. Unfortunately, Alanna knew, Carrick wouldn't readily admit it even if he knew it. He was as dense about these things as his father had been.

Glynis began to pace. Alanna said nothing, watching the younger woman work through her own thoughts. She guessed that Glynis Muldoon was trying to decide how to best go about moving their conversation from superficial pleasantries to the nitty-gritty plane of honest communication. And it wasn't going to be long in coming, either.

"Look," Glynis said suddenly, turning to face her. "Can I say something before I implode? Normally, I'm a bit better mannered and can wait for a smooth segue into a topic, but—"

"Of course, Glynis," Alanna replied graciously. "Say whatever you need to say. There's no need to mince words with me."

"I love Carrick."

"I can tell."

"I want him to love me."

"He does."

"Not enough."

Alanna gave Glynis two points for directness, a half-dozen for loving her son. She gave her a cartload for frustration. The young woman did indeed look as though she might have a meltdown at any moment. Deciding that the release would come all the sooner if she kept silent, Alanna met the green-eyed gaze searching her own and arched a brow.

"Okay, to hell with any attempt at finesse. Here's the whole ball of wax. Carrick tells me that you can transport me back to where I belong. If that's true, I want him to come with me."

"And he refuses to consider doing so," Alanna finished with a nod of understanding.

"Yes." She resumed her pacing.

"If it's any consolation, Glynis, I haven't fared any better with him, either."

"You've offered to send him across time, haven't you?" Glynis asked. At Alanna's nod, she sighed. "I figured you would have. Why won't he go? Why does he insist on dying?"

How many times over the years had she wrestled with these very questions? Alanna wondered. How many times had she failed to find answers? Perhaps this time it would be different.

"There are a number of reasons," Alanna began. "The primary consideration has to do with who Carrick is. He and Kiervan are both cut from the same cloth when it comes to seeing something through to the end. Neither one of them has the ability to see how things might have changed along the course.

"Second, but of no less importance, is the fact Carrick has to want to go. Magic will not work against a will set in another direction."

"I didn't want to come here, but Saraid managed to bring me anyway. How did she do that?"

"I suspect that a large part of the answer lies within you."

"Me?"

"Our magic is earth-based, Glynis. Those with a special affinity with the earth make the best conduits for magic. At the moment Saraid brought you across, were you more keenly aware of natural forces than usual?"

"Well, yes, I guess I was. It was a helluva storm and I was out in the open. I remember thinking that I had to get out of it. And fast."

"Then we have our explanation. Your awareness and desire unwittingly mirrored Saraid's at the same precise moment." Lady Alanna smiled. "There's good news in that. You'll be more easily sent back through the portal to where you belong."

Glynis nodded, her thoughts going to what had become a borderline obsession. "But if I can be so neatly zapped around in space and time, can't you just wave a wand over Carrick while he's sleeping and send him somewhere? Surely in his heart he wants to live. Wouldn't that be enough?"

"Although it would be exceedingly difficult and not without risks, it would be possible. And don't think that I haven't considered it."

"So why haven't you done it?" Glynis pressed.

"As I said . . . there are a number of reasons. All of them very complicated."

"Well, I'm not going anywhere at the moment."

Alanna decided there was no point in avoiding a head-on discussion of the realities. Glynis obviously knew quite a bit of the truth already. Alanna settled herself on the sofa. "Sit down, Glynis, and make yourself comfortable. What has Carrick told you of the nature of the Dragon's Heart's prophecies?"

Glynis sat and stared at a spot in the carpet in front of her. "He says they can't be dodged, that what the Dragon's Heart says will happen, will happen. You can try to change what's been foretold, but you'll fail."

"He's right," Alanna admitted, her heart heavy. "I don't know what he's told you of his vision of his death, but we know nothing of the particular circumstances leading up to it. Every time I consider sending him elsewhere in time, I'm forced to consider a horrible possibility: What if my attempting to save him is the catalyst for the events that lead to his hanging? What if in trying to save him, I actually set him up?"

"Oh."

Alanna leaned back into cushions and nodded sadly. "Yes, oh. One of the hardest things to accept about seeing is the fact that the future foreseen can't be altered. It's an absolute certainty that, sometime in this year, Carrick will be hanged. I can't help but be haunted by the possibility that the magic will go wrong and that in the end I may indirectly send him to the gallows."

Glynis didn't look up from the carpet, didn't seem to be aware that she took another sip of whiskey. "But at some point, don't you have to try?"

"I'm his mother, Glynis. I love him and I don't want to lose him. I've held out to this point, hoping for a miracle, for some sign that would show me the proper action to take and when to take it."

"And so far you haven't seen the light?"

Alanna shook her head, deciding that they'd dealt enough with grim realities and half-seen truths. "Would you like to talk about your return to your proper time and place?"

"Not right at the moment."

"It's possible, Glynis," she reassured her. "I've seen fragments of your future—enough to know that you're destined to go back to your Rocking M Ranch. I can and will see you safely back where you belong."

"Why don't I find that as comforting as I should?"

"Because you love Carrick and you desperately want a happily-ever-after with him."

Her gaze finally came up from the carpet. "And you're telling me as gently as you can that that's probably impossible."

Glynis's pain knifed through her heart and Alanna offered what solace she could. "Only if Carrick somehow miraculously survives a hanging."

"This sucks."

Alanna nodded. "Big-time."

"Well, I can't accept it," Glynis declared, vaulting to her feet, her hand clenched around her glass. "I think all of you are looking at this prophecy with fatalism. You've apparently seen the vision just as Carrick has. Have you actually seen him dead? I mean, really dead? Or was it just all the stuff leading up to it and you've drawn the logical conclusion?"

Alanna saw Glynis's desperation and her gathering tears. "I know from my own experience that miracles do happen, Glynis. I once saw a wall collapse on Kiervan. By all logic, he should have been killed. Obviously he wasn't. I hold the same kind of hope for my son."

"I refuse to accept it all with a sigh and a shrug. What if I insist on trying to change the course of events?" the younger woman persisted, her tone no less defiant than before. "Will you stand in my way?"

"Only if I think that you may do harm to Carrick."

"Then you should know that I'm determined to do whatever I can to keep him alive."

God, but Alanna remembered how it felt to be so young, to love so deeply, and to be so afraid. "I consider my son very fortunate to have had you come into his life, Glynis. But please take care that you don't become ensnared in the same deadly web in which Carrick will find himself."

Glynis made a scoffing sound and then tossed back the last of the whiskey. On the way to the beverage cart, she said over her shoulder, "You said I was destined to return to the ranch, remember? Obviously I'm gonna survive whatever happens here."

"Surviving can be a hollow victory, Glynis."

Glynis spun around, high color spreading across her cheeks. "I have to believe that my coming across time was for a reason, Lady Alanna. I'm not going down without a fight. And you can mark my words: I'm gonna win."

Alanna let her leave the room without another word. Had she ever been as young and reckless and certain of herself as Glynis Muldoon? Had she ever looked fate in the eye and denied its decree? Yeah, she had. And she'd been and done those things because she had fallen in love with Kiervan des Marceaux, her dark privateer. She'd have paid any price to keep him alive. And she still would. Love made you stronger and it made you braver than you could have ever imagined.

Alanna lifted her glass toward the empty doorway. "To love, Glynis Muldoon. May it keep you courageous." She took a deep sip. "And may it be strong enough to save Carrick."

Kiervan stopped in midsentence and followed his son's gaze out across the field. "Your mind is elsewhere," he observed after a few moments. "Would it happen to be on a pretty redhead?"

Carrick seemed to bring himself back to the present only with great effort. "It might be," he muttered, turning and starting toward the row of outbuildings behind the main house.

Kiervan fell into step beside him, his hands clasped behind his back. "Do you care for her?"

"She's a time traveler. I find her intriguing."

"If the bite in your voice is any indication," Kiervan observed, casting a quick glance at his son, "you're finding her a bit frustrating as well. Would you be willing to hear some fatherly advice?"

"It rather depends on the nature of it."

"Surrender, Carrick," he said solemnly. "You don't stand a chance in trying to control the fall."

"Is that the course you took with Mother?" Carrick asked, squinting into the setting sun, his brows furrowed.

"I wasted a lot of precious time resisting. In hindsight, I should have admitted to loving her long before I did."

"Well, there's the difference between us. I don't love Glynis Muldoon."

Kiervan snorted and rolled his eyes. "The hell you don't."

"She's different than any other woman I've ever known. What's between us is a good deal of curiosity and nothing more."

God. He had four children and the only one that drove him to madness was the one just like him. At Carrick's age he'd been just as determined to wall out everyone and deny that he felt anything beyond the simple emotions of lust and pride. Then Alanna Kathleen Chapman had come into his life and torn down his defenses day by day, stone by stone until he'd no other recourse but to admit the truth. And something told him that Carrick was fighting the battle much sooner than he himself had been forced to.

"Son," Kiervan said patiently, "you're as thickheaded as I am. Learn from my experience. You love Glynis Muldoon. Now, admit the truth and get on with living. You're wasting time."

"And time is something, Father, I don't have a whole lot of."

"Carrick . . . I'll say it again because it has apparently failed to sink in. What you see in the visions is not necessarily the full story."

Carrick looked toward the house. Regret shaded his voice when he said, "I've seen enough to know what my future holds. Glynis will have my child—a boy."

"And are you there for her? For my grandson?"

"I didn't see myself in the vision. I rather think she'll cross back to her own time to have the child. I don't know why I think that except that I didn't recognize the hearth she sat before. If she remained here, she'd be rocking the babe in front of the fire at Castle O'Connell." He paused a moment before he added, "I'd hope that you'd give her and the child a safe home, anyway."

"You mean you'd hope I'd fulfill your responsibilities."

Carrick's gaze went back to the setting sun. "I would if I could," he said quietly.

"Would you?"

Carrick turned to glare at him. "Of course I would. God knows I may be a lot of things, but a bounder isn't one of them. I accept my responsibilities."

"Would you accept them if Glynis Muldoon decided to take your child to her time? Would you travel with her? Be her husband and your child's father?"

"I wish the decision were that simple," his son answered sadly. "But it's not."

"I fail to see your reasoning," Kiervan pressed, seeing his son's regret as a hopeful sign. "All that's required is putting

Glynis and your child before everything else, as they should properly be, and then talking to your mother."

Carrick was silent. Then he squared his shoulders and said, "There are matters that have to be settled before I can consider going anywhere." He met his father's eyes. "Sean is dead," he said tightly. "The British tortured him to death. I'll see the officer who did it sent to hell."

"Vengeance belongs to the Lord."

Carrick asked dryly, "Have you found religion since I left home?"

"No. But since you never hear what I tell you, I thought I might try invoking a higher authority." Kiervan laid his hand on his son's shoulder. "Seeking vengeance is a fool's mission, Carrick. It doesn't bring back the dead. It doesn't make the wrongs right. It simply leads to more death, more vengeance. Leave it be and go on with your life, son."

Carrick took a step back, his expression resolute. "I owe it to Sean."

"Dead men don't keep balance ledgers, Carrick. Sean doesn't give a damn whether you avenge him or not. His book is closed."

"Mine's not. He died following me."

Kiervan's patience was fraying. "And killing a British officer will accomplish what? Getting yourself killed? Getting Robert killed? Or maybe Meyler? Is that what you want, Carrick?"

"No. I'll take care of the matter myself. No one else need be involved." His eyes darkened to the color of the twilight sky. "Cunningham's a predator. No one's safe as long as he breathes."

"And if you die instead of Cunningham?"

"It's a risk I'll have to take," Carrick said with a shrug, turning away.

Patience gone, Kiervan grabbed Carrick by the arm, pulling his son around to face him. "Your fatalism would drive a saint to violence. Doesn't it rankle to think that you might never hold your child? Never make love to Glynis again? Christ, Carrick! Isn't there a goddamn thing in this world that would make you want to fight to stay in it?"

His son glared at him but said nothing.

"Why don't you just put a bullet in your brain and be done with it?" Kiervan demanded, releasing his hold. He took a calming step back. "Why don't you save everyone the bother of watching you march blithely to the scaffold? Ireland has plenty of martyrs already."

"And she has enough cowards, too, Father. At least I'm trying to make a difference in the lives of those less fortunate than the des Marceauxs and the Concannons of this country. That's more than you can say."

If any man but his son had spoken those words . . . Kiervan chose to ignore the insult and go for the heart of the matter instead. "I won't be a party to your attempts to ease your conscience, Carrick. If you mean to die, then you'll have to walk up the steps to meet the hangman knowing that I refused to burn the bridge between us. If it's destroyed, it'll be by your own hand. I'm not about to make dying easy for you, son."

"You'd prefer to have me at Castle O'Connell strapped to Phelan's side, wouldn't you? You'd prefer to have me pretend that—"

"I'd prefer to see you fight like a man," Kiervan cut in. "And when you decide to do that, I'll fight with you."

"*When?* You make it sound as though it's a given."

"Aye. You'll choose to fight."

"What makes you so sure?" his son demanded. Defiance still rang in his words, but they were edged with a wariness that hadn't been there before. "Has Mother seen it in the Dragon's Heart?"

"No magic visions, Carrick," Kiervan answered, his anger gone. "I don't place much credence in them anyway. You know that."

"Then what makes you so damn sure that I'm going to fight to change my destiny?"

Kiervan smiled. "Son, I've seen the way you look at Glynis Muldoon. And one day very soon you're going to come to your senses and realize just how much she's worth." And then he walked away, leaving Carrick standing there looking like he'd been poleaxed.

21

Glynis wedged herself into the corner of the carriage cushion and looked around at the other occupants. Robert shared her seat. Lord and Lady des Marceaux sat opposite, both of them looking very much like cats who'd just dined on big, fat canaries. And the truth of the matter was that they'd looked like that all week.

"So," Glynis said, smoothing the green velvet of her skirt with a gloved hand. "Would someone please be kind enough to tell me why this is a good idea?"

"Did you want Carrick to ride with us?" his mother asked innocently, feigning surprise. "If I thought he'd be more companionable than he has been the last few days, I wouldn't have minded. But given his sour mood, I think Kiervan was wise to insist that he ride over with Saraid and Horace. Don't you?"

"The boy's obviously preoccupied with something," Kiervan agreed before Glynis could comment. "I've lost track of the number of hours he's spent out in that wood-wright's shop. I can't imagine what has him so knotted up."

The sparkle in his eyes belied his claim. Glynis groaned. It was a conspiracy, pure and simple. Everyone in the household had been enlisted to keep her and Carrick either separated or surrounded. And Kiervan had been the obvious ringleader from the start. She and Carrick had suffered both apart and together in frustrated silence. But she held hope that it would come to an end fairly soon. The look Carrick had thrown her as she'd been hustled off to his parents' carriage had promised that, come hell or high water, he'd find a way for them to be together once they reached Julia Conroy's.

Glynis settled herself even deeper into the corner. "I wasn't asking about Carrick in that sense," she said evenly. "I was asking why going over for Julia's ball was such a good idea. It seems to me that putting him in the midst of British officers is a little like waving a red cape in front of a bull."

The amusement disappeared from Kiervan's eyes. "It's a calculated risk. If he were to decline the invitation, British suspicions would be raised."

Robert cleared his throat quietly before adding, "And we've hopes of diverting whatever suspicions they might already hold. Eachann and Patrick are going to conduct a small raid while we're dancing and dining at Madam Conroy's. Nothing reckless or too bold, mind you. Just the straying of one or two of the Crown's fatted calves. With luck, the British will eliminate Carrick as a suspect in their search for the Dragon." He grinned. "Brilliant, huh?"

Glynis looked at him dubiously. "Does Carrick know about this plan of yours?"

"Well," Robert drawled, "in a manner of speaking, yes."

"What do you mean, *in a manner of speaking*?"

"He opposed the idea. We're going ahead with it anyway."

Glynis rolled her eyes. "Oh, won't he be thrilled when he finds out."

"With any luck, he won't find out."

"Counting kinda heavily on luck this evening, aren't you, Robert?"

At least Carrick's cousin had the good sense to look uneasy. Not that he'd entertained second thoughts soon enough to cancel the harebrained scheme he and whoever else had concocted.

Carrick's father stretched his long legs and crossed his arms over his chest. "Miss Muldoon, you surprise me," he said as though considering her anew. "I had rather thought of you as a young lady who knew how to take risks."

"Make no mistake, Lord des Marceaux," Glynis countered

without hesitation. "I know all about risk. And I'm not opposed to taking some when necessary. But I don't like depending on luck. I stack the odds whenever and however I can."

"As do I," he replied with a brief nod. "Don't worry about Carrick. We've taken care with the plan and we'll see that he understands the wisdom in it should he discover it."

Pulling the tail of the British lion seemed to be a dangerous thing even if done carefully. And judging by how Lady Alanna was biting her lower lip, it was obvious to Glynis that Carrick's mother was harboring the same sort of misgivings as she.

"May I say how lovely you look this evening, Miss Muldoon?" Robert offered, clearly trying to ease the tension. "I'm sure the British officers will be too busy courting your favors to be concerned about either the Dragon's activities or identity."

Oh, yeah, Glynis thought. *Like Carrick's gonna stand by and let that happen without a word.* This evening was a disaster in the making. She could feel it in her bones.

As though reading her thoughts, Lady Alanna cautioned, "You'll have to be very careful managing your dance card, Glynis. Remember all that Saraid and I told you. Make certain that Carrick has both the first and the last dance. That way his claim to you will be established and the likelihood for misunderstandings will be lessened. And regardless of how they might press, don't dance with any other gentleman more than once."

Glynis nodded, but in her mind every dance was Carrick's. She longed to feel the strength of his arms around her again and hear his laughing voice caress her. She wanted to spend every moment of the coming evening at his side. The week since his parents had arrived had been the longest of her life. Seeing him but not being able to touch him had wound her tighter than an eight-day clock. Publicly dancing wasn't the solution she wanted, but if it was all she could get, then she'd be content with it until they could find some time and someplace to be alone. Maybe they could find an opportunity to slip out into the gardens. Her pulse quickened at the thought. Perhaps no one would miss them if they were gone only a short while.

"And stay out of the gardens," Lord des Marceaux said pointedly. "Gentlemen feel compelled to defend a lady's honor if another man's beaten them into the moonlight with her."

Again Glynis nodded and said nothing. What was it about these people? Could everyone read her mind? Or was she just pathetically transparent when it came to Carrick?

"And don't let Carrick talk you into it," Robert added. "He'll try, and it's up to you to have enough common sense for the both of you."

Glynis wasn't sure whether she wanted to laugh or to cry.

"Leave the poor child alone," Lady Alanna said, glowering at her husband and nephew in turn. "You have her just as stressed out as you have Carrick. If the two of them manage to get through the evening without going off the deep end, it'll be a miracle."

Maybe it wasn't too late to call the whole thing off, Glynis thought. She could get them to stop the carriage and she could walk back to Saraid's house. She really wouldn't mind. Carrick was in the carriage ahead of them, but once he discovered that she'd abandoned ship, he'd beat feet back to Saraid's, too. Yeah, it was a plan. It was doable. Everyone else would be at Julia Conroy's and she and Carrick would be alone at the house. Okay, the kids would be there, but they'd eventually go off to their own beds.

"I've decided that I don't want to do this," she announced, sitting up straight. "I think I should go back to Saraid's. You can tell me all about it in the morning."

"Nonsense," all three replied in unison.

"No, really," Glynis persisted. "Just let me out and I'll walk back to Saraid's. You'll have a much better time if I'm not there. I'm the original party pooper."

"Saraid and I will guide you through the evening," Lady Alanna assured her. "There's nothing to worry about."

"I'll keep a watchful eye on you at all times, Miss Muldoon," Robert volunteered with a grin. "I'll be your constant shadow."

Lord Kiervan smiled broadly and delivered the coup de grâce. "And I shall ensure that Carrick remains otherwise engaged all evening."

Okay. This strategy wasn't going to work. To hell with dignity. Maybe she could just throw herself from the moving carriage. She'd been bounced out of the bed of a pickup truck once. She hadn't been hurt all that badly. And it had been moving a lot faster than this horse-and-buggy contraption was rocking along. But even as she eyed the door handle the carriage slowed and stopped.

"Ah," Lord Kiervan said with satisfaction. "We have arrived."

Damn. And double damn. Maybe she could twist an ankle or fall into a mud puddle. Either calamity would get her tucked away in some corner where she'd soon be forgotten. Only Carrick would come looking for her.

The door flew open. As though her thoughts had conjured him, Carrick instantly filled the space, his jaw hard. He gave his father and cousin warning looks before his gaze came to her. Her blood raced. This handsome man with the sky-blue eyes, raven hair, and unbrookable resolve was hers. And she loved him.

"Allow me to assist you, Glynis," he said, reaching for her hand, his expression dignified.

Instead of throwing herself into his arms as she wanted to, she gracefully put her hand in his and allowed him to guide her down the carriage steps.

The door snapped closed behind her in the same instant that Carrick caught her about the waist and spun them around. For a moment the details of the world were lost in a breathless blur. When it came back into focus, Glynis found herself held along the muscled length of his frame. Carrick's broad shoulders were pinned against the carriage door, his legs braced wide.

"Open this door, Carrick," his father ordered from inside the carriage.

Carrick grinned down at her wickedly and she laughed.

"Carrick," his mother called, her voice stern. "Don't you dare make a public spectacle on Julia's front porch. Do you hear me?"

"Kiss me," he whispered, drawing Glynis closer.

"Gladly," she answered, twining her arms about his neck.

Never in her life had she been kissed with such thoroughness. Her bones melted and her knees weakened. Carrick's arms tightened around her and she pressed closer, reveling in the strength of Carrick's possession.

And then the carriage door abruptly bumped them apart. Carrick leaned back, digging his heels into the crushed shells of the drive. His chest rose and fell with the same labored rhythm as her own. "Slip into the garden when you have a chance," he said quietly, his eyes ablaze with passion. "I'll join you there."

She nodded as Robert called, "Miss Muldoon, we're depending on you to exercise good judgment. Make Carrick step away from the door before we're forced to tear it from the hinges."

"They seem to want out," she observed, fighting a broad grin.

"I ought to nail the son of a bitch shut."

"Effective, but not very subtle," Glynis observed, easing out of Carrick's embrace as the door jostled them again and Lady Alanna called her son's name with obvious pique.

He let her go and shifted slightly. "As if what they've been doing to us the past week has been subtle."

"Well, you have to admit that the midnight hall patrols were a stoke of genius."

"A perverse kind of genius, if you ask me."

"True. But I think you really should let them out now."

"All right," he agreed. "But know that it's going against my sense of justice."

The door popped open the second Carrick stepped away. If Carrick hadn't stepped forward and snatched a handful of tailored jacket, Robert would have landed face down on the drive. Kiervan, with far more grace but no less speed, followed his nephew out.

Carrick didn't give his family members a chance to censure him and Glynis. As soon as Robert had regained his balance, he stepped back, and wordlessly extended his arm to Glynis. Her earlier trepidation fell away as she allowed him to lead her up the wide steps to Julia Conroy's home.

Alanna stood at her husband's side in the drive and watched them disappear into the house. "I do believe the boy is close to breaking," she quietly observed.

Kiervan shook his head and grinned. "Not yet. But the night's still young." He offered her his arm, saying, "Shall we join them?"

Walking beside him, she laughed softly. "He'll probably shoot you if he finds you wandering the hallway again tonight. You know that, don't you?"

Kiervan chuckled and drew them to a halt at the base of the steps. Pulling her into his arms, he brushed a kiss across her lips. As she slipped her arms about his neck, his hands slid down to caress her hips through the fabric of her skirt. "I do believe, dear wife," he whispered, gazing down into her eyes, "that I'll be otherwise engaged tonight."

Her heart skipped a beat, as it always did when she thought of making love with him. She rose on her toes and kissed him. "You're actually going to step out of their way?"

His dark eyes sparkling, he answered, "After our son's spent an evening watching other men court Glynis, only a fool would think of standing between them."

"And you're certainly no fool."

"Of course not," he agreed, his grin widening. "I had the good sense to admit that I love you and throw myself on your mercy."

She tugged at the curls lying along his collar. "It's mercy you want, huh?"

"Not particularly."

And his kiss proved that she wasn't going to have to endure any, either.

Glynis let Carrick guide her among the other dancers. "Don't let them stop playing."

"If only that were possible."

Glynis glanced over Carrick's shoulder. "Fox Face is drooling on the sidelines. What if he comes up and asks for the next dance?"

"Decline. Plead exhaustion. Tell him I've stomped your toes to pudding."

Resigned to her fate, Glynis shook her head. "He wouldn't believe it. How'd you get to be such a good dancer anyway?"

Carrick grinned and his blue eyes sparkled with mischief. "Practicing alone in my room at night."

"Yeah, right," she scoffed. "The only practice you've made a habit of is sweeping girls off the dance floor and onto moonlit terraces."

"I'm good at it. Want to see?"

God, she was tempted. But she let good sense prevail. "I think people would notice if we disappeared together so soon after arriving."

"If we move quickly, they'd have a hard time catching us."

"I don't want quick," she admitted in all seriousness.

Carrick groaned. "This is going to be the longest night of my life, Glynis."

"If it's any consolation, I'm not exactly looking forward to the front end of it, either."

"The front end?"

She quickly looked around them. "This part where we have to dance and dine and make nice to other people."

"What's the back end?"

Going home and making love to you.

"Christ, woman," he whispered, drawing her closer as he turned her about. "If you look at me like that again I'll make love to you right here on the dance floor."

Out of the corner of her eye she saw a flash of red near them. She looked up at Carrick and gave him a weak smile. "Damn. Fox Face is setting up to make his move. And just when things were getting interesting."

"Ignore him."

"I distinctly remember your mother telling me that sharing is required at such occasions as these."

"Glynis . . ." he warned.

"Carrick . . ." she countered, matching his tone.

"All right," he agreed as the waltz came to an end. "I'll be gracious. But not for one moment longer than propriety demands. And if one of the bastards makes an improper advance toward you, I'll—"

"I can take care of myself," she assured him, stepping

out of his arms even as Fox Face moved toward them. "Don't do anything that's going to make the redcoats mad at you. The last thing you need is one of them coming after you with a grudge."

"I can take of myself, too, Glynis."

She nodded and, acutely aware that the British officer hovered just behind her, said nothing more. Carrick glanced at the man and then back to her.

"Thank you for the dance," she said, dropping a slight curtsy as his mother had instructed. "I enjoyed it very much."

He bowed slightly. "I look forward to our next together." He once more looked at the man waiting before he walked away.

Glynis watched him thread his way through the dancers pairing up on the parquet floor and hoped he'd choose a partner from among the hopeful young women preening amid the potted palms at the edge of the room. When he snatched a flute of champagne from the tray of a passing waiter and tossed the contents down in a single swift movement, she silently groaned. The calm that had come over her as she'd entered the house with Carrick eroded as she saw him snag a second glass and make for a group of unattached men in the far corner of the room.

"Allow me to introduce myself," the uniformed man at her elbow said with a brief bow. "I am Major William Montgomery."

"A pleasure to meet you," Glynis managed to reply. "I'm Glynis Muldoon."

"Might I have the pleasure of this next dance?"

She nodded, deliberately looking away from Carrick. All of this would be over soon enough. She just had to be gracious in the meantime.

The major stepped before her, quickly slipping a gloved hand around her waist and lifting the other for her to take. His gaze dropped for a moment to her bodice and then came back to meet hers as he asked, "Are you an American, Miss Muldoon?"

The man's manner made her bristle. The way he said *American* made it sound like he used it as a synonym for *sleaze*. She squared her shoulders. "I am, sir," she answered as he guided her through the first steps of a waltz. *Wanna make something of it?*

"I was stationed for sixteen months in His Majesty's dominion of Canada. I had the opportunity to meet many of the Americans who crossed the border to trade."

"Oh? And what sort of trade were they engaged in?"

His hand slipped farther back along her waist. "All sorts, actually. I found them to be a generally interesting collection of persons."

It didn't take a rocket scientist to know where the major was going. "Really?" she asked, giving him room to run. "How so?"

"American men seem to accord their women a great deal of personal freedom." His hand slipped another fraction of an inch back. And slightly down. "And the American women of my experience seemed quite willing to take the lead they'd been given."

Glynis managed a strained smile. "Well, if you don't move your hand back to where it belongs, Major, you'll be experiencing a whole other kind of American woman."

It took him a couple of seconds, but his hand came slowly back to its original position. "I assure you that I meant no disrespect, Miss Muldoon."

The hell you didn't, Fox Face.

"But you are such a lovely creature that one can easily forget oneself. I do so hope you won't think me a cad of the first order."

"Not at all, Major," she lied with all the grace she could muster.

The rest of the dance passed in strained silence. His gaze dropped to her bodice too many times to count. When he bowed with his obligatory departing thanks, it took every ounce of her self-restraint to keep from kicking him in the shins.

And somehow she managed to trade in Fox Face for another British officer with similar interests, even faster hands, and far more persistence. She'd been forced to threaten him with gelding before their turn around the dance floor had come to a merciful end. The third one had used missed dance steps as a pretext for brushing his arm across her breasts. She'd turned the tables on him and repeatedly squished his toes. Lieutenant Stumbles-Gimpy had finally been sufficiently maimed that he'd accepted her invitation to retire the floor before the dance was done. He'd left her blessedly alone among the potted plants.

Glynis sagged against the wall the moment he was gone, thankful that she'd emerged from all three encounters without having called Carrick's attention to her struggles. It hadn't been easy. She'd frequently held her breath and her efforts at self-defense until a wall of dancers had blocked Carrick's view.

In the lull between the end of one waltz and the beginning of another, Glynis peered through the fronds for a glimpse of Carrick. She caught sight of Julia Conroy leading him out onto the floor. Certain that he'd be safely occupied for the next few minutes, Glynis decided to use the opportunity to find some safe alcove in which to hide from further British advances. As she made her way to the vantage point of the punch bowl, she reasoned that there had to be a group of little old ladies somewhere. She'd just nestle down in among them. Not even the biggest and baddest of the Kings's army would be man enough to take on a bevy of white-haired matrons.

But just as she accepted a cup of punch from a liveried servant, another, even better possibility presented itself. On the other side of the marbled foyer a wide set of mahogany doors opened and Robert emerged. Before he could pull them closed behind him, Glynis had a clear view of a green-felted table littered with playing cards and chips. Her mind was made up even as Robert turned and came toward her. Men playing cards were safe. They had to keep their hands in sight.

"Robert, dear," she said, rounding the punch table and blocking his way into the ballroom.

He stopped in his tracks, looking suspicious.

"What game are they playing in there?"

"Draw poker. Why?"

"Are ladies allowed to watch?"

"It's considered one of the better inducements to play,"

he answered, relieved. "A feminine whisper of awe can do wonders for a man's pride."

She took his arm and turned her newly appointed escort back toward the door. "Are they allowed to play?"

Robert laughed and promised to cover her markers as he opened the door for her.

22

Lord and Lady des Marceaux shared the carriage seat across from Glynis. Their hot-tempered, damn-the-consequences son sat next to her, his arms crossed and glowering at the toes of his boots. God, she could kill him. No jury of her peers would convict her. Hell, they'd probably give her a Darwin Award for having, for the benefit of all mankind, eliminated a significant set of moron genes from the reproductive pool.

The carriage jostled over what had to have been the hundredth bump in the road and Glynis took a deep breath, knowing that sooner or later someone would break the uncomfortable silence. Not that it seemed to bother Carrick's parents in the least. Even in the dim light she could see that they were wearing their cat-and-canary expressions again. And while they gave the outward appearance of being totally oblivious to the fact that she and Carrick shared the carriage with them, Glynis knew damn good and well that both of them were not only keenly aware of the tension between them, but inordinately pleased by it.

The carriage slowed slightly, made a sharp turn to the right, and bounced over another rut. Glynis, seeing Lady Alanna moisten her lips, braced herself.

"Julia wanted me to thank you both for making her party so memorable," Carrick's mother said evenly. "She said it's just the kind of event from which legends spring. And she was especially appreciative of the timing. Now no one will lack for dinner conversation. She said she couldn't have staged anything as entertaining if she'd set her mind to it."

"My pleasure," Carrick growled.

"I'm glad we made the Widow Conroy's evening," Glynis added.

Kiervan shook his head and settled back into the corner of the carriage cushions. "I don't think I'll ever forget the sight of Cunningham flying backward through the French doors. And his expression as his backside polished the dance floor . . . well, it was surpassed only by the look on his face when Carrick came storming after, ready to finish him off."

Lady Alanna laughed softly and curled into her husband's side. "And don't forget the look on our son's face when he discovered that Cunningham had told Glynis he'd won the right to walk her in the garden."

Carrick muttered, "I'd prefer to end this discussion, if you don't mind."

"I'm sure you would," his father countered with a chuckle. "Please remember that I warned you that playing Cunningham for courtship rights wasn't a particularly good idea."

Lady Alanna arched a dark blond brow. "You're being awfully quiet, Glynis."

"Trust me," she said softly, "it's for the best. You don't want to know what I'm thinking about this whole fiasco."

"Well, at least you're thinking," Carrick remarked, turning to face her. "It's more than you were doing when you sallied into that card game."

She drew herself up. "Excuse me?"

"You know exactly what I'm talking about," Carrick accused, leaning forward. "You were pumping everyone there for what they know about the Dragon."

"And just what's wrong with that?" Glynis demanded.

"It's my business and none of yours. We've talked about this in the past, Glynis. You're not to interfere."

The arrogant jackass. "I wasn't interfering, and don't tell me what to do. There was nothing wrong with the questions I asked. I learned a helluva lot about what you're up against."

"For instance?" he asked, his tone blatantly derisive.

"Okay," she said, leaning forward, more than willing to take up the gauntlet. "For instance, McKenna is a narrow-minded bigot who doesn't like to lose, can't do it gracefully, and will put his bruised pride before honor—what little of it he possesses. He talks big but doesn't have the backbone to go with it. Colonel Hewlett considers him a burr under the blanket and Cunningham generally ignores him. If you decide to pay McKenna another midnight visit, Hewlett will volunteer to hold Molan's reins for you. Cunningham won't waste the paper to write up McKenna's complaint.

"Hewlett, on the other hand, is an honorable man who doesn't like either the tithe policy or his role in the enforcement of it. But he's a man who's committed his life to the service of his King and he'll do as he's ordered. You find your butt in the wringer, Carrick des Marceaux, and Colonel Hewlett is going to be the only one who even thinks about cutting you some slack.

"It's a sure bet Cunningham won't. He's the one you have to worry about. He doesn't like to lose, either. But he doesn't stomp off indignantly like McKenna does. He stays and plays hardball. He wasn't the least bit interested in me, but he knew you were, and since you had my winnings, he went after them by trying to rattle your cage."

"Which he failed to do," Carrick inserted coolly.

"We'll come back to that in due time," Glynis countered. "Cunningham is the subject at the moment," she continued. "He's dangerous. He isn't interested in the rightness or the wrongness of what his King asks him to do. All he's interested in is what he can get out of it. He'll score major points from bringing in the Dragon. And don't count on him to play fair doing it. He'll go renegade in a heartbeat. Like he did with Sean."

"Very astute observations," Lord Kiervan said with a crisp nod. "And well stated."

Glynis met the older man's gaze, his compliment going a long way toward dissipating the anger and frustration which had driven her assessment. She took a steadying breath. "I happen to believe that one can learn a lot about a person by watching how he plays cards—and just as much again by listening to what he says when he's not guarding every word."

Carrick's father smiled slowly. "And what did you learn about me?"

"You weren't in that game. You were just holding cards, tossing chips, and watching. You sat back and let me have the reins. For which I thank you."

He nodded. "Hewlett was doing much the same. He let you beat up McKenna for him."

"I figured as much," Glynis admitted. "I like Hewlett. He has a heart under the red coat and all that gold braid. So what did you learn about me, Kiervan?" she challenged.

"I don't think I'd like to cross you," he admitted with a broad grin. "Beauty, brains, and nerves of steel are a formidable combination. If you decide to stay among us, I'll give you a ship to captain."

"I don't know anything about sailing."

"You can learn. It won't take you long."

"You obviously learned everything Jake had to teach you about gambling," Carrick declared flatly. "Including how to cheat."

"Who's Jake?" Lady Alanna inquired.

"My ex-husband, who couldn't have dealt off the bottom of a deck if his life had depended on it." Glynis turned to face Carrick. "And for your information, Mr. Gamble-the-Girl-Away, I didn't cheat to win. I stashed those two extra fours because I had a feeling McKenna wasn't going to go down without calling for my hand. I wasn't ready to give up my advantage at that point."

"Damn," Lord Kiervan said, shaking his head. "Now I'm feeling a tad guilty for those five hearts I dealt you."

"And smoothly done, too," Glynis quickly countered. "I'm sorry I had to let them go to waste, but I thought it better to let Cunningham take the hand. He was getting a little sore about losing."

Lord Kiervan nodded. "It took the edge off him very nicely."

"Yeah, well," Glynis admitted, "no doubt thanks to your son, he had plenty back on him when he cornered me on the terrace."

"You seemed intent enough on smoothing them when I came along," Carrick caustically observed.

"Don't *even* go there, Carrick," she warned. "I'm still too mad at you to pull my punches."

He leaned forward, his eyes narrowed. "Don't bother pulling. Just swing away, Glynis. Give it your best shot."

"Now, children . . ." Lady Alanna warned. "You're both going to say things you'll come to regret. We're almost back to Saraid's and—"

"Stay out of this, Mother. Please. This is between Glynis and me. And we *are* going to deal with it."

"Maybe when you sober up and I've had time to find some flimsy excuse for your behavior," Glynis retorted.

"Darlin' Glynis, I haven't even had close to enough to drink yet. And I don't need an excuse, thank you. You're the one in desperate need of an explanation."

"*Me?* I need to explain myself to you?" The carriage came to a stop and she had to catch herself with the door handle or tumble off the seat. Quickly deciding that fate had given her a sign, she turned the handle and flung open the door. "You're absolutely insufferable, Carrick des Marceaux," she declared, shoving herself and her skirts through the opening.

The driver was still climbing down from the box and she was halfway up the front steps of the Concannon home when she heard Carrick's boots hit the gravel drive.

"Don't you *dare* walk away from me, Glynis."

She didn't pause or look back. Pushing open the great front door, she yelled, "I refuse to deal with you and your bad attitude on top of everything else tonight, Carrick. I've had enough and I'm going to my room. Good night."

She'd stomped across the marbled foyer and started up the central staircase when he came through the front door.

"Goddammit!" he barked from the center of the foyer. "Glynis, get back here! We're going to finish this."

"No." She reached the top and glanced back to see if he was coming up the carpeted stairs after her. He stood at the base, one foot on the bottom stair and one hand on the newel post. The pale light of the oil lamps let her see what the relative darkness inside the carriage had hidden. Carrick was a thunderstorm in a cutaway coat and suede breeches. His blue eyes flashed with anger and his jaw was set hard as granite. The sight of him standing there sent a delicious fire coursing through her.

"Glynis," he said evenly, "don't make me come after you."

Her blood boiled. Of all the high-handed, imperious, overbearing men in the world, this one took first prize. "Go to hell!" she yelled, whirling about and hurrying down the hallway. She heard him bellow her name again. She answered it by slamming her bedroom door closed behind her and then ramming home the bolt.

Not five seconds later, the handle jiggled and the door rattled on its hinges.

"Open this door before I kick it in," Carrick demanded from the other side of it.

"You wouldn't dare," she called back, standing in the center of her room with her hands on her hips.

"Wanna bet? I'll give you to the count of three. One . . ."

He would. She could hear the determination in his voice.

"Two . . ."

She darted to the door, throwing back the bolt and jerking the panel open in almost the same movement. He stood on the other side of it, his lips compressed in a thin line, his hands balled into fists. Somewhere between the foyer and her doorway he'd removed his coat and neckcloth, pulled open the front of his shirt. The top button was missing entirely; the second clung to the cloth by a frayed strand of thread.

Her heart thundering, her pulse racing, Glynis met his fiery gaze and said, "You're gonna wake the children standing out there bellowing like some drunken sailor."

"Fine," he snapped, striding forward, the speed and determination of his advance pushing her back. "I'll come in and we'll discuss this in a civilized fashion." He shoved the door closed behind him.

"I'm not feeling the least bit civilized at the moment," she countered. "I'm so mad at you right now I could . . . could . . ."

"Could what?" he pressed, moving slowly toward her.

God, she was so angry with him that she could scream. She squared her shoulders and held her ground. She wouldn't give him the satisfaction. "How dare you put me up as the stake in a poker game!" she demanded. "How could you?"

"I had no intentions of losing," he answered, deliberately closing the distance between them. "This may come as a surprise to you, sweetheart, but you're not the only one who can read card players. You're not the only one who can take a hand on bluff."

"And what would you have done if, despite your over-whelming self-confidence, you'd lost? Huh? Would you have let Major Cunningham walk me through the roses?" she challenged.

"Would you have let him?"

"How can you even ask me that?"

"Because you were pretty well swaddled in red when I came out on the terrace looking for you."

She took a step forward, close enough that she could smell the starch of his shirt, and had to tilt her head back to look him in the eye. "Well, if you'd been a half-second later, Carrick des Marceaux, *you* could have watched *me* punch Cunningham through the French doors. Pardon me if your sense of timing was off and I took a second to gather my wits."

"You could have called for help," he said, his flashing eyes belying his controlled voice.

"*I* was trying to avoid a scene. Which of course *you* didn't even stop to think about."

"No, I didn't. And I'm not about to apologize to you or anyone else for having knocked the major on his commis-sioned ass."

"I haven't asked you for an apology for that. I don't want one."

"Then what *do* you want?"

"I want tomorrows," she retorted without thinking. Her heart lurched the instant she heard the admission spoken aloud. But there was no going back. The only way was to go forward, to admit to all of the truth. "And all the days after, Carrick. I want all the visions in the Dragon's Heart to disappear."

"Christ, Glynis! How many times have we been over

this? No matter how much I want to, I can't give you those things."

Her anger drained away, leaving her only sadness. She started away, determined to blink back the sudden moisture in her eyes before Carrick could see it. He caught her arm and stayed her, his touch sending the tears spilling over. Still, she turned her face away, unwilling to let him see. She wouldn't speak, she vowed. She wouldn't make a sound.

"This isn't about Cunningham, is it, Glynis?" he asked, looking puzzled. "It isn't about the card game or my wager for you, either. It's about what lies underneath all of that, isn't it?"

When she didn't answer, didn't look at him, his fingers tightened slightly about her arm. Exasperation edged his voice when he said, "God, Glynis, I could stand here all night and make guesses. Save us both the agony. Turn around and look at me. Tell me what you want me to do."

Pride said she should pull her arm from his grasp and icily demand that he leave her room. Her heart wanted more. She drew a shaky breath and lifted her chin. Slowly, she turned and looked up at him. "I want you to love me," she said softly.

"That I can do," he answered, releasing her arm to take her face gently between his hands. "I can love you, Glynis Muldoon." With the pads of his thumbs he brushed the tears from her cheeks.

"Not just *make* love to me," she protested, her voice catching. She closed her eyes. "*Love* me."

"With you, Glynis, they're one and the same."

He kissed her gently, a soft touch of his lips to hers as his hands slipped down and around to her back. She felt his tension, the tentativeness of his caress, and drew back to look up into his dark eyes.

Carrick read the question clearly in her green eyes. "There are two roads from here, Glynis," he answered, opening the hooks at the back of her gown. "Slowly and gently like a caring lover. . . ." He drew the heavy velvet down over her shoulders, pushed the sleeves down the length of her arms and past her fingertips. "Or I can take you with all the desperation I feel." The fabric pooled around their feet as he took a slow breath and said, "I'm trying very hard to be a gentleman."

A smile touched the corners of her mouth as she reached out and began to unbutton his shirt. She looked up at him, her eyes beckoning. "You can be a gentleman in the morning," she offered softly, abandoning his shirtfront to splay her hands over the planes of his exposed chest.

He'd never in his life wanted a woman the way he wanted this one and it was too late to worry about the wisdom of it.

"Or maybe tomorrow afternoon," she continued, nipping him playfully. "Or the morning after next."

"Or maybe never," he admitted, wrapping her in his arms and drawing her along the length of his body. He captured her lips with his own as his hands moved to hold her against the hardness of his desire.

She tasted the reckless smoke of whiskey, felt the intensity and strength that throbbed through the corded muscles and sinew that pressed against her softer flesh. Her heart matched the cadence of his and deep within her a fire sprang to life. She gasped before the power of the flames that Carrick fanned with his kisses, moaned as it consumed her and set her senses ablaze.

Her lips parted at his demand, her hands tugging his shirt from the waistband of his breeches and then slipping up the muscled planes of his back to hold him close. He wanted more, and patience be damned. She'd said he could be gentle later and he had no choice but to take her at her word.

His tongue boldly stroked the dulcet cavern of her mouth. She moaned as he freed her breasts from the sheer prison of her chemise. Her hands slid to his waist and tightened with silent demand as she pressed her hips closer and arched her back.

Glynis softly moaned as he kissed a broad path down the length of her throat. Her eyes shut and her breath coming raggedly from between swollen, parted lips, her hands came up to hold his head to her breast, the compelling sensations overwhelming all but her desperate need for release. He used his fingers, his tongue, and his teeth, tugging her taut nipples so that she felt the heat of desire melt into the hot center of her body.

She swayed, breathless beneath the masterful assault of his hands and mouth, her fingers tangled in his hair, holding him close. A sudden bolt of pleasure jolted exquisitely through her. Passion, primal and elemental, wild and sweet, swept her past logic and patience. And she didn't care. She lowered her hands to his waist, wanting all of him. But the buttons of his breeches resisted and, frustrated, she gave the cloth a fierce yank.

Carrick felt the soft thud as the buttons from his breeches struck the toes of his boots. And then Glynis pushed aside the fabric of his breeches and took the hard length of him into her hands.

Her possession was gently demanding, incinerating the last threads of his control. Her nipples held prisoner between his thumbs and forefingers, he closed his mouth over hers. He plundered and she moaned and shuddered, her hands tightening about him.

And then she moved against him, her hips pressing urgently, and he couldn't deny her; couldn't deny himself. He backed her toward the bed, his kiss deepening with promise, his hands quickly lifting and sliding beneath the thin lawn of her chemise.

She acquiesced with a soft moan that he felt in his belly as she eased down onto the edge of the feather mattress, her hands drawing him to stand between her parted thighs.

His pulse thundered and his breathing was shallow and fast. His hands slipped over the edges of her gartered stockings, up the insides of her satiny thighs, his palms caressing, his fingers brushing over her mound. He saw her eyes darken, heard the telltale catch in her breathing, keenly felt the delicious friction of her hands sleeved around his manhood.

Desire flared white-hot, searing the air from his lungs and nearly buckling his knees. Gasping, he closed his eyes and let her draw him to the very edge of oblivion, to the very edge of surrender. And then, as though she knew when he'd reached the brink of endurance, she slowly released him, easing back into the cradle of the feather mattress, her eyes dark with timeless invitation. He couldn't have resisted her if he'd wanted to. He didn't even bother to try. His gaze holding hers, he slipped his hands beneath her and lifted her hips.

He filled her body with his need. Not slowly or gently. Deliberately. Luxuriously. Savoring the wonder, and the pulsing tightness of her.

He thrust into her, pushing them over the edge. The world spun and collapsed around them as they exploded together, breathless.

Glynis lazily opened her eyes and moistened her swollen lips with the tip of her tongue. Carrick's eyes met hers in the same instant and she saw the smoldering embers of his desire, the hammering pulse in the deep hollow at the base of his throat. She drew a shuddering breath as her desire flared in response.

"Again," she whispered, moving her hips to hold him close, to hold him within her.

"Jesus, Glynis," he murmured, smiling as he hardened in response. He leaned forward to kiss her, tenderly, thoroughly. Her arms came up to rest on his shoulders, her fingers tangling in his hair. He released her lips slowly and she made a small sound of protest, pouting sweetly. He shifted his hands about her hips and pushed deeper. Her eyes widened as her lips curved upward and parted with a gasp of pleasure.

He moved down, taking a nipple into his mouth, suckling until she moved against him and moaned his name. Only then did he release her.

"More gently and slower this time, I think," he whispered.

"No thinking allowed," she replied, drawing his lips down to hers.

He didn't protest. Not then. And not when she rolled him onto his back.

23

Glynis smiled to herself and snuggled closer to Carrick's broad chest. He shifted his arms about her, holding her close. The beat of his heart thrummed against the palm of her hand, a lullaby for her sated senses.

And in that moment she knew there would never be anyone else. No other man had ever touched her as Carrick had. And she understood in her heart that no other man ever could. All that existed between them was magical. Neither of them had led, neither had followed. They'd made love in perfect tandem, their bodies and spirits one, their desires flawlessly bound. Somewhere in the universe the gods were nodding in approval.

"Sleepy?" he asked quietly, pressing a kiss into her hair.

God, she loved how his voice vibrated through her. "Not really," she answered truthfully. "More satisfied than anything."

"Well, thank you, God," he countered, feigning relief. "I was beginning to think I'd lost my touch."

She laughed and hugged him close. "You've just never met a woman as wanton and willful as you are."

"True. You know you've probably ruined me for any other woman, don't you? No one will ever be able to come close to loving me like you."

"Well," she drawled, "that just breaks my heart."

"Yeah, I can tell you're filled with regret."

She rolled atop him, her hair cascading over their shoulders, her chin on her hands. She smiled wickedly down at him. "Give me a few more minutes and I'll be glad to show you again what else I can do. But if you're looking for regrets, I'm afraid you'll have to go elsewhere."

"I have absolutely no intention of going anywhere." He wrapped his arms around her. "I'm going to lie right here and hold you until . . . well, I'm not precisely sure what it would take to make me leave this bed and you."

"Flames?" she ventured, her smile broadening.

"They'd have to be pretty damn spectacular."

"How about Robert?"

"Robert who?"

She laughed, feeling free and happy. "Have I told you that I love you, Carrick des Marceaux?"

His eyes sparkled. "I don't think so. Seems to me I'd remember anything you might have said along those lines."

"Well, I do. I love you."

"Body and soul?" he asked, cocking a dark brow.

"Uh-huh. Do you doubt it?"

He grinned. "Not at the moment. Unfortunately, my confidence has a way of faltering. You might have to reassure me one more time before the night's done."

"Just once?" she laughingly teased. "Are you sure that will hold you over?"

"You're right," he agreed. "Twice. At least. It's a long stretch between dawn and noon. I wouldn't want you to find me wandering the hallways at midmorning, a sad shadow of my present self, my confidence shattered."

"Noon, huh? And just what excuse are we going to use for retiring to our rooms after lunch?"

He looked mischievous. "Who said anything about our rooms? I'm surprised at you, Glynis Muldoon. I wouldn't have thought you'd be bound by such convention."

"You aren't thinking of riding over to Julia Conroy's for an afternoon stroll in her garden, are you?"

"Well, it's an idea. I'll put it on the list of possibilities."

"Is it a long list?" she asked, laughing quietly.

"I want you to know that I noticed that you weren't wearing any pantalets under that luscious green velvet gown."

She had no idea where he was going with this left turn,

but she knew she'd enjoy both the journey and the destination. "Oh, you did, did you? I was rather under the impression that once you'd gotten rid of the gown, you didn't notice much of anything else."

"Well, I did. And I appreciated not having to take the time to tear pantalets off you."

She grinned. "Is this your roundabout way of asking me to forgo them in the future?"

"We'll make far faster progress on the list if you leave them folded in a drawer."

"This list of yours—"

"Ours," he corrected.

"Okay, this list of *ours* . . . is it just places or is it more . . . ah . . . comprehensive?"

"I'm a very thorough man."

"Oh, indeed you are. I have no complaints at all."

"I'm inventive, too," he added, his voice silken with promise.

Her blood warmed. "Oh, really?"

"You sound like you doubt it. Honor demands that you let me prove my claim."

"Never let it be said that I'm not a fair wo—" The rest of her assertion was lost as he rolled her beneath him with a speed and determination that took her breath away. With a fluid movement, he sat up, his thighs carefully pinning her hips to the bed. Her hands went to his waist as she gazed up at him, wide-eyed and insanely exhilarated.

"Ah, thank you," he said, taking her hands in each of his. "These are just what I wanted." He brought them together, gently transferring them into one of his. With his free hand he reached up toward the pillows behind her head.

"What—"

"One of your stockings," he answered, trailing the length of it across her bare shoulder and then up and around her extended arms. She arched up beneath him, gasping for air and silently pleading for more. He shifted his weight ever so slightly and held her still.

"Oh, God," she moaned, watching as he loosely wrapped the length of silk around one of her captured wrists and then the other. "What are you doing?"

He leaned forward, pressing her hands into the pillows above her head with exquisite gentleness. His gaze caressed hers, promising. "Trust me?"

She was going to explode long before he was done with her. "This," she answered on a ragged breath, "is gonna count . . . as one of your . . . two times . . . before dawn."

"My darlin', Glynis," he whispered, leaning down to place a feathery kiss at the corner of her mouth, "I do believe I'll just have to make you forget all about this counting obsession of yours."

And he did. Thoroughly.

She lay beside him, the sheets tangled about their entwined legs, the pale moonlight spilling across her lush curves. He smiled. There were hours left of the night.

"Are you happy?" she asked, reaching out to drag a fingertip through the stubble on his chin.

"Very much so," he answered, taking her hand in his and bringing her fingertip to his lips. "Thank you."

"My pleasure, sir. Anytime."

Time. There wasn't going to be enough of it with Glynis. He wanted forever. He wanted to grow old with her, to make love with her a million times and in a million ways. He wanted to make babies with her and hold her in his arms as they watched their children grow and then have their own lives and loves. His heart ached. He clenched his teeth and stared up at the ceiling, silently cursing his desire for what he couldn't have.

"Carrick? Are you all right?"

"Fine," he lied, pretending to smile. Her expression was somber as she searched his face. Desperate to keep his troubles from her heart, he chose the surest course he knew to divert her concern. "Tell me about your home, Glynis. What does it look like?"

For a long moment she was silent. "It's God's country, Carrick," she finally said, her voice reverent. "He created it so that no one would ever forget that on the first day He made the heavens and on the second, the firmament. I've always thought that's why some people called the Flint Hills desolate and barren; it reminds them how man was created almost as an afterthought, how little it takes for nature to destroy him."

"You love it very much, don't you?"

She stared off into the distance, focused on another place, another time. "I remember coming back from Kansas City one day with Aunt Ria," she said softly. "I must have been about eleven years old. It was one of those summer days, when the heat builds through the day and by late afternoon the sky turns lead gray and slowly drops down to touch the earth. The grass was tall and so green, Carrick. A dark green. It was waving before the wind. And as far as you could see there was nothing but the green grass and the leaden sky, one against the other.

"I felt it here," she said, her voice catching as she pressed her fist to the center of her chest. "I still feel it here whenever I remember. Homecoming. I was going home." She savored the memory, blinking back tears. She looked at him and said quietly, "I've lived many lifetimes in that place, Carrick. It's where I have to be, where I belong. It goes beyond being a Muldoon."

"Would I find your Flint Hills as beautiful, as stirring as you do?"

"I think you would," she replied. "Ireland reminds me of it sometimes in little ways."

"Tell me about your aunt and uncle. What are they like?"

She smiled broadly. "Uncle Lloyd is what we call a tall drink of water. He's all sinew and bone wrapped around a big ol' heart. He was my dad's best friend from the time they were toddlers. Kinda like you and Robert, I imagine." She sighed quietly, and after a moment continued saying, "Anyway, Uncle Lloyd's always been on the Rocking M; the manager since my dad inherited the ranch from his father.

"Uncle Lloyd met Aunt Ria at the Royale, the annual stockman's show in Kansas City, when he was nineteen and Ria was eighteen. Her father raises prize Brahmans down in Oklahoma. It was one of those love-at-first-sight things. They met on Friday night and got married Sunday afternoon. And they've been together ever since.

"Ria's tall and very regal but not disdainful, if you know

what I mean. There's something about her that just tells you she's special. In a lot of ways she reminds me of your mom. And now that I think about it, Uncle Lloyd's a great deal like your father. If the two of them were to ever get together . . ." She chuckled softly and shook her head. "Heaven help us all."

"Did Lloyd and Ria like Jake?"

"Oh," she answered, thinking about his question, "I think initially they didn't have any strong feelings about him one way or another. He came from one of the old families and he had ranching in his blood. It had the potential to be a good match. It just didn't turn out that way. Jake changed. Almost the instant he said, 'I do.' But Uncle Lloyd and Aunt Ria loved me enough to keep trying to find some common ground with him, to find something good in him to like."

"And were they successful?"

"Nope. Ria baked a big cake and Lloyd brought home a bottle of champagne the day the divorce became final." She met his gaze, looking sad. "It's a shame they can't meet you. They'd approve of you."

"Oh, yes," he countered sardonically. "An outlaw with a price on his head. I'm sure they'd be quite happy to see me at your side."

"I somehow doubt that you'd be a 1997 poster boy at the Cottonwood Falls Post Office."

"Explain that one, if you would."

"You're an outlaw only in this time, Carrick. The slate's wiped clean if you cross through the portal."

There was no point in letting her think of impossibilities; it would be cruel to even glance down the path she so desperately wanted to believe they could travel. "I meant about being a poster boy at the post office."

She quickly looked away. It took several seconds, but she finally said, "They put pictures of wanted men and women in post offices so everyone can see them."

"Speaking of wanted women . . ." He slid his hand around her waist and drew her toward him.

"Ummm. And wanted men," she murmured as she

offered him her lips and molded her soft curves along his hard angles.

He felt her stomach rumble and heard his own rumble in response. "It would appear that we're hungry," he said, laughing as he drew back. "And Lord knows we certainly need to keep up our strength."

"Well, we did leave Julia's before we had a chance to eat."

"What would you say to me slipping downstairs and seeing what I can find for a predawn feast? I wouldn't be gone more than five minutes."

"Five minutes?" She pouted for effect and then grinned. "All right. But not one second more than that. If you're not back here by then, I'll come looking for you."

He kissed her and then rolled off the the edge of the mattress. "I think the kitchen's on the list a couple of times," he said, shoving his legs into his breeches.

She laughed as he stood there staring down at the mangled front of his pants.

"Jesus, Glynis," he muttered, shaking his head. "You left one button to stand between me and indecency."

"Yeah, well, when you get back here, I'll take care of that one, too."

Grinning, he snatched his shirt up from the carpet and pulled it on, counting on the loose shirttail to afford him some meager dignity should the surviving button decide to give way.

"Five minutes," he assured her. "Wait for me."

"Forever if I have to," she answered quietly, watching him go. A chill crept over her the instant he was gone and she wrapped her arms around her, tamping down the urge to run after him. "A fire's what we need," she muttered, climbing from the bed. "I should stir the coals and throw some wood on."

He put a tray on the worktable and then headed for the larder, his bare feet moving soundlessly over the flagstones. A moment later he returned to the dark kitchen, his arms laden with a loaf of crusty bread, two sizable chunks of cheese, and four apples. Depositing the items on the tray, he stood back and surveyed the food. A sharp knife and bottle of Horace's best red wine and it would be a decent meal. He wished there was more he could offer the woman he loved, but—

Carrick froze. *The woman he loved?* The world tilted and he struggled against the realization. His father's words echoed through his mind: . . . *come to your senses and realize just how much she's worth.* He drew a shaky breath as Robert's came in their wake. *Glynis can save your life. Let her.* He stood in the dark kitchen, knowing that he'd suddenly come to the most important crossroad of his life.

Even as he reminded himself that fate had given him only one choice, his heart demanded another. Glynis. And life. Children and laughter. Hope. He closed his eyes and tried to suppress the feelings overwhelming him.

He couldn't fight the truth. It was inescapable, undeniable. He needed Glynis. She had become his life. He loved her with all his heart, all his soul. She was his reason to live, to fight for the forever they deserved to have.

His gaze fell to the table and the tray of food he'd gathered. Glynis was waiting for him to bring it upstairs. Carrick smiled. Should he tell her he that he loved her, that he'd travel through time with her before or after they'd eaten? he wondered. Or maybe over a glass of wine?

He started toward the door that led to the wine cellar. Startled, he tensed, his heart pounding, his eyes narrowed. The door leading to the yard inched inward; a pair of eyes peered into the kitchen just above the level of the door handle.

As he watched, the door opened a few more inches and Meyler slipped silently into the kitchen. Carrick relaxed and quietly cleared his throat. "I assume you have a reason for skulking about at this hour?"

Meyler jumped and squeaked, spinning about to look up at him.

One look at the boy's face chilled his blood. "Christ! What's happened?"

Meyler brushed the back of his hand across his tear-stained cheeks and sobbed, "They have Eachann."

"Who has Eachann?" Carrick demanded, closing the distance between them in three long strides.

"The British," he hiccuped. "They set a trap for them."

"Them? Start at the beginning," Carrick commanded, taking Meyler by the shoulders. "Tell me the whole story."

The boy sniffled, drawing a shuddering breath. "Robert and Uncle Kiervan had this idea that while you were at Miss Julia's party Eachann and Patrick would go on a raid. That way the British would know you weren't the Dragon because you were at the party and the Dragon was out stealing the tithe collector's cattle."

Carrick's blood ran cold.

"Eachann and Patrick told me to stay here, but I followed them. I saw it all. They were waiting for them. And they caught Eachann." Sobbing, Meyler added, "I don't know what happened to Patrick."

Carrick drew a deep breath and deliberately unclenched his teeth. As calmly as he could, he asked, "Where did they take Eachann? Did you see?"

"They headed down the road toward Greystones."

Carrick bit back another curse. "All right," he said with a nod, squeezing the too-young shoulders. "Go upstairs, Meyler. I'll deal with it from here."

"Shouldn't we tell Robert and Uncle Kiervan?"

"I'll do what needs to be done, Meyler." He turned the boy toward the back stairs and gave him a gentle nudge. "Go now."

Meyler turned back, his expression tragic. "I'm sorry, Carrick. I should have done something."

"You're a little boy," Carrick whispered sadly. "There's nothing you could have done, Meyler. Nothing." He saw in the youngster's eyes a terror and devastation no child should have borne. "I should have taken you back to Castle O'Connell the very minute you showed up in camp," Carrick whispered in regret. "I shouldn't have let any of you come with me."

"Will Eachann be all right? Will you get him back?"

"Aye," Carrick promised. "I'll get him back. Now don't worry anymore about it. Go on. To bed with you."

He stood where he was, his face impassive until Meyler disappeared from sight. Only when he heard the boy's footfalls at the top of the stairs did he dare to consider the situation.

Sean had died at Cunningham's hands. Eachann would meet the same fate. Carrick fought the anger and revulsion welling deep within him. He hadn't known of Sean's capture in time to intervene. But Eachann's life could still be saved. Carrick made the only decision he could. He'd go to Greystones and do whatever it took to save Eachann's life. He'd find out what had happened to Patrick, too. If Cunningham had them both . . .

He turned toward the stairs, already planning his course of action. He'd get dressed, load his pistols, saddle Molan, and be in Greystones just after dawn.

And then his gaze fell on the tray of food.

Glynis.

Glynis set aside the fireplace poker when the door opened, and smiled as Carrick stepped silently across the threshold. "That was the longest five minutes of my life," she said, moving to close the door behind him.

"Mine, too," he answered, carrying the tray to the desk.

Something about him seemed different. Something had changed in a way that she couldn't identify but could sense nonetheless. "Is everything all right, Carrick?" she asked, following him, the chill returning as she moved away from the fire.

"It will be in about ten seconds," he replied, setting down the tray. He turned around, stripped the shirt from his shoulders, and dropped it to the floor. His breeches shortly followed.

"I hope you're a strong women, Glynis Muldoon," he said, taking her into his arms, his gaze searching hers with breathtaking intensity. "Because I don't have the patience to wait until after you've eaten."

"Carrick . . . ?"

He kissed her hard and deep, silencing her words. It took

him longer to still the niggling worries, but as he drew her down to lie with him before the hearth her doubts were swept away.

They returned later when he carried her to the bed. But they faded again as she lay in his arms. She slept then, safe in Carrick's arms and his love.

Carrick stood at the foot of the bed, watching her sleep. They'd made love until exhausted. He hadn't thought to count the times. It didn't matter.

God willing, he'd come back to her. He'd take her in his arms and tell her he'd decided to fight for their future together. He'd promise her that she'd never awaken alone again, that he'd always be there for her.

And if he couldn't come back . . .

Carrick whispered, "I love you, Glynis Muldoon," then turned and left her.

24

Carrick stood at the barred window of his cell and watched the activity in the city square below. The authorities hadn't wasted any time constructing the scaffold. Just after dawn a wagon had been placed in the center of the cobbled square and the carpenters had used it to judge the necessary height of their structure. Already the corner timbers had been set into place and, as he watched, the cross members for the platform itself were being hammered across the span. At the rate the crew was working, the flooring and the drop hatch would be in place before nightfall. Tomorrow would see the completion of the project. In the course of the day after he could watch the hangman practice his craft with a bag of sand in preparation for the real event.

There was some consolation, he supposed, in events moving as quickly as they were. A man too long alone with his thoughts and regrets was a particularly pathetic thing to see. And the sooner the deed was done, the less those around him would have to suffer. The sooner he was dead, the sooner they could go on with their lives.

Especially Glynis. Carrick closed his eyes, remembering her as she lay sleeping, a smile curving the corners of her mouth. What he wouldn't give for a lifetime of those moments, a lifetime of loving her. But cheating the hangman wasn't going to be his destiny after all. Thank God he'd had the wisdom to say nothing to her. For her to know that she'd had the dream within her reach and then lost it . . .

The sound of a key in the lock of the cell door pulled him from his thoughts. He turned as the guard pushed open the oak panel and stepped aside to admit Colonel Hewlett.

"Back from my sister's, Colonel?" he asked, casually leaning against the window frame and crossing one booted ankle over the other.

"Yes. You have a remarkable family, young man. They bore up well to the news."

"I hope they agreed with equal aplomb to abide by my requests."

Colonel Hewlett placed his hat on the scarred table and unbuttoned his jacket. "Your sister's husband agreed and asked me to tell you they would pray for you."

"That's kind of ol' Horace," Carrick observed with a crooked smile. He shrugged. "Not that I think praying's going to do me much good."

"Probably not, but it's a comfort to them." Hewlett pulled out the chair and sat down, extending his legs in front of him. "Your cousin said he would send the boy home but refuses to go himself. He says he'll see it through."

"Predictable." Carrick looked dispassionately at the sky beyond the rooftops of the little village. "My parents?"

"Your mother is a gracious woman, and especially under such difficult circumstances. She was shocked, of course, but hardly exhibited the kind of hysteria I've seen in other women. Your father said he would exercise great effort to see your wishes fulfilled regarding Miss Muldoon before he and your mother came here."

"And Glynis? Did she agree to go home?" Carrick tried to look disinterested.

"What do you think?"

The amusement in Hewlett's voice drew Carrick's attention back into the dim stone cell and made him smile. "I suspect she had a few choice words for you to deliver to me, Colonel. And I doubt they amount to a sweetly worded farewell."

"Her precise words were, "When pigs fly.""

Carrick laughed outright. "That's my Glynis." He grinned at the British officer. "But knowing her as I do, I know there's more. Is any of it repeatable?"

"She asked me to tell you that she loves you."

Christ, it hurt; a razor-sharp ache that stole his breath and slashed his heart to ribbons. He turned his face toward the window again, but his view of the world outside was obstructed by the pain.

"Your father promised to prevail on Miss Muldoon's sensibilities and change her mind."

"If Glynis loves me," he answered, deliberately forcing himself away from the window, "it's obvious that she doesn't have any sensibilities." He began pacing the width of the small room.

"Frankly, I can see many reasons for the high regard in which the young lady holds you."

Carrick looked over at him, startled, and said dryly, "My activities against the Crown and the death of Major Cunningham aside, of course."

Hewlett nodded and then rose to his feet. "I shall regret very much my role in your coming death, des Marceaux. It is not a duty to which I attend lightly or from which I derive the slightest bit of pleasure."

"Thank you, Colonel."

The English officer buttoned his coat, saying, "I have arranged rooms for your family at the King's Arms Inn and left word that I am to be immediately informed of their arrival. Are there any further messages you would like for me to convey on your behalf?"

Carrick considered the opportunity for a long moment and then resolutely shook his head. "Thank you, Colonel Hewlett. But no. It's best for all concerned if matters are left as they presently stand."

With a crisp nod, the officer moved to the door and rapped against the heavy oaken panel. A moment later the door opened and Colonel Hewlett stepped into the corridor. The cell door closed behind him with a heavy thud.

The silence immediately afterward caught Carrick's attention. The key hadn't turned in the lock. He listened and heard the low murmur of voices in the hallway. Even as he pondered the possibilities the door opened again.

Robert stepped across the threshold. When the door closed behind him, the key turned.

Carrick met his cousin's somber gaze for as long as he could. Then, looking out the window of his cell, he said, "I know that Colonel Hewlett conveyed my wishes for no visitors."

"He did indeed," Robert replied, coming farther into the small stone room. "But then I don't listen worth a damn. Never have."

Carrick said nothing. He watched the construction of the scaffold, but he heard every step Robert took.

"Have you been mistreated? Did they interrogate you?" Robert asked from behind him.

Knowing he had no choice but to deal with his cousin's presence as best he could, Carrick turned and forced a smile. "There was a minor scuffle after I shot Cunningham, but I doubt I have so much as a bruise to show for it."

"Good," Robert said quietly, his own gaze on the scaffolding.

Then, without warning, Robert struck him. Carrick doubled over, unable to breathe. The world grayed and he felt his knees buckling. He struggled against the collapse, locking his knees. "Sweet Jesus, Rob."

"You goddamn fool!" Robert snarled through his teeth, grabbing Carrick by the shirtfront and shoving his back against the stone wall of the cell. "Why?" Robert demanded, shoving him again. "Why the hell did you come here alone?"

"You know why," Carrick groaned. At Robert's next bone-jarring shove, he growled, "You're going to crack my skull."

"Good," Robert declared, giving him one last push before letting him go and storming to the far side of the room.

Carrick slid down the wall to the floor of the cell. He told himself that he'd had worse beatings and probably deserved more than Robert had given him. All things considered, he'd gotten off lightly.

"You son of a bitch," Robert snarled. "You goddamn son of a bitch."

"Yeah," Carrick replied, slowly climbing to his feet. "You're like a brother to me, too."

"They delivered Patrick in a wooden box to your father this morning," Robert supplied, his hands clenched into fists at his side. "Eachann's alive, but just barely. Aunt Alanna and Saraid were doing what they could for him when I left to come here. He'll never walk again. Never work the horses."

Carrick gingerly settled himself on the stone window ledge and asked quietly, "Where's Glynis?"

"What the hell do you care?"

"Where's Glynis?" Carrick repeated patiently. "Is she all right?"

"She'll never be all right. You've outdone yourself this time, Carrick. Truly outdone yourself."

"For God's sakes, Robert. You didn't bring her here with you, did you?"

"No. She's still back at Saraid's. Probably still crying."

Carrick closed his eyes, resting his head against the cool metal bars, his heart heavy.

"What happened, Carrick?" There was no anger in Robert's voice now. Just resignation and pain.

Carrick forced his body upright. He owed his cousin far more than he could ever repay. The least he could do was show him some courage.

"What did Hewlett tell you all?" he asked.

"That you were apprehended attempting to take Eachann from custody. That you killed Cunningham. That you then confessed to being the Dragon, implicating only yourself. Frankly, it all sounds too simple to me."

They were the darkest memories of his life. Nothing he'd ever done, ever seen, had prepared him for what he'd walked into at dawn. "I found them by following the screams," he explained dispassionately. "It was just the three of them in the smithy. Eachann was a bloody and blackened heap on the floor. Cunningham was working on Patrick at the forge."

"Oh, Jesus."

Carrick trudged on, determined to have it over and done. "Cunningham looked up as I came through the door. He smiled and I knew. . . . He called in six regulars from the back and introduced me as the Dragon; told them to take my pistol from me. In that second they hesitated, Patrick raised his head and looked at me."

The memory of the pain, the shame in Patrick's eyes stopped him. Before the grief could overwhelm him, he stared at the toes of his boots and hurried to finish. "He said, 'I'm sorry, Carrick.' And then Cunningham snapped his neck like a twig. While he laughed and the regulars stood there looking queasy, I shot the goddamn sadistic bastard." He met Robert's eyes square on, then tapped the center of his forehead. "Right here."

"In front of God and a half-dozen British soldiers."

"I suppose that's the essence of it. My confession was a mere formality at that point."

"Formality, hell. The word of a tortured man isn't sufficient to convict another of treason. Not in this day and age."

"It hardly mattered," Carrick countered with a shrug. "The Crown tends to frown on the shooting of its officers, you know."

"The lower ranks of His Majesty's Army don't seem to be too distressed over Cunningham's untimely demise," Robert observed. He crossed his arms over his chest and added, "The orderly downstairs who searched me for weapons asked me to convey his respects and his appreciation. There was a general murmur of agreement from the rest."

"Hewlett has been a decent fellow over the matter."

"He was quite the compassionate gentleman while telling us he was going to hang you at noon the day after tomorrow." In an affected English accent his cousin said, "So sorry, Lord and Lady des Marceaux. Duty is, on occasions such as this, a most odious master."

"He meant it, you know. He really is a decent man." At Robert's silent nod, Carrick decided to give him another truth. "I wish there was some way to have spared everyone that exchange; to spare you all of this."

"If you're interested in knowing," his kinsman said evenly, "Glynis took the news of her pregnancy quite well.

Not that your father's masterful playing of that gambit had the effect he hoped. Glynis isn't going to run, Carrick. She's hurting now. She doesn't know which way to go. But she'll make a stand before too much longer. You can bet on it."

His heart twisted. "Part of me hoped that she'd awaken to find me gone and be angry enough to hate me."

"And what did the other part of you hope, Cousin?"

He didn't have the strength to lie and so Carrick gave him honesty. "That it was all the worst of nightmares and that I'd awaken and find her still sleeping in my arms. That I could tell her I'd decided to fight for our future together."

Robert looked shocked. "When did you come to this decision? Before or after you came to Greystones?"

"Before."

"Then why the hell did you come?" He shook his head. "Never mind. I know the answer already. You came because you knew Cunningham had Patrick and Eachann. You came alone so no one else risked bearing the potential cost."

"Would you have done any differently?"

Robert returned to looking out the window. After several long moments he answered, "No. I'd have done the same."

Robert's acknowledgment eased the burden on Carrick's shoulders. His cousin was once again his ally. Everything was now endurable. "Don't tell Glynis about any of this, Rob," he quietly admonished. "It would be cruel."

"I won't. Does anyone else know what you intended to do?"

"No."

"Your mother is going to do what she thinks she must. You know that, right? You know that, sooner or later, she'll bring magic into this."

"God, I wish I could let myself believe that Glynis and I can have forever. But we all know that whatever Mother does won't be successful. I can't stop them from hoping, Rob. I can't keep them from trying. But I'm counting on you to be there to pick up the pieces when it all falls apart. I need to know that you're going to do that for them—for me."

Robert continued to stare out the window as he slowly nodded.

"And I have to know that you'll take care of Glynis through this."

Again Robert nodded. "I'll see that she gets back across time, back to where she belongs."

"Until then, hold her," Carrick pressed. "Don't let her mourn too deeply."

Robert didn't move, didn't make a sound. Carrick glanced over at him, instantly noting the hard set of his jaw, his flat expression. "Well, don't just stand there glowering. Spit it out, Rob."

"She doesn't love me, Carrick," his cousin said, his tone flinty. "She never will. If you're expecting me to step into your shoes in that respect . . . it isn't going to happen. I can hold her. I can dry her tears. But I can't fill the hole in her heart."

Carrick shrugged and looked at his toes. "It was worth a try."

"I'm sorry," Robert said, the gentleness returning to his voice. "I honestly wish I could do that for both of you."

"I'll tell you what it is you *can* do."

"What?"

He pushed himself from the window ledge and faced his cousin. "Leave, Robert. Don't come back."

A long silence stretched between them, and then finally Robert said, "You don't know how many times since that night I've thought about this moment; of what I'd say, what I'd do. It's been fourteen years, Carrick. And I still don't know how I'm supposed to walk away from you."

As much for himself as Robert, he answered, "One step at a time and without looking back."

"With no regrets?"

"If you can do that, I'd certainly appreciate knowing how."

The sound of the key sliding into the lock echoed in the silence between them. Colonel Hewlett pushed open the door, softly cleared his throat, and then announced that he could give them no more time. They both nodded and the officer withdrew to let them say their final farewells.

Robert studied him before saying, "I have a favor to ask of you."

Carrick managed a weak smile. "My resources are rather limited for the foreseeable future."

"When the magic comes," his cousin said evenly. "promise me you won't fight it. Promise me you'll take the chance."

"Thinking we might get lucky, huh?"

"We have before. Many a time. Just promise me."

It was a small thing to ask, a small thing to give. "All right, Robert. I won't fight it."

"Then I won't say good-bye." He extended his hand and as Carrick shook it, his cousin added, "I'll see you when it's all behind us."

"We'll get roaring drunk. I'll buy."

Robert smiled. It didn't reach his eyes. "Damn right you will," he asserted, releasing Carrick's hand and turning toward the door.

Carrick wanted to look away, to avoid the memory. He watched Robert open the door and step into the hallway. Once the door closed . . .

"Robert?"

He stopped, but he didn't turn around, didn't look back. "Yeah?"

"Take care of yourself."

His cousin squared his shoulders, nodded, and pulled the panel closed behind him.

The key turned in the lock with a cold finality that struck Carrick like a physical blow. He sank back against the window ledge. Closing his eyes, he tried to still the tremors that made his hands shake and his legs weak. He reminded himself that there were going to be a thousand moments like this between now and when he stood on the scaffold. The trial would be tomorrow. The spectators' gallery would be filled. He'd have to walk through the crowds filling the square the morning after that. And he'd have to climb the steps to face them all while the hangman fitted the noose around his neck.

He could hope his mother had a miracle in her storehouse of magic. He could hope it worked. He could pray that he and Glynis would have a chance for happiness and a life together.

But if the Dragon's Heart prophecy came to pass . . . if he hoped to keep from shaming those he loved . . . he had to find a way to bury his fear and his regrets.

25

Glynis turned and began another pass of her rented room. It was the damn waiting. She was past ready to do something besides count the ten steps it took to cross the length of the room, the seven it took to cover the width. Looking out the window was impossible. All she could see in the moonlight was the scaffolding in the village square, and that made her feel both queasy and intensely desperate.

She turned and started back across the room, certain that the innkeeper would want to bill someone when he discovered the rut she was wearing in the floorboards. A soft knock on the door stopped her pacing. She opened it to find Lady Alanna standing there.

"Ready?" Carrick's mother asked.

"Yes," Glynis answered, taking her traveling cloak down from the peg and throwing it around her shoulders as she stepped across the threshold. She pulled the door closed behind her and together she and Alanna moved down the hallway.

Alanna spoke with quiet urgency. "Remember that you have three very important tasks, Glynis. The first is to convince Carrick that traveling through the portal is the right course of action. He loves you with all his heart. He'll do things for you he wouldn't for anyone else on earth.

"The second is to select with Carrick a time and place for me to work the magic. Make it someplace public, someplace where I'll be able to see him, Glynis. I want to know in that instant whether the magic's worked."

"And the third thing is our insurance policy," she instructed. "Give him an image of the Flint Hills to visualize as I cast the spell. He stands a better chance of getting where we want him if he has some idea of where he's supposed to end up.

"Now, if it's possible, I'll send you through together. If it's not, I'll send Carrick first. You, second, and as quickly after him as I can. Is that acceptable?"

"No problem. Carrick's the one whose life is in danger," Glynis said as they reached the stairway and stopped.

"Good," Lady Alanna said, squeezing Glynis's hands with a determined smile. "Kiervan's waiting for you downstairs."

"May I ask a question?" Glynis ventured quietly. "I've been wondering about something."

"What?"

"Have you ever deliberately sent someone across time before?"

"No."

Oh, God. "Maybe accidentally?" Glynis offered hopefully.

"Not that I know of." Lady Alanna smiled. "But if Saraid can do it purely by accident, then it should be well within my deliberate capabilities."

Glynis marshaled her courage and pressed. "Do you know how to do it?"

"In theory." Lady Alanna laughed quietly. "Oh, for heaven's sakes, Glynis. You look like someone just ran over your cat. Have a little faith. I know I look like your average, garden-variety, mild-mannered mother, but you haven't seen me in my tights and cape. I'm pretty awesome."

Glynis wanted to laugh. She wanted to cry. Instead she took a deep breath and shook her head. "You're not mild-mannered and you're not anything close to garden-variety. You're Glenda, Good Witch of the North, meets General George S. Patton."

"What an interesting combination," Lady Alanna said with a grin. "I rather like the image of that. Yards and yards of glittering chiffon, accessorized with a riding crop and a steel helmet."

"Don't forget the combat boots," Glynis added as she started down the stairs. "They're a fashion must."

"I'm going to miss you, Glynis," Alanna called after her. "I hope you don't mind if I look in on you from time to time."

For some reason the thought of Alanna des Marceaux watching her life unfold brought her a great deal of comfort. Glynis paused and turned to look up. "I'd like that. Peek in anytime you'd like." A sudden thought made her hastily add, "Just give me some warning so I'm not caught naked, okay?"

"Poor Glynis," Lady Alanna said, shaking her head and looking like she wasn't really the least bit sympathetic. "I'm afraid that if we succeed in getting Carrick through time with you . . ." Her eyes twinkled and her smile broadened. "He's a des Marceaux male, Glynis. Which means you're going to spend very little of your life dressed."

With that, Carrick's mother blew her a kiss, then turned and walked away. Glynis stood there a moment considering the maelstrom of her emotions. There was hope. A plan had been fashioned. It was riddled with potholes, but it was a hell of a lot better than nothing. And in just a few minutes she would be with Carrick again.

That was the source of her dread: their imminent meeting. She knew Carrick. He wasn't going to jump up and down with joy when he heard of his mother's plans. He wasn't going to blithely agree to let her carry them through.

Glynis was determined to stay positive. She had to be totally together from this point on. She was in for the fight of her life and she couldn't afford to lose it. Glynis lifted her chin and gathered her skirts, then went to meet Carrick's father.

"I can't give you long together," Colonel Hewlett said quietly as he escorted Glynis along the narrow corridor of the jailhouse. "I shall stand watch near the end of the hall and signal with two small raps against the door. You must present yourself immediately."

"I understand. And thank you, Colonel Hewlett. For everything."

"I feel as though I must warn you, child. You are not likely to find yourself welcomed as you might want. It has been my experience that men facing their own death are not comforted by reminders of the happiness they are leaving behind."

Glynis nodded.

The colonel took the iron key from his pocket and unlocked the door, pushing it open for her and waiting until she'd stepped into the darkened cell before pulling it closed and locking it behind her.

She stood silently just inside the stone cell, letting her eyes adjust to the darkness.

"If you've come here to strangle me, sweetheart, you should know that the hangman's going to be real disappointed. He's been practicing all afternoon with a huge sack of sand."

She turned toward the sound of his voice and found him seated on a narrow cot, his back against the wall and his booted ankles crossed. She'd have thought him relaxed looking at him, but she heard the tension beneath his irreverence.

Carrick watched her sway on her feet, watched her struggle to hold herself together. He wanted to go to her, to take her in his arms. He remained where he was, telling himself over and over again that he couldn't risk letting her get past the walls he'd deliberately built around himself in the last two days. To admit that he loved her would reduce him to tears, would strip him of the courage he needed to face what lay ahead.

He had promised Robert that he'd accept the magic when it came. He'd promised himself that he'd accept its possible failure with dignity. A fine line separated the two courses and balancing between them was difficult enough without Glynis standing before him, needing him. There were no halfways with her. There never had been. And he knew beyond any doubt that he couldn't hold her and withhold his heart, couldn't comfort her and still hide from her the depth of his heartache, the vastness of his regrets. Her own burdens were heavy enough for her to bear. He couldn't add his to them. If the magic worked and they came through their ordeal together, he'd spend the rest of his life atoning for what he was about to do. But for now, for both their sakes, he had to send her away.

"Julia Conroy outdid herself at the trial today, don't you think?" he said, as much to distract himself as Glynis. "At least I assume it was of Julia's design, since I saw her moving everyone about in the spectators' gallery. I'm sure all those men leaping to their feet at the last moment to declare themselves as the Dragon will go down as one of the greatest performances in legal history. I hope none of the gentry hurt themselves. They're not accustomed to either the physical or moral exercise."

She stood perfectly still. Her voice came quietly out of the darkness. "You could have at least made some pretense of defending yourself, Carrick."

Her gentleness frightened him. He needed her anger between them to fortify his own defenses. "I thought my statement before the court was rather inspired," he countered blithely, trying to goad her. "I distinctly heard weeping from the gallery. I must admit, though, that I was a bit disappointed when no one unfurled the Irish flag."

"It *was* eloquent, Carrick. I'll give you that," she answered, an edge to her voice. "And it was about as public as confessions of treason get."

"Hewlett assures me that no charges will be brought against Meyler for his part in the general circus. It seems that leaping the bar, brandishing a gun, and charging the magistrate are forgivable offenses when you're twelve years old. Thank God. I hope Robert is finally on his way back to county Kerry with him?"

"Your father sent them both back to Saraid's," she supplied, her anger suddenly gone. "He said they'd all go home together."

Christ. There was nothing to do but push her harder. "And when are you going home, Glynis?"

"When I get damn good and ready, and not one second before."

She wasn't quite where he wanted her. But she was close.

He pushed again. "You shouldn't have come here, Glynis. This is a mistake for both of us. Be a good girl and go back to the inn."

"Your mother arranged it with Colonel Hewlett."

Icy reserve. He heard it and knew that it was meant to mask her growing anger. Good. "Was it her idea or yours?" he asked caustically.

"Your parents'. I agreed to be the messenger."

"Don't say another word, Glynis," he said, his voice as coolly controlled as hers. "I don't want to hear them."

"You don't even know what they are."

"Don't I? Let me see how close I can come. Mother's going to haul out the bag of magic tricks and find one that will be just right for spiriting me out of the hangman's noose and plopping me down somewhere where I'll be safe and cozy. And that someplace is the Rocking M Ranch in the Kansas Flint Hills in the year 1997."

He pressed closer to the cold stone wall and continued without pause. "And your task, Glynis . . . the reason you're here . . . is to convince me to allow this to happen. You're to prevail upon my love for you, to do whatever you must to get me to surrender pride, honor, and dignity." He gave her two seconds before he coldly asked, "How'd I do? Am I close?"

"There are a few significant details to add, but you have the gist of it."

She was struggling to hold back tears. He could hear them in her voice. He could feel his resolve weakening. "The answer's no, Glynis. Tell my parents to leave it be."

"I love you, Carrick. I can't give you up without a fight."

The pain drove him off the bed and to his feet. He stood, the backs of his legs pressed against the frame of the cot, his hands fisted at his side. "And I couldn't bear to look into your eyes years from now and see you remembering that I took the coward's way out."

She stiffened. "We've had this conversation before."

"And it's not going to turn out any differently than it did the last time, Glynis. Stand in my shoes and tell me you'd run away."

"I would," she answered hotly. "I swear I would. In a heartbeat."

"Then what are you doing here? Why haven't you run back to Kansas and the certainty of your life at the Rocking M?"

"It's different!"

"The hell it is," he instantly countered, finding comfort in his own anger. "All of this is killing you, breaking your heart. But your sense of honor won't let you run out on me. It demands that you stay here and fight until the bitter end. It's your pride that's keeping you from begging. And your dignity, Glynis . . . right now your dignity is the only thing between you and tears." He shook his head and slowly added, "Don't you dare come in here and tell me I should give up what you can't and won't."

"But I'm right, Carrick. And you're wrong."

"There is no right or wrong to this, Glynis. There's just my destiny and your destiny. For a time they came together. But they part ways here."

"And now?"

"I think it would be for the best. We're just reminding each other of what can't ever be."

Glynis trembled as a wave of grief swept through her. He was right. She knew it. But she also knew that she couldn't leave him this way.

"Do you have any requests for our child's name?" she asked quietly.

"I leave the decision in your hands, Glynis," he replied tiredly. "I trust you to choose one that will fit him and serve him well."

"Your mother wants me to take the Dragon's Heart with me when I go. She says our son will have the powers you and she do for seeing. I told her I'd think about whether or not I wanted to do that. What do you think I should do?"

"Christ Almighty!" he snapped, taking a half-step toward her. "Why are you asking me these things, Glynis?"

"Because I'm going to be raising our child without you. There are going to be a thousand decisions to make over the years and I'll have to make them alone. I want to be able to look at my choices and say to myself, 'Yes, I remember. Carrick wanted me to do this.' Or 'Carrick would have expected me to do it this way.' I'm asking you to tell me what I should do so that sometimes, when I'm scared . . ." Her voice broke and she rushed on before the words were lost in tears. "I want to hear your voice in my head so I can pretend, just for a little while, that you're there with me."

His shoulders slumped and he stared down at the floor. "Sweet Jesus."

Oh, God. What had she done to him? "I'm sorry," she said, frantically holding back the tears. "I didn't mean to lose it," she went on, her voice steadying with every word. "I'll be brave for you, Carrick. I won't cry and make this any harder on you than it already is. I promise."

He looked up at her. In the darkness she couldn't see his eyes. "Glynis . . ."

She heard the heartache and scrambled to do what she could to save him from it. "So do I take the Dragon's Heart with me or not?"

He stepped forward and stopped. For a long moment he just looked at her and then he slowly reached out and took her hand in his. "The Dragon's Heart goes with you, Glynis," he whispered, gently placing her hand against his chest. "I gave it to you long ago. It's yours forever and always."

"Please—"

He touched his fingertips to her lips and shook his head. "No more arguing, Glynis. We have better things to do with the time we have left."

He felt the tremor that shook her. "Tell me," he said, putting his hands on her hips and drawing her closer. "If I were to lift these skirts of yours, would I find a pair of pantalets?"

"No."

"You're a brazen woman, Glynis Muldoon."

"I rather thought that was one of the things you liked about me."

"That I love about you," he corrected softly. "But leave

me the buttons on my breeches this time, will you, darling? It's the only pair I have."

She laughed shakily and the sound destroyed the last of the walls he'd put up to protect them. Even as he felt them crumble around him, she took him in her arms and wrapped him in her love. He held her close and loved her with fierce tenderness, pouring into her all that he had to give. And in the silence, they clung to one another, giving what they could of their strength and courage, taking what they needed.

Later she left him without a word, rising from his arms at the gentle taps against the door and pausing only long enough to press one last kiss to his lips. He didn't move to stop her, didn't give voice to the anguish tearing at his heart. He watched her go and when the door closed behind her, he stopped fighting the tears.

Kiervan knew the minute he saw her. His gaze met Colonel Hewlett's in silent inquiry, but the Colonel shook his head sadly and said nothing as he escorted Glynis to him. Only after Kiervan had taken her arm did the Englishman release his own hold on her and step away.

"Thank you, Colonel," Kiervan said. "I'll see her safely back to her room."

"Were she my daughter, I would not leave her alone for some time to come."

"We'll care for her."

The colonel touched Glynis's cheek softly, his eyes clouding in the second before he turned and walked away. Glynis gave no outward sign of being aware of the gesture. Indeed, she seemed to have turned inward, to have gone to some place where the pain could not touch her.

Kiervan slipped his arm around her shoulders and started forward. She came along without resistance, without a flicker of life in her eyes. They were skirting the village square, almost to the corner where they were to turn away from it, when her steps faltered.

"Glynis? Are you all right?"

She bolted from him, running toward the scaffold.

Kiervan sprinted after her, fear for her pushing him. He was only halfway to her when she stopped and scooped up a piece of timber.

"Glynis!" he called as she squared up to the scaffolding.

"Goddamn his sense of honor," she sobbed, swinging the board with all her might at one of the bracing timbers. The impact of wood against wood sent her staggering back. She righted herself as Kiervan grabbed for her, twisting away from his grasp. She swung the board again. "Goddamn his pride."

"Christ Almighty," he swore, catching her about the waist with one arm and hauling her back. She flailed against his control, heartbreaking sobs wracking her body and making her efforts useless. "Stop before you hurt yourself," he commanded, catching her wrists in one hand and shaking the timber from her grasp. The wood clattered to the cobblestones as he said, "We'll think of something else, Glynis. We're not going to give up."

She went limp against him and he quickly wrapped his free arm around her and hoisted her up, pinning her back to his chest.

"He can't die, Kiervan," she moaned. "I can't live without him."

"We're not going to let him die."

"Oh, God."

"You've got to dig deep, Glynis. Find whatever it takes for you to face this. You're not going to do Carrick any good if you let yourself wallow in grief and self-pity. Do you hear me, Glynis Muldoon?"

"I hear you," she said weakly. "I hear you," she said again, this time with a note of conviction in her voice.

He eased her down until her feet touched the cobblestones. Slowly, he let her take her own weight back, let her find her balance. And when he felt her take a shuddering breath, he knew the time had come to begin devising a plan.

"If I let you go now, will you promise to behave somewhat rationally?" he asked.

She nodded and wiped the palms of her hands over her cheeks.

"All right." Kiervan released her and stepped back. He gave her to the count of three before he put his hands on her shoulders and turned her around to face him. She looked up at him, her eyes swollen, her lips compressed into a thin line that trembled despite her effort. But the tilt of her chin told him she was ready to fight.

26

Glynis strode down the inky dark hallway of Saraid's home. Lady Alanna could think magic resided in spells and visions if she wanted to, but Glynis knew better. Magic was a pair of faded Levi's and scuffed boots. It was a set of worn leather chaps, a drover's coat, and a battered Stetson pulled low over your eyes. It was a set of saddlebags hanging over your left shoulder and a loaded Winchester in your right hand. But above all else, magic was an attitude with a Capital A. And she had found it.

She didn't bother to knock. She simply flung open the door and strode into Robert's room. He stood at the window, fully clothed, looking out at the sunrise with his arms crossed over his chest. He turned his head as she stepped over the threshold.

"We have a plan, Robert," she said. "We're riding in ten minutes. And we need to saddle the horses. I'll get Meyler."

Robert didn't say anything. He simply reached over, picked up the flintlock pistol lying on the bureau, and proceeded to tuck it into his waistband at the small of his back. She left him and moved down the hall.

Meyler was still asleep. At the sound of her entrance he came from the bed as if he were spring-loaded. "We need to help Robert saddle the horses. Yours and his, plus five extras," she said, standing just inside the doorway. "We're racing the sun. Haul ass, Meyler."

He nodded and scrambled for his clothes. She left him,

heading for her final destination before leaving this place forever.

Pausing outside Saraid and Horace's door just long enough to knock on the panel and say, "I hope you're decent, 'cause I'm coming in," she pushed open the door.

"Miss Muldoon?" Horace rasped, struggling to sit up.

Saraid was quicker. "What's happened?" she asked, flinging the blankets aside and climbing from the bed with remarkable agility.

"I'm taking Robert and Meyler and five of your best horses. I won't be coming back and I just wanted to thank you for your hospitality." She tugged the brim of her hat as she added, "Much appreciated. And it's been a pleasure knowin' ya."

"Glynis, what are you doing? Where are you going?"

"Greystones. And then home," she added, already turning to leave. "You might pray for a good string of luck between those two."

She headed down the hallway, Saraid exhorting her husband to dress and ready a carriage to follow her. She smiled grimly. Unless they hurried, those two were going to miss the show. She couldn't afford to wait for them.

Ten minutes later she rode down the graveled drive, Bert trailing her on a lead. Robert rode on her right, Meyler on her left, each of them leading two spare mounts. They headed east, into the faint light of dawn, over the same road she'd ridden less than twenty minutes before. The thunder of hooves pounded through her and into the last hours of the night.

Kiervan sat astride Molan in the shadows of the trees and watched the road that snaked from the western hills. They'd had less than twelve hours to put together their plan. They needed another six to deal with all the finer points. But they didn't have that luxury. Noon was less than an hour away. They had no other choice but to act, and hope for a string of miracles. He glanced up at the sun. Time was running out.

The sound of riders in the distance instantly brought his attention back to the road and gave him a sense of relief. They came straight at him, moving fast, with their riderless mounts trailing behind on leads. He urged Molan forward into the roadway and fell in with them as they continued on without pause.

"We're as ready as we can be," he said over the pounding of hooves. He saw Glynis nod crisply once, her eyes on the road. It occurred to him in that moment that he'd never fully seen her before. The brocade and velvet gowns had been costumes and she'd been playing only one part of herself. The strange clothing she wore now, the way she sat the saddle, the wordless purpose with which she pushed ahead—they all spoke clearly of the Glynis Muldoon who existed under the feminine trappings and bright smiles. At her core she was flinty determination and cool resolve, a woman who faced hard realities and high risks with quiet courage. She met the world square on, willing to grant quarter to those who deserved it but asking none for herself. A sense of peace settled over him. No matter how it all turned out, his son had known the wonder of a great and glorious love. Few men got that out of life.

"We take the left fork," he said as they neared a curve in the road. "Alanna's waiting for us."

Carrick settled deeper onto the windowsill and studied the goings-on below. The village square had been transformed into the site of a lively public festival. There were horses and carts and people everywhere. Vendors had set up their booths, offering the gathering spectators everything from brightly colored ribbons to hot meat pies to hanks of hair purported to be from the head of the Dragon himself. He scanned the sea of faces, searching for those he knew. There was no one.

"Confessing your sins will ease your soul," the priest said for the second time.

Carrick shook his head in exasperation but didn't spare the man a glance. "I can appreciate your dedication, Father, but there isn't any point to it. I'm not Catholic. And I figure the Good Lord was watching me the whole time anyway. He knows what I've done. He also knows that I'm not the least bit repentant."

"Surely you have some regrets that trouble—"

"Pray for those who'll be left living, Father," Carrick snarled, turning to glare at the man. "Go offer them your comforting words."

The priest closed his book quietly, mumbled in Latin as he made the sign of the cross in Carrick's direction, and then moved to the door. No sooner had he been allowed to exit than Colonel Hewlett and three British regulars entered.

"I'm afraid the appointed time has arrived," the colonel said quietly. "If I might ask you to stand, turn, and place your hands behind your back . . ."

"It's not necessary, " Carrick assured the officer as he abandoned his seat. "I give you my word of honor that I will make no attempt to escape."

"I have no latitude in this matter, Mr. des Marceaux. I am sorry."

Carrick shrugged and went to stand before him. He turned, presenting his hands as requested and saying, "They've come for a show. I suppose the least we can do is make it worth their time and effort."

As he followed Hewlett out the door of the jail and down the steps, Carrick decided that there was something to be said for having watched yourself die for fourteen years. There were no surprises. Everything was exactly as it was supposed to be. Dirty cobblestones. A crowd milling about the square, the new wood of the scaffolding bright in the noon sunlight. The dead wagon waited beneath the trapdoor of the gallows. And yes, there the headstone was, propped against the rear wheel. That he wasn't close enough to read the carving didn't matter. He knew what it said.

And just as he'd seen himself do a thousand times, he followed Hewlett through the parting crowd and moved toward the waiting scaffold. The hooded executioner waited as well, although Carrick couldn't imagine why a hood was necessary at this juncture. The man hadn't worn one during the hours he'd spent hanging that blasted bag of sand. He had no anonymity except to those who had arrived in Greystones that morning.

Ah, and the little priest was up there with the hangman just like he was supposed to be, his worn prayerbook in his hands, his robes fluttering in the breeze. They'd all have to wait until he'd finished praying for a lost soul that really didn't give a damn where his soul went.

They reached the bottom of the stairs and Hewlett stepped aside, saying, "I will see that you are delivered into your family's care for proper burial."

Thanking the man seemed a rather odd thing to do, but he did it anyway and then started up the steps alone. The breeze felt good. As he climbed above the crowd, he thought about how much he'd missed the feel of it in the last few days. The sun felt good on his shoulder, too. And then, as though God had decided that he wasn't properly miserable for the occasion, a cloud passed over the sun and blocked the warmth just as he reached the top of the stairs.

The murmuring of the crowd didn't stop, but the volume and pitch of it subtly shifted as he turned and walked toward the center of the stage of the King's justice. He looked out into the sea of upturned faces, half-wanting to see some he recognized, half-dreading the same possibility.

Glynis! The sight of her instantly merged with all that he remembered of the vision. She was striding over cobblestones at the far edge of the square, the edges of her tattered drover's coat fluttering about her legs, the battered felt hat pulled low over her eyes. Just as he'd seen in the watery image, she held her rifle in her right hand and quickly threaded her way through the passing crowd. Everyone was coming toward the gallows. Glynis was the only one walking away. How the hell no one seemed to notice her he couldn't imagine, but no one did.

His heart raced. He hadn't put the two separate visions together. He'd never thought to see them as connected. But he should have, he realized. God, he should have. He should have known that she wouldn't hide in her rented room, wouldn't watch in tearful passivity. Not his sweet, steely Glynis.

Glynis scrambled up the makeshift steps Kiervan had built for her out of stacked wooden boxes and barrels and onto the low roof of the building. Crouching down and quickly making her way over the tiles, she searched the crowd below. She saw that Robert and Meyler were in position, thank God. Now if only they moved when and where they were supposed to. Molan remained tethered where she'd left him, where she needed him to be if they managed to pull off the first part of this miracle.

She couldn't see Carrick's parents. She could only hope that they were having success with their tasks. If Kiervan and Alanna failed, none of them would get out of Greystones alive. Her heart thundering, Glynis slipped into position, lying flat on her stomach just back from an opening in the building's crenellated facade.

Less than two seconds later she was ready, her legs braced and her elbows set, the butt of the Winchester pressed securely into her shoulder. She drew a long, slow breath, held it, and then slowly let it out. She did it twice more, watching the priest's lips move, watching the hangman tighten the noose around Carrick's neck. She judged the wind and set the sights. Laying her fingertip over the trigger, she prayed for a perfect shot.

The hemp was good quality, Carrick decided. It didn't prickle against his skin as he'd expected. He'd always heard that the better the rope, the cleaner the break, and consequently the quicker the death. The priest was still droning on as Carrick glanced up at Glynis and then quickly away so as not to betray her presence.

What was she doing up there? What was she thinking? He'd seen executions that hadn't gone smoothly. That's why some families hired boys to throw themselves around the legs of the condemned if the rope didn't break the neck cleanly the instant the trapdoor dropped away. Perhaps, if the rope failed to do its job properly, Glynis intended to put a bullet in his brain and prevent his suffering. There wasn't a doubt in his mind that she had the courage to do it. There wasn't a doubt in his heart that she loved him enough to bear that burden.

He looked out into the crowd as the priest closed his book and the hangman checked the placement of the knot one last time. His mother and father stood at the farthest edge of the crowd, their faces drawn and tight. Suddenly he found himself no longer relieved that they hadn't come to his cell to say their farewells. At the time the written message had seemed best, had seemed like a mercy. Saying goodbye to Glynis had torn his heart from his chest and frayed his courage. The prospect of facing his parents, of seeing his mother's tears, had been more than he'd been able to face. To their credit they'd apparently known that and stayed away. And now he regretted it.

He met his father's gaze and held it. Pride, courage, and resolution were all there for him to see. He nodded. Just once, just slightly, so as not to undo the hangman's careful placement of the knot. His father returned the gesture, then squared his shoulders. Carrick's gaze slid to his mother's. Heartbreak and fear looked back at him. He offered her a smile of reassurance, of love and thanks. The tears spilled down over her cheeks and she buried her face in her hands. His father took her in his arms and held her close, pressing a kiss into her dark honey hair.

Out of the corner of his eye he saw the hangman begin to ease the lever forward, saw the priest close his eyes and begin to silently mouth the words of a prayer. Carrick looked up to the rooftop across the square, saw the muzzle of the rifle trained at his head.

I love you, Glynis.

"Fire!" he heard a voice bellow.

It all came at once. The gasp of the crowd. The click of the trapdoor mechanism. He heard a sharp crack as he closed his eyes and the world fell away.

27

The shot was true. Glynis sagged with relief, taking it all in—the severed end of the rope, the hole in the floor of the scaffold, Carrick tumbling into the wagon bed. But she didn't have time to dwell on what had happened. They weren't done yet.

She automatically levered the rifle again, her attention riveted on the square below. Robert stole the team of horses from the hands of the soldier detailed to hold them, and the wagon shot from beneath the gallows with Meyler in the back, his small body shielding Carrick's. Her heart hammering, she watched them careen from the square, prepared to cover their flight with a rain of bullets if need be. Only when they sped around a corner and out of sight did she expel the breath she'd been holding and focus on the activity below.

She caught a glimpse of Alanna and Kiervan just as they disappeared into the throng surging toward the fire-engulfed building on the far side of the square. Red-coated soldiers scrambled like ants over the cobblestones. Only one of them was apart from the growing panic. Colonel Hewlett stood on at the base of the scaffold . . . perfectly still amid the turmoil . . . looking right at her.

If he was going to be a problem, she'd just have to deal with it. The wagon was going to need a rear guard. She rolled onto her back and let the weight of her body draw her down the sloping tiles. As she neared the edge, she set her heels and quickly climbed to her feet. She didn't bother with the makeshift stairs. She jumped, landing neatly in a pile of hay and rolling out of it in the same smooth motion. She crossed to Molan in long even strides, pulled his reins free with her left hand, and vaulted up into the saddle.

He spun instantly and leaped from the shadows between the buildings and into the smoke and chaos filling the square. He raced toward the narrow road that led into the hills beyond the small town. Setting herself firmly in the saddle, she set him back hard on his haunches. He fought her control, but his determination was no match for hers and in the end he surrendered with an angry snort and a stamp of his front hooves.

Glynis glanced around her, orienting herself, while Molan danced beneath her. Her gaze met Colonel Hewlett's across the square. His head jerked up in recognition. And then, a split second later, he grinned and snapped to a sharp salute. She lifted the Winchester in return greeting and silent farewell, then wheeled Molan about and drove him across the square.

There was noise and movement everywhere. Vendors were desperately trying to protect their wares from quick hands taking advantage of the chaos. A bucket brigade was in the first stages of formation. Those that hadn't committed themselves to either looting or fighting the blaze were desperately trying to maneuver wagons and horses toward the dirt lanes that led out of the village center. British soldiers darted among them, brilliant flashes of red in the frantic activity. Amazingly, everyone had both the presence of mind and the agility to get out of her way. Glynis smiled. It was going perfectly, even better than they'd hoped.

In the next second she frowned. The British were quicker than she'd expected. She found a squad assembling at the far side of the square, their leader shouting and swinging his arms wildly as his men hurried to lead a horse and cart across the dirt road out. His gaze met hers as Glynis brought Molan to a clattering stop. The man's gaze slipped to the makeshift roadblock and then back to her. He smiled triumphantly.

The smug son of a bitch. Did he really think she was going to let him and that puny little wagon stand between her and Carrick?

She wheeled Molan about, took him three paces back into the square, and turned him sharply back. She paused just long enough to meet the redcoat's gaze again, touch the barrel of the Winchester to the brim of her hat, and smile. Then she kicked Molan hard in the flanks and sent him pounding forward.

The soldier blanched and darted away with the rest of his men as Molan sailed effortlessly up and over the cart, landing neatly on the other side with a resounding *thud* of hooves against hard-packed earth. Glynis let the animal find his balance and then drove him forward again, sparing nothing and no one a second glance as she raced to catch up with Carrick.

Only as she swept past the edge of the town and into the open land beyond did she hear her own ragged breathing, feel the white-knuckled tension with which she held the Winchester and the reins. Her heart thundered faster and harder than Molan's hooves against the turf, every slamming beat resonating with one thought, one hope . . . *Carrick*.

Relief shot through her as she crested the hill and saw the scene below. The wagon had been drawn up beneath the spreading branches of an oak tree. Robert was struggling to get Carrick across Bert's back as Meyler raced to unhitch the horses from their traces. Molan needed no urging.

"Carrick!" she cried, drawing Molan to a stop beside the wagon.

He lifted his head and looked at her, his eyes clouded with confusion. He wasn't all there, but he was alive and that was what mattered.

"Hit his head on the way down," Robert quickly supplied, putting his cousin's foot in the stirrup. "He'll be okay. It'll just be a while yet."

She hoped Carrick pulled it together soon because the next time she saw him she had every intention of kissing him senseless.

"They can't be too far behind us," she reminded them. Nudging Molan forward, she reached for the lines of the horses Meyler had freed from the wagon. "The three of you head on. I'll take these two and head off in the other direction. The Brits will have to make a choice or divide here. Either way it'll buy us some time. Meyler," she called, stopping him before he could mount. She pointed to the bed of the wagon and the length of cord that had bound Carrick's hands, the noose that had nearly taken his life. "Hand me those ropes. I'll toss 'em down for the Brits to find. It should make the decision easier for them."

Meyler did as she asked and then scrambled up onto his own horse.

Robert turned in his saddle, a troubled look in his dark eyes. "You don't know where we're going. How will you find us?"

"When I'm clear, I'll cut an arc and pick up your trail."

He looked at the sky and shook his head. "The storm's coming in fast. If it washes out our—"

"Don't worry about me, Robert," she interrupted. "Just get Carrick to his parents and don't waste any time in doing it. I'll be there as soon as I can."

He nodded crisply. "Godspeed, Glynis."

"Godspeed, Robert!" she called, pulling Molan hard to the right and setting out across the rolling green hills with the two horses trailing behind her.

She spared only a glance at the sky when she tossed the ropes away. Robert had every reason to be concerned. It looked like it was going to be one hell of an impressive storm. With any luck it would hold off until she reached Carrick again. With even better luck, the sky would open up before the British found them all.

Full awareness returned to Carrick with a jolt . . . and brought with it an overiding fear. Carrick reined Bert in and whirled about to look in the direction they had come. Robert and Meyler brought their own mounts to a halt.

"Did you let Glynis go off on her own?" he demanded, fastening his cousin with a lethal look. "Do I remember that correctly?"

"Christ, Carrick! *You* try telling Glynis Muldoon what to do!"

Bert danced beneath him, anxious to move on. "Where'd she go, Rob?"

"Hell, I don't know! She's laying down a false trail."

He swore bitterly and fought back the building fear. She shouldn't be out there alone; he had to find her. If the British did, they'd kill her.

"No way in hell!" Robert snarled, reaching out to grab Bert's reins. "You're not going after her, Carrick! For once in your goddamned life, you're going to do what *I* say!"

Carrick looked into his cousin's eyes. He saw the anger and the determination. And the devotion that anchored Robert's stand against him.

"We've brought you this far and by God you *will* let us finish it our way. I'm *not* giving you a choice."

Carrick gave in reluctantly and in that instant the bond between them had forever changed. "If something happens to her—"

"Then you can hate me till your dying day. I'll accept it." Robert met his gaze for a long moment, then released the reins and sat back in his saddle. The silence echoed with a thousand memories, a lifetime of kinship and love.

"Aunt Alanna and Uncle Kiervan are waiting for us," Meyler said softly. "We need to go."

"She'll be all right, Carrick," Robert said, his tone certain. "Have faith in her. In me."

It took every measure of Carrick's faith in his cousin, every measure of his own self-control, to turn Bert about and nudge him forward. But he did it.

As they rounded the bend and came into the wide meadow, Carrick saw his mother whirl about, took one look at her face, and knew with absolute certainty that he was going to be at the receiving end of her wrath. He'd been there often enough before. He knew how it would go this time, too. And Lord knew he deserved everything she was going to heap on him. Thunder rolled through the valley as they drew their winded mounts to a halt before his parents.

He was just swinging down off Bert when his mother came at him.

"You ever do this to me again, Carrick des Marceaux, and I'll thrash you within an inch of your life. Do you hear me?" And then she was reaching for him, pulling him into her arms. "I'll thrash you," she whispered, hugging him with all her might.

"I hear you, Mother," he said, holding her close, feeling the silent sobs that shook her slender shoulders. "I hear you. Never again. I promise."

She drew away and quickly looked him up and down. "Are you all right?" she asked, her composure returning. "Are you hurt?"

He smiled to reassure her. "I have a helluva headache, but all things considered, I won't complain." Out of the corner of his eye he saw his father nod and then turn to Robert and Meyler.

"Both of you," his father commanded, "change horses and get yourselves to Bray Harbor as fast as you can. The *Wind Dancer* will sail for Boston the instant you're aboard. You're to stay with your Uncle Donal until I come and fetch you. Do you understand me, Robert? Meyler? Have I made myself clear?"

"Yes, sir," they said in unison, quickly swinging up onto the fresh horses Alanna and Kiervan had brought with them from Greystones.

A sense of loss tightening around his throat, Carrick stepped forward and caught the bridle of Robert's mount. "I'm going with Glynis."

Robert nodded. "Well, it's either that or spend the rest of your life hiding from the British. Of the two, I'd say it's the better choice."

"You know I'd already made the decision to go with her."

His cousin smiled at him. "I'm glad you found her, Carrick. I'm happy for you." He cocked a brow and added, "Actually, I'm bordering on envious."

"You'll find a Glynis Muldoon of your own someday, Robert."

Robert laughed and shook his head. "I don't think there could be two of her. The world wouldn't be safe."

"True," he managed to say with a smile. "But I'll hope for it anyway. You'll need someone to make your life interesting after I'm gone."

"Frankly, I'm rather looking forward to the boredom and rest."

"Take care of yourself, Cousin."

Robert instantly sobered. "You do the same," he said softly. He looked off into the hills and swallowed. Suddenly his face brightened and he looked back down at Carrick. "Say, maybe if Aunt Alanna thinks she can manage it, I'll come visit you and Glynis someday."

It was a tiny hope but enough to sustain them through the moment. "You're welcome anytime, Robert. Anytime at all."

Carrick turned away before his smile faltered. "Meyler," he said, grasping the boy's foot and tugging it. "You do what Robert tells you." He winked. "Just don't let him get you into any trouble. All right? You know how he is."

"I'm never going to see you again, am I?" Meyler asked, his chin quivering.

"Naw. You'll see me. Make Robert bring you with him when he comes to visit."

The boy thought for maybe half a second before he fixed Robert with a stern look and said, "All right. I will."

"Enough!" Kiervan boomed. "Get going!"

Carrick lifted his hand, palm out, and Robert and Meyler each did the same before they rode away. His heart aching, he watched them go until they disappeared in a fold in the land. Only then did he turn toward his parents.

His father's smile was an odd mixture of sadness and pride. "I'm relieved to know that you're going, son. I was afraid we'd come to this point and I'd have to beat some sense into you."

He tried his best to smile in return. "I may be reckless, but I'm not stupid." He looked from his father to his mother and felt the full cost of what he was about to say to them. "I love her. I want to go."

"There will be no farewells, Carrick," his mother said firmly. "I won't have them. In my heart I know we'll see you again."

"A man should properly be the one to provide for his wife and family," his father said, reaching into his coat pocket. He withdrew a bulky leather pouch and handed it to him, saying over the jangle of coins, "It's only a portion of what you would inherit if you were to remain here, but it's all I could gather together in the time we had to prepare. If I can find a way to send you more, I will."

His mother didn't give him a chance to offer his thanks. She took his shirtsleeves in her hands and looked up at him earnestly. "One of the most loathsome things about the twentieth century is their damn insistence on numbers and a wad of papers to prove you exist. You need to go to Ouray. Glynis will know how to get there. Find a man named Cracker Jack. Tell him Alanna Chapman sent you and that you need an identity. It'll cost you, but he's good and worth every penny." She studied him for a long moment. A heavy volley of thunder rolled across the meadow, and over it she said, "Ouray. Cracker Jack. Got it?"

"I got it, Mother," he said, bending down to kiss her cheek. "Ouray and Cracker Jack."

"And you take care of Glynis," his father admonished, taking him by the shoulder. "You make her exercise some good sense about riding while she's carrying this baby."

Carrick laughed softly. "That ought to be an interesting—"

"Here she comes," his mother interrupted, pointing off into the hills to the east.

All three of them turned to watch Glynis come down over the crest of the hill, her coat streaming in the wind behind her as she drove Molan toward them at breakneck speed. Carrick smiled, his heart swelling at the sight of her. In that instant all the sadness he felt about leaving fell away and he knew he'd pay any price to go with her, sacrifice anything to be with her however she'd have him. He pulled open the front of his shirt and dropped the money pouch inside.

His father observed, "And of course she's riding hell-bent like she always—"

Carrick's heart stopped as the four red dots crested the hill behind Glynis. He swore just as a jagged bolt of lightning arced across the sky above them. The thunder pounded down, reverberating through him.

His father drew two flintlocks from his waistband and tossed one to him as they both spun about and sprinted to their horses. Over his shoulder Lord des Marceaux yelled, "Alanna, get ready!"

Bert leaped forward the instant Carrick hit the saddle and he leaned out over the animal's neck, fixed on the scene unfolding before him. He saw the British stop halfway down the hill, saw the muskets fitted to their shoulders.

They all fired at once, a narrow wall of flame and smoke. In the same instant he saw the battered hat fly from Glynis's head, saw her lurch forward over Molan's neck and slip to the side.

"No!" he screamed, his blood frozen in his veins. "Glynis!"

The storm answered, sweeping into the meadow with a howling vengeance. Through the slamming wall of rain he caught a glimpse of Glynis righting herself in the saddle. Relief washed over him.

And then she was gone.

She tumbled from Molan's back as his front hooves struck the ground. For a long moment she lay there stunned, feeling only the unholy pounding in her head, her racing heart, and the rush of the wind.

It was the feel of the rain on her back that finally drew her attention. She was home. She was back in the Flint Hills. Fighting a wave of dizziness, she pushed herself to her feet, searching for landmarks. She was right where Lady Alanna had said she'd put her—right in the middle of the draw from which Saraid had carried her into another time and place. Into Carrick's life.

Carrick. She whirled about, straining to see through the rain. She saw only Molan, lathered and exhausted, heard only her own breathing. She had to find Carrick. He had to be out here somewhere. Lady Alanna would send him.

Her hands trembled as she gathered Molan's reins and climbed back on him. "Just a little farther," she assured him raggedly. "Carrick would never forgive me if I hurt you. To the other side of the rise is all, Molan. Just to the other side. I'll get some help and you can rest."

Lloyd saw her as she rode over the hill, and came away from the side of the wagon as though he'd been launched from a cannon. "Glynis! What the hell . . . ?" He didn't finish, just reached up and physically hauled her down from Molan's back.

Ria was there in the same instant. "Oh, dear God. You're bleeding! What happened? Let me look at you."

"Where's Bert?" Lloyd demanded. "Where'd you get this animal?

"I'll explain later," Glynis said, pushing past them. "I need a fresh mount. Any one will do." She met the wide-eyed gaze of one of the tourists. "You," she said, striding toward the woman. "Give me those reins."

The woman nodded frantically and promptly dropped them. Glynis swore and snagged them up.

"You're not going anywhere until I check your head," Ria stated, catching her arm.

Glynis pulled from her grasp, threw the reins over the horse's neck, and slammed her foot into the stirrup.

"Glynis Muldoon!"

"His name is Carrick des Marceaux," she said, settling across the saddle. "And I have to find him." She looked between her aunt and her uncle. "I have to find him. Help me. Please."

Tears filled her eyes. "Please."

28

Carrick wiped the rain from his eyes and turned Bert in another circle. Even if there had been a moon, it wouldn't have made any difference. Despite the darkness it was easy to see that there was nothing around him but a vast expanse of rolling hills. Not a tree anywhere. No road or even a wagon rut. No lights glimmered in the distance.

He rode to the top of the nearest rise, a rise that was far higher than he'd thought and far more distant than it had appeared. From the top of it he saw that the land rolled on before him, just as barren and featureless as the land behind him. And to the left of him. And to the right of him.

The wind gusted suddenly, plastering his shirt to his body and chilling his skin. Rain came down, rain that was only a fitful reminder of the torrent through which he and Bert had come to be in this place. Carrick cupped his hands around his mouth. "Glynis!"

Her name rolled out over the land and then disappeared beneath the wind and the patter of raindrops against the saturated earth.

His gaze drifted over the land as he methodically recalled every word Glynis had ever told him of her home. She had loved it, telling him it was earth and sky and the place where she had to be. How had she described it through the eyes of others? Barren and desolate, she'd said. That many didn't like it because it made them realize how small they were and how little it took for nature to destroy man.

He could see how some would feel that way about this

place. But he couldn't, not completely. There was a sense of peace in the solitude, a sense of freedom in the expanse. And in a way he felt that if he were to surrender to the power of it, it would protect him from all harm. It would make him feel invincible, as though all things were possible.

Carrick smiled. His mother had instructed him to hold Glynis's spirit in his heart, to focus on that which made Glynis the woman he loved. And it had worked. These were the Flint Hills. He was certain of it. Glynis had survived; he'd seen her struggle back into the saddle. They had both come to this place; he sensed that, too. He could only hope that they'd come during the same century.

It had been a mistake to let Lloyd and Ria talk her into coming back to the house. She knew it the instant she walked into the kitchen and Ria snapped on the lights. Glynis spun on her heel and headed back toward the door. Lloyd quit fighting the wind, let it have the screen door, and filled the open doorway with his body, blocking her way.

"I shouldn't be here," she said, trying to step around him. "I need to go back out."

"Glynis," Ria said softly, "you're scaring us."

"You're not half as scared as I am." She tried to step past Lloyd again, and again he refused to let her pass.

"We can see that," he said as Ria turned on the faucet and pulled a bowl from the cupboard.

"Sit down and let me look at that head wound," her aunt instructed.

"It can wait," Glynis assured her. "It hurts like hell, but if I'm not dead, it's not serious."

"Glynis, if I have to restrain you bodily, I will," Lloyd ground out, lowering his chin the way he always did when he'd reached the end of his rope. He pointed to the kitchen table. "Now do as Ria tells you and park your butt in that chair!"

She closed her eyes and drew a ragged breath. It didn't do a damn bit of good; she couldn't seem to stop shaking. "If I sit down, I'll never get up again. I haven't slept in two . . . no, it's been three days. Hell, I don't know. Maybe it's been four."

"Then your judgment's shot to hell. Sit down!"

Ria set the bowl and the towels on the tabletop while she quietly asked Lloyd, "Think maybe we should take her to the emergency room?"

Glynis looked between the two of them, fighting back the desperation. "No! I'm not going anywhere. I'm staying right here."

"Honey, you're hysterical," Ria replied, pulling two chairs out from the table. "We don't know what happened out there, but obviously something did. Now, if you won't let us help you, then we have to find someone who can."

"So it's either you calm yourself down," Lloyd added, "or we'll hog-tie you and cart you into town. We'll have Doc Walters sedate your ass until you're rested enough to talk some sense."

She knew they'd do it. And if they got her away from here, if they took her to a doctor, she'd end up in the nut ward at the state hospital. She wouldn't be here for Carrick. Marshaling every bit of her determination, she took a slow, deep breath. "No," she said calmly. "I'll be okay. Just give me a minute to pull it together."

"Make it quick, Glynis."

She paused, trying to gauge how to best go about it all. "I don't know where to start. There's so much."

"All right," Lloyd said, pointing to the chair Ria had pulled out for her. "I'll give you a place. Start with that horse."

She sat. "That's Molan. He's Carrick's. Carrick's got Bert."

"Why?" Lloyd asked, joining them at the table.

The words tumbled out in a torrent. "Because I needed a fast horse to come out of Greystones. One that could go a long distance. We were supposed to trade when we met up and left the wagon, but Carrick wasn't strong enough to handle Molan, so I kept him. Robert put Carrick on Bert and they went on. Meyler went with them and I took the other two horses off in the other direction."

She saw the look that passed between them and knew that they thought she'd lost every last one of her marbles.

"I know it sounds insane," Glynis hurried to assure them. "I know it all seems impossible. But it happened. It really happened. I've been gone. I've been gone at least a month. Maybe longer. I don't know for sure. So much has happened."

"Honey . . ." Ria said soothingly, taking Glynis's hands in hers.

Glynis closed her eyes. The more she told them, the worse it was going to get. If only she had some concrete, physical proof to offer them. Too bad she hadn't thought to snag a newspaper before . . .

"Look!" she cried, vaulting to her feet and stripping off her coat. She thrust it into Lloyd's hands. "Look at the left shoulder." She pointed as Lloyd adjusted the folds. "That's a bullet hole. In the back, out the front. Those are blood-stains. Saraid tried her best to get them out, but they'd set by the time we got to her house." She popped open the front of her shirt and pulled it down over her left shoulder. "And look here. Look at my shoulder. See?"

"Goddamn," Lloyd whispered, his gaze darting between her coat and her shoulder.

"It's healing," Glynis continued, angling her shoulder so that Ria had a clear view of it. "Doesn't it look like it's a month old to you? Did I have this when we rode out of here this morning?"

"How'd you get it?" Lloyd asked, draping her coat over the back of a chair.

"Same way I got this crease in my head. Running from the British." She managed a smile of sorts. "Damn good thing they're lousy shots, huh?"

"The British."

She heard the skepticism in his voice, but she was stronger than she'd been a few minutes ago and she was ready to do whatever she had to do to make them understand. To hell with finesse. She didn't have the time or the energy for it. "Okay. Brace yourselves. This is comin' hard and fast. I've spent the last month in Ireland. In the year 1832. And no, I'm not crazy. *Pregnant,* but not crazy."

"Oh, God," Ria whispered, sinking down onto a chair. "You think you're pregnant?"

"The baby's Carrick's."

"This Carrick de something or other," Lloyd said, the

condemnation in his voice unmistakable as he grasped the back of a chair.

Glynis sighed and nodded. "Carrick des Marceaux."

"Did he marry you?"

The memories hit her in that single instant and she buried her face in her hands, laughing, nearly sobbing. She pulled herself back from the brink with great effort, telling herself that she couldn't afford to lose it at this point. "Oh, Uncle Lloyd," she said, lowering her hands and giving him the best smile she had in her, "I'm sorry. But if you knew all that I've been through, all that Carrick and I've been through together, you'd understand how unimportant that is." She laid her hand over his as she added, "But thank you for buying into what I'm telling you enough to be worried about it."

"I'm trying, honey, I'm really trying."

"And you think your Carrick is out in the hills somewhere," Ria said, rising to her feet. She dunked a washcloth into the bowl of water and barely wrung it out.

Glynis let her aunt tilt her head and, as Ria gently dabbed at the wound, answered, "If he can find a way, Carrick'll come after me, Ria. He will."

Lloyd stared down at the tabletop. "You're placing a lot of faith in this man."

"I know Carrick," Glynis assured him. "I know that he loves me. If his mother can find a way to send him, he'll come across time."

"When?"

"I don't know." She winced as Ria touched a particularly tender spot with the rag. "From what I gather, magic isn't real precise sometimes. But Lady Alanna, Carrick's mother, must be pretty good at it because she got me back here. Exactly when and where we'd planned."

Because when Lady Alanna had cast the spell and sent her through the portal, Glynis had been thinking about home and how badly she wanted her and Carrick to reach it. Her heart twisted.

Ria laid a hand on her shoulder. "What's wrong, Glynis?"

"Carrick wouldn't let me describe how the Flint Hills

looked," she whispered, despair filling her. "His mother wanted me to tell him so there'd be a clear image in his mind to bring him across if we had to come separately. But he wouldn't let me tell him."

"Maybe he didn't want to know," Lloyd suggested. "Maybe he really didn't want to come with you and chose that way out of it rather than being man enough to tell you the truth."

Everything in her felt battered and defeated. "They'd sentenced him to hang at noon the next day, and that night Colonel Hewlett let me go see him." She remembered the quiet hunger in Carrick's eyes as they'd made love, the unyielding tenderness with which he'd held her afterward. "Oh, God," she moaned, wrapping her arms around herself. The tears came and she didn't even try to blink them back. "Walking away from him hurt so much."

"And letting you do it ripped my heart out. What do you say to taking the Greystones jailhouse off our list?"

Her heart knew, but she couldn't be sure until she saw him. She looked up and found him standing in the kitchen doorway with her Stetson in one hand, his eyes drinking her in, and the gentlest of smiles on his lips. Sweet, pure joy flooded through her as the tears spilled down her cheeks.

Carrick knew the other two people in the room looked up in the same instant Glynis did, but that was the last thought he had of them. The relief, and the joy in her eyes, were all that existed in the world, all that mattered. She came to her feet in a split second and flew into his arms.

He kissed her, his welcome as fierce and hungry as her own. God, he couldn't hold her close enough, couldn't get enough of her. He could live for a thousand years and never have enough of her. But he'd spend every last day of his lifetime—and the next ten—trying.

She drew away from him, her fingers tangled in his hair. She didn't say a word; she didn't have to. He saw it in her eyes.

"I missed you, too," he whispered. "Let me see," he said, taking her chin gently in his hand and turning her head so he could check the wound. "Are you all right?"

"I am now," she answered, wrapping her arms around his waist and pressing her cheek to his chest. "I am now."

Carrick hugged her close, kissed the top of her head, and then tucked her carefully beneath his chin. "Christ Almighty, you scared me."

She laughed softly. "Like you haven't done that to me a time or two. Consider it partial payback."

It was at that point that he realized there were still two people there with them. The relief he'd felt on finding Molan's tracks had been tempered by the certainty that he'd have to face this very moment. Carrick shifted Glynis into the curve of his left arm and met the stern, blue-eyed gaze of the man. "You must be Lloyd," he said, extending his hand. "I'm Carrick des Marceaux."

The man took it firmly, assessingly, saying with a slight movement of his head toward the woman standing at his side, "My wife, Ria."

"Madam," Carrick said with a courtly nod. The woman had dark eyes, the kind that held secrets well. But she was making no effort to hide her feelings at the moment. She was clearly pleased by the sight of Glynis in his arms.

"I want to know if you plan to shoulder your responsibility and marry my niece."

"Lloyd!" the woman admonished, glaring at her husband.

Carrick smiled and met the man's direct gaze. "If she'll have me," he answered. "The last time I asked her, she turned me down flat."

Glynis drew back just enough to look up at him. "You never asked me."

He smiled down at her. "I did so, sweetheart. In the shepherd's cottage in the upper meadow. Right after we finished stealing the King's cattle. Remember?"

"That doesn't count. We were speaking hypothetically. It wasn't a real proposal."

"All right," he said, setting her from him and taking her hands in his. He looked deep into her wondrously emerald-green eyes. "Miss Glynis Muldoon, will you do me the distinct honor of accepting my proposal of marriage?"

He saw the answer. He also saw a mischievous light flicker to life.

"What if I told you no?"

He grinned. "I'd ask you again tomorrow. And the day after that and every day until you said yes."

"Sounds like you're planning to be here for a while."

"Forever."

"I love you, Carrick."

"Is that a yes, Glynis?"

She nodded and whispered, "It's a yes."

Glynis closed the bedroom door as quietly as she could. She was almost to the bureau when Carrick rolled onto his side and smiled at her.

"What's that?"

She used the edge of the tray to move the gold coins and the Dragon's Heart out of the way while answering, "Ria brought us some food. She says it's been two days and she's afraid we may starve to death."

"Honestly? Two days?" he asked, climbing from their bed. "It doesn't seem like it's been that long."

Good God. Would seeing him naked ever stop making her crazy? "I vaguely recall waking up long enough one time to see a sunset," she said, watching him come toward her.

His blue eyes sparkled mishievously. "I remember a particularly glorious sunrise."

"Yeah, I remember that one, too," she admitted, feeling the flush of renewed desire warm her skin. "It was glorious, wasn't it?"

"Let's dispense with this," he said, as he undid the sash holding her bathrobe closed.

The terry-cloth covering pooled around her feet a moment later and she laughed. "Your mother told me I'd spend very little of my life dressed."

"Well, that's hardly a great stretch of prediction," he scoffed, taking her hands and drawing her after him. "She's married to my father."

"Where are we going, Carrick?"

"In here," he supplied, leading her into the bathroom.

"I can see that. Why?"

"I like this shower contraption."

"Oh, yeah?" she asked, arching a brow as he pulled open

the glass door and turned on the tap. "Any particular reason?"

"It offers some intriguing possibilities," he admitted, his grin broad and delightfully wicked.

"So you put it on our list, huh?"

He winked. "Several times." Then he stepped into the steaming spray, his eyes dark with promise. "Come here," he commanded gently, drawing her toward him.

She happily obliged. Several times.

And when, much later, they finally set aside the empty tray and snuggled beneath the sheets in each other's arms, she knew that Carrick wasn't going to have the slightest problem adjusting to the twentieth century. He was going to walk straight into it and seize every possibility he encountered. She smiled. And she was going to be there right beside him every step of the way. They had fought for and earned their happiness, their right to be together. And in her heart she knew that neither man nor fate would ever come between them again.

Epilogue

The Rocking M Ranch
June 1998

Carrick cantered into the yard and drew Molan to a halt. Glynis came down the back steps toward him, the wind fluttering the hem of her sundress about her bare calves, the sun glinting brightly in her copper hair. He sat where he was, watching the most beautiful woman he'd ever seen and marveling that she was his. A smile touched the corners of his mouth. He'd bet every last head of cattle they owned that the dress and those little crocheted slippers were all his delectable wife had on.

"Well, well, Mrs. des Marceaux," he drawled, tilting his Stetson back on his head and looking her up and down. "You're wearing a dress. What's the special occasion?"

She took Molan's bridle in her hand and smiled up at him serenely. "Your son's gone into town with his Aunt Ria. They're going to do the grocery store and Wally World circuit."

"Oh, yeah?" he asked, leaning down and crossing his forearms over the saddle horn.

"And his Uncle Lloyd has gone to the sale barn."

He straightened slowly, a broad grin spreading over his face. "Are you telling me that we're alone? We're alone in the middle of the afternoon?"

"We are indeed," she answered invitingly.

"Well, Mrs. des Marceaux," he said with a low chuckle, extending his hand and pulling his foot out of the stirrup, "you just put your little foot in here and climb right up."

Glynis laughed and let him pull her up and settle her across his lap. She slipped her arms around his waist and leaned her head against his shoulder as he turned Molan and started out of the yard. She'd always ridden on her own, but there was something to be said for sharing a horse. Especially with an incredible man like this one. Lord. And to think Carrick was all hers. It still amazed her. It probably would until the day she died.

"Are we going to do another one of your pasture tours?" she asked. "I remember the last one quite fondly."

He kissed her before he replied, "It's been a while since we've been out to the southwest section. How does that sound to you?"

"Anywhere's fine."

Molan ambled on across the prairie, gently rocking them in the sunshine and the breeze. She snuggled against Carrick, feeling the strong, steady beat of his heart all along the length of her body, feeling the warmth of his arms around her. "The mail came a little while ago," she said dreamily. "I brought the letter along. Wanna read it now or later?"

"Have you read it already?"

"Of course," she admitted, chuckling. "I couldn't resist. It's better than being on the road with Charles Kuralt."

He grinned. "Then tell me about it. What are my parents up to now?"

"They're in San Francisco."

"They move fast. Last week it was Las Vegas."

She laughed outright. "And apparently it was a very good week, too. Your father won big in a high-stakes poker game. They traded in the Lincoln and bought a Ferrari."

He pulled Molan to a sudden halt and looked down at her. "A Ferrari? Jesus, Glynis. My father has his hands on a Ferrari?" He shook his head before he nudged Molan forward again. "Check the piggy bank when we get home, sweetheart. It's only a matter of time before we have to bail them out of jail."

"Actually, I'm more concerned about them flying off a

cliff. They're heading up Highway 101 on their way to Oregon. You know your father's gonna push those curves."

"Oregon's next?"

"Yeah, your mother thinks maybe California would be a bit too much for Robert to handle."

"Hell, California's too much for anyone sane to handle." A moment later he added quietly, "But they're going to have to find somewhere for him. I still say they ought to send him to us."

"I sorta imagine that's how it will end up," she offered, trying to draw him from his troubled thoughts. "In the meantime, they're having a helluva lot of fun scoping out the possibilities."

"Are they still planning to be back here for the Fourth of July? Or have they decided to go home for Julia and Colonel Hewlett's wedding?"

"Your mom said they were coming back here."

"We'll talk with them about Robert again."

If Lady Alanna was right, and she always was, Robert's difficulties were a few years down the line. There was no point in worrying about them right now. When they needed to find a solution, they would. But she knew Carrick and understood that time and distance had not weakened the bond that tied them. He'd brood over it until something sufficiently distracted him.

"Have I mentioned that I'm not wearing any pantalets under this dress?"

Carrick knew what she was doing, why she was doing it. And he loved her for it. "Darlin'," he drawled, grinning, "I knew that the minute I laid eyes on you in the yard." His eyes grew serious. "Have I ever told you how happy I am?" he asked.

Her voice came softly. "You don't have to. I can tell."

Carrick cupped her cheek in his palm. She turned to look into his eyes. "I know I don't have to, sweetheart," he said. "But I want to."

She slowly tilted her head and pressed a kiss to the inside of his wrist.

"Most men can't hope for more out of life than a roof over their heads and food in their stomachs. I've got so much more, Glynis. So much more. I don't know what I did to deserve you in my life, but I'm so very grateful that you are. I love you, Glynis. Thank you for not giving up on me when things got tough."

"I'd do it all again if I had to."

"No regrets?"

She shook her head and kissed him, gently, with all her heart.

Carrick gathered his wife closer, knowing that no luckier man had ever walked the face of the earth, and sent Molan into a canter across the windswept prairie.

About the Author

LESLIE LAFOY grew up loving books and telling stories. From *Bamba, the Jungle Boy* to Early American history, she was hooked. After growing up, leaving home, and earning tons of college degrees, all as a voracious reader, Leslie entered the Real World, and decided to get a job. Looking around at her Real World options, she chose to become a teacher. As a teacher she got to read a lot, which she loved, but she didn't actually have time to write. The decision was difficult, but Leslie left teaching in the fall of 1996 to write full-time. She, her husband, their son, a sheltie, and three cats live on ten acres of wind-swept Kansas prairie . . . fifteen miles east and three miles north of the Real World.

THE VERY BEST IN CONTEMPORARY
WOMEN'S FICTION

SANDRA BROWN

___28951-9 Texas! Lucky $6.99/$9.99 in Canada   ___56768-3 Adam's Fall $5.99/$7.99

___28990-X Texas! Chase $6.99/$9.99   ___56045-X Temperatures Rising $6.50/$8.99

___29500-4 Texas! Sage $6.99/$9.99   ___56274-6 Fanta C $5.99/$7.99

___29085-1 22 Indigo Place $6.99/$8.99   ___56278-9 Long Time Coming $5.99/$7.99

___29783-X A Whole New Light $6.50/$8.99   ___57157-5 Heaven's Price $6.50/$8.99

___57158-3 Breakfast In Bed $6.99/$8 .99 ___29751-1 Hawk O'Toole's Hostage $6.50/$8.99

___10403-9 Tidings of Great Joy $17.95/$24.95

TAMI HOAG

___29534-9 Lucky's Lady $6.50/$8.99   ___29272-2 Still Waters $6.99/$9.99

___29053-3 Magic $6.50/$8.99   ___56160-X Cry Wolf $6.99/$9.99

___56050-6 Sarah's Sin $5.99/$7.99   ___56161-8 Dark Paradise $6.50/$8.99

___56451-x Night Sins $6.99/$9.99   ___56452-8 Guilty As Sin $6.99/$9.99

___57188-5 A Thin Dark Line $6.99/$9.99

NORA ROBERTS

___10834-4 Genuine Lies $19.95/$27.95   ___27859-2 Sweet Revenge $6.50/$8.99

___28578-5 Public Secrets $6.50/$8.99   ___27283-7 Brazen Virtue $6.50/$8.99

___26461-3 Hot Ice $6.50/$8.99   ___29597-7 Carnal Innocence $6.50/$8.99

___26574-1 Sacred Sins $6.50/$8.99   ___29490-3 Divine Evil $6.50/$8.99

DEBORAH SMITH

___29107-6 Miracle $5.99/$7.99   ___29690-6 Blue Willow $5.99/$7.99

___29689-2 Silk and Stone $5.99/$6.99

___10334-2 A Place To Call Home $23.95/$29.95

Ask for these books at your local bookstore or use this page to order.

Please send me the books I have checked above. I am enclosing $_____(add $2.50 to cover postage and handling). Send check or money order, no cash or C.O.D.'s, please.

Name _____

Address _____

City/State/Zip _____

Send order to: Bantam Books, Dept. FN 24, 2451 S. Wolf Rd., Des Plaines, IL 60018

Allow four to six weeks for delivery.

Prices and availability subject to change without notice.   FN 24 8/98